THE
Regency
RAKES

2 Glittering
Regency Romances

GALLANT WAIF
by Anne Gracie

MR TRELAWNEY'S PROPOSAL
by Mary Brendan

THE
Regency
RAKES

by

Anne Gracie & Mary Brendan

MILLS & BOON®

*First published in Great Britain 2002 by
Harlequin Mills & Boon Limited,
Eton House, 18-24 Paradise Road,
Richmond, Surrey TW9 1SR*

THE REGENCY RAKES © Harlequin Books S.A. 2002

The publisher acknowledges the copyright holders of the
individual works as follows:

Gallant Waif © Anne Gracie 1999
Mr Trelawney's Proposal © Mary Brendan 1998

ISBN 0 263 83662 2

138-1002

*Printed and bound in Spain
by Litografia Rosés S.A., Barcelona*

GALLANT WAIF
by
Anne Gracie

Anne Gracie was born in Australia but spent her youth on the move, living in Scotland, Malaysia, Greece and different parts of Australia before escaping her parents and settling down. *Gallant Waif* was a finalist in the Romance Writers of America's Best First Book competition. Anne lives in Melbourne, in a small wooden house which she will one day renovate.

Also by Anne Gracie
in Mills & Boon Historical Romance®

TALLIE'S KNIGHT
AN HONOURABLE THIEF

Look for
THE VIRTUOUS WIDOW
(within **The Regency Brides** short story collection)

Out now

Prologue

Kent, England. Late summer, 1812.

'No, no, Papa. I won't. You cannot make me!'

'Please, my sweet, I beg of you. It will not take long and I fear he will take no notice of me.'

The tall dark-haired man waiting alone in the drawing-room reacted to the voices, which seemed to come from outside. He turned sharply and let out a soft expletive, his face tensed in pain. Moving more cautiously, he flexed his leg carefully, supporting himself with his cane. His sudden pallor gradually disappeared as the pain ebbed slowly away.

He glanced towards the sound of the voices and swallowed, tugging nervously at his cravat, thus ruining the effect that he'd taken hours to achieve. His clothes were of the finest quality, although somewhat out of date; they seemed to have been tailored for a slightly larger gentleman, for the coat that should have fitted snugly was loose everywhere except across the shoulders. The gentleman himself was rather striking to behold as he stood staring blankly out of the window, tall, broad-shouldered and darkly handsome, yet thin, almost to the point of gauntness.

Jack Carstairs had done enough waiting. It had been bad

enough being closed up in a carriage for hours upon end to get here…then to be left closeted in the front parlour for almost half an hour was too much for a man who'd spent the last three years out of doors, commanding troops under Wellington on the Peninsula. He opened the French doors on to the terrace and stepped outside into the cool, fresh air, and was immediately rewarded by the sweet, melodic tones of his beloved.

Jack stepped forward impatiently. Three years, and now the waiting was at an end. In just minutes he would hold her in his arms again, and the nightmare would be over. He limped eagerly towards the sound of the voices coming from the open French windows further along the terrace.

'No, Papa, you must tell him. I do not wish to see him.' Julia's voice was petulant, sulky. Jack had never heard it so before.

'Now, now, my dear, I will speak to him and put him right, never fear, but you must see that it is necessary for you to at least come with me, for you know he will not believe me otherwise.'

Jack froze. He had received a letter full of sweetness and love from Julia, only a month ago, just before he was wounded. It was in the same batch of letters that had told him of his father's death. Months after the event, as was all mail received on the Peninsula.

The lovely, well-remembered voice became more petulant, almost childish. 'I don't want to see him, I don't. He's changed, I know, I saw him from the window.'

Her father's voice was coaxing. He'd always been wax in the hands of his beautiful daughter, but for once he was standing relatively firm. 'Well, now, my dear, you have to expect that. After all, he has been at war and war changes a man.'

Julia made a small sound, which from anyone less exquisite would have been called a snort. 'He…he's ugly now, Papa; his face is ruined.'

Unconsciously Jack fingered the harsh, still livid scar that bisected his cheek from temple to mouth.

'And he can hardly even walk.' Her voice grew soft and coaxing. 'Please, Papa, do not make me speak to him. I cannot bear even to look at him, with his leg sticking out in that peculiar-looking way. It would have been better if he had died than to come back like that.'

'My dear!' Her father sounded shocked.

'Oh, I know it seems hard,' Julia continued, 'but when I think of my beautiful Jack and how he is now I could weep. No, Papa, it's just not possible.'

'Are you sure, my dear?'

'Of course I am sure. You told me yourself his father left him nothing. I cannot marry a pauper.' She stamped her foot. 'It makes me so angry to think of it—all that time wasted, *waiting*! And, in any case, he can barely walk without falling over, so you can be very sure that he will never dance with me again as he used to…'

Her voice tailed off as she recalled the magic moments she had spent on the dance floor, the cynosure of every eye, the envy of every other woman in the room. She stamped her foot again, angry at being deprived of all she had expected.

'No, Papa, it is quite impossible! I am glad now that you would not allow us to announce the betrothal formally, though I thought you monstrous cruel at the time.'

Jack had heard enough. His face white and grim, he drew back the draperies which had concealed him and stepped into the room.

'I think that says it all, does it not?' he said in a soft, deadly voice.

There was a small flurry as the two absorbed what he might have heard. There was no telling how long he had been outside. Jack limped quietly to the door and pointedly held it open for Julia's father to make his exit.

'I believe your presence is no longer required, Sir Phillip,' he said. 'If you would be so good as to leave us alone, sir?'

Sir Phillip Davenport began to bluster. 'Now see here, Carstairs, I won't be ordered about in my own house. I can see it must be a nasty shock for you, but you are no longer in a position to support my daugh—'

'Thank you, sir.' Jack cut across him. 'I understand what you are saying, but I believe I am owed the courtesy of a few moments alone with my betrothed.'

The voice which had spent years commanding others had its usual effect. Julia's father began to look uncomfortable and took a few steps towards the door.

'Oh, but...' Julia began.

'As far as I am concerned our betrothal has not yet been dissolved and I believe I have the right to be told of it in person.' Jack gestured again for her father to leave. Observing that gentleman's hesitation and concern, his lip curled superciliously. He added silkily, 'I assure you, Davenport, that, while I may be changed in many respects, I am still a gentleman. Your daughter is safe with me.'

Sir Phillip left, leaving his daughter looking embarrassed and angry. There was a long moment of silence. Julia took a quick, graceful turn about the room, the swishing of her skirts the only sound in the room. The practised movements displayed, as they were meant to do, the lush, perfect body encased in the finest gown London could provide, the fashionable golden coiffure, the finely wrought jewellery encircling her smooth white neck and dimpled wrists. Finally Julia spoke.

'I am sorry if you heard something that you didn't like, Jack, but you must know that eavesdroppers never hear any good of themselves.' She shrugged elegantly, glided to the window and stood gazing out, seemingly absorbed in the view of the fashionably landscaped garden beyond the terrace.

Jack's face was grim, the scar twisting down his cheek standing out fresh and livid against his pallor.

'God damn it, Julia, the least you could have done was told me to my face—what's left of it,' he added bitterly. 'It's partly because of you that I'm in this situation in the first place.'

She turned, her lovely mouth pouting with indignation. 'Well, really, Jack, how can you blame me for what has happened to you?'

His lips twisted sardonically and he shrugged, his powerful shoulders straining against the shabby, light, superfine coat.

'Perhaps not directly. But when my father ordered me to end our betrothal you cast yourself into my arms and begged me to stand firm. Which of course I did.'

'But how was I to know that that horrid old man truly *would* disinherit you for disobeying him?'

His voice was cool, his eyes cold. '*That horrid old man* was my father, and I told you at the time he would.'

'But he doted on you! I was sure he was only bluffing...trying to make you dance to his tune.'

His voice was hard. 'It's why I purchased a commission in the Guards, if you recall.'

The beautiful eyes ran over his body, skipping distastefully over the scarred cheek and the stiffly extended leg.

'Yes, and it was the ruination of you!' She pouted, averting her eyes.

He was silent for a moment, remembering what she had said to her father. 'I am told that I will never dance again. Or ride.'

'Exactly,' she agreed, oblivious to his hard gaze. 'And will that horrid scar on your face go away too? I doubt it.'

She suddenly seemed to notice the cruelty of what she had said. 'Oh, forgive me, Jack, but you used to be the handsomest man in London, before...that.' She gestured distastefully towards the scar.

With every word she uttered, she revealed herself more and more, and the pain and disillusion and anger with himself was like a knife twisting in Jack's guts. For this beautiful, empty creature he had forever alienated his father. Like Julia, he had never in his heart of hearts believed his father would truly disinherit him, but it seemed his father had died with Jack unforgiven. It was that which hurt Jack so deeply; not the loss of his inheritance, but the loss of his father's love.

Feeling uncomfortable under Jack's harsh scrutiny, Julia took a few paces around the room, nervously picking up ornaments and elegant knick-knacks, putting them down and moving restlessly on.

Jack watched her, recalling how the memory of her grace and beauty had sustained him through some of the worst moments of his life. It had been like a dream then, in the heat and dust and blood of the Peninsula War, to think of this lovely, vital creature waiting for him. And that's all it was, he told himself harshly—a dream. The reality was this vain, beautiful, callous little bitch.

'Oh, be honest, Jack.' She twirled and stopped in front of him. 'You are no longer the man I agreed to marry. Can you give me the life we planned? No.'

She shrugged. 'I am sorry, Jack, but, painful though it is for both of us, you must see it is just not at all practical any more.'

'Ahh, not practical?' he echoed sarcastically. 'And what exactly is not practical? Is it my sudden lack of fortune? My ruined face? Or the idea of dancing with an ugly cripple and thereby becoming an object of ridicule? Is that it, eh?'

She cringed in fright at the savagery in his voice.

'No, it is not practical, is it?' he snarled. 'And I thank God for it.'

She stared as she took in the meaning of his last utterance.

'Do...do you mean to say *you* don't want to marry *me*?' Her voice squeaked in amazement and dawning indignation. It was for her to give *him* his *congé*, not the other way around.

He bowed ironically. 'Not only do I not wish to marry you, I am almost grateful for the misfortunes which have opened my eyes and delivered me from that very fate.'

She glared at him, her bosom heaving in a way that had once entranced him. 'Mr Carstairs, you are no gentleman!'

He smiled back at her, a harsh, ugly grimace. 'And you,

Miss Davenport, are no lady. You are a shallow, greedy, cold little bitch, and I thank my lucky stars that I discovered the truth in time. God help the poor fool you eventually snare in your net.'

She stamped her foot furiously. 'How dare you? Leave this house at once…at once, do you hear me? Or crip—wounded or not, I'll have you thrown out!'

He limped two paces forward and she skittered back in fright.

'Just give me back my ring,' he said wearily, 'and your butler won't be put to the trouble and embarrassment of man-handling a cripple.'

She snatched her left hand back against her breast and covered the large diamond ring with her other hand.

'Oh, but I am very attached to this ring, Jack,' she said in a little-girl voice. 'I did love you, you know. Surely you want me to have something to remember you by?'

He looked at her, disgust filling his throat, then turned and silently limped from the house.

Chapter One

London. Late autumn, 1812.

'**G**ood God! Do you mean to tell me my grandson did not even receive you after you'd travelled I don't know how many miles to see him?' Lady Cahill frowned at her granddaughter. 'Oh, for goodness' sake, Amelia, stop that crying at once and tell me the whole story! From the beginning!'

Amelia gulped back her sobs. 'The house is shabby and quite horrid, though the stables seem well enough—'

'I care nothing for stables! What of my grandson?' Lady Cahill interrupted, exasperated.

'His manservant told me Jack saw no one.'

The old lady frowned. 'What do you mean, no one?'

'I mean no one, Grandmama, no one at all. He—Jack, that is—pretended to be indisposed. He sent a message thanking me for my concern and regretting his inability to offer me hospitality. Hospitality! His own sister!'

Amelia groped in her reticule for a fresh handkerchief, blotted her tears and continued, 'Of course I insisted that I go up and tend him, but his man—a *foreigner*—would not even allow me up the stairs. I gathered from him that Jack was not ill…just…drunk! He won't see anyone. And, according to his manservant, he's been like that ever since he returned from Kent.'

There was a long pause while the old lady digested the import of this. 'Kent, eh? I wish to God he had never set eyes on that poisonous little Davenport baggage.' She glanced up at her granddaughter. 'I take it, then, that the betrothal is definitely at an end.'

'Unfortunately, yes, Grandmama.'

'Good!' said Lady Cahill vehemently. 'He's well rid of that little harpy and you know it.'

'But, Grandmama, it appears to have broken his heart.'

'Nonsense! He's got a fine strong heart. He's got my blood in him, hasn't he? When you're my age, you'll stop prating of broken hearts and other such nonsense. Bodies mend and so do hearts.'

There was a long silence.

'But that's just it, isn't it, Grandmama?' Amelia said at last. 'Bodies don't always mend, do they? Jack's servant said that Jack's leg is still very bad and painful, although he can walk.'

Lady Cahill thought of the way her favourite grandson had looked when he'd come back from the wars in Spain. Such a fine tall, athletic lad he had been, too, before he left. But now…

She glared at her granddaughter. 'Don't let me ever hear you speaking such rubbish, do you hear me, gel? Never! That boy is as fine a lad as ever he was, you mark my words! He's got a fine fighting spirit in him.'

'I saw no fighting spirit, Grandmama.'

'Do you try to tell me, gel, that my grandson has had the stuffing knocked out of him and hides himself away from the world merely because his betrothal to that beautiful, heartless little viper is at an end? Faugh!' Lady Cahill snorted. 'You'll not make me believe that, not in a month of Sundays.'

'No,' said Amelia slowly. 'But that, on top of everything else… He will never ride again, they say. And so many of his friends have been killed in the war… And, Grandmama, you *know* how much Papa's will hurt him—to be left with virtually nothing…'

'Lord knows what maggot was in your father's mind at the time,' agreed Lady Cahill. 'Bad enough to disinherit the boy, but to leave him "whatever is found in my pockets on the day I die"… Faugh! Utter folly! 'Twas the veriest coincidence that he died after a night of cards at White's. Had he not just won that deed to Sevenoakes, the boy would not even have a roof over his head!'

Lady Cahill snorted in disgust. Yes, Jack had taken some terrible blows, one on top of another. But even discounting Amelia's dramatics it seemed he was taking it badly. He could not be allowed to brood like that. He needed *something* to snap him out of it.

There was a soft knock at the door. 'Yes, what is it, Fitcher?' the old lady snapped, her temper frayed by concern for her grandson.

'Pardon me, milady.' The butler bowed. 'This letter was delivered a few moments ago.' He bowed again, proffering a letter on a silver salver.

Lady Cahill picked up the letter, wrinkling her nose in disdain at the undistinguished handwriting which gave her direction. 'Humph,' she muttered. 'Not even franked.'

She turned it over and broke the seal. She frowned over the letter, muttering crossly to herself as she did. Finally she threw it down in frustration.

'What is it, Grandmama?'

'Demmed if I can read the thing. Shockin' bad hand and the spelling is atrocious. Can't think who'd be sending me such rubbish. Toss it in the fire, girl!'

The young woman picked the letter up and smoothed it out. 'Would you like me to try?'

Taking the snort she received from her grandmother to be assent, Amelia read it out, hesitating occasionally over misspellings and illegible words, of which there were many.

Milady I be right sorry to be addressing you like this
it being above my station to be writing to Countesses but
I cannot think of who else to turn to…

'A begging letter!' the Dowager Countess snapped in outrage. 'On to the fire with it at once!'

'I think not, Grandmama,' said Amelia, scanning ahead.
'Let me finish.'

…for my poor girl is now left all alone in the world
with no kin to care what become of her but it do seem a
right shame that the daughter of gentlefolk should have
to skivvy to stay alive…

Lady Cahill's eyes kindled with anger. 'By God, she's trying to palm one of your father's by-blows off on to us!'

'Grandmama!' Amelia blushed, horrified.

'Oh, don't be so mealy-mouthed, girl. You must know your
father had any number of bits o' fluff after your dear mother
died, and they didn't mean a thing, so don't pretend. But it's
nothing to do with us. Your father would have left any base-
born child well provided for. He was a gentleman, after all,
even if he was a fool! Now toss that piece of impertinence in
the fire at once, I say!'

But her granddaughter had forgotten her blushes and was
avidly reading on. 'No, wait, Grandmama, listen to this.'

And being as I was her old nurse even if some as did
say I wasn't good enough to be nurse to Vicar's daughter
it falls to me to let you know what my girl has come to
being as you was godmother to Miss Maria her poor
sainted mother…

Lady Cahill sat up at this and leant forward, her eyes sharp
with interest.

…and her only remaining child so now there be nothing left for her but to Take Service her not willing to be took in by myself and truth to tell there be little enough for me alone so I beg ye Milady please help Miss Kate for as the Lord is my witness there be no other who can yours truly Martha Betts.

'Do you know any of these people, Grandmama?' said Amelia curiously.

'I believe I do,' said her grandmother slowly, picking up the letter and scanning it again. 'I think the girl must be the daughter of my godchild Maria Farleigh—Maria Delacombe as she used to be. She married a parson and died giving birth to a daughter…must be nigh on twenty years ago. She had two boys before that, can't recall their names now, and I lost touch with the family after she died, but it could be the same family.'

She peered at the address. 'Is that Bedfordshire I see? Yes. Hmm. No kin? What can have happened to the gel's father and brothers?' Lady Cahill frowned over the letter for a short time, then tossed it decisively down on a side table.

'What do you mean to do, Grandmama?'

Lady Cahill rang for sherry and biscuits.

Amelia's husband arrived and they all went in to dinner. Over cream of watercress soup, Lady Cahill announced her decision.

'But, Grandmama, are you sure about this?' Amelia looked distressed. 'It's a very long journey. What if Jack won't receive you, either?'

Lady Cahill gave her granddaughter a look of magnificent scorn. 'Don't be ridiculous, Amelia!' she snorted. 'I have never in my life been denied *entrée* to any establishment in the kingdom. I go where I choose. I was a Montford, gel, before my marriage to your grandfather, and *no one*, not even my favourite grandson, tells me what I may or may not do!'

She dabbed her mouth delicately on a damask napkin and poured her sherry into the soup. 'Tasteless rubbish!'

Later, as she pushed *cailles à la Turque* around her plate, she said, 'I'll call upon Maria's gel on my way to visit Jack. I cannot let her starve and I'll not allow Maria Farleigh's child to enter into service! Faugh! The very idea of it. Maria's mother would turn in her grave. She was a fool to let her daughter marry a penniless parson.' Lady Cahill's eyes narrowed as she considered the shocking mésalliance.

'The Farleighs were a fine old family,' she admitted grudgingly, 'but he was the last of his line and poor as a church mouse to boot. Church mouse. Parson! Ha!' She cackled, noticing her unintended pun, then fell silent.

She heaved a sigh and straightened her thin old shoulders wearily. She pushed her plate away and called for more sherry.

'Yes, I'll roust the boy out of his megrims and keep him busy.' Lady Cahill ignored the Scotch collops, the lumber pie, the buttered parsnips and the chine of salmon boiled with smelts. She helped herself to some lemon torte. 'Can't leave him brooding himself into a decline up there in the wilds of Leicestershire with no one but servants to talk to.' She shook her head in disgust. 'Never did believe in servants anyhow!'

Amelia tried valiantly to repress a gasp of astonishment and met her husband's amused twinkle across the table. For a woman who considered a butler, dresser, cook, undercook, housekeeper, several housemaids and footmen, a scullery-maid, coachman and two grooms the bare minimum of service needed to keep one elderly woman in comfort, it was a remarkable statement.

'No, indeed, Grandmama,' Amelia managed, bending her head low over her plate.

'Don't hunch over your dinner like that, girl,' snapped the old woman. 'Lord, I don't know how this generation got to be so rag-mannered. It wouldn't have been tolerated in my day.'

* * *

The knocker sounded peremptorily, echoing through the small empty cottage. This was it, then, the moment she had been waiting for and dreading equally. The moment when she stopped being Kate Farleigh, Vicar Farleigh's hoydenish daughter, and became Farleigh, maidservant, invisible person.

Now that the moment had come, Kate was filled with the deepest trepidation. It was a point of no return. Her heart was pounding. It felt like she was about to jump off a cliff… The analogy was ridiculous, she told herself sternly. She wasn't jumping, she had been pushed long ago, and there was no other choice…

Squaring her shoulders, Kate took a deep breath and opened the door. Before her stood an imperious little old lady clad in sumptuous furs, staring at her with unnervingly bright blue eyes. Behind her was a stylish travelling coach.

'Can I help you?' Kate said, politely hiding her surprise. Nothing in Mrs Midgely's letter had led her to expect that her new employer would be so wealthy and aristocratic, or that she would collect Kate herself.

The old lady ignored her. With complete disregard for any of the usual social niceties, she surveyed Kate intently.

The girl was too thin to have any claim to beauty, Lady Cahill decided, but there was definitely something about the child that recalled her beautiful mother. Perhaps it was the bone structure and the almost translucent complexion. Certainly she had her mother's eyes. As for the rest… Lady Cahill frowned disparagingly. Her hair was medium brown, with not a hint of gold or bronze or red to lift it from the ordinary. At present it was tied back in a plain knot, unadorned by ringlets or curls or ribands, as was the fashion. Indeed, nothing about her indicated the slightest acquaintance with fashion, her black clothes being drab and dowdy, though spotlessly clean. They hung loosely upon a slight frame.

Kate flushed slightly under the beady blue gaze and put her chin up proudly. Was the old lady deaf? 'Can I help you?'

she repeated more loudly, a slight edge to her husky, boyish voice.

'Ha! Boot's on the other foot, more like!'

Kate stared at her in astonishment, trying to make sense of this peculiar greeting.

'Well, gel, don't keep me waiting here on the step for rustics and village idiots to gawp at! I'm not a fairground attraction, you know. Invite me in. Tush! The manners of this generation. I don't know what your mother would have said to it!'

Lady Cahill pushed past Kate and made her way into the front room. She looked around her, taking in the lack of furniture, the brighter patches on the wall where paintings had once hung, the shabby fittings and the lack of a fire which at this time of year should have been crackling in the grate.

Kate swallowed. It was going to be harder than she thought, learning humility in the face of such rudeness. But she could not afford to alienate her new employer, the only one who had seemed interested.

'I collect that I have the honour of addressing Mrs Midgely.'

The old lady snorted.

Kate, unsure of the exact meaning of the sound, decided it was an affirmative. 'I assume, since you've come in person, that you find me suitable for the post, ma'am.'

'Humph! What experience do you have of such work?'

'A little, ma'am. I can dress hair and stitch a neat seam.' *Neat? What a lie!* Kate shrugged her conscience aside. Her stitchery was haphazard, true, but a good pressing with a hot flatiron soon hid most deficiencies. And she needed this job. She was sure she could be neat if she really, really tried.

'Your previous employer?'

'Until lately I kept house for my father and brothers. As you can see…' she gestured to her black clothes '…I am recently bereaved.'

'But what of the rest of your family?'

This old woman was so arrogant and intrusive, she would doubtless be an extremely demanding employer. Kate gritted her teeth. This was her only alternative. She must endure the prying.

'I have no other family, ma'am.'

'Hah! You seem an educated, genteel sort of girl. Why have you not applied for a post as companion or governess?'

'I am not correctly educated to be a governess.' *I am barely educated at all.*

The old lady snorted again, then echoed Kate's thought uncannily. 'Most governesses I have known could barely call themselves educated at all. A smattering of French or Italian, a little embroidery, the ability to dabble in watercolours and to tinkle a tune on a pianoforte or harp is all it takes. Don't tell me you can't manage that. Why, your father was a scholar!'

Yes, but I was just a girl and not worth educating in his eyes. In her efforts to control the anger at the cross-questioning she was receiving, it did not occur to Kate to wonder how the old woman would know of her father's scholarship. If Mrs Midgely wished Kate to be educated, Kate would not disappoint her. Some women enjoyed having an educated person in a menial position, thinking it added to their consequence.

'I know a little Greek and Latin from my brothers—' *the rude expressions* '—and I am acquainted with the rudiments of mathematics…' *I can haggle over the price of a chicken with the wiliest Portuguese peasant.* It suddenly occurred to Kate that perhaps Mrs Midgely had grandchildren she wished Kate to teach. Hurriedly Kate reverted to the truth. It would not do to be found out so easily.

'But I cannot imagine anyone offering a tutor's position to a female. I have no skill with paints and have never learnt to play a musical instrument…' No, the Vicar's unwanted daughter had been left to run wild as a weed and never learned to be a lady.

'I do speak a little French, Spanish and Portuguese.'

'Why did you not seek work as a companion, then?'

Kate had tried and tried to find a position, writing letter

after letter in answer to advertisements. But she had no one to vouch for her, no references. Someone from Lisbon had written to one of her female neighbours and suddenly she was *persona non grata* to people who had known her most of her life. It hadn't helped that the girl they remembered had been a wild hoyden, either. There were many who had predicted that the Vicar's daughter would come to a bad end. And they were right.

Life in service wouldn't be so bad, she told herself. As one of a number of servants in a big house, she would have companionship at least. A servant's life would be hard, harder than that of a companion, but it was not hard work Kate was afraid of—it was loneliness. And she was lonely. More lonely than she had ever thought possible.

Besides, a companion might be forced to socialise, and Kate had no desire to meet up with *anyone* from her previous life. She might be recognised, and that would be too painful, too humiliating. She had no wish to go through that again, but none of this could she explain to this autocratic old lady.

'I know of no one who would take on a companion or governess without a character from a previous employer, ma'am.'

'But surely your father had friends who would furnish you with such?'

'Possibly, ma'am. However, my father and I lived abroad for the last three years and I have no notion how to contact any of them, for all his papers were lost when…when he died.'

'Abroad!' the old lady exclaimed in horror. 'Good God! With Bonaparte ravaging the land! How could your foolish father have taken such a risk? Although I suppose it was Greece or Mesopotamia or some outlandish classical site that you went to, and not the Continent?'

Kate's eyes glittered. Old harridan! She did not respond to the question, but returned to the main issue. 'So, do I have the position, ma'am?'

'As my maid? No, certainly not. I never heard of anything so ridiculous.'

Kate was stupefied.

'I never did need a maid anyway, or any other servant,' the old lady continued. 'That's not what I came here for at all.'

'Then...then are you not Mrs Midgely, ma'am?' Kate's fine features were lit by a rising flush and her eyes glittered with burgeoning indignation.

The old lady snorted again. 'No, most decidedly I am not.'

'Then, ma'am, may I ask who you are and by what right you have entered this house and questioned me in this most irregular fashion?' Kate didn't bother to hide her anger.

Lady Cahill smiled. 'The right of a godmother, my dear.'

Kate did not return the smile. 'My godmother died when I was a small child.'

'I am Lady Cahill, child. Your mother was my goddaughter.' She reached up and took the girl's chin in her hand. 'You look remarkably like your mother at this age, especially around the eyes. They were her best feature, too. Only I don't like to see those dark shadows under yours. And you're far too thin. We'll have to do something about that.'

Lady Cahill released Kate's chin and looked around her again. 'Are you going to offer me a seat or not, young woman?'

This old lady knew her mother? It was more than Kate did. The subject had been forbidden in the Vicarage.

'I'm sorry, Lady Cahill, you took me by surprise. Please take a seat.' Kate gestured to the worn settee. 'I'm afraid I can't offer you any refresh—'

'Never mind about that. I didn't come here for refreshments,' said the old lady briskly. 'I'm travelling and I can't abide food when I'm travelling.'

'Why did you come here, ma'am?' Kate asked. 'You've had little contact with my family for a great many years. I am sure it cannot be chance that has brought you here just now.'

Shrewd blue eyes appraised her. 'Hmm. You don't beat

around the bush, do you, young woman? But I like a bit of plain speaking myself, so I'll put it to you directly. You need my help, my girl.'

The grey-green eyes flashed, but Kate said quietly enough, 'What makes you think that, Lady Cahill?'

'Don't be foolish, girl, for I can't abide it! It's clear as the nose on your face that you haven't a farthing to call your own. You're dressed in a gown I wouldn't let my maid use as a duster. This house is empty of any comfort, you can't offer me refreshment— No, sit down, girl!'

Kate jumped to her feet, her eyes blazing. 'Thank you for your visit, Lady Cahill. I have no need to hear any more of this. You have no claim on me and no right to push your way into my home and speak to me in this grossly insulting way. I will thank you to leave!'

'Sit down, I said!' The diminutive old lady spoke with freezing authority, her eyes snapping with anger. For a few moments they glared at each other. Slowly Kate sat, her thin body rigid with fury.

'I will listen to what you have to say, Lady Cahill, but only because good manners leave me no alternative. Since you refuse to leave, I must endure your company, it being unfitting for a girl of my years to lay hands on a woman so much my elder!'

The old lady glared back at her for a minute then, to Kate's astonishment, she burst into laughter, chuckling until the tears ran down her withered, carefully painted face.

'Oh, my dear, you've inherited you mother's temper as well as her eyes.' Lady Cahill groped in her reticule, and found a delicate lace-edged wisp which she patted against her eyes, still chuckling.

The rigidity died out of Kate's pose, but she continued to watch her visitor rather stonily. Kate hated her eyes. She knew they were just like her mother's. Her father had taught her that…her father, whose daughter reminded him only that his beloved wife had died giving birth to a baby—a baby with grey-green eyes.

'Now, my child, don't be so stiff-necked and silly,' Lady Cahill began. 'I know all about the fix you are in—'

'May I ask how, ma'am?'

'I received a letter from a Martha Betts, informing me in a roundabout and illiterate fashion that you were orphaned, destitute and without prospects.'

Kate's knuckles whitened. Her chin rose proudly. 'You've been misinformed, ma'am. Martha means well, ma'am, but she doesn't know the whole story.'

Lady Cahill eyed her shrewdly. 'So you are not, in fact, orphaned, destitute and without prospects.'

'I am indeed orphaned, ma'am, my father having died abroad several months since. My two brothers also died close to that time.' Kate looked away, blinking fiercely to hide the sheen of tears.

'Accept my condolences, child.' Lady Cahill leaned forward and gently patted her knee.

Kate nodded. 'But I am not without prospects, ma'am, so I thank you for your kind concern and bid you farewell.'

'I think not,' said Lady Cahill softly. 'I would hear more of your circumstances.'

Kate's head came up at this. 'By what right do you concern yourself in my private affairs?'

'By right of a promise I made to your mother.'

Kate paused. Her mother. The mother whose life Kate had stolen. The mother who had taken her husband's heart to the grave with her... For a moment it seemed that Kate would argue, then she inclined her head in grudging acquiescence. 'I suppose I must accept that, then.'

'You are most gracious,' said Lady Cahill dryly.

'Lady Cahill, it is really no concern of yours. I am well able to look after myself—'

'Pah! Mrs Midgely!'

'Yes, but—'

'Now, don't eat me, child!' said Lady Cahill. 'I know I'm an outspoken old woman, but when one is my age one becomes accustomed to having one's own way. Child, try to use the brains God gave you. It is obvious to the meanest intelligence that any position offered by a Mrs Midgely is no suitable choice for Maria Farleigh's daughter. A maidservant, indeed! Faugh! It's not to be thought of. There's no help for it. You must come and live with me.'

Come and live with an aristocratic old lady? Who from all appearances moved in the upper echelons of the *ton*? Who would take her to balls, masquerades, the opera—it had long been a dream, a dream for the old Kate...

It was the new Kate's nightmare.

For the offer to come now, when it was too late—it was a painful irony in a life she had already found too full of both pain and irony.

'I thank you for your kind offer, Lady Cahill, but I would not dream of so incommoding you.'

'Foolish child! What maggot has got into your head? It's not an invitation you should throw back in my face without thought. Consider what such a proposal would involve. You will have a life appropriate to your birth and take your rightful position in society. I am not offering you a life of servitude and drudgery.'

'I realise that, ma'am,' said Kate in a low voice. Her *rightful position in society* was forfeited long ago, in Spain. 'None the less, though I thank you for your concern, I cannot accept your very generous invitation.'

'Don't you realise what I am offering you, you stupid girl?'

'Charity,' said Kate baldly.

'Ah, tush!' said the old lady, angrily waving her hand. 'What is charity but a foolish word?'

'Whether we name it or not, ma'am, the act remains the same,' said the girl with quiet dignity. 'I prefer to be beholden to no one. I will earn my own living, but I thank you for your offer.'

Lady Cahill shook her head in disgust. 'Gels of good family earnin' their own living, indeed! What rubbish! In my day, a gel did what her parents told her and not a peep out of her—and a *demmed* good whipping if there was!'

'But, Lady Cahill, you are *not* my parent. I *don't* have to listen to you.'

'No, you don't, do you?' Lady Cahill's eyes narrowed thoughtfully. 'Ah, well then, help me to stand, child. My bones are stiff from being jolted along those shockin' tracks that pass for roads in these parts.'

Kate, surprised but relieved at the old lady's sudden capitulation, darted forward. She helped Lady Cahill to her feet and solicitously began to lead her to the door.

'Thank you, my dear.' Lady Cahill stepped outside. 'Where does that lead?' she asked, pointing to a well-worn pathway.

'To the woods, ma'am, and also to the stream.'

'Very pleasant, very rural, no doubt, if you like that sort of thing,' said the born city-dweller.

'Yes, ma'am, I do,' said Kate. 'I dearly love a walk through the woods, particularly in the early morning when the dew is still on the leaves and grass and the sun catches it.'

Lady Cahill stared. 'Astonishing,' she murmured. 'Well, that's enough of that. It's demmed cold out here, almost as cold as in that poky little cottage of yours. We'll resume our discussion in my coach. At least there I can rest my feet on hot bricks.'

Kate dropped her arm in surprise. 'But I thought…'

The blue eyes twinkled beadily. 'You thought you'd made yourself clear?'

Kate nodded.

'And so you did, my dear. So you did. I heard every word you said. Now, don't argue with me, girl. The discussion is finished when I say it is and not before. Follow me!'

Gesturing imperiously, she led the way to the coach and allowed the waiting footman to help her up the steps. Swathed in furs, she supervised as Kate was similarly tucked up with a luxurious fur travelling rug around her, her feet resting snugly on a hot brick. Kate sighed. It seemed ridiculous, sitting in a coach like this, to discuss a proposal she had no intention of accepting, but there was no denying it—the coach was much warmer than the cottage.

'Comfortable?'

'Yes, I thank you,' Kate responded politely. 'Lady Cah—'

The old lady thumped on the roof of the coach with her cane. With a sudden lurch, the coach moved off.

'What on earth—?' Kate glanced wildly around as the cottage slipped past. For a moment it occurred to her to fling herself from the coach, but a second's reflection convinced her it was moving too fast for that.

'What are you doing? Where are you taking me? Who are you?'

The old woman laughed. 'I am indeed Lady Cahill, child. You are in no danger, my dear.'

'But what are you doing?' demanded Kate in bewilderment and anger.

'Isn't it obvious?' Lady Cahill beamed. 'I've kidnapped you!'

Chapter Two

'But this is outrageous!' Kate gasped. 'How dare you?'

The old lady shrugged. 'Child, I can see you're as stubborn as your dear mother and, to be perfectly frank, I haven't the time to waste convincing you to come and stay with me instead of hiring yourself out as a maid or whatever nonsense you were about. I intend to reach my grandson's house in Leicestershire tonight and, as it is, we won't reach it until well after dark. Now, be a good girl, sit back, be quiet and let me sleep. Travelling is enough of a trial without having a foolish girl nattering at me.' She pulled the furs more closely around her and, as if there was nothing more to be said, closed her eyes.

'But my house…my things…Martha…' Kate began.

One heavy-lidded eye opened and regarded her balefully. 'Martha knows my intentions towards you. She was most relieved to hear that you would, in future, make your home with me until such time as a suitable husband is found for you. A footman is locking up your house and will convey the keys to Martha.'

Kate opened her mouth to speak, but the blue eyes had closed implacably. She sat there, annoyed by the ease with which she had been tricked, and humiliated by the old lady's discovery of her desperate straits. She sighed. It was no use fighting. She would have to go wherever she was taken, and then see what could be done. The old lady meant well; she did not know how ill-placed her kindness was.

…*until such time as a suitable husband is found for you.* No. No decent man would have her now. Not even the man who'd said he loved her to distraction wanted her now. She stared out at the scenery, seeing none of it, only Harry, turning away from her, unable to conceal the revulsion and contempt in his eyes.

Harry, whom she'd loved for as long as she could remember. She'd been nine years old when she first met him, a tall, arrogant sixteen-year-old, surprisingly tolerant of the little tomboy tagging devotedly along at his heels, fetching and carrying for him and his best friend, her brother Jeremy. And when Kate was seventeen he'd proposed to her in the orchard just before he'd left to go to the wars, and laid his firm warm lips on hers.

But a few months ago it had been a totally different Harry, staring at her with the cold hard eyes of a stranger. Like all the others, he'd turned his back.

Kate bit her lip and tried to prevent the familiar surge of bitter misery rising to her throat. Never, ever would she put herself in that position again. It was simply too painful to love a man, when his love could simply disappear overnight and be replaced with cold disdain…

The coach hit a deep rut and the passengers lurched and bounced and clung to their straps. Kate glanced at Lady Cahill, but the old lady remained silently huddled in her furs, her eyes closed, her face dead white beneath the cosmetics. Kate returned to her reflections.

So she would never marry. So what? Many women never married and they managed to lead perfectly happy and useful lives. Kate would be one of them. All she needed was the chance to do so, and she would make that chance; she was determined. Maybe Lady Cahill would help her to get started…

* * *

Bright moonlight lit the way by the time the travelling chaise pulled into a long driveway leading to a large, gloomy house. No welcoming lights were visible.

In a dark, second-floor window a shadowy figure stood staring moodily. Jack Carstairs lifted a glass to his lips. He was in a foul temper. He knew full well that his grandmother would be exhausted. He couldn't turn her away. And she knew it, the manipulative old tartar, which was, of course, why she had sent her dresser on ahead to make things ready and timed her own arrival to darkness. Jack, in retaliation, had restricted his grandmother's retinue to her dresser, sending the rest off to stay in the village inn. That, if nothing else, would keep her visit short. His grandmother liked her comfort.

The chaise drew to a halt in front of a short flight of stairs. The front door opened and two servants, a man and a woman, came running. Before the coachman could dismount, the woman tugged down the steps and flung open the door. 'Here you are at last, my lady. I've been in a terrible way, worrying about you.'

Lady Cahill tottered unsteadily on her feet, looking utterly exhausted. Kate felt a sharp twinge of guilt. The old lady clearly wasn't a good traveller, but Kate's attempts to make her more comfortable had been shrugged aside with so little civility that, for most of the journey, Kate had ignored her.

Kate moved to help but the maidservant snapped, 'Leave her be. I will take care of milady. I know just what needs to be done!' Scolding softly, she gently shepherded the old lady inside, the manservant assisting.

The chaise jerked as it moved off and Kate almost fell as she hastily scrambled out of it. She took a few wavering steps but, to her horror, her head began to swim and she swirled into blackness.

The man watching from the window observed her fall impassively and waited uninterestedly for her to scramble to her feet. No doubt this was another blasted maid of his grandmother's. Jack took another drink.

Damned fool that he was, he'd clearly mishandled his sister, refusing to see her. He'd been heavily disguised at the time, of course. Even drunker than he was now. Good thing his grandmother hadn't asked to see him tonight. He'd have refused her too. Jack continued staring sourly out of the window, then leaned forward, intent. The small, crumpled figure remained motionless on the hard cold gravel.

What was wrong with the girl? Had she hurt herself? It was damned cold out there. Any more time on the damp ground and she'd take more than just a chill. Swearing, he moved away from the window and limped downstairs. There was no sign of anyone about. He heard the sound of voices upstairs— his grandmother was being tended to by the only available help. Jack strode into the night and bent awkwardly over the small, still figure.

'Are you all right?' He laid his hand lightly on the cold cheek. She was unconscious. He had to get her out of the cold. Bending his stiff leg with difficulty, he scooped her against his chest. At least his arms still had their strength.

Good God! The girl weighed less than a bird. He cradled her more gently. Nothing but a bundle of bones!

Jack carried her into the sitting-room and laid her carefully on a settee. He lit a brace of candles and held them close to her face. She was pale and apparently lifeless. A faint, elusive fragrance hovered around her, clean and fresh. He laid a finger on her parted lips and waited. A soft flutter of warm breath caused his taut face to relax. His hands hovered over her, hesitating. What the deuce did you do with fainting females? His hands dropped. Ten to one she'd wake up and find him loosening her stays and set up some demented shrieking!

Jack went to the doorway. 'Carlos!' No response. Dammit! He poured brandy into a glass and, slipping one arm around the girl, tipped a generous portion into her mouth. Instantly she came alive in his arms, coughing, hands flailing against him.

'Gently, gently,' he said, irritated.

'What—?' Kate spluttered as he forced another mouthful of fiery golden liquid into her. She gasped as it burnt its way down her throat and glared indignantly at him.

'It's only brandy.'

'Brandy!' She fought for breath.

'You needed something to bring you around.'

'Bring me around?' Kate glanced round the strange room. She stared up at the shadowed face of the man who had an arm around her. Her pulse started to race. Blind panic gripped her and she tried to wrench herself away, to hit out against him. She was restrained by strong hands, gentle but implacable.

'You fainted outside.' He held her a moment until she calmed slightly, then released her and stood back. 'Mind you, if I'd known you were such a little wildcat I'd have thought twice about rescuing you from the cold, wet driveway and giving you my best brandy.'

Kate stared blankly at him. Fainted? Rescue? Best brandy? She still felt decidedly peculiar. 'I...I'm sorry... My nerves are a little jumpy these days...and I tend to overreact.'

Especially when I awake to find myself in strange company, not knowing what has come before it. Her head was pounding. Had she fainted for just a few minutes, as he said, or would she find a gap in her memory of days or weeks, as she had once before? Her hand reached to touch the faint ridged scar at the base of her skull, then dropped to her lap. She glanced down and a wave of relief washed over her. She remembered putting on these clothes this morning...Lady Cahill...the long trip in the coach. It was all right. It wasn't like before...

But who was the man looming over her? She was aware of a black frown, a long, aquiline nose, a strong chin, and blue, blue eyes glinting in the candlelight. She blinked, mesmerised.

He shifted uncomfortably under her gaze and moved abruptly beyond the candleglow, his face suddenly hidden in shadows again.

'I…I really do beg your pardon,' she said. 'I didn't…I was confused.' She tried to gather herself together. 'It's just—'

'Are you ill?' His voice was very deep.

'No, I don't think so. It's just…it must be because I haven't eaten for several day—for several hours.'

Jack frowned. The slip of the tongue was not lost on him.

Kate tried to sit up. Another wave of dizziness washed over her. Jack grasped her arm and thrust her firmly but gently back against the cushions. 'Don't try to move,' he ordered. 'Just stay there. I'll return in a moment.' He left the room.

Kate sat on the settee, one hand to her head. She felt weak and shaky. Brandy on such an empty stomach. She shook her head ruefully, then clasped it, moaning. She closed her eyes to stop the room from spinning around her.

'Here, this will make you feel better.' The harsh deep voice jolted Kate out of her daze. She opened her eyes. Before her was a plate with a clumsily cut slice of bread and cold meat on it. It looked wonderful. She glanced quickly up at the man towering over her and smiled.

'Oh, thank you so much. It is very kind of you,' she said, then added, blushing, 'I'm afraid that brandy made me quite dizzy.'

She applied herself carefully to her meal, forcing herself to eat with tiny bites, chewing slowly and delicately.

Jack watched her, still faintly dazzled by the sweetness of her smile. She was pretending uninterest in the food, he realised, even though she was starving. Well, who was he to quibble at pride? But she was certainly an enigma, with her pride and her shabby clothes.

'Who the devil are you?'

The sudden question jolted Kate out of the rapture of her first meal in days.

'My name is Kate Farleigh.' She returned to the food.

'And who is Kate Farleigh when she's at home?'

Kate pondered as she chewed. Who was Kate Farleigh now? She was no longer the Reverend Mr Farleigh's daughter, nor

Jeremy and Benjamin Farleigh's sister. She certainly wasn't
Harry Lansdowne's betrothed any more. And she didn't even
have a home.

'I don't suppose she's anyone at all,' she replied in an attempt at lightness that failed dismally.

'Don't play games.' The frown had returned to his face.
'Who are you and what are you doing here? I know you came
with my grandmother.'

His grandmother? So this was the master of the house, Mr
Jack Carstairs. His food was doing wonders for her spirits.
She felt so much better. Kate almost smiled at his aggrieved
tone. He obviously didn't want her here. Well, she hadn't
asked to come.

'Oh, you mustn't blame me for that.' She licked the last
crumb delicately from her lips. 'It wasn't my choice to come,
after all.'

'Why? What the deuce do you mean by that?' He scowled,
watching the movement of the pink tongue. 'What is your
position in relation to my grandmother?'

What was her position? Kidnappee? Charity case? Spurious
great-goddaughter? None of them would exactly delight a dot-
ing grandson. Besides, it would be very ungrateful of her to
upset the man who'd fed her a delicious meal by calling his
relative a kidnapper. Although the idea was very tempting.

'I'm not at all sure I can answer that. You will have to ask
Lady Cahill.' Kate got to her feet. 'Thank you so much for
your kind hospitality, sir. The meal was delicious and I was
very hungry after my journey.'

She took two steps towards the door, then faltered, belatedly
realising she had nowhere to go. 'Could you tell me, please,
where I am to sleep?'

'How the deuce should I know?' he snapped. 'I don't even
know who you are, so why should I concern myself where
you sleep?'

Rudeness obviously ran in the family, decided Kate. It mattered little. With a full stomach, she felt quite in charity with

the whole world. She would find herself a bed without his assistance—having found billets all over Spain and Portugal she would be lacking indeed if she could not find a bed in one, not terribly large English country house.

'Very well, then, sir, I will bid you goodnight. Thank you once again for your hospit…' She paused, then corrected herself wryly, 'For the food.' She began to climb the stairs in a determined fashion. Halfway up, her knees buckled.

'Dammit!' Jack leapt stiffly towards the stairs and caught her against his chest as she fainted for the second time. He carried her into a nearby bedchamber and laid her gently on the bed. He stood looking down at her for a long moment. Who the devil was she?

In the soft light of a candle, he assessed her unconscious form. She was thin, far too thin. Clear delicate skin was stretched tightly over her cheekbones, leaving deep hollows beneath them. His gaze lingered where the neck of her shabby, too loose dress had slipped, revealing a smooth shoulder, hunched childlike against the chill of the night. Had he not chanced to be watching when she fainted, she would still be lying unconscious on the front driveway. It was an icy night. Doubtless she would not have survived.

He'd get no answers tonight. Best to tuck the girl up in bed and take himself off. He bent and removed her shoes, then stopped in perplexity. He was sure he should loosen her stays, but how to go about that with propriety? His mouth quirked. Propriety! It was quite improper enough for him to be in this girl's bedchamber. He shrugged and bent over the supine body, searching gingerly at her waist for stay laces. God, but the chit was thin! With relief he ascertained that she wore no stays, had no need of them, probably didn't even own any.

Carefully he covered her with warm blankets. She shifted restlessly and flung an arm outside the bedding. He bent again to cover it and as he did so her eyes opened. She blinked for a moment, then smiled sleepily and caressed his face with a cool, tender touch. 'Night, Jemmy.' Her eyelids fluttered closed.

Jack froze, his breath caught in his chest. Slowly he straightened. His hand crept up to his right cheek, to where she had touched him. As they had done a thousand times before, his fingers traced the path of the ugly scar.

He grimaced and left the room.

The thunder of galloping hooves woke Kate at dawn next morning. She stared around the strange room, gathering her thoughts. It was a large chamber. The once rich furnishings were faded, dusty and worn.

She sat up, surprised to find herself fully clad except for her shoes. How did she get here? She recalled some of the previous night, but some of it didn't make sense. It was a frightening, familiar feeling.

Kate could have sworn she saw her brother Jemmy last night. She vaguely remembered his poor, ravaged face looking intently into hers. Only that could not be, for Jemmy lay cold and deep in a field in Spain. Not here in Lady Cahill's grandson's house. She got out of bed and walked to the window, shivering in the early morning chill.

The view was beautiful, bare and bleak. The ground glittered silver-gilt with sun-touched frost. Nothing moved, except for a few hardy birds twittering in the pale morning sunlight. Immediately below her window was a stretch of rough grass. A trail of hoof prints broke the silvery surface of the frost.

Her eyes followed the trail and widened as she saw a riderless horse galloping free, saddled, reins dangling around its neck. It seemed to be heading towards a small forest of oaks. It must have escaped its restraints. She could sympathise. She too would love to be out in that clear, crisp air, galloping towards the forest, free and wild in the chill of dawn. How she missed her little Spanish mare and her early morning rides, that feeling of absolute exhilaration as the wind streamed through her as if she were flying. Dawn was the only time she could ride as fast and as wildly as she liked. Her father was never an early riser.

Turning, Kate caught a glimpse of herself in the glass that hung on one wall. She giggled. It looked as if she'd been dragged through a haystack backwards. Wild brown curls tumbled in every direction. *The veriest gypsy urchin*—how many times had she been called that? Swiftly she pulled out the remaining pins from her hair and redid it in her customary simple style. She brushed down her clothes, pulling a wry face at the wrinkles. She looked around for a pitcher of water with which to wash, but there was nothing in sight.

Walking softly, so as not to disturb the sleeping household, she left her room and went downstairs in search of the kitchen. There was not a soul around. A house of this size should surely have many servants up and about their duties at this hour, in preparation for when their master woke.

The more she saw, the more Kate goggled with surprise. What kind of establishment had Lady Cahill brought her to? The floors were gritty underfoot. Dustballs drifted along skirting boards and under furniture. The furniture, no longer fashionable, was covered in a thick layer of dust. The early morning sunshine was barely able to penetrate the few grime-encrusted windows which were not shrouded by faded curtain drapery. She shuddered at the number of cobwebs she saw festooned across every corner—she loathed spiders. Everything spoke of neglect and abandonment, yet the house was, apparently, inhabited.

This shabby, dirty, rambling house did not at all fit in with the impression given to her by Lady Cahill's manner, clothes, and servants. It was her grandson's home. Why did he not command the same sort of elegant living his grandmother so obviously took for granted? Kate shrugged. The mystery would be solved sooner or later; in the meantime she needed hot water and something to eat.

Finally Kate discovered the kitchen. She looked around in disgust. The place was a pigsty. The floor hadn't been swept in weeks, there was no fire burning in the grate and cold ashes mingled with the detritus on the floor. The remains of past meals had been inadequately cleared away and piles of dirty dishes lay in the scullery.

It might be the oddest gentleman's establishment she'd ever had the doubtful privilege of visiting, but here was one way she could earn the large breakfast she planned to eat. Kate rolled up her sleeves and set to work. It was ironic, she thought, clearing the ashes from the grate and setting a new fire—the misdeeds of her youth had given her the one truly feminine skill she possessed.

The only time Reverend Farleigh had spoken to his hoydenish daughter had been when she'd misbehaved. Kate's crimes had been many and various: climbing trees; riding astride—bareback—hitting cricket balls through windows; coming home in a straggle of mud with skinned knees, tangled hair and a string of illegal fish. Her father had soon learned it was not enough to confine his wild and errant daughter to her bedchamber—she simply climbed out of the window. He'd learned it was more effective to give her into the custody of the housekeeper, who'd set her to work, cleaning and cooking.

The youthful Kate had despised the work, but years later she'd become grateful for knowledge generally considered unnecessary and unbecoming to a girl of her class. It had proven invaluable. Most girls of her station in life would have recoiled with genteel disgust at the task she faced, but Kate's experiences in the Peninsula War had inured her to the horrors of filth and squalor.

This kitchen was nothing compared to some of the unspeakable hovels where she and her father and brothers had been billeted during Wellington's campaigns. In those hovels, the Vicar's impossible daughter had discovered an ability to create a clean and comfortable environment for her family, wherever they were. And had glowed in the knowledge that for once she, Kate, had been truly *needed*.

Her skills were needed here, too, she could see.

* * *

Almost an hour and a half later Kate looked around the room with some satisfaction. The kitchen now looked clean, though the floor could do with a good scrub. She'd washed, dried and put away all the crockery, glasses, pots and pans. She'd used sand, soap and water to scrub the table and benches. And she'd even taken her courage in both hands, tackling the worst spiderwebs and killing two spiders with a broom. A fire now burned merrily in the grate and a huge iron kettle steamed gently. She poured hot water into a bowl in the scullery and swiftly made her ablutions.

A rapid search of the provision shelves unearthed a dozen or so eggs. Kate checked them for freshness, putting them in a large bowl of water to see if they sank to the bottom. One floated; she tossed it out. A flitch of bacon she found hanging up in the cool room. And, joy of joys, a bag of coffee beans. Kate hugged them to her chest. It had been months since she had tasted coffee.

She roasted the beans over the fire, then used a mortar and pestle to crush them, inhaling the aroma delightedly as she did so. She mixed them with water and set it over the fire to heat. She sizzled some fat in a pan, then added two thick rashers of bacon and an egg.

The floor did need scrubbing, Kate decided. She would do it after breakfast. She went to the scullery to fetch a large can of water to heat. The largest can she could find was wedged under a shelf, stuck fast. She tugged and pulled and cursed under her breath, then the heavenly aromas of bacon, egg and coffee reached her nostrils. Oh, no! Her breakfast would be ruined! She raced into the kitchen and came to a sudden halt.

Lady Cahill's grandson sat at the table, his back and broad shoulders partly towards her. He was tucking into her breakfast with every evidence of enjoyment.

'What do you think you're doing?' Kate gasped crossly.

He didn't stop eating. 'I'll have another two eggs and four rashers of bacon. And some more of that excellent coffee, if you would be so good.' He lifted his empty cup without even turning to face her.

Kate stared in growing indignation.

'More coffee, girl, didn't you hear me?' He snapped his fingers impatiently, still not bothering to turn around.

Arrogance obviously ran in the family too! 'There's only enough for one more cup,' she said.

'That's all I want.' He finished the last bite of bacon.

'Oh, is it, indeed?' Kate said, pulling a face at his impervious back. The exquisite scent of the coffee had been tantalising her for long enough. She'd cleaned and washed his filthy kitchen. All morning her mouth had been watering in anticipation of bacon and eggs and coffee. And he'd just walked in and without so much as a by-your-leave had devoured the lot!

'There's only enough for me,' she said. 'You'll have to wait. I'll make a fresh pot in a few minutes.'

He swung around to face her. 'What the deuce do you mean—only enough for you?'

Jack was outraged. To his recollection, he'd never even heard a kitchen maid speak, let alone answer him back in such a damned impertinent manner. And yet who else would cook and scrub at this hour of the morning?

She stared defiantly back at him, hands on hips, cheeks flushed, soft pink lips pursed stubbornly. One hand moved possessively towards the coffee pot and her small chin jutted pugnaciously. She was a far cry from the pale, exhausted girl he'd met by candlelight the night before.

Despite his annoyance, his mouth twitched with amusement—there was a wide smear of soot reaching from her cheek to her temple. She stared him down like a small grubby duchess. Her eyes weren't grey, after all, but a sort of greeny-grey, quite unusual. He felt his breath catch for a moment as he stared into them, and then realised she was examining his own face just as intently. He stiffened, half turned away from her, keeping his scarred side to the wall, and unconsciously braced himself for her reaction.

She poured the last of the coffee into her own cup and proceeded to sip it, with every evidence of enjoyment.

Jack was flabbergasted. He was not used to being ignored—let alone by a dowdy little maidservant with a dirty face. And in his own kitchen! He opened his mouth to deliver a crashing reprimand, but she met his eye again and something held him back.

'I think I've earned it, don't you?' She gestured at the sparkling kitchen.

He frowned again. What else did kitchen maids do but clean and scrub? Did the chit expect to be thanked? Did she realise who she was addressing? He opened his mouth to inform her, then hesitated uncertainly, a novel sensation for Major Carstairs, late of the Coldstream Guards.

How the devil did one introduce oneself to a kitchen maid? Servants knew who one was, and acted accordingly. But this one didn't seem to know the rules. And somehow it just didn't seem right to roar at this pert little urchin when only a few hours before he had held her in his arms and felt just how frail she was. Despite her effrontery.

He cleared his throat. 'Do you know who I am?'

'Lady Cahill's grandson, Mr Carstairs, I presume?'

He grunted.

Why had he mentioned it? Kate looked gravely at the tall dark man leaning back in his chair. He didn't look particularly out of place in the kitchen, sprawled at the large scrubbed table, his long booted legs crossed in front of him. He was very handsome, she realised. Maybe he felt it would not be appropriate to eat in here with her when they had not been properly introduced.

'Would you rather I brought your breakfast to another room? A breakfast parlour, perhaps?'

His scowl deepened. 'I'll eat it here.' Long brown fingers started to drum out an impatient tattoo on the wooden surface of the table.

'Please try to be patient. I'll finish my coffee, then cook enough bacon and eggs for both of us.'

Jack stared at her, debating whether to dismiss her instantly or wait until she'd cooked the rest of his breakfast. The egg had been cooked just how he liked it, the bacon had been crisped to perfection and she did make the best coffee he'd tasted in months. But he was not some scrubby schoolboy, as she seemed to imagine—he was the master of the house!

Jack's lips twitched with reluctant amusement. His manservant's cooking had, he perceived ruefully, seriously undermined his authority and his resolution. The men in his brigade would have boggled at his acceptance of this little chit's effrontery, but they had neither drunk her coffee nor looked into those speaking grey-green eyes. Nor had they carried her up a flight of stairs and felt the fragile bones and known she had been starving. He couldn't dismiss her—he could as soon rescue a half-drowned kitten then kick it.

She sat down opposite him at the kitchen table. He stiffened awkwardly as her gaze fixed on his face.

'So,' she said, 'it was you in my bedchamber last night.'

His mouth tightened abruptly, his face dark with bitter cynicism. What was she going to accuse him of?

'When I woke up this morning I couldn't quite remember how I got to bed. I thought I remembered seeing Jemmy, but now that I see you, of course, that explains it.'

Kate didn't notice the stiffening of his body and the way his eyes turned to flint.

'Jemmy caught a bayonet wound, too, in just the same place, only his became terribly infected. Yours has healed beautifully, hasn't it?'

She stood up, stretched luxuriously and smiled. 'Isn't coffee wonderful? I feel like a new woman, so I'll forgive your barefaced breakfast piracy and cook some more for both of us.'

He stared at her in stunned silence. Who the devil was this impertinent, shabby, amazingly self-possessed girl with the wide, lovely eyes? And how could she recognise a bayonet wound and, what was more, refer to his shattered cheek so calmly when every other blasted female who had laid eyes on it had shuddered in horror, or wept, or ostentatiously avoided looking at him? He had the evidence of his own mirror that it was not a pretty sight.

And, he thought, watching her slight body move competently around the kitchen, who the devil was this Jemmy she kept mentioning? Jemmy with the scars, who was not, apparently, out of place in her bedchamber!

They were just finishing the last bacon and eggs and coffee, when the outside door opened and in walked a dark, stockily built man. He took one comprehensive look at Kate and smiled, a dazzling white smile which lit his swarthy face.

'*Señorita.*'

Kate smiled slightly and inclined her head.

He sniffed the air and let out a long, soulful sigh. 'Ah, coffee.'

Kate chuckled. 'Would you care for a cup, sir?'

'The *señorita* is very kind.' The white smile widened in the dark face and he bowed again.

Kate dimpled. 'Then please be seated, sir, and I will fetch you a cup directly.' She went to fetch the coffee pot.

The two men began to converse in Spanish. Kate slowly stiffened. Three years in Spain and Portugal had resulted in a certain amount of fluency in both languages. She could understand every word the men said. And she was not impressed.

'So, Major Jack, who is the little brown mouse with the pretty eyes, the terrible clothes and the dirty face?'

Kate peered at her reflection in a spoon, then scrubbed at her face with a clean dishcloth.

'Damned if I know, Carlos. Some servant of my grandmother's.' His tone was indifferent, bored.

A chair scraped on the floor and footsteps came towards her. Kate bent over the pots, then jumped nervously as a warm hand touched her lightly on the shoulder. She turned quickly and found a pair of dark blue eyes regarding her from a great height, a glimmer of amusement in their depths. Did he find it amusing to give her a fright? Or had he noticed the clean face? She blushed.

'If you would be so good…' He waved her aside, bent, took a burning twig from the fire, lit a cheroot and returned to the table, limping heavily.

'Jumpy, isn't she, the little mouse?' said Carlos in Spanish.

Kate could almost feel the shrug of the broad shoulders.

'Skinny too.'

'Probably hasn't had a square meal in a good few weeks,' the deep voice agreed. 'I don't know what my grandmother could want with such a little waif.'

Kate flushed in mortification. Was it that obvious?

Carlos continued, 'Pretty, though. Those eyes are beautiful. Needs some meat on her bones yet. Me, I like a woman to feel like a woman.'

Jack Carstairs grunted. 'You think too much about women.'

'Ah, Major Jack, do not say so, you, with your fine handsome face and wicked blue eyes that all the ladies sigh over.'

Jack's hand went unconsciously to the shattered cheek.

'Ah, Major Jack, that little scratch will never make you safe from the ladies' attentions. It will only—'

'Hold your tongue, Carlos,' Jack snapped brusquely.

There was a short silence. Kate pushed some more sticks into the fire, her face rosy.

'Yes,' Carlos continued, 'that little bird is as flat as a board at the moment, but with some of your good solid English beef in her curves will grow—oh, yes, they will grow most deliciously.'

His soft laughter washed over Kate's rigid body. How dared they discuss her like that? She was no innocent, not any longer, but they did not know it.

No one who had travelled with an army could retain the total innocence of men that was so necessary for an unmarried English lady. Still, for most of that time she'd had the protection of her father and brothers and the broader protection of the soldiers who knew them. Kate had walked freely among the troops, tending wounds, writing letters to loved ones and doling out soup and cheerful greetings, secure in the knowledge that not one of them would offer her the sort of insult that she was now having to endure in the home of a so-called English gentleman! Even if it was in a foreign tongue.

Of course, given how she had left the Peninsula, she should be inured to this sort of insult by now—but these men knew nothing of that. And she was *not* inured to insult and never would be!

Carlos's voice penetrated her consciousness again. 'And when those curves do grow, Major Jack, I will be there to worship them. I, Carlos Miguel Riviera.'

'That's enough!' Jack's voice was suddenly harsh. 'You'll do no such thing.'

'Ah, Major Jack…' the other smiled with dawning comprehension '…you fancy the little mouse yourself, do you?'

'Not at all,' snapped Jack furiously. 'I have no interest in tumbling scrawny kitchen maids. But I won't have you sniffing around her. She's…she's my grandmother's servant and you're not to go near her, understand?'

The men of the Coldstream Guards all knew that particular tone and not one of them would have dreamed of answering back or disobeying. Carlos's hands rose in a placatory fashion. 'No, no, of course not, Major Jack. I will have nothing to do with the girl, nothing, I promise you.' His voice was soothing, conciliatory, then his evil genius prompted him to add, 'She is all yours, Major Jack, all yours.'

Jack sat up and glared at Carlos, but a clatter from the other end of the kitchen distracted him. Both men turned to look at Kate.

The small body was rigid with fury, the grey-green eyes blazing tempestuously. 'Your coffee, *gentlemen*.' She emphasised the last word sarcastically, then, to both men's utter amazement, she lifted the coffee pot and hurled it straight at them.

Chapter Three

Reactions honed by years of fighting sent both men instantly diving out of the way, but nothing could save them from being splattered with hot coffee as the earthenware pot shattered against the wall behind them. They cursed and swore in a fluent mixture of Spanish, Portuguese and English and turned to face the source of their anger. But there was no one to be seen. Kate had not waited to see the results of her action, but had stormed out of the kitchen while they were still ducking for cover.

'Blast the wench!' Jack growled. 'What the hell's the matter with her? Damned coffee all over me.' He pulled off his shirt, now sodden with brown coffee, and used it to mop down his dripping face and chest.

Carlos, similarly engaged with the aid of a drying cloth, looked across at him. 'You think, Major Jack, that maybe she understand what we were saying?'

Jack stared at him. 'An English kitchen maid, in the middle of Leicestershire, understand Spanish?' His tone was incredulous. 'Impossible! Though she did clean that soot off her face.'

He absent-mindedly rubbed the shirt over his arms and chest, then shook his head. 'No. Ridiculous. She's English.'

He stood up and roughly towelled the remains of the coffee from his unruly black hair.

'Unless she has Spanish blood in her.' He considered her clear, pale skin, the grey-green eyes and the curly, nut-brown hair, then he shook his head again. 'Hasn't got the colouring for it.'

Carlos shrugged. 'Then why?' His hands spread out eloquently, indicating the devastated coffee pot.

'How the hell should I know why?' Jack growled. 'The chit ought to be in Bedlam for all I know. Damn her, but she'll not get away with it this time!'

'This time?' queried Carlos, the beginnings of a grin appearing on his broad face. 'Do you say, Major Jack, that the little mouse has crossed you before?'

A pair of icy-blue eyes turned on him. 'Clean up this mess at once,' snapped the crisp voice so familiar to the men of the Coldstreams.

'*Sí, sí.* At once, Major Jack, at once.' Carlos bent to the task instantly as Jack strode from the room with a frown like a black thundercloud on his face.

'Oho, little mouse, you've roused the lion in him, to be sure,' Carlos muttered. 'I hope you've hidden yourself safe away, for Major Jack is greatly to be feared when he has the devil in him.'

Jack entered the hallway and glanced swiftly around. No sign of the chit. His hands clenched into fists. He'd give the little hussy a good shaking before he sent her packing! The chill morning air quivered against his bare skin, and with a muttered curse he moved quickly up the stairs towards his room, favouring his stiff leg quite heavily. Turning the corner on the landing, he ran smack into Kate storming along the corridor. They collided with such force he had to grab her to steady himself.

Kate, too, reached out instinctively and found herself clasped against a broad, strong, very naked male torso. His chest was deep and lightly sprinkled with dark hair, his shoulders broad and powerfully muscled. His skin was warm and smooth and his scent, the scent of a powerful male, surrounded her, filling her awareness.

'Oh!' she gasped, and tried to pull away.

'Not so fast, my girl!' he grated. 'How dare you toss that thing at us? You could have caused a serious injury.'

'Nonsense,' she scoffed, tugging at his grip, 'I've played cricket for years—I'm an excellent shot and I aimed to miss.'

'Cricket? Rubbish! Girls don't play cricket. You need a lesson in behaviour, young woman!'

'Let go of me,' she spat, struggling in his arms. 'How dare you?' She wriggled and writhed, but he held her effortlessly. It was no use trying to fight him, she realised; the big brute was far too strong. He chuckled, a low rumbling from deep inside his chest.

'If you keep wriggling against me like that, little spitfire, I just might begin to enjoy this,' he murmured into her ear.

Kate froze. The wretch was seeking to put her to the blush—she would have to use other tactics.

'Ohh, ohh, you're hurting me…ohh…' She sighed dramatically and sagged abruptly in his arms.

'Bloody hell!' he muttered.

Kate felt the hard grip on her arms instantly gentle.

'Hell and damnation,' he muttered again. The girl was so small and frail. And he had caused her to faint. A wave of remorse passed over him. He felt a brute, a savage. He'd known she was half starved. There was no need to frighten her to death, even if she had hurled a pot of hot coffee at his head. He'd have to carry her to her room, he supposed. His grip shifted and he bent to swing her into his arms.

Instantly Kate moved. In a flash she escaped his arms and dealt him a smart slap across the face. 'Brains before brute force every time!' she flashed, and took to her heels down the corridor.

As she reached her room, she turned. 'And girls do play

cricket!' She slammed the door behind her, turned the key and leant against it panting, laughing, oddly exhilarated.

He stared after her, frustrated, cursing her in English and Spanish. Then he turned and limped as quickly as he could towards his grandmother's room, his face black as thunder.

'Grandmama!' He burst into her room. 'Who the devil is that…that little hell-cat?'

The beady blue eyes examined her grandson's face closely. He was in a fierce temper—it was positively blazing from his eyes. Splendid! Lady Cahill thought. No sign of the lacklustre absence of spirit that Amelia spoke of. Something, or rather someone, by the sounds of it, had stirred him up beautifully. And his loving grandmother would continue the process.

She glared at him. 'What the devil do *you* mean, sir, to come storming into my boudoir at this time of day, cursing and swearing and raising your voice?' The blue eyes were frosty with displeasure. 'In *my* day, no gentleman would dream of entering a lady's presence in such indecent attire, or should I say lack of it? Be off with you, boy, and don't return until you are properly clothed! I am shocked and appalled, Jack, shocked and appalled!' She turned her head from his naked chest in a pained, offended manner.

Jack opened his mouth, then shut it with a snap. Blast it, he could hardly give her a piece of his mind. She was his grandmother, dammit. He glared at her, fully aware of her game. She was the most outrageous old lady he knew—he would bet his last guinea that she was no more shocked at seeing a man without a shirt than he was. And as for his swearing…the old hypocrite, peppering almost every phrase she uttered with oaths, then pretending to blush at his! He was damned if he'd stay and let his grandmother rake him over the coals for the entertainment of herself and her dresser! Jack bowed ironically and left the room.

He slammed the door and Lady Cahill relaxed back against the pillows, grinning in a most unladylike way.

'Oh, how shocking, milady,' said the hovering woman dressed severely in grey.

'Oh, don't be such a ninny, Smithers. You've seen a man without his shirt before, haven't you?' Lady Cahill cast a quick glance at her poker-faced maid. 'Well, perhaps not. It'll widen your education in that case.'

'Milady!' said Smithers indignantly.

'Oh, fetch me my wrap,' said the old lady. 'I'm getting up.'

'Before eleven!' gasped Smithers.

Lady Cahill regarded the shocked face of her maid in amusement. 'Perhaps not,' she decided. 'You can fetch that child I brought with me. Ask her to come and take hot chocolate with me here, if such a thing can be found in this be-nighted place.'

Her maid stiffened in displeasure. 'That…that shabby young person, milady?'

The old lady's voice turned to ice. 'That "shabby young person", as you refer to her, is the daughter of my beloved goddaughter, Maria Farleigh, and as such, Smithers, is to be treated as my honoured guest. Do you understand?'

The woman curtseyed. 'Yes, milady,' she murmured humbly.

Kate stiffened at the knock on her door. She hunched her shoulder away from it and remained curled up on the bed. The knock sounded again. 'Go away!' she said.

There was a short silence.

'Miss?' The voice was unmistakably female. Kate slipped off the bed and ran to the door. The disapproving face of Smithers met her eye. 'Lady Cahill invites you to join her in her bedchamber to take chocolate.' The cold, pale eyes ran quickly over Kate's shabby outfit and the long nose twitched almost imperceptibly in disdain.

Kate's chin rose. 'Have you prepared the chocolate?' she asked bluntly.

The stare grew contemptuous. 'I am her ladyship's dresser, not the cook. I will direct Mr Carstairs's man to arrange for the cook to prepare it immediately.' The cold stare informed Kate that even a guttersnipe would know better than to expect an important personage like Lady Cahill's dresser to lower herself with the preparation of foodstuffs.

Kate repressed a grin and took two steps in the direction indicated by Smithers. She would have liked to see this woman's face when she realised there was no one to prepare breakfast for herself or Lady Cahill. Then a stab of compunction halted her. Lady Cahill was an elderly lady who had been exhausted by her journey into the country. And Kate knew that she had eaten nothing at all during the trip.

'Please inform Lady Cahill that I will join her directly. I will see to her ladyship's breakfast first.'

The eyebrows rose in displeasure. The prim mouth opened. 'But her ladyship gave me the clearest instructions—'

'If you would be so good as to convey my message to Lady Cahill,' Kate interrupted in a cool voice which, despite its soft huskiness, left no room for argument.

'Very good, miss.' The woman sniffed disparagingly, but left without argument, hiding her surprise. Despite her hideous clothing, this girl had some breeding in her.

Kate ran downstairs, keeping a wary eye open for the two men, but they were nowhere to be seen. In the kitchen she quickly built up the fire and set the kettle to boil. There was no chocolate to be had. She surveyed the barren storeroom ruefully and shrugged. She'd just have to do the best she could.

She found a large tray and set it with a cloth. In a few minutes it bore crockery, a pot of tea, two soft boiled eggs and some lightly buttered toast. It was not what Lady Cahill was used to, no doubt, but it would have to do. She carried the heavy tray upstairs.

'Ah, my dear,' said Lady Cahill. 'But what are you doing carrying that heavy tray, you foolish child? Get one of the servants to do that for you.'

Kate deftly set the tray down on a table beside Lady Cahill's bed. 'Good morning, ma'am,' she said cheerfully. 'I trust you slept well.'

The old lady grimaced. 'In this bed? My dear, how could I?' She gestured towards the shabby hangings and worn furniture. 'I suppose I must be grateful that I have a chamber at all, since my dear grandson refused even to see his sister. Thank heavens Smithers had the forethought to pack bedding. I don't know what sort of place my grandson is running here, but I can tell you—I intend to have words with him on the subject.'

The old lady twinkled beadily at her and Kate found herself smiling back. She poured the tea.

'Tea?' said the old lady pettishly. 'I told Smithers chocolate.'

'I fear there is none to be had in the house.'

'No chocolate?' said the old lady incredulously. 'I know the countryside is uncivilised, but this is ridiculous.' She pouted. 'I suppose there are no fresh pastries either?'

Kate shook her head. 'No, indeed, ma'am. But I did get you some freshly boiled eggs and a little toast. Here, eat it while it is still hot,' she coaxed.

Ignoring the old woman's *moue* of distaste, Kate placed the food before her. After some grumbling, Lady Cahill consumed the repast, pretending all the while that she was only doing it to please Kate. Finally she sat back against her pillows and regarded Kate speculatively. 'Now, missy,' she said. 'I gather you've met my grandson.'

'What did he say about me?' Kate asked warily.

The old lady chuckled. 'Nothing much, really.'

'Oh,' said Kate. Clearly Lady Cahill did not intend to enlighten her. 'He...he doesn't know who I am, does he, ma'am?'

The old lady noted with interest the faint colour that rose on Kate's cheeks. 'Didn't he ask you?'

Kate looked slightly embarrassed. 'No...I mean, yes, he

asked me, and of course I told him my name. But I don't think he understands my position.'

'What did you tell him?'

Kate looked uncomfortable. 'I told him to ask you.' She was annoyed to find that her voice had taken on a faintly defensive tone and added boldly, 'Indeed, ma'am, I could not answer him, having been kidnapped! I do not know why you have brought me to this place or what you intend me to do.'

Lady Cahill acknowledged her point with a slow nod. 'Truth to tell, child, I had no clear intention at the time, except to get you away from that dreadful cottage and prevent you from ruining your life.'

'Ruining my life? How so, ma'am?'

'Tush, girl. Don't poker up like that! Once you'd been in service that would have been the end of any possibility for an eligible alliance.'

'An eligible alliance!' Kate spoke in tones of loathing.

'Yes, indeed, miss!' snapped Lady Cahill. 'You're not on the shelf yet. You have good blood, good bones and you have no business giving up on life in such a stubborn fashion!'

'Giving up on life? I'm not giving up on life. I am endeavouring to make my way in it. And I fully intend to do so— in the way *I* choose to do it!'

Kate jumped up from her seat at the end of the bed and began to pace around the room. It was vital that she get Lady Cahill to understand. It was simply not possible for Kate to make an eligible alliance any longer. She was ruined and, even if she attempted to hide the fact, it must come out eventually. But she had no desire to explain the whole sordid tale to this autocratic old lady whose sharp tongue hid a kind heart. It was cowardly, she knew, but if she could retain this old lady's respect, even by false means, she would. She must convince her some other way.

'I know you mean well by your charity, but I cannot bring myself to accept it. I have been too long accustomed to running my father's household, and have had responsibilities far in excess of other girls of my age and station.'

'Charity be damned!' snapped Lady Cahill.

'Ma'am, just look at me. Look at my clothes. You say you wish me to live with you as your guest, to take me into society. Can you see me paying morning visits and attending balls in this?' She gestured angrily at her shabby garments.

Lady Cahill stared at her incredulously. 'Well, of course not, you ridiculous child! I wouldn't dress my lowest skivvy in those rags.' She leant back in the bed, shaking her head at the folly of the girl. 'Naturally I will provide you with all that you will need—dresses, gowns, gloves, hats, parasols, trinkets—all the fal-lals that you could wish for. '

'Exactly, ma'am. I would have to ask you for each little thing, and that I could not bear.'

'Ah, bah!' snorted Lady Cahill.

'Besides, ma'am, I have no social skills to speak of. You seem to have overlooked the fact of my upbringing. I have no musical skills, I have never learnt to paint watercolours, I can patch and darn anything, and have even sewn up wounds, but I cannot do fancy embroidery. I can dance, but I do not know how to chat of nothing day in and day out. I have worked for most of my life, ma'am, and that is what I do best. I simply do not have it in me to act the social butterfly and that is what you want me to do.'

Oh, Lord, Kate prayed, let me not have to tell her the truth. Her arguments were valid enough; it would be difficult for Kate to accept charity—that was true. She knew herself to be overly stiff-necked about such things. But to attend routs and balls, to learn her way in society, to bury herself in frivolity for a time—a foolish part of Kate longed for those very things.

Lady Cahill stared, utterly appalled. 'Child, child, you have no idea what you are saying. Most of those things are not necessary and the others you can learn. Entering society does not mean becoming a social butterfly and chatting of nothing—though, I grant you, a great many people do little else. But there are fools in every stratum of society.'

She fell silent for a moment, then waved her hand at the girl sitting so silently at the end of the bed. 'You fatigue me, child, with your foolish intractability. I must give this matter further consideration. Leave me now. We will talk of this further.'

Kate rose, feeling a trifle guilty for causing the old lady distress. It was not her fault, she told herself defensively. She had not asked to be brought here. She had the right to make decisions for her own life and she owed Lady Cahill nothing except politeness. So why did she feel that she was in the wrong? Was it wrong to wish to owe nothing to anybody? Was it wrong to want to earn her own money, to refuse dependence on others? No, it wasn't wrong…it just felt wrong when she had to refuse an old lady's kindness, she reluctantly acknowledged.

She picked up the breakfast tray and left, closing the door softly behind her. A door ahead of her opened and Jack Carstairs appeared in the hall. Kate halted abruptly. He was between her and the stairs. She could flee to her own room, return to Lady Cahill's bedchamber or face him out.

Folding his arms, Jack leaned against the wall and awaited her arrival, a sardonic look on his face.

Kate's chin rose stubbornly. She would not be intimidated by mere brute force! Even if he was over six feet and with shoulders as wide as…well, as wide as any shoulders had a right to be. But she wasn't nervous of him. Certainly not! She gripped the heavy tray more tightly in her hands, taking obscure comfort in the fact that it was between them, and walked forward, her head high.

A faint glimmer of amusement appeared in Jack's eyes. She was calling his bluff, was she? After tossing that coffee pot, she had a right to expect that he might want to throttle her. And then she'd slapped him—slapped the master of the house. So foolhardy. He could snap her in two if he chose; she would surely know that. She wasn't to know he'd never hurt a woman in his life. But did she quail? No, on she came, chin held defiantly high. His amusement deepened. Such a little creature, but with so much spirit.

Even if she didn't fear violence from him, after that outrageous act of hers in the kitchen, she must surely expect to be dismissed without a character. It was, he knew, a servant's biggest dread, for it meant they were unlikely ever to gain employment again. She must know that. Her dreadful shabby black clothes, clearly made for another woman and adapted to her thin frame, showed she was well acquainted with poverty. And starvation was obviously a recent experience.

But her precarious position hadn't stopped her hurling that pot of hot coffee straight at his head. Or over his head, as she claimed. Cricket, indeed! He almost snorted. But why had she thrown it in the first place? Unlikely though it seemed, perhaps this little English kitchen maid did speak Spanish. Jack decided to test the theory. He remained leaning casually against the wall, watching her.

Kate swept past him, apparently indifferently, though her heart was beating rather faster than usual. She reached the steps, and he said in Spanish, '*Señorita*, there is an enormous black spider caught in your hair. Allow me to remove it for you.'

He waited for her to turn around, to scream, to start tearing at her hair or to continue, ignorant of what he had said.

She simply froze. Jack waited for a moment, puzzled, and then strode towards her. '*Señorita?*'

She did not move. Jack touched her shoulder. Good God! The girl was shaking like a leaf. He could hear the crockery on the tea tray rattling faintly.

Swiftly he turned her around to face him and was appalled to see naked terror in her eyes. Her face was dead white and the clear smooth forehead was beginning to bead with perspiration. She was swallowing convulsively. Through dry, pale lips she whispered piteously, 'Please get it off me.'

Jack stared at her for a few seconds, stunned by the unexpected intensity of her reaction.

'Please,' she whispered again, shuddering under his hands.

'My poor girl. I'm so sorry,' he said remorsefully. 'There is no spider. None at all.'

He took the tray from her unresisting hands and laid it on a nearby table, not taking his eyes off her.

She stared at him, uncomprehending. He placed his hands on her shoulders again and gave her a tiny shake to jolt her out of her trance-like terror.

'There is no spider. I made it up,' he explained apologetically. 'It was a trick.'

Her mouth opened and she started to breathe again in deep, agonised gasps.

'I'm sorry,' he repeated. 'I wanted to see if you understood Spanish.'

She looked up at him in confusion, her mind still numbed by the remnants of her uncontrollable fear of spiders.

'I spoke in Spanish, you see.' His hands rested warmly on her shoulders. She was still trembling and, despite himself, he was moved. Not knowing what else to do to atone, he drew her against him, wrapped her in his arms and held her tight against him, uttering soothing noises in her ear. He inhaled slowly. What was that fragrance she wore? It was hauntingly familiar. His arms tightened.

It did not occur to him that it was utterly inappropriate for him to be behaving in this way with a mere kitchen maid. As a boy, Jack had frequently brought home creatures in distress—half-drowned kittens, injured birds—and if he had thought of it now he would have explained to anyone who asked that he was merely offering comfort and reassurance. And she felt so right just where she was.

Kate's cheek was pressed against his chest, her head tucked in the hollow between his chin and his throat. She could feel the warmth of his breath, the roughness of his unshaven cheek catching in the silk of her hair as he moved his face gently against it. She heard the steady thud of his heart. His strong body cradled hers, protecting, calming.

It had been so long since Kate had been held so comfortingly, the impulse just to let herself be held was irresistible. She felt his broad, strong hand moving soothingly up and down her spine and a shiver of awareness passed through her.

Gradually, Kate realised just who was holding her and why. She tried to wriggle out of the strong arms. He did not immediately release her, so with all the strength she possessed she thrust hard at his chest and emerged from his embrace dishevelled and panting, her face rosy with embarrassment.

'I suppose this is another one of your tricks!' She tried to smooth her hair and brushed down her clothes.

Jack felt his guilt intensify at her words and, unreasonably, anger flooded him.

'No, it damn well isn't, you little shrew! I'm not in the habit of entertaining myself with scruffy kitchen maids. I was merely offering comfort.'

She glared at him, not knowing which made her angrier, his actions of the past few minutes or his description of her.

'Well, I don't need your sort of comfort and I wouldn't have needed comforting in the first place if you hadn't played that beastly trick on me!'

'How was I to know you'd make such a devilish to-do about a spider?'

Kate's temper died abruptly and she looked away. She had always been deeply ashamed of her fear of spiders and had tried valiantly to conquer it, to no avail. Her brain might tell her that the horrid creatures were small and for the most part harmless, but the moment she was confronted with one she panicked. It was a weakness in herself she despised.

'You're right,' she muttered stiffly. 'I'm sorry I made such a fuss. It won't happen again.' She turned to pick up the tray.

'Not so fast, my girl,' he said, and his hand shot out to grip her wrist. He turned her to face him again. 'Who the devil are you?' he said slowly, his eyes boring into her.

'I told you my name last night. It is Kate Farleigh, in case you have forgotten,' she retorted, twisting her arm to escape his grip. 'Will you please release my hand?'

'I haven't finished with you yet.'

Kate pursed her lips in annoyance. 'I suppose you think your position entitles you to make game of others!'

'What?' He frowned down at her in puzzlement.

'Evidently you consider you're perfectly entitled to treat those less fortunate than yourself in any fashion you care to! Well, I take leave to dispute you on that. No matter who I am, I have the right to go about my concerns as I see fit, without interference from you or any other member of your family!' Kate looked pointedly down at her wrist, imprisoned by his large strong hand.

He noted the short, blunt, unpolished nails, so different from the smooth, polished ovals on every lady of his acquaintance. He turned her hand over and his large thumb moved gently back and forth over the work-roughened skin. There was no doubt that this girl was accustomed to menial work, but she was an enigma all the same.

'You are the damnedest kitchen maid!' he murmured at last, shaking his head. 'How the devil did you come to be brought here by my grandmother?'

Kate looked up at him in surprise. The dark head was still frowning over her hand. She repressed a rueful grin. She supposed she couldn't blame him for that. She was surely dressed for the part and he had seen her working in the kitchen, obviously at home. Well, if the master of the house insisted on calling Kate a kitchen maid, Kate would oblige him—and serve him right! She had an imaginary spider to pay him back for, after all!

'Sir.' She tugged at her hand.

His thumb still absently caressed her.

'I must get back to my duties, sir. The kitchen floor needs scrubbing.' She tried to pull her hand free again, becoming increasingly unsettled by the gentle motion of his thumb on her skin.

'But where on earth did you learn to speak like a lady?'

Oh, drat the man! Would he never leave off? Kate's sense of humour got the best of her. 'A lady, sir?' She goggled in mock-surprise, and did her best to simper. 'I never thought I sounded like a real lady.' She pronounced it 'loidy'.

'I kept house for an old gentleman for a long time and he insisted I learn to speak proper-like. He was a true scholar, sir, and a Reverend he was, too, and he hated what he called the mangling of the English language.'

He did not appear to notice that her accent had broadened considerably during this speech, a fact which Kate found immensely encouraging. She twisted her hands awkwardly, as she imagined a rustic wench would, when confronted by a handsome gentleman.

'He taught me to read and write and cipher an' all,' she added ingenuously, regarding him with wide, innocent eyes—which she was tempted for a moment to cross, but didn't.

'But you understand Spanish,' Jack persisted. 'Where does a kitchen maid come to know a foreign tongue like that?'

'I imagine there are hundreds of kitchen maids in Spain,' she responded pertly, her eyes downcast to hide the mischief in them.

'Don't be impertinent, girl; you know perfectly well I was asking how an English kitchen maid like you came to know Spanish. It's obvious to me that you have no Spanish blood.'

She beamed up at him foolishly. 'You're absolutely right, sir—no Spanish blood at all. You are a clever gentleman. Coo, so you are.'

The chit was playing games with him again! He was hard put to it not to laugh—except that he had an equally strong impulse to turn her over his knee. How on earth had this cheeky little miss survived this long without being strangled, let alone kept a position in a household? He couldn't imagine his grandmother putting up with this type of cheek from a maidservant. His mouth quirked in some amusement. His grandmother would not take kindly to competition in the art of impertinence and this little baggage was every bit her equal.

'Enough of your sauce, girl. I asked you how an English maid came to understand Spanish.'

'Oh, the gentleman did a lot of foreign travel and it were easier for him to take me than leave me behind, so a'course I was bound to pick up some of the lingo, wasn't I? Will that be all, sir?' she asked humbly, her head bent to hide her laughter.

She could see perfectly well that she hadn't satisfied his curiosity, and that he didn't like it. He was used to being in control. Well, he wasn't going to control her. He'd be furious when he found out who she really was, but it served him right for jumping to conclusions. And for the spider.

'Hmm. Yes, all right,' he mumbled ungraciously.

Kate bobbed him the sort of rustic curtsey her old nurse used to make to her father, and picked up the tray. She stepped lightly down the stairs, her mouth trembling on the verge of laughter as she imagined his face when his grandmother finally explained who she was.

Jack watched her slight figure disappear, then turned and knocked at his grandmother's door.

Chapter Four

'Where the devil did you find that girl, Grandmama?' he demanded on entry.

His grandmother regarded him coolly. 'I am very well, Jack, thank you for asking.'

'Dammit, Grandmama...' he began, then, noting the light of battle in the beady blue eyes, decided it would be politic to capitulate. His grandmother, Jack knew from long experience, was quite capable of parrying his questions all day. Curse it, he sighed, what had he done to be plagued with such females? Only a few days ago, life had been so peaceful.

He sat himself down on the edge of her bed, his stiff leg out before him, ignoring the strangled gasp of horror from his grandmother's maid at the impropriety.

'Oh, get out, Smithers, get out if you cannot stomach the sight of a man seated on my bed!' snapped Lady Cahill. She waited until the maid removed herself, after having favoured her mistress with a look of deep reproof.

'Stupid woman!' muttered the old lady. 'But she's worth her weight in gold at *la toilette*. Makes an old woman like me look less of an old hag.'

Jack smiled, his good humour restored. 'Old hag, indeed! What a shocking untruth, Grandmama. As if you haven't remained an acknowledged beauty all your life. You've clearly recovered from the ordeal of the journey, for I must tell you that you are in great looks, positively blooming in fact.'

'Oh, pish tush!' said his grandmother in delight. 'You're a wicked boy and I know perfectly well that you're only trying to turn me up sweet.'

Jack's lips twitched, as he recalled the time his grandmother had read his sister a blistering lecture for using exactly that piece of slang. 'Turn you up sweet, indeed?' he quizzed her. 'Good God, Grandmama. What a vulgar expression. I'm shocked!'

'Don't criticise your elders and betters, young man,' she retorted, her twinkling eyes revealing she was fully aware of her inconsistency. 'Now, what's all this I've heard about you falling into the megrims? It's not like you, Jack, and I won't have it!'

Jack took a deep breath, struggling to overcome the surge of annoyance that rose within him at her blunt statement. 'As you see, Grandmama,' he responded lightly, 'your sources have misinformed you. I'm in the pink of health despite being a cripple.'

Lady Cahill frowned at him. 'You're no more a cripple than I am,' she snapped. 'What's a stiff leg? Your grandfather had one for years as a result of a hunting accident and it never stopped him from doing anything he wanted to.'

'As I recall, ma'am, my grandfather was still able to ride to hounds until shortly before his death.'

A short silence fell. Lady Cahill considered the cruel irony of her grandson's injury. A noted rider to hounds until his injury, Jack had received as his only inheritance a house in one of the most famous hunting shires in the country. Now, when he was unable even to sit a horse.

Jack stood up awkwardly. He still found it hard to face discussion of his wounds. 'Can one enquire as to what brought you to my humble home?' he asked, changing the subject.

'You may well ask that,' she said crossly.

'Yes, I just did,' he murmured irrepressibly.

'Don't be cheeky, boy! I came to find out what was happening to you. Now, tell me, sir, what did you mean by denying your own sister hospitality?'

'Grandmama, you can see for yourself that this place is not yet fit to receive guests... Besides, I was castaway at the time. I do regret it, but I've had enough of women weeping and sighing over my...my disfigurement,' he finished stiffly.

'Disfigurement, my foot!' She snorted inelegantly. Her eyes wandered to the scar on his right cheek. 'If you are referring to that little scratch on your face, well, you were always far too good-looking for your own good. You look a great deal more manly now, not so much of a pretty boy.'

He bowed ironically. 'I thank you, ma'am.'

'Oh, tush!' she said. 'I think I will get up now, so take yourself off and get one of those lazy servants of yours to bring me up some hot water.'

'I regret it, ma'am, but I cannot.'

'What do you mean, boy?'

He shrugged indifferently. 'I don't employ any indoor servants.'

Lady Cahill sat up in bed, deeply shocked. 'What? No servants?' she gasped. 'Impossible! You must have servants!'

'I have no interest in the house. I've bivouacked in enough dam—dashed uncomfortable places in the last few years and now it's enough for me to have a roof over my head and a bed to sleep in. I have no intention of forking out a small fortune for a horde of indoor servants, merely to see to my comfort, even if I had a small fortune to fork out, which as you know I do not.'

Lady Cahill was appalled. '*No* indoor servants?'

He shrugged again. 'None but my man, Carlos, and he sees to my horses as well.' He held up his hand, forestalling any further comment from her. 'There are only those servants you brought with you yourself. I'm afraid you'll have to get them to wait on you. Only I sent them to stay in the village at the inn—all except for your dresser and maid. They can see to your needs as best they can.'

Lady Cahill snorted. 'You won't see Smithers demeaning herself by heating water.'

He shrugged. 'Get your other maid to do it. She seems capable enough.'

'What other maid? What are you talking about, boy?'

Jack sighed. 'Grandmama, don't you think it's time you stopped calling me "boy"? I am past thirty, you know.'

'Don't be ridiculous, boy! And stop changing the subject. What other maid are you talking about?'

'The little thin creature in the dreadful black clothes. I must say, Grandmama, that I am surprised that you haven't noticed them. You're usually so fastidious about your servants' appearance. And how is it—' his voice deepened with indignation '—that you allowed the girl to almost starve herself to death? She swooned last night in the driveway and there was no one to assist her.'

'Swooned?' said Lady Cahill, watching him narrowly.

'Fell down in a dead faint. From hunger, unless I miss my guess. She's nothing but skin and bones, with the most enormous eyes. Pale skin, curly brown hair, looks as if a breeze would blow right through her, a tongue on her like a wasp but, apparently, scared stiff of spiders.'

Jack halted, suddenly aware that he had said far too much. He knew from past experience that his grandmother could add two and two and come up with five.

'Frightened of spiders, is she? That surprises me. I wouldn't have said that that young woman was afraid of much at all. I would've said she has a deal of courage. But she's not my maid,' Lady Cahill added finally. 'Is that what she told you?'

Jack frowned. 'No,' he said slowly, thinking back. 'I suppose I rather jumped to that conclusion.' His eyes narrowed, recalling Kate's performance of a few minutes ago. 'If she isn't your maid, who is she?'

'Her name is Kate Farleigh.'

'I know that, ma'am. She did inform me of that. But what is she doing here?' Jack hung on to his patience.

His grandmother shrugged vaguely. 'Now, how should I know what she is doing, Jack? You know perfectly well I haven't left this room since I arrived last night. She could be picking flowers or taking tea. How the deuce should I know what she is doing, silly boy?'

Jack gritted his teeth. 'Grandmama, why has this girl come to my house?'

The old lady smiled guilelessly up at him. 'Oh, well, as to that, dear boy, she had no choice. No choice at all.'

'Grandmother!' Jack's lips thinned.

'Now don't get tetchy with me, boy; it doesn't work. Your grandfather used to rant and rave at me all the time.'

'I fully understand why, and heartily sympathise with him!' her undutiful grandson snapped. 'Now enough of this nonsense, Grandmama. Who is she?'

'Her name is Kate Farleigh and she is the only daughter of my goddaughter, the late Maria Farleigh, *née* Delacombe.' In a few pithy sentences, Lady Cahill put Jack in possession of the bare bones of Kate's story, as she knew it.

He frowned. 'Then she is a lady.'

'Of course.'

'Well, she doesn't behave like one.'

'I saw no sign of any lack of breeding,' said his grandmother. 'A temper, yes. Glared at me out of those big blue eyes of hers—'

'Not blue. A sort of grey-green.'

The old woman repressed a grin. So he had noticed the colour of her eyes, had he? 'Whatever you say,' she agreed. 'The gel glared at me, but there was no sign of panic—stayed as cool as you please as I whisked her off to heaven-knew-where.'

His eyebrows rose at this. 'What do you mean, you whisked her off?'

'Oh, don't look like that, Jack. It was the only possible

thing. You said yourself the girl was on the verge of starvation. She was in dire straits. She is an orphan with no blood kin to turn to and has not a penny left in the world, unless I miss my guess.'

Jack frowned, stretching his bad leg reflectively. 'I still don't understand.'

'The girl has far more than her share of stubborn foolish pride. Just like her dratted father in that respect. Maria's family wanted to make a huge settlement on her when she married him, Maria being their only child, but he would have none of it. Didn't want it to be thought he was marrying her for her money. And look what has come of it! His own daughter dressed in rags and almost starving! Faugh! I have no patience with the man!'

'But Kate…er…Miss Farleigh, Grandmama,' he prompted.

'Said she wasn't interested in taking charity from me or anyone else. Well, I had no time to stand around bandying words with her in her poky little hovel. So I kidnapped her.'

'You *what*?' Jack stared at his grandmother in amazement. Truly, she was an outrageous old lady. His lips twitched and suddenly he couldn't help himself; the chuckles welled up from somewhere deep inside him. He collapsed on the bed and laughed till his sides hurt.

His grandmother watched him, deeply pleased. It was the first glimpse she'd had of the beloved grandson who had gone off to the wars. A scarred, silent, cynical stranger had returned in his place, and until she saw him laughing now, with such abandon, she had not realised how frightened she'd been that the old Jack had truly perished for ever in the wars.

Something had shattered the deep reserve he'd adopted since he came home from the Peninsula War, crippled, disinherited, then jilted. He'd remained unnaturally calm, seeming not to care, not to react. Except that he'd withdrawn into himself and become a recluse.

Now, in the space of an hour or so, Lady Cahill had seen her grandson boiling with fury, then laughing uninhibitedly.

And a slip of a girl seemed to have caused it all. Lady Cahill thanked heaven for the impulse that had caused her to call on Kate on the way to Leicestershire. The girl could not be allowed to disappear now.

The old lady pushed at Jack's shoulders, which were still heaving with mirth. 'Oh, get out of here, boy. I've had enough of you and your foolishness this morning.' She spoke gruffly to cover her emotion.

'It's time I got dressed or Smithers will be having hysterics. It's clear to me that this place of yours needs a woman to set things in order, so I suppose I must shift myself and set to work. See if you can get me some hot water, there's a good boy. Now move, Jack, or I will get out of bed in my night-gown right now and that would most certainly cause Smithers to fall in a fit and foam at the mouth!'

Jack grinned at her. 'You are, without doubt, the most scandalous old lady of my acquaintance. I'm surprised that poor woman hasn't died of shock long since.' He rose from the bed and, still chuckling, limped from the room.

Jack headed downstairs, the laughter dying from his face. Now to find Miss Kate Farleigh without delay and put her straight on one or two things. A kitchen maid? Hah! Only interested in scrubbing the floor? Hah! To think he'd been worried about her! No doubt the little wretch was sitting somewhere with her feet up, laughing up her shabby sleeve at the fine trick she had played on him.

Entering the kitchen, he came to a dead halt. Kate was down on hands and knees, vigorously scrubbing the large flagstones of the kitchen floor, exactly as she'd said she would.

'What the *devil* do you think you're doing?' he roared.

Kate jumped, then turned, laid down the hard-bristled scrubbing brush and sat back on her heels. She noted the black frown, the clenched fists and the outrage. Her eyes twinkled. So, he had finally discovered who she was. And was feeling rather grumpy about it. She pressed her lips firmly together to stop them quivering with laughter.

Jack's violent reaction to the sight of her scrubbing his floor confused him. He battled with anger and an equally strong desire to lift her up and whisk her upstairs. She looked so small and delicate. She had no business attempting such a dirty and demeaning task. 'I said, what do you think you're doing?'

She glanced at the floor, still swimming with dirty water, then at the discarded scrubbing brush. 'It's called scrubbing the floor,' she explained helpfully, unable to resist teasing him a little. 'I would have thought a man of your age—'

'Don't play games with me, girl!' he growled. 'What the devil is my grandmother's guest doing scrubbing my floors and cooking my breakfast?' He glared at her. 'I won't have it, do you hear me? I won't have it!'

Kate, kneeling in a pool of scummy water, endeavoured to look soulful. 'But you did, don't you remember? Three eggs, six rashers of bacon, and almost a whole pot of coffee.'

'Dammit, I'm not talking about that—'

'But you were. You accused me of cooking your breakfast and then said you wouldn't have it,' she interrupted gently. 'I'm sorry if you didn't like my food.'

She attempted to make her lower lip quiver sorrowfully, but abandoned the effort and rattled on, well aware that she was fanning his temper to flames and oddly excited by the prospect. 'If you prefer, I won't cook your breakfast again. Indeed, I hadn't intended to do so, for it was my own breakfast I was cooking and you stol—commandeered it.'

With a grubby hand she pushed a straggling curl off her face, leaving a smear of dirt in its place. Unaware, she continued, 'I gather you didn't like it after all. But I dare say you are one of those people to whom the mere thought of breakfast is anathema. Perhaps the consumption of food at such an early hour made you feel…unwell? Certainly, if you'd been drinking the night before… I do seem to recall…' She lowered her eyelashes discreetly.

'I…that's not…I wasn't… The breakfast was very goo—' Jack glared at her again. The interview was not going at all as he had planned it. The cheeky little urchin. She was tying him into knots with a flow of polite-seeming nonsense, for all the world as if she were sitting in his grandmother's drawing-room, instead of at his feet in a puddle of water with dirt on her face.

'Why are *you* scrubbing this floor?' He bit out each word.

'I thought it was the best way to clean it. Perhaps there's a more modern method you would prefer?' She looked up at him as if for enlightenment, her gaze wide-eyed and artless.

'No, there isn't!' he snapped, infuriated.

'Well, in that case...' Kate hid a grin and picked up the scrubbing brush.

'Put down that blasted thing!' he roared.

Kate obligingly put it down, in the manner of humouring a lunatic. 'I see. You don't wish me to use the brush. Perhaps you would like me to use another implement?' She looked around the room, apparently seeking an alternative.

'I don't wish you to use anything!' he growled.

'But how else can I clean the floor?'

'I don't wish you to clean the floor at all!' he snapped.

Kate's eyebrows rose. 'Oh, I see. You *like* it dirty.' She shook her head in amazement. 'Well, if you *prefer* to live in filth...'

'I prefer nothing of the sort,' he roared, goaded beyond endurance. Bending down, he grasped her shoulders and dragged her to her feet.

'You impudent little baggage! Don't bandy words with me! I won't have you scrubbing my floors. Curse it, you're my grandmother's guest! Guests do *not* scrub floors!' He shook her in frustration. 'Do you understand me?'

It was one thing, Kate found, to tease him into losing his temper. It was quite another to be hauled unceremoniously to her feet and treated like a naughty child.

'Let go of me!' she gasped angrily, struggling in the iron grip. She swung back her foot, ready to kick him in order to free herself, but he was ready for her.

'No, you don't, you little vixen!' He lifted her at arm's length; her feet dangled six inches from the floor. 'My grandmother said you were a lady but, by God, she doesn't have any idea of what a shrew you really are!'

'Well, no doubt your grandmother is also under the impression that you are a gentleman!' Kate flashed back. 'I'm sure she has no knowledge of your...your manhandling habits!'

She freed herself at last with a final twist and darted behind the kitchen table.

'My what?' he said wrathfully.

'Well, what else would you call it?' she responded, pushing back several more curls which had come loose in the struggle. She glared at him, eyes bright, cheeks flushed, panting. 'I haven't been in this house above a day and on several occasions you have...have used violence on me!'

'Violence?' he repeated incredulously. 'And who threw a pot of hot coffee at my head not an hour ago?'

'And who deserved it, and more, for sitting there discussing me so horridly, as if I was...was...a...?' Kate flushed.

Jack looked uncomfortable. 'Well, how was I to know you understood what we were saying?'

'A gentleman would never have put me in that position.'

'A lady would never have been in the kitchen in the first place!'

'Oh, so I'm a lady now, am I? Pity you didn't think of it earlier.'

'My grandmother told me about you.'

'And you're prepared to take your grandmother's word on it, are you?' she said dryly.

'Are you calling my grandmother a liar?' he said in the soft tone that would have been a warning to anyone who knew him well.

'She's undoubtedly a kidnapper, so why not a liar?'

It was a complete facer, Jack had to admit it. His grandmother had confessed to kidnapping Kate without a shred of self-consciousness or guilt. He called down a silent curse on all women, particularly those currently under his roof.

'We will not discuss my grandmother,' he said with dignity. 'The fact remains that it was *your* behaviour which led me to assume you were a kitchen maid and treat you as such.'

'Oh, so it's perfectly respectable to insult honest kitchen maids, is it? Pray forgive me for not understanding the finer points of a gentleman's code of conduct!'

Jack's hands clenched in frustration. 'Of course it isn't, you little shrew! How in hel— Hades was I to know you understood Spanish?'

'Oh, so that makes it my fault too, does it?' Kate had been unsuccessfully trying to twist her hair back into its usual simple style; she tugged at the knot in frustration, bringing the rest of her hair tumbling over her shoulder.

'Then perhaps I'd better warn you that I also speak Portuguese, French, Latin and Greek, in case you ever find yourself wishing to insult me in those languages!'

'I didn't mean that and well you know it!' snapped Jack, his gaze following the glossy tumbled curls. Her hair smelled of that faint fresh fragrance that so eluded him, but her comment had put him in mind of another grievance. 'And how did you learn to speak those languages in the first place?'

'I told you!' said Kate.

'You told me some faradiddle about working for some eccentric old gentleman—'

'My father!' snapped Kate. 'And it was no faradiddle! Everything I told you was true.'

'Including the nonsense about being a poor little kitchen maid?' He leaned forward over the table.

'Well, no,' she admitted, 'I was my father's housekeeper. I never told you I was a kitchen maid—you jumped to that conclusion. I merely did not contradict your assumption.' A gleam of pure mischief shone in the green-grey eyes. 'Besides, it was quite entertaining. I simply couldn't resist.'

He suddenly lunged forward across the table and caught her

hand before she knew what he was doing. She struggled to snatch it back but his grip was firm. He turned her hand over and examined it, gently rubbing a red mark caused by the scrubbing brush.

Kate, embarrassed, tried again to pull her hand away. 'I know I don't have a lady's hands. I never have. In fact, as I told your grandmother, I doubt very much I can even be called a lady. What I allowed you to believe wasn't so far from the truth. Soon I will indeed be the maid you took me for.'

His grip on her hand tightened. 'Nonsense!'

'It is not nonsense,' she said quietly. 'Now, if you would please release my hand—again.'

He dropped it as if it were a hot coal. 'So, what do you intend to do?'

'Finish washing the floor,' said Kate, ignoring his real meaning.

'For the last time, girl, you will *not* scrub that floor!' He thumped a clenched fist onto the table.

Kate shrugged. 'I refuse to cook in a pigsty.'

'You're not going to do any cooking at all! Good God, woman, don't you *ever* do what you're told?' said the harassed erstwhile Major of the Coldstream Guards, running a hand through his unruly dark locks.

'Not when I'm told such foolish nonsense,' she answered composedly.

Calm grey-green eyes met fiery blue ones.

'Tell me, Mr Carstairs, who is to make luncheon for your grandmother if I do not?'

Jack's mouth opened, then closed. Kate's eyes twinkled.

'Exactly. Stale bread and cold meat will not do for her ladyship. On the other hand, neither my father nor my brothers ever had any cause to complain about my culinary skills, therefore I will prepare luncheon for your grandmother and, of course, the rest of the household. But I will *not* cook in such dirty surroundings, and so...' She bent gracefully to pick up the dish of water and the scrubbing brush.

'You will *not* scrub that floor! Carlos will do it. It's bad enough that I must accept your offer to prepare luncheon for my grandmother, but I won't allow you to sully your hands any more with such menial and degrading tasks! Don't argue with me, girl!' he growled, seeing her mouth open.

'I'll see to it at once!' He stormed to the door, which opened on to the courtyard. 'Carlos!' he bellowed. There was no answer, so with a muttered oath Jack stepped outside, preparing to search for his servant. Then he halted, remembering something. He stood for a moment, seemingly a little embarrassed.

'My…er…grandmother is…er…in need of some hot water… Could you please…er…would you mind setting some on to heat?'

'Of course,' said Kate. He closed the door behind him. Kate turned to fetch the water. She jumped as the door crashed open again.

'And don't even *think* of carrying it up to her, you hear me?' he roared at her.

Kate stared at him in surprise.

'I'll take it up. It's too heavy for you,' he mumbled, and left again.

'I cannot stay here in these primitive conditions,' Lady Cahill announced.

Jack repressed a jubilant grin. He'd hoped to be rid of her and it seemed that his prayers were about to be answered. 'I did warn you, Grandmama, that this house is not fit for guests.'

'No need to sound proud of it, boy,' she snapped. 'I have directed Smithers to get my things ready. I will stay a sennight or so at Alderby, before returning home.'

'Well, if you wish to reach Alderby in good time, you should leave here by two o'clock.' He rose.

'Sit down, boy. I haven't finished with you yet. I need to discuss that gel.'

Jack frowned, then a look of complete indifference settled

on his face. He shrugged. 'I thought she was to go and live with you. Changed your mind, have you?'

'No, I haven't! It is still my most ardent wish that she come and live with me and make her entrance into society, as is her birthright.'

'Well, then, it's settled.' He stretched his long, lean frame.

'It's no such thing!' said the old lady tartly. Her grandson turned and raised his eyebrows in enquiry.

'The stupid gel will have none of the scheme.'

The thick dark brows came together in a frown. 'What? You mean that girl out there—' he jerked his head in the direction of the door '—that half-starved little ragamuffin has turned you down?' His voice was incredulous. 'Refused an offer to be fed and clothed in the first style of elegance and taken to all the most fashionable places?' He ran his hands through his tousled dark hair. 'I don't believe it.'

'It's true enough!' said his grandmother acidly. 'Turned me down on no less than two separate occasions.'

'Does she know what she's refusing?' he said. 'Did you explain it to her? Describe to her what her life could be like?'

He received a withering look in reply.

'Yes, yes, I suppose you did,' he muttered, shaking his head in amazement. He could imagine no female of his acquaintance even considering the rejection of such a magnificent offer, let alone a girl in such dire straits as this one. Women, in his experience, were after all they could get.

'Lord, the chit must have bats in her belfry.'

'No,' said his grandmother dryly. 'She suffers from the same complaint as you.'

He stiffened and looked down his nose at her. 'And what is that, may I ask?'

'Excessive, stubborn, stiff-necked pride.'

'Excessive…er…pride?' he exclaimed stiffly. 'I don't know what you are talking about.'

He could feel the knowing blue gaze boring into him and clenched his teeth. She was referring to her offer to finance him, made when he'd first returned to England. He had refused it in no uncertain terms then and was damned if he was going to give her the satisfaction of discussing it now.

'The two situations have nothing in common.' He ignored the disbelieving arch of her elegantly pencilled brows. 'In any case, what has her situation to do with me?'

'The girl intends to hire herself out as a maidservant.'

'What?' His voice thundered. Kate had mentioned it earlier, but naturally he hadn't believed her. For a gently born girl to seriously consider such a thing was unheard of, particularly if she had other options.

'That's utterly ridiculous!' Aware of his revealing overreaction, he lowered his voice. 'She can't be serious. What's the chit playing at?'

'Of course it's ridiculous,' said his grandmother, 'but I do believe she means it. She intends to earn her own way. When I first met her she took me for her new employer.'

'Well, then, if she is so determined to ruin her life, what can you do?' he said in a show of indifference that deceived no one.

Lady Cahill smiled the sort of smile which had always made her family uneasy in the past. Jack watched her suspiciously.

'I intend to provide her with the kind of position she says she wants.'

'As your maid?' Jack was incredulous. 'I must say, Grandmama, that seems rather shabby to me—'

'Not as my maid,' the old lady interrupted. Jack's eyes narrowed, dark suspicion forming even as she spoke. 'As yours.'

'Mine!' he exploded. 'I'm damn—'

'As your housekeeper, I should have said,' continued his grandmother imperturbably. 'It's as clear as daylight to me that you need someone to prevent this house from crumbling into complete barbarism, and you have told me yourself that you are not willing to waste your money employing anyone to do it. I, however, am not prepared to allow a member of my family to live in such a disgraceful state. And you must admit this admirably solves the two problems.'

'I'll admit nothing of the sort!' he said angrily. 'I won't tolerate such unwarranted interference in my affairs, Grand-mama!'

'So you don't wish to help the girl?'

'Help her? To social ruin by employing her as my maid…housekeeper? I don't think—'

'No, Jack, you don't think. Naturally I will send some re-spectable woman to act as her chaperon. And I'm not consid-ering any ordinary terms of employment. I intend to put this to the girl: if she will consent to run your household for six months, turn it into a gentleman's establishment instead of a ramshackle place where a lady cannot even get a cup of choc-olate to break her fast, then I will consider—and, what's more to the point, so will *she*—that she will thereby have earned my sponsorship for a season in London. *She* can keep her pride, *you* can live like a moderately civilised human being and *I* can introduce Maria's gel to society.'

Lady Cahill sat back and regarded her grandson with some satisfaction. 'And, in the meantime, it will give me some time to have someone look into the matter of Kate's finances. I cannot believe that she's been left completely destitute. So, she stays here while I organise things. And setting this house in order will keep her nicely occupied, so that's settled.'

'It is *not* settled.'

'Jack, if you say no to this scheme, it will mean the end of that girl, for I tell you she is as stubborn and foolish as you are and she tells me she will not accept charity from me, or from anyone else.'

Jack met her level glance.

'Ah! Dammit!' He slammed his hand down on the table in frustration.

His grandmother smiled. She reached up and patted his chin. 'I knew you'd agree with me in the end.'

'I don't,' he snapped.

'But you will have her here.'

'It is the most ridiculous, ill-considered, inconvenient and damnably outrageous scheme I have ever heard of!'

'Good, then you'll do it!' nodded his grandmother complacently.

He glared at her and clenched his hair with his fingers.

'Yes, all right, you leave me no choice, though without doubt I should be clapped up in Bedlam for agreeing to it!'

'Don't be silly, boy,' she said, suddenly businesslike again. 'Now send that man into the village to tell my coachman to come and collect my baggage. Oh, and before you do fetch young Kate here. I'll just explain to her what it is you want her to do.'

'What *I* want?' he began. Fortuitously, he noticed the provocative glint in his grandmother's eye. 'Yes,' he said, goaded, 'you do that, Grandmama,' and strode from the room, slamming the door after him.

'And so, my dear Kate, you can see that my grandson's domestic circumstances are in a shocking state and yet Jack has no one to see to the smooth running of the house.' Lady Cahill applied a delicate wisp of lace to a wrinkled eyelid to emphasise her distress.

Kate became thoughtful. Lady Cahill had not resumed her arguments in favour of taking Kate to London with her and presenting her to society. Kate felt equal measures of disappointment and relief at that. A very small part of her, the wild, rebellious, frivolous part of her that her father had tried so hard to crush, wistfully longed for the prospect of a London season. Kate ruthlessly suppressed it. It was too late for all that.

An idea occurred to Kate. This could be her chance. Her domestic skills might once more be the saving of her. With Lady Cahill's backing, Kate might be able to carve herself a niche in this household and earn herself a home, a living, some security.

'Ma'am,' she said hesitantly, 'if you wish…I mean, if you think I am suitable…I could become the housekeeper here.'

'*You*, child? Don't be ridiculous! You couldn't possibly act as my grandson's housekeeper!' said the dowager spider to her youthful fly.

'Indeed I could, ma'am. I'm young, but I've had a great deal of experience. I was my father's housekeeper for many years. And it would be a better position than I would be likely to find elsewhere.' Kate fought to keep the eagerness out of her voice. 'I would take good care of your grandson, and you could rest assured that I was safe and in a secure position.'

Lady Cahill tapped her finger thoughtfully on the small table in front of her, then grimaced at the dust it had collected.

'Faugh!' she exclaimed in disgust. 'This place is a disgrace! And you think you can improve it, do you?' She looked at Kate. 'It won't do, you know.'

'Ma'am?' said Kate, a worried pucker between her brows.

'Oh, I don't doubt you could do the job,' she added, seeing Kate's readiness to argue the point. 'But I could not possibly pay Maria Delacombe's daughter a *wage*!' She made a wage sound like some unspeakable insult.

Kate's heart sank. She could not survive without money.

'I must confess, however, that I'd worry about my grandson a lot less if I could be sure someone sensible were here to look after him. 'Tis bad enough he will never ride again—that I must accept, as he must…'

Kate frowned. Jack's limp was bad, to be sure, but she had observed it closely. It seemed to her no worse than Jemmy's limp had been… Perhaps— Lady Cahill's voice cut into her thoughts.

'But allow him to sink into sloth and misery I will not.' The old lady looked at Kate speculatively.

Kate held her breath.

'All right, Kate Farleigh, I'll strike a bargain with you. You work here as my grandson's housekeeper for the next six months without wages. At the end of the six months you come to live with me in London and I'll present you to society.'

Kate blinked at the old lady in surprise. It was a magnificent offer. Too magnificent, she realised slowly, and utterly impossible. She opened her mouth to refuse.

'Well, child, what do you say? Do I rest easy tonight, knowing my grandson is in good hands, or not?' Lady Cahill touched Kate's hand gently, confidingly. 'My dear, I know that living with an old woman like me in London isn't what every young girl would want, but I do like a bit of youth about me. You'd be doing an old widow a great favour.'

A lump in Kate's throat threatened to choke her. She had never thought to find such kindness again. It was almost too much to bear. Yet she could not take advantage of the old lady's ignorance.

Lady Cahill had made the offer without knowing the real reason why Kate could never enter society, would never be able to marry, why no decent man would have her. Kate would have to tell her, explain once and for all. And afterwards she would no doubt have to leave and return to the life she had planned for herself before Lady Cahill's well-meaning interference.

Chapter Five

'Lady Cahill,' said Kate, 'I do thank you, but your offer is made in ignorance of my circumstances. If I were to accept, you would surely despise me once you learned the truth. And society would condemn you or think you a fool to have been so taken in.'

When Lady Cahill saw the look on Kate's face she bit back the pithy comment she had been about to make on her complete indifference to society's opinions on anything.

'May I ask why, child?'

Kate was very nervous. She didn't want to tell Lady Cahill, didn't want to lose her affection and her respect. But there was no choice. The story would eventually come out—it always did. Better to get it over with, instead of having the threat hanging over her.

'I am not regarded as fit for marriage,' said Kate at last.

'Will you tell me why, child?'

'It's a long story,' said Kate. 'When my brothers, Jemmy and Ben, went to the war on the Peninsula, my father and I accompanied them. I've spent the last three years living with the army.'

'Child. How dreadful for you!' Lady Cahill looked appalled.

Kate shook her head. 'No, ma'am, it wasn't at all. In fact

those three years, while the boys and my father were alive, were the best years of my life.'

Lady Cahill made a shocked sound of disbelief and Kate smiled ruefully. 'I'm afraid it's true. I...I've always been a bit of a hoyden, you understand, and I found the life suited me— much better than at the vicarage. I was never lonely and...and my father valued me as he never had before.' She looked down at her hands. 'You see, when my mother died, Papa blamed me—she died giving birth to me.'

'But, child, that was not your—'

'Oh, I know, but Papa could never see that... You said I had my mother's eyes... Papa was a good man, but when he looked at me all he could see was my dead mother...so he never looked at me. *Never*.' Kate choked on the word.

'Oh, my dear...'

'But somehow, on the Peninsula, things changed. Perhaps, with death and danger all around us, everything else faded into insignificance. I don't know... And because, in such a difficult situation, comfort comes to mean a great deal...' Kate looked at Lady Cahill. 'I became quite a good housekeeper, you see. And hot food at almost any hour, a warm, dry place to sleep and clean clothing mean a lot to men at war...'

She sighed. 'They truly needed me and I was happier than I have ever been in my life...until poor Ben was killed at Ciudad Rodrigo...' She fell silent for a moment, then continued, 'And then everything fell apart at Salamanca.'

Lady Cahill frowned. Jack had been wounded at Salamanca.

As she spoke, Kate's hands unknowingly began to pleat the stuff of her skirt in tiny, deliberate folds. 'Last July, our army was retreating from the Douro River, back towards Salamanca—you may have read of it; the newspapers hate it when we retreat. The French were close behind us. At times they were even parallel with us and so close that you could see them through the swirling clouds of dust.' She gulped.

'Jemmy was hit in the chest... We got him on to our

cart…but with all the dust and confusion we fell a long way behind.'

She turned the wad of pleated skirt over and methodically began to unpleat it. Her voice was flat, bleak. 'Then Papa was hit. In the stomach. I…I managed to get him and Jemmy away to a deserted building. It was half destroyed, but at least it was shelter… Jemmy died the first night…Papa lasted two more days… I had a little laudanum and at least I…I was able to ease his passing…'

Lady Cahill leaned forward. 'You poor child—'

'I didn't remember anything after that…until more than a month later.' She straightened her skirt with shaking hands, smoothing out the wrinkles. 'I awoke one morning and found myself in a French camp. An officer, Henri Du Croix, was interrogating several recently captured prisoners—English prisoners. I had no idea how I got there.'

She shivered and continued, 'It was the most terrifying feeling… Later, I learned that the officer, Henri, had found me wandering after Salamanca. I had been wounded—on the head.' Her hand crept unconsciously to the scar almost hidden by her hairline. 'Apparently I was unable to remember my name or anything, although he knew, of course, that I was English. I became his prisoner…and his mistress.'

Kate flushed at the small sound from Lady Cahill. She could not look at the old lady. Her hands began their intricate pleating again.

'I discovered that for the last month I had lived with him, slept with him in his tent…' Kate swallowed in embarrassment, and forced the words out '…living as man and wife.' She flushed a darker rose colour and added, 'I know it was true—I remember it. You must not think he was a totally wicked man—in his own way, I think he was fond of me…but I swear to you I did not realise what had happened until a month after Salamanca…when it was too late.'

She took a deep shaky breath and continued, determined to

get it all out in the open. 'In Lisbon afterwards they called me
the Frenchman's whore…and a traitress.'

Lady Cahill made a shocked sound.

'Traitress, because I'd tended the wounds of French soldiers. I have some small skill with injuries, you see. And
though they were the enemy I see no wrong in what I did.
They were only men, like our men—tired, hungry, in pain,
and longing to be with their loved ones, not fighting this dreadful war. That part, I do not regret…'

She shrugged, her eyes downcast. 'So, now you know.'

The material of her skirt was crushed and twisted. Her voice
rose again in distress. 'But I did *not* consent to be Henri's
mistress—he told me he was my *husband* and I *believed* him.
I found a ring on my finger, though I did not know how it got
there. I could not even remember my own name at the time,
and so I believed him! He was very convincing. He said I was
his English wife. I never knowingly—'

'Hush now, child! Do not distress yourself. I don't doubt
your word,' interrupted Lady Cahill

Huge, swimming grey-green eyes regarded her doubtfully.

'Oh, tush, child,' the old lady said gruffly, patting Kate's
knee. 'As if I did not know you are the soul of honour.'

Kate inhaled, a long, tremulous breath. Tears trembled on
her lashes. 'Then you are very singular, ma'am, for few others
believed me. They thought me a wanton, a liar, a traitress.'

'Lud, child. Anyone with a grain of sense could see you are
none of those. As far as I am concerned, you did nothing
wrong. And I respect you for tending their wounded. Tell me,
how did you return to English territory?'

'Well, as I said, my memory came back to me when Henri
was interrogating English prisoners—perhaps it was the sound
of English being spoken that caused it to return. It took me a
day or two to find out what happened and make my plans to
escape. Then I stole a horse and rode into Allied territory. It
was not difficult to pass from behind the French lines—a

woman is not so suspect as a man.' She flushed. 'But you see why I cannot possibly enter society, or marry.'

'I see nothing of the sort,' said Lady Cahill. 'There is no reason for anyone to know of this—'

'It is a matter of public record,' said Kate regretfully. 'I returned to the English forces almost six weeks after my father's death. Naturally I was interviewed, in case I was a spy. Some of the officers who interviewed me didn't believe I'd lost my memory. Others were only interested in what I could tell them about the French. It was supposed to be kept secret, but when I reached Lisbon everybody there knew the worst,' she concluded bitterly.

There was a long silence. 'It is not mere wilfulness or false pride preventing me from seeking a husband, you know,' Kate added. 'Ever since I was a little girl I've dreamt of my wedding day, waited for the man whom I could love for ever...and played with other people's children, preparing myself for the day when I had children of my own.' She smoothed twisted fabric with unknowing hands.

'I have put this dream away...but *not* of my own volition.'

Lady Cahill opened her mouth to argue, but Kate continued, 'In Lisbon I received a taste of what would face me if I ever again tried to enter society. Ma'am, I was shunned, reviled...even *spat* on—by English ladies, some of whom I'd regarded as friends...' Her throat swelled and tightened, remembering whispers and sidelong glances, prurient curiosity and outright hostility.

'And men whom I thought I knew, whom I thought were decent Christian gentlemen, tried to *touch* me, made obscene suggestions.' *The Frenchman's whore*—she was fair game.

'Even Harry...my betrothed...' Kate shuddered. Harry's eyes had run over her body in a way they never had before. The realisation had entered Kate's heart like a blade of ice. He was no different from the rest.

'It was unspeakably vile...and I could not bear to face it again.' She looked wearily at Lady Cahill. 'That is why I cannot accept your very kind offer, why I cannot seek a husband or go about in society. I could not bear to meet someone who knows what happened.'

She tried to smile. 'It is not so very bad, you know. I cannot miss what I've never had. I've not had the sort of upbringing that other girls have. And I'm young and healthy and—' she wiped her eyes '—generally not such a dreadful watering pot. If I could only find a position as a children's nurse or companion... You could help me with that, could you not?'

Lady Cahill was deeply moved. Kate had been badly wounded, she could see that. There was no point in pushing her to agree to any plans at present. She was still too vulnerable to risk her heart and her hopes again—she needed time to recover. Lady Cahill would help Kate, but not to a position as a children's nurse. No, if an old woman had any say in the matter, Maria Delacombe's child would have her dream. She reached out and took Kate's hand in a tight grasp.

'Of course I will help you, child. Try to put the whole horrid business behind you. You found yourself in a difficult situation, but you conducted yourself with honour as a true Christian lady. I am sure that both your father and your mother would have been very proud of you. I know I am.'

Tears spilled from Kate's eyes. Kindness, she suddenly found, was so much harder to withstand than cruelty. The old woman gathered the girl into her arms and held her tightly for a moment or two.

'Lady Cahill, you see—'

'I see nothing at all at the moment,' Lady Cahill interrupted, wiping her eyes. 'This dratted face paint has run and I refuse to do or say another word until it is repaired. Fetch my maid to me, and in the meantime go and wash your face and comb your hair. Return to me in twenty minutes.'

Kate stared at her, dumbfounded. Suddenly laughter began to well up inside her and she sat back and laughed until the tears came again.

Sympathy and warm, wicked humour gleamed back at her

from the admittedly smudged face of the old woman. 'That's right, my girl. A good cry and a good laugh. That's what the doctor ordered. Now,' she continued briskly, 'fetch Smithers to me and go and wash your face. You look a sight!'

Later that afternoon Kate helped the old lady climb into her travelling chaise, and stood in the driveway, waving her off. Lady Cahill had promised to 'do what I can to help Maria's gel', and Kate felt sure that she would find her a position as a children's nurse in some quiet, pleasant household.

In return, Kate's job was relatively simple—she had to put Mr Jack Carstairs's house in order. That was well within her capabilities. She might not enjoy housework very much, but there was no doubt that Sevenoaks was badly in need of attention, and there would be real satisfaction gained from restoring a ramshackle house to a graceful residence. And her old nurse, Martha, was to come and live here. That would be wonderful, thought Kate. Martha was a dear and would keep Kate from feeling too lonely. Martha had also known and loved Jemmy and Ben.

Moreover, Kate thought, mentally ticking off her advantages, she was surrounded by lovely countryside and could go for long rambles whenever she wanted to. In fact, she could do whatever she wanted, whenever she wanted to. She was her own mistress and she meant to enjoy that rare freedom while she had it.

And she was needed.

Kate had no doubt whatsoever that Lady Cahill's grandson needed her skills, and that once he saw how much easier his life would be with Kate as housekeeper he would be grateful. Perhaps she could also use her healing skills—possibly even help him to strengthen his injured leg and reduce that dreadful limp. They might even become friends, she thought optimistically. To be sure, he had proved a trifle autocratic and difficult to get along with at first, but that was largely her own fault for teasing and tricking him.

Kate felt sure that Jack Carstairs would prove to be exactly like Papa and the boys and all the other men she had ever known—as long as his surroundings were clean and comfortable and his stomach was full of good cooking, he wouldn't care what she did.

Carlos grinned as he heard the sound of his master's voice raised yet again, this time from the direction of the breakfast-room. He crept closer to peer in at the open window.

'I've told you before, I *won't* have you scrubbing floors!' The deep, angry voice was raised in frustration.

'Ah, yes, I'd forgotten your preference for dirt.' Kate's voice was dry.

'Oh, don't be ridiculous!' snapped Jack.

'Then what would you have me do?' she retorted crossly. 'You can see for yourself that these floors need scrubbing. Someone must do it and you know perfectly well that Martha is too old to do such a task. I am young and strong and, no matter what you may say, if something needs scrubbing, then I will scrub.'

'It is not fitting!'

'Now you are being ridiculous!' Kate said, exasperated. 'Tell me, what is fitting for a housekeeper? When I take down the curtains to wash them, you roar and forbid me to do it! If I clean the windows, so I can see out of them instead of gazing at a view of dirt, you appear out of nowhere and bellow that it is not for me to be doing that! Your interference is quite insupportable! Please, Mr Carstairs, go away and let me get on with my work!'

'I said, I will not have you scrubbing! Look at you, you're a mess! You've got dirt on your chin, a smudge of something else on your nose and your hair is falling all over the place!'

'Oh, yes, mock me for doing honest work!' Kate scrubbed furiously at her face with one hand, dashing curls from her eyes with the other.

'You missed a spot.' He reached out and flicked her small tip-tilted nose, his lips twitching with reluctant amusement.

Kate made an infuriated noise and returned to her scrubbing, ignoring the man standing in front of her.

'I said I *won't* have you scrubbing.'

Carlos grinned. He knew that tone. There would be fireworks if Señorita Kate didn't do as she was bid. He moved closer for a better view, then ducked hastily as a bucket was flung through the window.

'Oh, for goodness' sake!' exclaimed Kate. 'How very child-ish!'

Carlos's eyes widened. To answer back to Major Jack! In that mood! And call him childish! Carlos cautiously raised his head to look in again, then ducked as he noticed his master striding towards the window. Desperate not to be caught eavesdropping, he dived into a nearby bush.

'Carlos!' yelled Jack, thrusting his head out of the window. 'Carlos!'

'Er…*sí*, Major Jack,' mumbled Carlos, sheepishly emerging from the bush.

'What the devil are you doing down there?'

Carlos opened his mouth. 'Er…'

'Oh, never mind. There's a bucket out there somewhere. Fetch it and fill it with hot water. Then get in here and scrub this floor. On the double!'

Carlos's mouth drooped. '*Sí*, *sí*, Major Jack, at once,' he muttered. Scrubbing! Again! Dolefully he fetched the bucket and headed for the scullery. Scrubbing was no job for a man! Señorita Kate wanted to do it, so why did Major Jack not let her do it?

'On the double, I said!' came the bellow from the window.

'*Sí*, *sí*, at once, Major Jack.' Carlos scurried away to do his master's bidding.

Kate got to her feet. She could not scrub without water, and in truth she would be relieved to have Carlos do it—she loathed scrubbing. In any case, she could do nothing while Jack Carstairs stood guard over the scrubbing brush.

She glared at his handsome profile, in two minds about his bossiness. He had no business interfering with her work. On the other hand, he kept saving her from chores she hated. It was very confusing. Papa and the boys never minded what she did. Jack Carstairs was almost a stranger, and yet he was oddly...she could only call it protective.

That reminded her. 'Er...Mr Carstairs,' she said diffidently.

'What the devil do you want now?'

'I...I want to thank you.'

Jack's head whipped around in amazement.

'Yesterday I found Carlos in my room.'

Jack's brows snapped together.

'He said it was on your orders.'

Suddenly Jack knew what she was going to say. 'Oh, that,' he mumbled gruffly, and turned to go.

Her hand on his arm stopped him. 'He was there to clean away all the cobwebs and kill any spiders. And I believe you told him to do the same with all the other rooms. It was a very kind and thoughtful gesture and it would be remiss of me not to thank you, and I do so, very much.'

Jack felt a rush of warmth as he looked down at the sweet face. He gazed into the clear eyes and felt the soft pressure of her hand on his arm. He could smell that faint elusive scent she had, unlike any lady's perfume he knew of, but oddly familiar, nevertheless.

'What *is* the name of that perfume you wear?' he asked abruptly.

Kate dropped his arm and stepped back a little. Jack was annoyed to see a faint trace of wariness in her eyes.

'I wear no perfume. I cannot afford it.'

'But I can smell it whenever I stand close to you, some faint fragrance.'

Kate blushed slightly. 'It's only rosemary.'

'Who?'

'The fragrance you have noticed. It is rosemary, a herb. I make a rinse of it for my hair, and put sprigs of it in my clothes to keep them fresh. It grows plentifully and is free and I am very fond of its scent. Obviously I am too lavish with it,' she said defensively. Definitely too lavish, she thought, if he could talk to her about the way she smelled.

He stared at her thoughtfully. 'No, not too lavish. It's very nice.'

'Carlos. That farm you visit,' said Jack later that afternoon.

'Farm?' said Carlos cautiously.

'The one you visit so frequently. The one with all the daughters,' said Jack impatiently. 'I want you to go there at once.'

'*Sí*, Major Jack.' Carlos brightened visibly.

'Bring back a couple of girls.'

Carlos goggled at his employer.

'Wipe that ridiculous look from your face, you fool! I want those girls to come here to work.'

Carlos hesitated. 'To scrub, you mean, sir?'

'Yes, and whatever else needs doing. Miss Farleigh cannot do all the work that she seems to think necessary.'

A grin split the dark face. '*Sí*, Major Jack! I will fetch them at once!' Carlos moved with alacrity.

'And, Carlos—' His master's voice halted him. 'There will be no fraternising with the wenches while they are employed here, understand?'

'*Sí*, Major Jack,' sighed Carlos dolefully.

He headed off towards a nearby cottage where the unfortunate farmer had seven daughters to feed, clothe and somehow marry off. There would be no trouble in persuading two of them to come and work for a gentleman like Major Jack.

Trudging across damp, muddy fields, Carlos gradually brightened. He might not be allowed to fraternise with the girls, but at least he would no longer have to demean himself scrubbing floors. And, if Miss Kate had a couple of girls to

help her with the work, she would not be making Major Jack
so angry all the time.

'What the devil do you mean, you wouldn't wear them?'

'Mr Carstairs, you must realise that I cannot accept clothing
from you.' Kate's tone was mild but her chin was defiantly
high.

'Why the devil not?'

'It isn't proper,' said Kate composedly. 'And besides, I have
sufficient clothing for my needs here. Martha brought the trunk
containing my things.'

'Balderdash!' he exploded. 'You are the stubbornest female
it has ever been my misfortune to meet! You know perfectly
well that those rags you wear are fit only for burning!'

Kate bit her lip on the retort that had risen to her tongue.
There was some truth in his statement. The trunk containing
all the clothes she had worn in Spain, as well as all her father's
papers and things, had been lost when she had been captured
by the French. The clothes she'd left in England were from a
time when she was a young, carefree girl. Faced with total
poverty, Kate had sold all clothes with any claim to fashion
and style. Those that remained were old and worn and now
dyed black for mourning.

'My clothes may not meet with your approval, sir, nevertheless, they are perfectly adequate for my position.'

'That they are not! You are my grandmother's ward!'

'No, Mr Carstairs, I am housekeeper here!'

Jack ran his hand through his hair in frustration. The chit
opposed him at every turn! 'Do you think I wish it said that
I pay you so poorly that you cannot afford to dress like a
civilised human being?'

'As you have no visitors and virtually no contact with anyone, I cannot imagine that anyone will have anything to say
about it, so it need not concern you,' Kate retorted. 'Besides,
you do not pay me at all.'

'Not for want of trying!'

'Mr Carstairs, I was put in this position by your grand-mother, not you. It has nothing to do with you, and you must see that I could not accept money from you under any circum-stances. Your grandmother and I have an agreement, and that is my last word on the subject.' Kate turned to walk out of the room, but Jack caught her arm and pulled her close. He glared down at her and spoke in a low and furious voice.

'All right, Miss Katherine Farleigh, then here is *my* last word—if you won't accept a wage and you refuse my offer of new clothes, then I'll have no alternative but to dismiss you!'

Uncomfortably aware of his firm grip on her arm and the proximity of his warm body to hers, Kate had to force herself to look up at him. For a moment of two she stared into his glittering blue eyes, only a few inches from her own. She felt his hand tighten and her pulse quickened at the suddenly intent look in his eyes. His effect on her was most unsettling—she had to fight it. She pulled free of him, and brushed down her skirt, buying a few seconds in which to compose herself, aware that his unnerving gaze had not altered.

'You cannot dismiss me. You haven't the power.'

'The devil I haven't!'

He took a few steps towards her. Kate retreated rapidly to the door. 'My agreement is with Lady Cahill, not you, and only *she* can dismiss me.' She poked her tongue out at him, then slipped out the door and down the stairs as fast as she could.

It was a kind offer, Kate thought, but he knew as well as she did that it would be most improper for him to buy her clothing. A man only did that for his wife...or his mistress. Kate bit her lip. It was probably the grossest hypocrisy for the ex-mistress of a French officer to be quibbling about such a thing. But it was precisely because she was so vulnerable to accusation that she had to maintain the highest level of pro-priety.

Propriety was a frail web of protection at best, but without it she would be crushed. Propriety was what kept her feeling like the Reverend Mr Farleigh's daughter instead of a fallen woman. Without it, she would never be able to go about her daily work with a light heart, feeling free to tease and provoke Jack Carstairs if she felt like it, defying him when his bossiness became too provoking and arguing with him if she disagreed with his pronouncements.

She was thinking a little too much about Jack Carstairs these days, she realised. He was the first thing she thought of when she awoke…and the last, before she went to sleep. Even their frequent quarrels she found exhilarating. And, even when he was infuriating her with his interference, deep down she could not help feeling touched by his concern for her…warmed by it. And feeling warm feelings towards him in return…such feelings were dangerous.

Nothing could come of them. She would only hurt herself if she allowed herself to weaken. If—no, *when* he learned about her background, Jack Carstairs would be no different from any other man.

Jack glared at the closed door and clenched his fist at it, swearing softly. The chit had defied him yet again, blast it! But she wouldn't get the better of him this time. She might think she had won the battle, but Major Jack Carstairs knew it was just a preliminary skirmish. And he had served under the Beau, the Marquis of Wellington, the ultimate master at turning retreat into victory.

A slow smile appeared on his lean face and he limped towards the writing desk, sat down and began to pen a letter to his grandmother.

Chapter Six

'Señorita Kate,' called Carlos from the hallway. 'Something here for you.'

Kate stepped back from her task, and glanced around her with some satisfaction. With the aid of Millie and Florence, the girls from the farm, she had wrought a remarkable improvement in the room. The old, mismatched furniture looked infinitely better, gleaming softly from vigorous applications of beeswax. The dusty curtains had been taken down and laundered and brilliant late autumn sunshine streamed through the newly washed windows. The oak floor was freshly polished, and the old Persian carpet had been taken out and ruthlessly beaten until the rich colours glowed.

Housework might not be Kate's favourite activity, but at least it showed results she could be proud of. The room looked warm and inviting, a far cry from when Lady Cahill had snorted at it so disparagingly. All that was needed now was a bowl of flowers or leaves. Perhaps she could find some in the tangled garden. Kate gathered up her cleaning rags and stepped into the hall.

'What is it, Carlos?'

'These arrive for you, *señorita*.' He gestured towards a large number of bulky packages resting on the long hall table.

'For me?'

'You like me to carry them upstairs for you, *señorita*?' Carlos offered politely. These days he treated her with the utmost respect. Once he might have thought her a skinny little mouse of a thing, with her huge greeny eyes and her shabby clothes, respected only because he was ordered to. But no one who had seen this little creature coolly stand up to his master would need to feign respect. Carlos had not forgotten the coffee pot, either.

'That would be very kind of you, Carlos,' Kate murmured abstractedly, puzzling over these unexpected and mysterious items. She followed him upstairs to her room, her arms full of parcels, and he even more heavily laden.

When he left, Kate opened the packages, slowly at first, then faster and faster, her head in a whirl. They contained everything she could ever think of needing. A wonderful warm merino pelisse. No cold winter wind would dare penetrate that to send her shaking and shivering. Dresses, in fine warm cloth, the colours dark—lavender, grey, black and a beautiful soft dove—nothing to offend her state of mourning.

And underclothing, some of fine, soft linen, trimmed with lace, some of silk and satin, the like of which Kate had never in her life seen or felt. Surely it would be positively sinful to wear garments such as these exquisite things next to your skin? As for the nightgowns and chemises—they bore no earthly resemblance to the patched, sturdy, voluminous garments Kate had worn most of her life.

She stared dumbfounded at the tumble of lovely things spread out across her bed. Jack had bought them, of course. He hadn't listened to a word she'd said... But, oh, they were so beautiful. It had been so long since she'd had anything new, and these were of the finest quality. She wouldn't wear them, but it wouldn't hurt, surely, to hold them up against herself and look in the mirror and imagine, just for a moment, that they were hers.

She lifted the dove-coloured dress and stood in front of the mirror, holding it against her. It was very elegant—high-waisted, with a border of embroidered leaves around the hem—simply but beautifully cut. And the material felt so light and yet so warm. She rubbed her cheek against its soft folds and inhaled, savouring its new, delicious smell.

One after another, Kate held the dresses against her slender frame, draping them this way and that, trying to imagine how they would look if she were to wear them—which, of course, she could not.

She picked up a nightgown. Fine silk slipped through her fingers like water. She held it up, imagining herself wearing it, and blushed. It was…would be quite immodest. The Reverend Mr Farleigh's daughter had never owned, or even imagined, such a garment. It was so fine that surely you could see through it. She slipped her fingers inside the nightgown and, sure enough, her skin glowed pinkly through the delicate fabric. She blushed a deeper rose and hastily put it down and then picked up the dove dress again.

'That colour suits you,' said a deep voice from the doorway.

Kate gasped and whirled around, clutching the dove frock against her, for all the world as if she were naked. Jack Carstairs stood in the open doorway, leaning casually against the door frame.

'H-how long have you been there?' she stuttered.

He did not respond, but a slow smile told her the answer and her blush deepened. He'd seen her looking at the nightgown.

'I've brought you a letter.' He glanced down at the welter of clothes that covered the bed and the lurking smile widened. Kate followed his gaze. He was looking at the underclothes and nightgowns. Hurriedly she snatched them up and thrust them under the dresses, her cheeks burning.

'Wh…what did you say you wanted?' she muttered, unable to meet his eyes.

'A letter has arrived for you,' he said softly. 'And I see that that's not all.'

Jack couldn't resist teasing her. The sight of that nightgown sliding sensuously over her skin had caused his body to tighten, imagining her clothed in nothing but that fine translucent silk. And the blush that rose so easily to her cheeks would no doubt be repeated elsewhere on her body. He knew it. And she knew he knew it; he could tell by her loss of composure. Kate Farleigh wasn't easily rattled, and by God he was going to enjoy it while he could. The little termagant was adorable like this, flushed and embarrassed and uncertain.

'Please give me the letter,' said Kate, still flustered by the amusement in his deep voice. He held it out. She reached for it, but he swiftly raised it out of reach.

'Say "thank you" first,' he drawled, still grinning.

'Give it to me, please,' she repeated, annoyed. The big lummox! Did he think she was going to grapple with him for it? She had been teased by experts—her brothers—and she wasn't so foolish as to think she could get the better of him by trying to snatch the letter. He was far too tall, for one thing.

In any case, she'd sworn never to let him get his hands on her again. Her encounters with Jack Carstairs were nothing like the tussles she'd had with her brothers. His touch had no brotherly feel about it at all; it made her feel oddly helpless and fluttery inside and it took all her will-power to break away from him.

'I've come all the way upstairs to bring it to you. Don't I deserve something?' he teased, enjoying her discomfiture.

'You deserve something, all right,' she muttered beneath her breath.

He heard her and laughed. 'Little wildcat. Here's your letter, then.' He tossed it on to the bed.

'Thank you. Now please leave.' Kate went pointedly to the door. 'And you can take all of your things with you,'

He looked at her in mock-amazement. 'My things? What ever do you mean, Miss Farleigh?'

Kate nodded at the pile of clothing on her bed. 'All of those. I told you before, I cannot accept such gifts from you.'

He stared at her in exaggerated surprise. 'My things? You

think these are *my* things? My dear Miss Farleigh…' He bent and, before Kate could see what he was about, drew the silk nightgown from its hiding place. He held it up against his lean, strong frame.

'You think that *this* is *mine*?' His blue eyes quizzed her wickedly. Kate fought against the rising tide of embarrassment that threatened her again.

'Oh, don't be ridiculous!' she snapped, trying not to smile. The frail wisp of silk only served to emphasise the masculinity of the man. 'You know exactly what I mean.'

He let the delicate silk trail through his long brown fingers, then tossed the offending garment to one side. 'But *I* haven't offered you these.'

'But—'

'You'll find that this letter from my grandmother explains everything,' he interrupted smoothly. 'It arrived with the rest of these things. It wasn't *my* taste that selected these…although for once in my life I find myself in total accord with my grandmother.' He smiled, a slow, teasing smile that had Kate fighting those fluttery inner feelings again.

'Your grandmother?'

'Yes. She told me in my letter that she'd sent you some clothing more suited to your position.'

'You mean you didn't send me all of this?'

'No, indeed. I hope, as a gentleman, I wouldn't dream of so insulting you.' He added piously, 'A lady could certainly not accept such gifts from a gentleman, Miss Farleigh. I am shocked you would even suggest it.' He pursed his mouth primly, his eyes twinkling wickedly.

Kate tried to avoid his gaze. She had been made to feel very foolish. He'd known very well that after their previous discussion of her wardrobe she would jump to the conclusion that he'd sent these things. He might not have actually sent them himself, she realised, but he most certainly was behind his grandmother's charitable actions.

'But I cannot—'

'I hope you're not suggesting there is any impropriety attached to an elderly lady buying a few bits and pieces for the daughter of her godchild?' he interrupted in a cool voice. 'Her own mantua-maker made them from measurements Smithers took from your old clothes.'

Kate hadn't realised Lady Cahill had taken so much trouble. She felt a little embarrassed, but she didn't want to back down while he was standing over her like this. 'No...but...it is too much...too generous...'

His face hardened, his eyes lost their twinkle.

'Understand me, Miss Farleigh. These things are from my grandmother and you can and will accept them!'

Kate resented his tone. 'You have no right to tell me what I may or may not accept.'

'I care nothing for that. You will oblige me by appearing in one of these dresses within the half-hour.' Lord! The chit was stubborn.

'I will do nothing of the sort,' Kate responded defiantly. 'I resent your high-handed manner, sir, and take leave to tell you I will *not* wear these clothes.'

He took two menacing steps towards her and she skittered away out of his reach. 'Understand me, miss! You will wear these new clothes and burn the old ones!'

'Oh, will I, indeed?' She pulled a face.

Jack took his watch out of his pocket and glanced at it. 'You'll dress yourself in one of those new dresses within the half-hour, or...'

'Or what?'

'Or, Miss Katherine Farleigh, I will come in here and dress you myself.' There was a hard glitter in his eyes that suggested he was not jesting.

She wrinkled her nose at him. 'You wouldn't dare!'

'Just try me, missie!' he snapped. 'You have half an hour.' He left the room.

Kate locked the door firmly after him and sat down on the bed. He'd thrown down the gauntlet and naturally she'd picked it up. It was time Jack Carstairs learned once and for all that he was *not* her master. He had no authority over her whatsoever. If she didn't choose to wear these clothes, she wouldn't, and no bossy great interfering man would tell her otherwise.

A little over half an hour later there was a knock on her door. 'Who…who is it?' Kate called, annoyed at the involuntary quaver in her voice.

'It's me, miss, Millie.'

Kate unlocked the door. 'Come in, Mil—'

Millie stood twisting her apron nervously. Jack Carstairs loomed darkly behind her. Kate drew herself up straight and stared defiantly at him. He snapped his fingers at the maid.

Millie swallowed. 'I'm here to collect your old clothes, miss.'

'That won't be necessary,' replied Kate smoothly.

Millie looked doubtfully back at Jack. 'But Mr Carstairs—'

'Mr Carstairs has nothing to do with it, Millie. My clothes belong to me, not Mr Carstairs.'

'Excuse me, Millie,' said Jack softly. He moved past her and approached Kate determinedly. Mistrusting the look in his eye, she skipped around to the other side of the bed. He opened the door of the wardrobe and started to drag her old clothes from it, tossing them to Millie.

'Stop that at once!' snapped Kate, outraged. He ignored her and moved next to the chest, which he similarly emptied into Millie's waiting arms.

'How dare you?' cried Kate, and ran to restrain him. He whirled and took her shoulders in a firm grip. Their eyes locked for a moment. Slowly his hands slid down her arms and he held her wrists in a light but unbreakable grip.

'Let me go, you big bully!'

'I thought I made my instructions clear to you before.' He looked meaningfully down at the shabby old dress she was still wearing in defiance of his orders.

Kate's mouth grew dry. He could not surely mean to carry out his threat to dress her in the new clothes himself? She struggled to escape, but to no avail. He was a very powerful man and she had no hope of pitting her strength against his.

'That will be all, Millie,' he said.

'Don't leave, Millie,' cried Kate.

'I said, that will be all, Millie. Take those rags outside and burn 'em. Carlos has a fire ready.'

'*Burn* them?' The Reverend Mr Farleigh's daughter was appalled. 'But that's a shocking waste of perfectly good clothing—'

He snorted.

'But it is,' she persisted. 'I am very sure that the vicar's wife would be glad of them for some of her poorer parishioners. You have no idea how difficult it is to ensure that people are adequately clothed.'

He raised an ironic eyebrow. 'Believe me, Miss Farleigh, my appreciation of that particular problem grows hourly.'

Kate stamped her foot in frustration.

Jack grinned. 'Take 'em to the parson's wife, Millie, with my comp—' he glanced at Kate's face and changed his mind '—with Miss Farleigh's compliments.'

'At least leave me one of the old dresses,' Kate cried. 'I cannot possibly carry out some of my duties in such elegant outfits as those.'

'What sort of duties do you mean?' enquired Jack silkily.

'Well, things like scrub—' Kate floundered to a halt and glared at him, realising the full extent of his trickery.

'Exactly,' he concluded, enjoying his victory. 'Take 'em out, Millie.'

Millie did not dare disobey. 'I'm sorry, miss,' she muttered, casting a sympathetic look at Kate. She left, taking Kate's clothes with her.

Kate struggled in Jack's grip for a moment longer and then changed her tactics. She held herself stiffly and forced herself to meet the angry blue eyes.

'Unhand me, sir,' she demanded, her eyes glittering with haughty indignation.

'I told you,' he grated. 'You had half an hour. The time is up.'

'How dare you steal all my clothes?'

'Not quite all, I think.' He glanced down at the dress she was wearing. 'I did warn you.'

At that she started to struggle again, but he effortlessly held her arms behind her and then held them in the grip of one large strong hand. She was pressed hard against him, chest to chest. She could feel his heart thudding. He seemed to be breathing rather harder than usual.

'And now, Miss Katherine Farleigh,' he said softly, his breath warm against her ear, 'will you agree to accept these clothes from my grandmother or not?'

'No, and you cannot make me!'

'Oh, no?' His free hand went behind her and to her horror she felt his hand tug free a button at her neck. He looked at her, and one long, strong finger gently stroked the soft skin of her nape. Kate stared defiantly back, struggling to maintain her composure, willing her body not to respond to the delightful sensation.

He undid a second button and waited, stroking, circling, smoothing her skin. His eyes darkened. His body seemed to surround her and it took every bit of Kate's self-discipline not to lean into him. And he knew it, the beast, she told herself, desperately resisting the tiny seductive caresses. His tactics were utterly unfair, totally despicable, Kate decided, so she tried to kick him. Her legs were restrained by the pressure of his powerful thighs. He reached for the third button, but Kate had had enough.

'Yes, all right, then, I accept the clothing,' she snapped, adding under her breath, 'You big bully!'

He heard her and chuckled. 'This time, Miss Farleigh, I believe brawn has won the day.' He released her and stood back triumphantly. 'You'd better mean it,' he added, 'for if you defy me once more—'

'You need not go on about it so—I gave you my word,' she muttered crossly.

'So you did.' His eyes mocked her anger.

Kate glared at him, wishing she could think of something—anything to wipe that infuriating grin off the wretched man's face. 'Get out of my room,' she ordered.

His grin grew wider. 'Sore loser,' he said softly, and left.

In a whirl of temper Kate flung off her old clothes and donned new ones—new underclothing, the soft, warm, dove-grey dress she had liked so much and a grey spencer, smartly frogged with black and gold braid. The sensual pleasure of the fine new clothes did nothing to alleviate her annoyance with Jack Carstairs. He had no right to force her to accept them…after all, she was entitled to choose what she wore, wasn't she? She wasn't his slave or anything, was she? If they truly did come from Lady Cahill, she supposed she had no moral qualms about accepting them. But whether she did so or not was *her* choice—not his!

Oh, but the man was infuriating—always sticking his nose in where it was neither needed nor wanted! She kicked her old clothes into a heap in the corner, wishing they were Jack Carstairs instead.

A short time later there was a knock on the door.

'What do you want now?' she exploded. There was a brief silence.

'If you please, miss,' said Millie's hesitant voice, 'Mr Carstairs sent me up to fetch the rest of the things to go to the parson.'

Kate handed the bundle to Millie and watched as the girl took the last remaining remnants of her old life.

It was not such a bad thing, she realised suddenly. Her old clothes had carried old associations—and none of them good. Some had been given to her after she'd escaped from the French—reluctant charity to a disgraced woman. Some dated from her girlhood before they all went to war. All of them were dyed black with grief. She had put those times behind her now, and was building a new life. The new clothes were symbolic of that.

She smoothed down the long woollen sleeve of the grey spencer. Never had she worn such lovely, fashionable, expensive clothing. She noticed Millie's sidelong glance as she did so and smiled a little ruefully.

Millie grinned back at her. 'Aye, 'tis sad to lose old clothes—some seem like old friends, don't they, miss? But, well, it's a beautiful jacket, miss. And all the rest. The old lady sent them, I hear.' There was a question in her voice, and Kate hastened to reassure her.

'Yes, Lady Cahill. It was very kind of her.'

Millie nodded. 'Ah, well, that be all right, then.' She paused. 'Like a cup of tea, miss?'

Kate hesitated.

'It's all right,' said Millie, reading her thoughts accurately. 'Mr Carstairs is off up the Bull.'

'I beg your pardon?'

'The Bull, miss—the Bull and Boar Tavern. He'll not be back till late, I reckon.'

'Oh, well, then, in that case, yes, I'd love one.'

Later that evening Kate donned one of her new nightgowns and slipped into bed, shivering. The nights were getting very cold—soon she'd have to think about heating a brick to take to bed with her. Or perhaps using that bedwarmer she'd found. She burrowed down into the bedclothes, enjoying the feel of the soft linen nightgown against her skin. She had taken out the silk one and looked at it for a moment of two, then put it wistfully away. She could not imagine a time when she might have a use for it. Such a garment was not meant as clothing to warm a girl at night—rather, it aimed to warm a man...

For the first time in months, Kate thought of Henri and the things he had done to her in the privacy of his tent. She had not disliked them...but any pleasant memories had been driven out by the realisation that she was not wed to him after all, that he was a stranger who'd lied to her, tricked her, taken marital rights illicitly. And she'd felt used and angry and guilty...

She wondered what it would be like to share those pleasures with Jack. She thought of the silken nightgown—as it had looked draped incongruously against his big, masculine body. Having seen the creamy silk sliding through his fingers, it was easy to imagine the same creamy silk sliding over her body, and those same tanned fingers stroking, caressing, exploring...

Suddenly her face flamed in the dark. Such thoughts! It was shocking. She knew now why girls were kept so ignorant until marriage—the whole thing was far too unsettling. She burrowed her face into the pillow, cooling her cheeks on the cold linen.

She'd been blaming that quarrel over the clothes on Jack Carstairs but, in truth, she'd provoked most of it herself. It had been Kate who'd thrown down the gauntlet, not him—she'd known very well how he would react if she refused the clothes, and he had. Giving her the excuse to defy him...

She squirmed in mortification as she realised it was she who had first laid hands on him, she who had provoked that whole physical tussle. Worse, she'd enjoyed it, had liked the feeling of being in his arms, had wanted him to keep touching, stroking, caressing...imagining Jack doing to her what Henri had done...

Bleakly Kate faced the truth: those women in Lisbon were not so wrong about her after all—she *was* a wanton hussy— she'd just proved it. Miserably she pulled the covers over her head and tried to think pure thoughts. It didn't work. All she could think of was the way she had felt when Jack Carstairs held her. Kate curled herself into a ball in the big bed. The only thing to do was to recite every psalm, prayer and passage from the Bible that she knew and hope they would drive the thoughts from her head. It would take a long time, for she had frequently been made to memorise passages from the Bible as a punishment. And she had been a *very* naughty child...

* * *

At the Bull and Boar Tavern, Jack sat nursing a brandy, staring into the fire, oblivious of the noise of his fellow drinkers.

His face softened into a half-smile as he recalled the way she'd boldly faced him down, a stubborn little ragamuffin in her dreadful black hand-me-down dresses, sternly rejecting the clothes she desired so badly. And she did desire them; there was no doubt about it in his mind.

He could tell by the way she'd touched her cheek to the material, like a child caressing a puppy or kitten, by the way she'd slid her fingers through the silk of that nightgown, as if she'd never even imagined such a garment was possible.

Only Kate was no child. He'd been unable to resist teasing her, flirting, flustering her…

He tossed down the last of the brandy and signalled to the landlord to bring him another. A buxom tavern wench brought it instead, pressing up against him invitingly as she did so. Jack's eyes automatically went to the gaping neckline that was presented for his enjoyment and he registered that she was both attractive and willing. He glanced up and shook his head, smiling to soften his rejection. No, a tumble with a willing tavern wench would not solve his problems.

He recalled the dreamy way Kate had draped the fine silk nightgown against her soft skin and felt his body tighten again, imagining her in it.

Impossible…unthinkable…

Perhaps he should take up the tavern wench's offer after all… He glanced across at her again, but somehow she seemed too buxom, too willing, too… He realised the way his thoughts were heading and tried to quash them firmly.

Bloody hell! Was *that* what that scene in her bedroom had been all about? He couldn't deny that he had been aroused by the sight of her with that damned silk thing. Was that what had prompted him to go so far, undoing the very buttons at her back? He recalled the feel of the warm silken skin of her nape and the scent of her body and swore darkly.

What the hell was he going to do? If he wasn't more careful, things with Kate Farleigh would get out of hand. They almost had. Her teasing sense of fun, the wholehearted way she threw herself into a quarrel, her very defiance spurred him to want to push it further with her each time. He felt entirely too stimulated by her very presence. If she'd been a different sort of woman, he'd have no hesitation in making her his mistress— and what a mistress she'd make, he thought. All fire and passion and silky limbs and hair. He felt aroused just thinking about it.

But Kate was no kitchen maid, nor a tavern wench—she was a respectable lady, and after Julia Davenport he'd forsworn all dealings with respectable ladies for ever.

Damn it all to hell and back!

He wondered how his grandmother was faring with her enquiries into Kate's situation. He hoped it was going well. The sooner she was out of his hair the better—for both of them.

He called for another drink.

Chapter Seven

Kate awoke very early one morning. She slid out of bed, padded across the chilly floor and peered outside. It was almost dawn, faint shards of morning light dimming the last of the stars. Winter had begun—outside it looked cold, but inviting. For the last week she had worked unceasingly indoors, and she was feeling stale and housebound. A good brisk walk was what she needed.

The house seemed deserted as she slipped out of the back door. Her boots crunched across the frosted grass. As the pure, cold air bit into her lungs, Kate felt a surge of exhilaration. The rich earthy scent of rotting leaves and the sharp contrast of pine was in the air and it felt good to be alive. Suddenly she felt free of all the constraints of her life—her poverty, her past, her concerns about the future, her problems with Jack Carstairs.

It had been more difficult than she'd expected, working in such close proximity, feeling as she did about him. Such shameless, entirely inappropriate feelings, too. Every night. Sometimes *even during the day*. It was dreadful. Kate had done her best to fight them with passages from the Bible, but even that failed to eradicate the problem. It was very lowering to discover how steeped in depravity she had become.

She told herself a thousand times a day that such dreams

were foolish, as well as wicked. She was a disgraced woman. She could never enter his world. He would be disgusted if he ever found out about Henri.

Such dreams were impractical, too—even had she been as pure as the day she was born, she was still poor and Jack needed to marry an heiress to make up for the fortune he had lost when his father had disinherited him.

In fact, she told herself severely, Kate Farleigh had no business to be thinking anything at all about Jack Carstairs except what she would cook him for dinner. She knew the correct behaviour for a woman in her position and, even if she couldn't make her feelings behave, she could try.

So she'd tried to keep out of his way, tried to keep a formal barrier between them, tried to follow Lady Cahill's instructions to ensure her grandson lived in a civilised fashion, tried in all ways to be the perfect, invisible housekeeper.

But all her good resolutions had been ruthlessly undermined by Jack Carstairs himself. He always seemed to be watching her—appearing from nowhere, opening doors, seating her at table as if she were a fine lady. Glaring gimlet-eyed if he found her doing anything he deemed 'inappropriate', storming off in a temper when she pointed out in the most reasonable of tones that she knew what she was doing.

And she'd tried, so very hard, to resent it.

He was being ridiculous, she'd told herself. What did a man know about housekeeping anyway? He had no business interfering with things which were none of his domain. He was a bossy, meddlesome, arrogant pest!

But it was more difficult than she'd imagined. Her strength of mind was weakened by the realisation that he was concerned for her welfare, that he cared whether she was comfortable, that he wished to shelter her from the harshness of her everyday life. Even if he was just being gentlemanly and polite, even if he treated all his housekeepers like this, it was still very…weakening.

And that, combined with her own wanton tendencies, made life with Jack Carstairs very dangerous.

Kate sighed, then rallied herself—listing his character defects was a useful strategy. She did so as she marched down the garden path, enjoying the cold air, the droplets of dew still shivering on the plants as she passed. He was frightfully bossy, even for a major in His Majesty's Coldstream Guards. And arrogant. Stubborn. Yes, indeed—worse than any mule she had wrangled with on the Peninsula. And infuriating, especially when he had trapped her in some misdeed, then laughed at her with those wicked blue eyes.

And moody. Some days he would be warm and friendly, then, from out of nowhere, a blaze of intensity would emanate from him. His blue gaze would seem to burn right into her, then just as suddenly he'd turn away and storm out of the room in cold, bitter withdrawal.

Mornings were the worst; he usually slammed into the kitchen from outside, flinging himself down at the table, surly and uncommunicative for some time, drinking cup after cup of her coffee. Sometimes he would refuse to eat the breakfast she'd cooked, and limp straight through the kitchen, grey-faced and grim. On those days he would retire upstairs to his private parlour where, Kate gathered, he quietly drank himself into oblivion, preferring to drown his demons rather than face them.

On those days his unhappiness ate away at her, burning away all her good resolutions like acid. On those days it was hardest of all to remember that she was only his housekeeper, there on sufferance…she wanted to be so much more… She longed to have the right to put her arms around him, to comfort him and to coax and tease him out of his black depressions. But she had no right.

On those days she threw herself into the jobs she hated most, the hard, dirty, filthy jobs—rendering mutton fat, cleaning and black-leading the grates, sifting wood ash and boiling it up to make lye. Boiling the cottons and linens in a big copper boiler, filling the laundry with steam. Tossing other clothes in flour and then beating them until clouds of flour flew, leaving them clean and sweet-smelling but her hair and nostrils clogged.

In spite of it all, Kate found herself dreaming about him day and night—even when making soap, when the stink of the sheep fat and home-made lye made her eyes water! He was so impossibly attractive, particularly when he looked at her with that smile lurking wickedly in his eyes, inviting her to share his amusement. And when his voice deepened and took on that low resonance it shivered though her bones, turning them to honey...

Kate headed towards the forest. It was magical. Dawn was stealing over the hushed landscape, highlighting the purity of the bare, frost-etched branches. Her breath escaped in misty tendrils and hung in the motionless chill. Far away she could hear a cockerel crowing, and beyond that a dog barking. It was as if she was the only person astir in the world. Kate hugged the delightful sensation to her and strode on.

Suddenly she heard the sound of rapid hoofbeats close behind her—too close. She dived off the narrow pathway just as a riderless horse pounded past her, reins dangling free, stirrups flapping.

Shaken, she clambered out of the tangled underbrush, smoothing her skirts and brushing mud from her hands. Some-one had had an accident—a rider had been thrown. Should she go back and see if they were all right, or should she try to catch the horse first? If its reins got tangled or caught, it could injure itself. She ran along the path and came to a stile, where a large roan stallion stood, snorting and tossing his head, unable to go any further. Calmly Kate approached, talking quietly and coaxingly, while he watched her in suspicion, poised for flight.

It was one of Jack's horses, she was sure, though why he should keep so many horses when he couldn't ride was beyond her comprehension. It was the same horse she'd seen on her first morning at Sevenoaks. Clearly he was a rogue, and one in need of more exercise than he was currently receiving. She had seen him running free several times before, Carlos in hot pursuit.

Had a thief tried to ride it? If so, he'd made a big mistake—that particular horse had only ever been ridden by Jack, according to Carlos. Jack had bred the horse himself, broken him to bridle and trained him to do his every bidding. He'd even taken the horse to war with him. And now no one rode him at all. Jack should have sold the horse, she thought, not kept it here, under his eye, where every sight of it was a bitter, festering reminder that he could no longer ride.

'Come on, there…good boy…there, there…' she murmured, wishing she'd brought an apple with her. She held out her hand as if offering something and continued slowly and deliberately to approach the horse. Curiously, it thrust out its neck, sniffing to see what titbit she was holding. Kate deftly and calmly took hold of the dangling reins.

The big horse tried to jerk away, but she held him firmly, soothing him with murmured endearments and steady hands. She'd always loved horses, and they seemed to know it. Jack's roan was no exception—under Kate's calming influence he stopped his nervous trembling, and was soon blowing affectionate snuffles into the front of her dress. She quickly checked him over, running experienced hands down his legs, and was relieved to find no sign of damage. Now to see if he would accept her on his back.

With some difficulty, for he was still nervous of any other rider, and she was hampered by her long skirts, Kate managed to mount the big horse, using the stile as a mounting block. He reared up and snorted in fear at first, but Kate clung on tightly, and her firm hands and low, soothing voice soon had him under control again. Then, sidling and dancing under her unaccustomed light weight, the roan headed back down the narrow pathway at a brisk trot, shying skittishly at every falling leaf or shifting shadow.

For the first few moments, Kate was wholly engrossed in controlling her mount, then, as it became clear that the stallion accepted her mastery, pleasure filled her—it was so long since she had ridden a horse. And this was such a fine horse. She could understand why Jack had been unable to bring himself to sell the animal. The thought occurred to her that perhaps she could ask if she might exercise him. He certainly needed it.

As the path opened out, she saw a trail of hoofprints crossing the field nearest the house, and remembered her task. Someone might be hurt, even if it was a thief who deserved punishment! Castigating herself at her selfish pleasure in the ride, she urged the stallion into a canter. Rounding the back of the stable, she saw a prone figure lying on the frozen ground.

Kate's heart missed a beat. No, surely not. She urged the horse closer, then flung herself off, retaining just enough presence of mind to tie it to a nearby bush. The figure on the ground was ominously still.

Breathing hard, she fell on her knees beside him, heedless of the cold, wet mud, and gently turned him over. Dear Lord, she prayed, let him not be badly hurt!

'Jack. Are you all right?' There was no answer. She laid her cheek to his chest. His heart was beating steadily. Thank God! Swiftly she ran her hands over his limbs. Nothing was broken. She gently examined his head but could find no extraordinary bump or cut. He was as white as a corpse, and almost as cold.

Kate whipped off her pelisse and tucked it around him, then eased his head and shoulders into her lap, abandoning all modesty, surrounding his body with her legs. She would ensure his warmth, at least. Later, if he did not regain consciousness, she would have to leave him and go for help. But while he was so pale and frozen and helpless she could not leave him.

She held him close, praying silently that he would be all right and that someone would come soon to help them. One hand cupped his rough, stubbled chin, tenderly cradling his head against her breast, the other smoothed his hair back off his forehead. She murmured soothing words in his ear, her breath mingling with his in the crispy air.

She was just deciding reluctantly that she might have to leave him to fetch help when Jack's eyes flickered open. He stared up at her blankly for a moment or two and muttered, 'You?' in a tone of bemusement, then closed his eyes again.

'How do you feel?' Kate asked softly, his head still against her breast.

'Bloody,' he muttered, still with his eyes closed.

'Oh, no, there is no blood,' she assured him.

One blue eye opened and regarded her sardonically. 'Good.' He lay heavily against her for another few moments, then, seeming to become aware of just how intimately he was lying against her, he sat up, groaning. He swore as a sudden wave of pain shot through his leg, and he stilled his movements suddenly, bending to examine his leg more closely.

'You haven't broken anything either,' Kate said reassuringly.

'And you'd know, I suppose,' he said.

Kate didn't allow herself to rise to his bait. 'Well, yes, I would know, but I don't expect you to believe me. Now, it's extremely cold on this ground and you'd better move if it's at all possible.'

He glanced at her again, and a frown darkened his forehead as he noticed that she was shivering. Then his eyes fell to her pelisse, tucked securely around him. He swore, dragging it off him and almost angrily thrusting it at her. 'Put that on at once, you little fool! Do you want to catch your death?'

Kate ignored him. 'Do you think you can stand up?'

Jack moved his bad leg a little and groaned. 'I think I can manage to walk, but the question is, can your ears bear the bad language that will doubtless result from the effort?'

Kate laughed aloud at this. As if he did not already curse

with almost every breath he took! 'Here, put your arm across my shoulder and see if you can stand.'

He sat up and she wedged her shoulder under his armpit. Using his good leg and herself as a lever, he slowly rose to his feet. His lips were tightly compressed, but he did not utter a word. By the time he was upright, he looked exhausted. White lines around his mouth told Kate he was in considerable pain.

'Do you really think you should be trying to walk on your bad leg?' said Kate hesitantly. 'I could easily run for help and fetch someone to carry you on a litter.'

'I'll be damned if I'll let the blasted thing make me a cripple,' he muttered bitterly.

'Oh, well, that's a relief,' murmured Kate provocatively.

He shot her a look of hard enquiry.

Her lips twitched with amusement. 'I feared the strain would be too much for you.'

'I fail to understand what you find to amuse you in this situation,' he grated.

'Oh, nothing, to be sure, sir,' she said. 'Only that I feared that your effort to refrain from cursing would be too much for you. However, I perceive that your tongue is in its usual fine form, so I need feel no anxiety on your behalf.'

He stared for a few seconds and then recalled his use of the word 'damned'. Despite himself, his lips twitched. Leaning heavily on her, he began to move slowly towards the house. After a few minutes he glanced down at her. 'You really are the oddest girl.'

'What makes you say so?'

'Ninety-nine women out of a hundred would be turning this into a major dramatic occasion, weeping and having hysterics over me, and here you are, having the audacity to tease me about bad language.'

'Would you prefer me to have hysterics, then, sir?' Kate pretended to consider it seriously. 'I must confess that I haven't had a great deal of experience in the matter, but if it would make you more comfortable, then I'm sure that I could undertake to stage a very convincing bout of hysterics. If you prefer it, that is.' Her eyes danced mischievously, but all the time she urged him onward, hoping her nonsense would distract him from the pain.

He threw back his head and laughed outright at that. 'Good God, no! Heaven preserve me from hysterical females!'

They continued their laboured progress for a few more minutes, then stopped for a brief respite.

'You have no idea how refreshing it is to have a sensible female to deal with,' he said earnestly.

At this Kate was forced to lower her head and compress her lips to prevent herself laughing out loud.

He noticed, however. 'What is it now?' he asked and, when she did not respond, he put a hand under her chin and turned her face up to his. Finding it brimful of suppressed merriment, he frowned in suspicion.

'Well, what have I said to cause this?' With a light finger he flicked at the dimple which peeped elusively out.

Her eyes danced irrepressibly. 'For weeks now you have been calling me "the stubbornest, most infuriating female it has ever been my misfortune to meet"!' she growled in a deep gruff voice. Then she allowed her mouth to droop mournfully. 'And *now*, when you call me *a sensible female*, alas, there are no witnesses!'

His lips twitched. 'Well, most of the time...' he began.

Kate burst into peals of infectious laughter and reluctantly he joined in. As they laughed, she met his eye and felt the jolt of warm good humour pass through her. Slowly the laughter died in his eyes and she felt his gaze intensify. Suddenly Kate became hotly aware of the intimacy of their position, her body held tightly under his arm, wedged firmly against his hard, warm body, his mouth only inches away from hers. For a moment they stood there, their eyes locked, then she felt, rather than saw, his mouth moving down towards hers.

Abruptly she turned her head away, her heart racing, her mouth dry.

'Come on now,' she murmured. 'We'd best keep moving and get you in out of this chilly morning. Your leg will need to be examined by the doctor.' She felt him withdraw as they moved off.

'I'm not having any damned leech or sawbones maul me around any more. I had enough of them to serve me a lifetime on the Peninsula.'

'Oh, but surely you cannot compare the physicians we have here in England with some of the butchers that passed for surgeons during wartime?' Kate said incautiously.

Jack stopped and looked at her in surprise. 'Do you know, you're the first person in England that I've ever heard with an accurate notion of some of those bloody devils? Apart from anyone who was there, I mean. You sound as if you actually have an inkling of what it was like.'

Kate smiled slightly. 'Do I, indeed?' Her face sobered. 'Well, I did have two brothers and a father who died there. Now, have you had enough of a rest to continue, or do you wish to rest a moment or two more?'

That got him moving again. Kate was relieved, but, more than that, he'd given her the opening she'd wanted. 'Not all doctors are butchers, you know,' she said after a time.

He snorted.

'It's true,' she insisted. 'I once met the most wonderful physician, descended from a long line of physicians, right back to the Moors, who used methods of treatment that enabled some terrible wounds to heal almost like new.'

'Humph!'

'For instance, with a bad leg like yours,' she persisted, 'where the wound had healed, but the muscles had lost their strength, he would order that the leg be massaged three times daily with hot oils, the oil being rubbed well in and each part of the leg stretched and pummelled.'

'Ah…' he said ironically. 'A torturer. I have heard that

some of those oriental types have the most subtle and fiendish methods.'

'I know it sounds like that, but it is truly efficacious, though it is not at all comfortable at first.' Kate remembered the groans of anguish that her brother Jemmy had uttered when the treatment first began, and how it had taken all her will-power to continue the treatment.

'After a few short weeks, the limb begins to strengthen and, with added exercise, I believe that almost full power can be returned in some cases.'

'Rubbish!' he snapped curtly. 'Unscrupulous leeches prey-ing on credulous fools.'

Kate understood his hostility. Hope could be very painful.

'Possibly,' she said quietly. 'I suppose it depends on the wound, but this treatment had my brother walking after our English doctors had told him he would never be without crutches again.'

She paused to let that sink in. 'And his wound was very bad, enough to have them planning to amputate.'

Kate would never forget frantically clinging to the surgeon's arm, begging him to wait for another opinion, and then the final relief when her father had burst into the tent and wrested the saw from the man's drunken hand.

'Perhaps the method may help your leg.'

'I doubt it!'

'It could not hurt to try, surely?' she coaxed.

'Dammit! You know nothing about it, girl! I have been mauled enough by incompetents from the medical fraternity and I will have nothing to do with any more quack cures, especially those dreamed up by mysterious oriental fakirs!'

Kate felt a wave of frustration surge through her. It was perfectly obvious to her that he had been attempting to ride his horse in defiance of the medical prognosis he had been given and despite the pain his leg was so clearly giving him. It was sheer insanity to attempt to use a barely healed limb for strenuous exercise.

'Don't be so stupid. You cannot simply ignore damage done to muscles and sinews and ride by will-power alone. You are just a man, with a man's body. You were dreadfully injured and I am sorry for it, but you must face the fact of your injury, instead of pretending it does not exist.'

'What the devil would you know about it? I'm damned if I'll give in to it,' he growled, attempting to thrust her away.

Kate glared right back at him. 'And who said you should give in to it?' she demanded. 'Not I—I said face facts, not give in.'

'Dammit, girl, you go too far. This is none of your concern!'

'Well, if you wish to ride that horse instead of falling off it all the time, you will have to do something differently,' Kate said furiously. 'You may be able to walk on that leg, but it is so stiff and weak you cannot grip on to a horse. And if you keep doing what you are doing you will end up giving yourself a much more serious injury. You need to retrain your muscles and exercise them. The treatment I spoke of is specifically aimed to restore flexibility and muscle strength…'

The words died on her tongue. Jack was staring at her with such a mixture of humiliation, outraged pride and sheer fury that she recoiled, thinking for a moment that he might strike her.

'Damn you to hell and back, girl! Mind your own blasted business!' he exploded. 'I don't need your damned unwanted advice, I don't need your blasted quack miracle cures and I don't need your damned assistance. I can make my own way to the house!'

Kate knew she should stop, but she had to have one last try, using an analogy he might accept. 'What would you think of a trainer, who, after a horse had fallen and injured itself, put it straight at the highest jump, and expected it to succeed? Would you not think him a fool?'

He was silent. Not knowing whether to feel encouraged or not, Kate continued, 'A man who wants such a horse to jump again would surely walk it over low jumps, gradually raising them until it is strong enough and confident enough to jump anything. Well, wouldn't he? Think about it, Mr Carstairs.'

He stared at her, and for a moment Kate thought her argument might have reached him. But, gritting his teeth against the pain, Jack pushed her roughly away and began to stump painfully towards the house.

'You stupid stubborn man!' raged Kate, going after him and inserting her shoulder under his again. 'If you don't want to listen to what I say, well, of course, that is your right, short-sighted as it may be... No, I *won't* be pushed away! How ridiculously...' she cast around for an adequate adjective '...manlike...to reject my practical assistance when you know you need it.'

Jack stopped and glared furiously down at her, his fingers biting into her shoulder.

'All right,' she said hastily, meeting that fiery blue gaze. 'I have said my piece now and I promise you I will say nothing more on the subject.' She began to head once more towards the house, forcing him to move too.

They made slow, painful progress to the house, Kate silently cursing her runaway tongue. For the first time ever, they'd been completely easy with each other, even joking and laughing, despite his awkwardness at being discovered, helpless on the ground. And then she'd ruined it. Knowing what she knew.

As she'd sat on the cold ground, cradling his head against her, the whole picture had come together—the sound of a galloping horse when she first arrived, hoofprints on frosted grass, day after day, his early morning bad temper, white lines of pain around his mouth.

He'd been doing this for weeks, sneaking out before dawn to try and learn to ride again. His mental anguish, the desperation that drove him to try to ride, secretly, day after day, *knowing* he would fall—Kate's heart contracted at the thought. It had taken courage—mad, proud, stubborn courage. But without treatment he would never be able to do it. And sooner or later he was bound to do himself a grave injury.

It need not be that way, she was sure of it, and so she had spoken—too much. Offending the very pride she admired. He would never listen to her now, never forgive her. She was only his housekeeper, existing, not to put too fine a point on it, on the goodwill of his family. *When* would she learn to accept it?

Finally they reached the house and she helped him to a chair in the kitchen. 'I'll fetch Carlos,' she said quietly, and moved towards the door.

He did not acknowledge her; he just sat there, his face a white and bitter mask.

Chapter Eight

'What's this? Looks delicious.'

Before Kate could say a word, Jack had scooped a fingerful of the creamy mixture and popped it in his mouth. She clapped a hand over her mouth, attempting unsuccessfully to repress her mirth. Giggles escaped her as his eyes filled first with disbelief, and then with disgust. He rushed outside and she heard the sounds of vigorous spitting, as he attempted to rid his mouth of the foul taste of her latest domestic effort.

Kate collapsed in a chair, and laughed until the tears rolled down her cheeks. It served him right. He had been hanging around the kitchen all day, popping in and out for no apparent reason—lurking! Several times she'd asked him if there was anything he wanted, but he'd almost snapped her nose off! It was his kitchen, wasn't it? Well, of course it was, the silly man! She knew that!

Normally it wouldn't have bothered Kate so much, but to-day was proving to be one of those days; first a bird's nest had fallen down the chimney right into the bouillon which had just reached aromatic perfection. And it was baking day, but the dough stubbornly refused to rise. And the kitchen had been cluttered with damp washing for days.

And she'd been sleeping badly, ever since the accident. That was his fault, too!

Kate saw him only at breakfast. She would not have admitted it to a soul, but she knew she only really started to breathe each morning when he limped through the kitchen door, those tell-tale white lines of pain around his mouth. It was only a matter of time before he injured himself seriously, and they both knew it, but the man was so stubborn!

Last night she'd slept even worse than usual, alternately dreaming of him and worrying about him. She'd awakened feeling scratchy and irritable. And then the wretched man had lurked! Underfoot! All day! Observing each disaster!

So now justice was served, and the sounds of his violent expectorations were as music to her ears. Still chuckling, Kate wiped her eyes with a corner of her apron. He re-entered the kitchen, wiping his mouth, which was still puckered at the lingering after-taste.

'Are you trying to poison me?' He grimaced again and scrubbed at his mouth with his handkerchief. 'What the hell was that foul stuff anyway?'

'Spermacetti oil, white wax, almond oil,' she said, between giggles. 'I haven't yet added the lemon oil and lemon juice.'

He choked. 'Spermacetti oil? You were planning to feed me *whale oil*? That's for burning in lamps!'

Kate giggled again. It was a new recipe she was trying—guaranteed to remove freckles. 'I do not usually feed my cold cream to gentlemen, no matter how hungry—or greedy—they are.'

'Cold cream?'

'Cold cream.'

'Hrmph!' He turned away. His ears turned slightly pink.

Another giggle escaped her.

He continued to fidget for some minutes, then finally he spoke. 'Pour yourself a cup of coffee and sit down, Miss Farleigh. I wish to talk to you.' His voice was serious.

She fetched two cups and placed them on the table, still trying to keep a straight face. Eventually she met his gaze. He looked away, and the laughter died in her eyes. This really was serious.

'That brother of yours—you say he was able to regain the use of his leg?'

'Yes, completely,' she murmured, her pulse beginning to race.

'Because of the treatment you described to me?'

'Yes,' she confirmed, trying hard to suppress her rising jubilation.

'And you think my leg may benefit from similar treatment?'

'I am no medical expert but, yes, I think it would help.' She swallowed convulsively. 'At least…I cannot say if your leg will be completely restored, but I firmly believe there would be significant improvement.'

'Because of your brother.'

There was considerable scepticism in his voice, but Kate detected a grain of hopefulness. It was time to tell him the truth. It might cost her his respect, but if he could be convinced to try the treatment he might regain full use of his leg. Faced with that option, there was no choice but to risk it.

'Not only because of my brother—there were many others.'

'Others?'

'Yes, I saw this treatment used on many of our soldiers and, in almost every case, it brought some improvement.'

'And naturally there were hundreds of wounded soldiers in the village in…where did you say my grandmother found you—Bedfordshire?'

'No, of course not, but I saw hundreds of wounded soldiers in Spain and Portugal.'

He was incredulous. '*You* were in Spain and Portugal?'

She nodded.

'In wartime?'

'Yes.'

'When?'

'For the last three years.'

'On your own?'

She flushed. 'With my father. And my brothers, where possible.'

'What was your father doing there? Surely he was too old to be in the army.'

'My father felt he was needed more on the Peninsula than in his parish in Bedfordshire.'

'So he just packed up his Bible and went?' he said sceptically.

'Yes, indeed. Though you would have to have known my father to understand. Once he had made up his mind there was no gainsaying him.'

'But what of you?'

She looked at him in mild surprise. 'I went with him, of course. He was a brilliant scholar, but hopelessly impractical in the domestic field. He had no notion at all of how to procure lodgings or food or any of the other things so necessary to life in a country torn by war.'

'And you had?'

She looked at him in surprise. 'Yes, of course.' She flushed, realising she must sound boastful. 'Well, not at first, but I soon learned. And once I was able to speak some of the language it became much easier.'

'Incredible. You were—how old—seventeen, eighteen?'

'At first, yes.'

'And you did not mind?'

She opened her eyes at that. 'No, I did not mind.' She grimaced wryly. 'Remember my unladylike hands? They're a sign of a terrible hoyden, I'm afraid. I had some of the best times of my life travelling with the army... I see I've shocked you.'

'No, not at all. But...did you not experience a great deal of hardship?' Jack knew several officers' wives who had gone to war, but all of them had had servants to see to everything. And a husband to protect them. A girl who wore the sort of clothes Kate had arrived in certainly would not have had many servants.

'Oh, naturally there were times I wished we were not having to sleep in a dirty, vermin-infested village, or ride for hour after hour in the pouring rain or the sweltering heat—I am not unnatural, you know! But at least it was never dull. There was always something to be done and someone to talk to.'

She could not explain to him how she'd almost welcomed such discomforts because they highlighted her usefulness to her father, making him value her for the first time in her life.

'But the danger. Did your father not consider that?'

'Oh, yes, of course!' She was indignant at the slur. 'Why, at Badajoz he kept me virtually confined to my tent for more than a week.'

Jack gasped. 'You were at *Badajoz*?' He could not believe it. That bloody siege with its even bloodier aftermath! And her father had protected her from blood-crazed rampaging troops with a piece of canvas!

'Yes, and at Ciudad Rodrigo and all the other battles that are now famous, but always I was well to the rear during the fighting,' she said crossly, 'for several officers spoke to him and after that Papa was most insistent about it.'

'I should think so too!' he muttered, his hair raising on his scalp as he recalled some of the bloodier incidents in his experience of the war.

'Yes, but it was very impractical, for how could I tend the wounded when I was so far to the rear all the time?'

'Tend the wounded?' His tone was incredulous.

Kate flushed, knowing the reason for his surprise. He thought her immodest. Harry too had been incredulous when he had discovered that she had been helping wounded soldiers, not simply her brothers. He had been furious, forbidding her to do anything so indelicate again. Her refusal had caused him to thin his lips and walk off angrily. Obviously Jack Carstairs felt the same—well, his good opinion of her was a small thing to risk, if it meant he might ride again.

'Well, I had to do something to help—there was so much need. And that is how I came to know the Moorish doctor.'

She looked earnestly at him. 'And why I have such a strong belief in his methods of treatment.'

He reached across the table and took her small hand in his large one, his thumb rubbing gently over the skin of her small, grubby 'hoyden's hands'. He gazed at her face, noting the delicacy of her features, the small tip-tilted nose, the wide, innocent-looking eyes that had witnessed so much hardship and suffering. 'You truly are the most amazing girl.'

Suddenly she became acutely aware of the warmth of his hand, the large brown thumb that was moving caressingly back and forth across her skin, and she flushed and awkwardly pulled her hand away.

'Nonsense,' she muttered gruffly. She started clearing away the cups, intensely aware of his eyes following her every movement. 'Would you like me to prepare the hot oils for the treatment? It is not difficult—it only takes persistence.'

Now it was his turn to look awkward. 'Can you not explain to Carlos what is required?'

'It would be better if I did it myself,' Kate said. 'I can show Carlos once I have ascertained the treatment needed—it is not difficult, but there are a few tricks to it that are better demonstrated than explained.'

Kate saw the look on his face and flushed. He *was* shocked at her indelicacy. Well, there was no need for him to be concerned—she was no delicate flower—but it was very difficult to force herself to disillusion him.

'It is...I...' she began, stumbling over the words. With her face averted she continued woodenly, 'Mr Carstairs, I am not the innocent you seem to believe me. I have seen the male form before, have cared for a number of wounded men, not only my brother, so, you see, you have nothing to be concerned about.' She avoided his eye, her cheeks rosy. 'So, shall I prepare the oils now?'

'No, no, I was only enquiring out of interest,' he said hurriedly, unnerved by her willingness to begin at once.

'But you will think on it.'

He smiled faintly at her intensity. 'I shall,' he agreed, 'but I have much to do today.'

He stood up and left the room. Kate watched him go, a frown on her face. He had nothing at all to do, she knew. He would probably spend the remainder of the day brooding. Drinking. The man had suffered more than physical damage. It was almost as if he was afraid to hope. Well, she could hope enough for two.

That evening, however, Jack did not retire in his customary solitude, but invited Kate and Martha to join him in the parlour where Carlos had lit a fire. He had a bottle of port beside him when they arrived, but he was not drunk. He poured Kate and Martha a glass of sherry, and they settled down in front of the cosy fire and chatted. Kate, initially wary of his motives, soon relaxed, perceiving he was making a genuine effort to play the polite host.

Gradually Jack turned the conversation around to more recent events. Her tale of being with the army had stunned him. He had to know more.

'So tell me, why did your father drag you off to travel in the tail of an army?' Jack tried to keep the anger out of his voice. It was ill to think badly of a man he had never met, a man who was dead and gone, what was more, but he could not forgive Kate's father for exposing such an innocent young girl to the horrors of war, valiant little creature though she might be.

'In the tail?' Kate grinned. 'You can't think I would be so poor-spirited as to travel at the tail with all the heavy baggage and complaining wives and impedimenta! Nothing so dreary, I'm glad to say. Jemmy found me a charming little Spanish mare and I was able to go where I wanted.'

'Good God!' he muttered, appalled. Had none of her family recollected she was a sheltered young girl of eighteen or so?

'Oh, it was much more convenient, for then I was free to ride back and forth, keeping an eye on Papa, for he was dreadfully absent-minded at times, and also the baggage, which travelled with Luis, our Portuguese servant. And then, you know, I was always on hand to snaffle a good spot when we stopped for the night and make sure everything was comfortable for them and a hot meal ready.'

She smiled as she sipped her sherry. 'We were lucky—Jemmy was hunting mad. Even when we were returning to Portugal after Talavera, and food was so scarce that almost everyone was starving, he managed to shoot a hare or something for the pot, just when I thought my stomach was going to stick to my backbone.' She rubbed her stomach reminiscently. 'Jemmy could turn even a retreat into a hunting trip.'

Jack moved uncontrollably in his chair, flooded with anger, fighting an impulse to sweep her into his embrace. He, too, had fought at Talavera. He recalled only too well the horrors of that retreat, the starving men, the sheer bloody hell of being unable to provide enough food. That she should ever have been put in such a frightful position! How many times had this little creature faced starvation? He would never forget how thin and frail she had felt in his arms the first time he met her! How he wished he had known her earlier. He would have ensured she was never in danger, or frightened or hungry.

Kate blushed suddenly. 'I'm sorry, I know it is unladylike to mention such things.'

Jack was amazed. She could casually refer to the experience of living through a frightful battle and retreating with an exhausted and starving army, then blush because it was unladylike to mention such a thing as a stomach. His eyes caressed her. She was unique, this little Kate.

'I was at Talavera,' he said quietly.

'Then you will recall that dreadful trip back into Portugal too.' She nodded. 'Were the Coldstreams at Busaco? Jemmy was wounded there. Was that where you caught your facial wound?'

'No.' His hand crept up to his ravaged cheekbone. 'This is a souvenir of Badajoz.'

They both fell silent, remembering Badajoz. The fire crackled loudly as a knot of sap burst. A log fell and sparks twirled madly up the chimney. In her comfortable wing chair, Martha stirred, then returned to her heavy doze. Kate regarded her with compunction. She was an old woman, and she should not be dozing uncomfortably in a chair at this hour, but tucked up warmly in bed. But none of Kate's arguments could shift her—she was Kate's chaperon, and her reputation would be safely guarded by her old nurse. Even though Martha knew there was no reputation to guard.

'You seem remarkably calm, relating your experiences.' Jack's deep low voice pulled Kate out of her reverie. 'Were you never frightened before a battle, for instance?'

'Lord, yes, utterly terrified,' she said simply. 'Before every battle I was a mess—unable to eat, leaping six feet at every sound…even a little grumpy.'

His warm chuckle washed over her. 'Grumpy? Now why do I not find that difficult to believe?'

Kate wrinkled her nose. 'Yes, fear brings out the virago in me. I used to snap at Ben for being such a big, slow stupid!'

She paused and stared into the flames for a moment. 'Ben was the eldest. He was the sort of person you could not for one moment imagine in a hurry, or a flap, about anything. Yet he invariably got things done just as fast and with none of the drama that Jemmy or I seemed to cause.'

She said in a slow, gruff voice, '"This sweaty haste doth make my head spin all the day"'—Ben was always saying that to Jemmy or me, and Father would always take him to task about mangling Shakespeare and mentioning sweat in front of me.' Her voice quavered a little.

Jack watched her from the shadows, his eyes unreadable. A father who didn't want her ears sullied with the word 'sweat', but who took her into situations where she was surrounded by blood, sweat and far, far worse.

'Jemmy used to roast Ben about his unflappability too, but he was a wonderful brother. They were so different, those two—like quicksilver and stone... No, I don't mean stone precisely because that suggests Ben was cold and he wasn't—he was a big darling.' Her eyes blinked rapidly and her lips quivered with emotion.

Jack wanted to gather her into his arms and kiss her grief and distress away. Poor, gallant little waif.

'Ben never saw Badajoz. He was killed at Ciudad Rodrigo... Were you at Ciudad Rodrigo?'

He shook his head.

She continued, 'I remember that first day there so clearly. It was terribly cold, and the snow was frozen and crunchy underfoot from the frost that night. But the morning was so still and perfect—simply beautiful, you know, the sort of day when you long to go for a good gallop, then come home to a lovely hot breakfast...

'And then the big guns shattered the morning, pounding and pounding until I thought my eardrums would shatter too, though I was a long way from them, you know. And I stuffed my ears with rags to stop the noise... Ben was killed the next day. I suppose you could say he was lucky, for he caught a ball in the temple and probably didn't know what hit him before he was dead.'

She bit her lip. 'You probably think I am unnaturally cold to say he was lucky, but there are so many more terrible ways for a man to—'

He could restrain himself no longer. He had to touch her. He reached across and took her small, cold hands in a warm grip.

'He *was* lucky, Kate. There couldn't be a better way to go than instantly, in the open air, in the heat of action.' His hands enveloped hers in warmth.

They lapsed into silence. The only sounds were the crackling of the fire and the slow, rhythmic sound of Martha sleeping. His thumbs stroked back and forth across her skin. Soothing, wordless reassurance.

'How did Jemmy and your father die?'

She blinked the tears back for a few moments, then said softly, 'They were both caught by snipers on the way to Salamanca. You recall the way our army and the French were travelling parallel and exchanging shots every now and then to relieve the tedium?'

He nodded. They had been in so many of the same places and yet their paths had never crossed.

'Jemmy was wounded in the chest and, a short time later, Papa was caught in the stomach. Both wounds were fatal. They could not bear the jolting of the cart, so I found a deserted farmhouse and stayed with them until they died.'

The simple statement hid a world of grief and Jack felt his heart stir. 'I think it is time you took yourself to bed.' He rose, reached down a hand to help her up, then, without conscious volition, drew her into his arms, cradling her securely against his big warm body.

There was little passion in the embrace, just warm, protective, comforting strength, and she nestled against him, listening to the pounding of his heart, wishing the moment could last for ever. Kate had not expected to be held like this again in her life, and she clung to him, desperately, revelling in his warmth and strength and tenderness.

He reached down and gently tipped her face up to his and they gazed into each other's eyes, then his dark head bent over hers and their lips met in a long, tender kiss.

Martha snorted in her sleep and stirred, awakening, and in moments the two were standing in separate parts of the room, Kate bending over her old nurse, assisting her to stand, Jack leaning casually against the wall, his face in shadow again.

It was probably the port anyway, Kate told herself for the umpteenth time as she separated curds from whey in the kitchen, making cottage cheese. They'd barely spoken since that night. In fact, he'd obviously been going out of his way to avoid her. Kate realised he was regretting the impulse which had caused him to kiss her. And, though she could never regret anything so magical, she knew she *should*.

So she had decided to forget the conversation by the fire, the wonderful embrace that had sent her to bed floating on air. It was not an easy resolution, but she was managing quite well, the memory of his kiss occurring to her no more than a dozen times a day before being firmly banished. It was very wearing, being wanton.

'Señorita Kate, Major Jack, he say he is ready for your torture treatment to begin. This morning.' Carlos grinned. 'He no try to ride today, no hurt himself.'

Kate was stunned. Jack had listened to her after all! He was prepared to trust her. She grinned back at Carlos, delighted, then hastened to prepare everything before Jack could change his mind.

Holding the small pot of hot, aromatic oil carefully, she mounted the stairs and walked slowly with Carlos towards Jack's bedroom door. She was absurdly nervous. Don't be ridiculous, she told herself. You've done this a dozen times or more. There's no reason to behave in this missish fashion, just because you're in an English country house and not a Portuguese cottage or a tent in Spain.

Yes, a small voice answered her silently. But this is Jack…

She pushed open the door. Jack lay on the bed, dressed in a nightshirt, his lower body swathed in a sheet. He looked at her, glanced down at the sheet, clutched it more firmly around himself and his colour darkened.

'This is a damned stupid idea. I've changed my mind,' he announced. 'Leave the stuff with Carlos. I'm sure we can work out what needs to be done.'

Kate perceived he was thoroughly embarrassed by her presence. All her nervousness dissolved like magic and she tried not to smile. 'Now don't be foolish. I told you before, it is not simply a matter of rubbing in a few oils. It is a special technique that must be taught.'

She noted his heightened colour and said softly, 'You must

not worry that I am here. I have performed many much more difficult tasks. Try to imagine that I am simply one of those who tended your wounds in Spain.'

He snorted. His imagination could not do it. Kate was small and slender, with a smooth, clear complexion, and soft pink lips. The last person to touch his wound in Spain had been a big brawny soldier, bald, toothless, tattooed and with the most extensive vocabulary of obscenities that Jack had ever encountered.

He braced himself as she reached for the sheet and clutched it tighter.

'Now don't be silly,' she said firmly. 'I must be able to see the leg, if I am to apply these oils to it in the proper way.' She flushed slightly and said in a lower tone, 'I told you before, I am not unacquainted with the male form. It will not embarrass me to view your leg.'

Jack found he could not release the sheet. It was not so much that he was worried about offending her maidenly modesty, he realised, it was not wanting to see her look of revulsion when she saw the mess that was his leg.

Briskly she twitched the sheet away. Jack clenched his teeth, awaiting her disgusted reaction. She bent over it silently. The leg was white and hideously criss-crossed with violent red and purplish scars. The muscles were shrunken and slightly twisted in places, as if pulled out of alignment by the puckered scarring.

She examined it carefully, not letting her feelings show. He truly had been mauled about but, apart from the dreadful scarring, it didn't look too bad. She ran her hand gently down the leg, feeling the lines of the muscles. She felt him flinch under her touch and quickly met his gaze.

'Did that hurt?'

He was watching her, an odd look in his eyes. She had shown no sign of horror or disgust, no sign of sympathy or pity either.

'Did I hurt you, sir?' she repeated.

'Er…your hands are cold. I did not expect it, that's all.'

'Oh.' Kate continued to examine the leg.

'Now, Carlos,' she said, 'I am going to work first on these muscles.' Carlos bent his head over the leg curiously. 'See how they are pulled tight by the scarring here. That is what makes it so hard to bend. Now, a little of this oil just so, and then…' She applied it to the leg and began to massage it in. Jack Carstairs groaned slightly and shifted awkwardly.

'Is the oil too hot, sir?'

'No, no…it's not that,' he muttered, not meeting her gaze.

Kate continued the treatment, explaining softly to Carlos all the time. Her small strong fingers rubbed and pummelled and pushed at the shrunken muscles. Jack lay on the bed, his face a mask of control. Kate alternated small intensive localised movements with long, soothing strokes up and down the whole leg, pulling and pushing with a strong, smooth, rhythmic action. During one of these movements Jack uttered a muffled moan. Kate's head went up abruptly. This action was meant to be soothing and relaxing, not painful.

'Am I hurting you, sir?'

Jack flushed. 'No, no…er…don't you think Carlos can take over now?'

'No, sir, not yet. I thought it would be best if I took him through a complete treatment first. It should take no more than fifteen or twenty minutes.'

'Oh, God!' groaned Jack, and shifted under the sheet again.

'I must be hurting you,' Kate said, distressed. 'I am so sorry. This part of the treatment should not hurt at all. Perhaps there is something I have missed. Can you tell me exactly where the pain is located?'

He glared at her for a moment, examining her face for any sign of mischief. She looked back, troubled grey-green eyes innocently meeting his gaze. She really had no idea what her touch was doing to him.

'Dammit! No!' Jack growled crossly. 'You're not hurting me at all. Just get it over with as quickly as possible!' His eyes darted past her, over her shoulder, to where Carlos was standing; Kate felt a spurt of surprise at the withering look Carlos received.

Kate bit her lip. Of course she was hurting him, or why was he moaning? Men were so stubborn at times. She didn't mind if he cursed or groaned, but she did need to know if the treatment was hurting or not and where. She continued in silence. He was getting tenser and tenser under her hands. It was puzzling. He should be relaxing. She redoubled her efforts, rubbing in the warm, aromatic oils with firm, rhythmical strokes along the length of his leg. Suddenly he groaned again and with a surge of sheets he turned over on to his stomach, sending Kate sprawling on the bed.

She sat up, flustered and astonished. 'What on earth do you think you are doing?' she demanded crossly. 'Turn over, please; I haven't finished there yet.'

'Oh, yes, you have, Miss Farleigh,' came the uncompromising reply, slightly muffled by the pillow. 'That's quite enough from you.'

Kate shrugged. 'Oh, well, I suppose I can work on the back of the leg as well as the front.' She reached out and began to rub it again.

'Damn and blast it, woman!' The words exploded from the pillow. He jerked his leg away from her and tried to thrust it back under the sheet. 'Out, Miss Farleigh, now!'

'But—' Kate began.

'Carlos!'

Kate felt Carlos's hand on her shoulder. 'Please, Señorita Kate,' the man said. 'You must go now.'

'But I have not finished showing you everything.'

Carlos grinned. 'Oh, *señorita*, you have shown me plenty, I think.'

'Carlos!' the deep angry voice from the pillow growled warningly.

'At once, Major Jack!' Carlos said hurriedly. His eyes glinting with private amusement, he turned back to Kate again. 'It is certain that Major Jack can bear no more of your treatment today. Perhaps another time in the future…'

'Carlos!' There was no mistaking that tone.

'*Sí, sí*, Major Jack. Now, *señorita, por favor*.' He ushered Kate rapidly out of the room and shut the door behind them.

Kate stopped on the landing. 'I don't understand it at all,' she said worriedly. 'What I was doing should not have hurt him so much. He's not the sort of man who would complain of a little pain. His leg must be worse than I thought.'

Carlos grinned down at her wickedly. 'It was not his leg which was troubling him, *señorita*,' he said meaningfully.

'What do you mean?'

Carlos shrugged. The English were so prudish about things such as this. She had brazenly entered Major Jack's bedroom and bared his leg without so much as a blush, so she was no innocent.

'Señorita Kate, it is a long time since the Major has been with a woman, and when you touched him…' He shrugged. 'Well, he is a man, after all…'

Kate stared at him a moment, assimilating what he was telling her. Then a fiery blush surged up over her face and she was flooded with embarrassment. 'Oh,' she gasped, and fled.

Chapter Nine

For perhaps the twentieth time that evening Carlos glanced towards Kate with foreboding. The little mouse was behaving more like a cat tonight, pacing back and forth, clearly disturbed about something, and from the looks that she was casting towards the ceiling it concerned Major Jack.

Naturally. Carlos sighed gently. If she was touchy and moody, it was nothing to what his master had been. Ever since Major Jack had been unable to disguise his body's response to her.

Carlos shook his head. It was the simplest matter in the world. These English made such a fuss over things. So the Major was attracted to the little mouse. It would be something to be concerned about if he was not, in Carlos's opinion, for she had blossomed lately and was looking very pretty. But instead the Major must go to all lengths to avoid her, even having Carlos sneak around heating oils in secret, in case she found out he was continuing the massage treatment without her. Such foolishness.

Kate kicked one of the logs in the fire angrily, releasing a shower of sparks up into the chimney. How could he give up after only one attempt? she asked herself for the hundredth time. She was utterly convinced that massage would improve his leg, possibly even enable him to ride again.

Obviously he didn't have her faith. But to try it only once and then give up! Merely because he was affected by lust.

That was what was so upsetting. It was partly her fault— men were unable to control their baser natures, she'd been told. They took their lead from women, she'd been told. And she'd behaved so indelicately.

Assuring him she was not embarrassed to see his leg! Telling him she was no innocent! That she was well acquainted with the male form! No wonder he'd reacted as he had.

It was clearly eating away at him, for every evening since he had retired to the upstairs parlour and commenced to drink himself into oblivion. He even seemed to have given up on his morning attempts to ride.

Well, she would not stand for it any longer. There were two faces to guilt, she knew—it could fester inside a person, or it could be got rid of, by turning it outward, by turning it to anger. And a healthy dose of anger, Kate decided, was exactly what Mr Jack Carstairs was going to receive.

Carlos eyed the slender, pacing figure with misgiving. If she had a tail she would be lashing it. A wise man would hide himself discreetly away until the fireworks were over. Stealthily he rose. His movement caught Kate's eye. She stopped and turned towards him, decision and resolution in every inch of her. Carlos's heart sank. Too late, he thought mournfully.

'Carlos, come with me if you please. And bring that large bucket from the scullery.' Dolefully he did so and followed her out of the room. She marched upstairs to Jack's private parlour. Carlos felt his hands growing damp. Surely she would know better than to disturb Major Jack at this time of night, when he would be in his blackest, bitterest mood—he would have consumed two bottles, maybe, by now. *Ay de mí!* It was madness.

Jack lay sprawled in a chair before the fire, a glass of brandy dangling perilously from his long, strong fingers. He gazed into the dancing flames, his eyes half-closed. Damn her. Damn

her. Damn her! It had been so much easier before she had
come into his life. So much easier…and so much duller. He
should have forced her to go off with his grandmother.

She wouldn't have been here long enough to plague him,
to provoke him, to insinuate herself into his…life.

She had no business being here, scrubbing his floors, cooking his meals, with no one to talk to in the evenings but a
foolish old woman, a rascally Spanish groom, two illiterate
farm girls and a crippled wreck. She should be in a ballroom,
dressed in silk and satin, swirling round the floor as light as
thistledown, engaging in light social *badinage* with a score of
men hanging on her every word.

Six months! How would he ever stand it? It was hard
enough to keep his hands off her as it was. She was like no
woman he'd ever met. She'd been through so much. And yet,
to look at her, see that fresh, sweet face, no one could believe
she had spent three years at war, seen death, destruction, men
at their worst, while in the process losing her entire family.

Curse her father! What the devil did he think he was about,
taking a young girl into that hell-hole? Getting himself killed
so that she had nobody to look after her, nobody to call her
own. Jack lit a cheroot and puffed sullenly, brooding on the
iniquities of the Reverend Mr Farleigh. His grandmother had
said the damned fool had even refused to let Kate's grandparents settle money on Kate's mother. Stiff-necked bloody
idiot. Pride was one thing—but to leave his daughter in such
straits! Good thing he was dead, Jack thought, or he'd probably have throttled the man…

Dammit, his grandmother had no business leaving her here.
She should be in London, finding herself a rich husband, some
titled fellow who would pamper her and protect her for the
rest of her life, who could give her all the fine things she had
been denied. Any man should be grateful to win her… His
mouth twisted at the unpalatable thought.

She was so damn naïve. She had no idea what her touch
had done to him that time when she was massaging him. She

was so full of unconscious sensuality and unawakened passion. Would probably fall for the first handsome face she saw. The *ton* was infested with damned blackguards. He would have to speak to his grandmother about it. Make certain she protected her from the wrong type, make sure she chose well for little Kate.

He drained the glass, then carelessly refilled it, slopping brandy on to the fine polish of the table at his elbow. Whatever he did, he was going to have to get her out of his house and up to London soon, for, the Lord knew, he was having the devil's own job keeping away from her. And that simply would not do. She was too fine a person to get herself chained to a poverty-stricken, embittered cripple. Scrubbing his floors the rest of her life. He thought of those small, work-roughened hands. No. If it killed him, he would get her out of here and into a fine London drawing-room.

He drank deeply again, and his mood darkened, recalling each and every time he had touched her. His body responded even at the memory and his mouth curled cynically. He had to stop this, had to get her out of his mind and out of his life. He was finished with women, finished with ladies anyway— even floor-scrubbing ladies with tender, beguiling eyes who smelt so sweet and fresh. They were a trap. Women thought differently from men.

Even the best of them wanted a man for what they could get.

He thought of Julia and the heavy bitterness rose inside him again. Was Kate any different? What would a penniless, homeless orphan want with him—a crippled wreck—an ugly, crippled wreck…? A home, perhaps? Even a run-down one like this might look good to a homeless waif. And, while he might consider himself poor, his sort of poverty was relative; he would never be in danger of starvation—she had already experienced that, several times. No, he would never be in danger of having nowhere to go, no one to turn to.

He had a home, a family and he was his grandmother's heir.

It didn't take a genius to realise that all of that would look good to a girl with nothing. And if the price was having to live with a broken-down ruin of a man, well, Kate was a girl full to overflowing with good Christian virtues—charity, self-lessness, pity… Yes, it wasn't hard to see what Kate might see in him. A girl could put up with a lot for the sake of a home, security and family…

'*Señorita,*' Carlos whispered tentatively. 'I do not think this is a good idea.'

Kate glanced at him scornfully. 'No, naturally you would not,' she snapped. 'You are the one who purchases those bottles of poison he pours down his throat every night.'

Carlos shrugged. 'He is my master, after all.'

'Well, if you had any concern for your master, you would refuse to do his bidding in this. Can you not see, he is destroying himself?' She stamped her foot. 'Well, I won't have it! I am employed by his grandmother to see to his welfare and I will put a stop to this right now.' She stepped towards the door.

'*Señorita,* I beg you, it is not a good time.' Carlos grabbed her sleeve in desperation. 'Please, wait until morning.'

'By morning, he will have consumed a great deal more of that filthy stuff,' she responded briskly. 'Now, let go of me, Carlos.' She flung open the door.

'*Señorita,* it is too dangerous to cross him when he is like this,' Carlos hissed urgently.

'Coward!' Kate flung off his hand and strode boldly into the room. She lit a brace of candles from the flickering fire and, placing them on the carved wooden mantelpiece, turned to face Jack. He remained silent and motionless, the glittering eyes regarding her broodingly from under heavy dark brows. She noted the glass balanced carelessly between long, elegant fingers, the half-empty decanters on the low mahogany table by his chair, the splatters where he had spilled the liquor while pouring it with unsteady hands, the mess of half-smoked cheroots where he had stubbed them out in a particularly beautiful china bowl.

'Carlos,' she said. 'Bring the bucket here at once if you please.'

Reluctantly, Carlos shuffled forward, irritating Kate by throwing a sheepish grimace of apology towards Jack as he did so.

'Hold it up,' she ordered, and before Carlos or Jack had any idea of what she was planning she hurled the decanters and bottles into the bucket. The sound of smashing crystal echoed shockingly in the silence. With a sweeping movement she tossed in the cheroot stubs and ash and finally nipped the glass from out of Jack's hand and tossed it into the mess in the bucket.

'There, that's better,' she said, brushing her hands together. 'That will be all, Carlos.'

'*Madre de Dios!* It will indeed,' he mumbled, and fled the battlefield.

Kate took two steps back. Jack was beginning to recover from his astonishment, exhibiting all the signs of a man in the beginnings of the black throes of rage. Kate hid her satisfaction.

'What the devil do you think you're doing, woman?' he roared, rising from his chair and moving purposefully towards her.

'What I should have done a long time ago,' she answered composedly, and skipped behind a chaise longue. Her heart was beating fast, but although she was a little nervous of what he might do to her in his drunken state she didn't think he would actually kill her, despite the fury in his eyes. And besides, there was something exhilarating about confronting him like this, just the two of them in the darkened room.

'You must know it is very bad for you to be up here like this, night after night, brooding and being miserable and drinking yourself into a stupor.' She moved from behind the chaise longue to a small refectory table. 'So I decided it was time you stopped drinking.'

'Oh, did you, indeed?' he growled, and made a swipe to grab her. She darted from the shelter of the refectory table to that of a wing chair. 'And just what the hell business is it of yours what I do, madam?'

She watched him warily. 'Your grandmother employed me to look after you—'

'The meddlesome old harpy foisted you upon me to drive me insane!' he roared, and made another grab in her direction. She eluded him just in time. 'And, by God, she has succeeded beyond her wildest expectations!'

'Oh, nonsense!' responded Kate sensibly. 'If you feel a trifle put out just now, I can understand that, but you are undoubtedly finding the effect worse because of all that brandy or port or whatever the horrid stuff is you've been drinking!'

He stopped and stared at her in stupefied fury. *'A trifle put out? A trifle put out?* I'll show you a trifle put out! I'm going to teach you a lesson, my girl, a lesson that damned father of yours should have taught you a long, long time ago, about not interfering with a gentleman's pleasures!' He lunged clumsily forward again.

'Don't be rude about my father,' snapped Kate.

'I'll do whatever I please in my own damned house, my girl, and that includes giving you that beating that your father should have given you the first time you treated him to the first taste of your damned impudence!'

'I was never impudent to my father in my life!' Kate lied indignantly, resolutely ignoring the dozens of birchings she had received for impudence and worse. 'And how dare you threaten me, you big bully? If you dare to lay one finger on me, I...I'll scream.'

'And who will rescue you, pray tell?' He grinned evilly. 'If I know Carlos, he'll be as far away as possible from this little fracas, Millie and Florence will be home by now, and as for Martha—' he grinned even wider '—well, you know as well as I do that I can do no wrong in Martha's eyes. She will probably egg me on.'

Kate gritted her teeth. Within minutes of stepping over the threshold of Jack Carstairs's house, Martha had conceived the absurdest *tendre* for him. And he dared to make mention of it! Boast of it, even! Kate glared at him across a bowl of greenery that she'd placed there only that morning.

'I don't need to scream,' she panted, 'I can protect myself.' She picked up the bowl and flung it. It missed him, smashing on the wall behind, but the foliage and water hit their target most satisfactorily. Kate grinned triumphantly.

Jack plucked greenery from his hair and dashed the water from his face. 'Ha! Missed, little vixen! So much for cricket.'

'That was deliberate,' she said airily, 'but I promise you, I won't miss next time.'

He leaned over the table. 'You certainly enjoy throwing things, don't you? I suppose I ought to be grateful that there is not a pot of boiling oil to hand, or no doubt you would fling that at me, wouldn't you?'

'Probably.'

'Well, just for that, I'm going to give you the biggest beating you've ever had in your life.'

There was amusement in his eyes, despite his anger. Kate resolved to remove it—she was certainly not going to let this deteriorate into a game.

'Well, at least now you've got an ambition in life! And about time too.'

Jack stiffened. 'And just what do you mean by that?'

Kate's chin lifted defiantly. She hadn't meant to be quite so blunt—it had just slipped out—but she couldn't back down and ruin the effect she had worked so hard to achieve.

'I said, at least you have an ambition in life now,' she enunciated, quailing inwardly as she did so. 'I mean, of course, apart from that of drinking yourself to death! Not that threatening to beat a woman is exactly an ambition to be proud of…'

Jack's face whitened with rage and shock. 'How dare you? I've never beaten a woman in my life!' he grated. 'Now, get out of my house now—before I break your neck and throw you down the stairs,' he added, sublimely unaware of his inconsistency. His long fingers dug into the back of the Queen Anne chair between them. Kate could hear the fine old brocade shredding under the pressure.

Kate was shaking, her pulse was pounding with excitement, unsure whether she was thrilled or terrified. It looked as if he really did want to kill her, now. But something deep inside her told her that, no matter how he was behaving and what he threatened, he would not actually harm her. Not really.

'Oh, yes, that would suit you very well, wouldn't it?' she taunted, dancing from behind one piece of furniture to the next. 'Get rid of me and there would be no one to prod you out of your shell again. Well, if you want me out of here, you will have to throw me out, Mr Carstairs, for I will not leave here unless of my own free will and I do not choose to go just yet.'

He made a lunge for her and as Kate skipped out of his way her foot caught on a loose rug. Without hesitation his arm shot out, preventing her from falling.

'I have you now, little vixen,' he growled, drawing her closer. Kate struggled against the unbreakable grip and he stared down at her, his eyes blazing. Effortlessly he pressed her back against a nearby table, imprisoning her legs with one muscular thigh and enclosing her narrow wrists in one large hand. Ignoring her struggles, he pulled her hard against him, chest to chest, breathing heavily, causing a light, tantalising friction. Silence fell, except for the sounds of their breathing and the crackling fire.

'I really ought to beat you, you know,' he murmured at last, his eyes darkening.

Kate knew she was in no such danger. His hold on her might be unbreakable, but it was also quite gentle. Almost possessive. It was another kind of danger altogether she was in. She gazed up at him for a long moment, her eyes clinging to his, then dropping to his mouth. She should not encourage this, should not allow it. She might want it with all her heart, but it was not proper to want it. 'Please…' she gasped, and wriggled, meaning him to release her.

He looked down at her enigmatically and groaned. 'If you must look at me like that with those eyes…' he muttered, and lowered his mouth to hers.

It was no gentle embrace and Kate had never experienced anything like it. She struggled half-heartedly against the invasion of her self-possession, but his lips, at first hard and demanding, softened and were tenderly teasing and coaxing hers until, without conscious volition, she responded to their demands and her lips parted.

Fire shot through her with such force that she let out a small whimper. His grip instantly gentled and he lifted his face and stared into hers. Kate was helpless—his muscular arms were all that kept her from sliding to the floor, her head was thrown back and her damp lips remained parted.

'What did you mean about my eyes?' she finally said.

'Only that every time I look into them I want to do this—'

He lowered his mouth to hers again in a long, passionate kiss.

Kate's senses were reeling but, more, she could not believe what he had said—her eyes made him want to kiss her? *Her eyes?*

He lifted his head back and smiled into her dazed face. She knew she should do something, say something, but she could not. Her eyes clung to his and he seemed to see the silent message in them for he murmured, 'See—you're doing it again,' and lowered his mouth, with agonising tenderness, to hers.

Without warning, he brushed his fingers across her breasts. Kate gasped and arched her back in response. Her nipples were unbearably tender as his hands rubbed the material of her frock and chemise across them. Her body was racked with wave after wave of the most exquisite shudders, and she could not help but push herself against him. At the same time, his mouth, lips and tongue were creating the most amazing sensations, intensifying the feeling she had of needing to get closer to him, to feel him against, around, inside her.

She could taste the brandy he had been consuming, the to-bacco he had smoked, but also, something indefinable, the maleness and uniqueness of Jack. She wanted to touch him, taste him, feel him. One of her hands embedded itself in his thick, crisp dark hair, while the other cupped his jaw, rubbing tenderly back and forth, revelling in the texture of his un-shaven chin. His mouth moved away from hers for a moment and she whimpered softly in protest at the deprivation and followed it.

His body was pressing against hers, moving in a slow, rhythmical motion, male to female, holding, tasting, wanting. His arms moved around to her back, and Kate thrust forward into the circle of his body, rubbing her breasts against the hardness of his chest. She felt him withdraw from her in some indefinable way, then gradually became aware of a growing draught at her back.

Abruptly she realised that Jack was unfastening her dress, trying to slip it from her shoulders. She pulled back, uttering a small exclamation of surprise, and found herself clutching her dress to her and staring him wordlessly in the face.

'Jack…' she whispered, an unanswerable question in her eyes.

His gaze fixed on her face for a moment. He swore and thrust her away. Running a hand through his hair, he turned and headed for the table where he habitually kept the brandy. He pulled up short and swore again, recalling its recent fate. He dug his hands into his pockets and stared moodily into the fire. He kicked it once with his bad leg and sparks flew and danced like whirling dervishes up the chimney, while the pain brought him to his senses.

Kate hurriedly fastened up her dress as best she could, then waited for Jack to turn around. They stood there for long, silent minutes, Jack staring into the fire, his chest heaving, an unreadable look on his face, Kate, her face delicately flushed in the candlelight, wide-eyed and nervous.

Jack clenched his jaw. One tender word from him now and she would be in his arms again. And this time there would be no stopping him. He was poised on a knife-edge as it was. He'd never wanted any woman in his life as much as he wanted her.

But Kate was a lady, and if he touched her now they would be calling the banns next Sunday in church, and he couldn't do that to her: tie her for life to a miserable wreck when, with his grandmother's help, she could have almost anyone, and a life of ease and pleasure. No, he wasn't much of a gentleman, but he had enough pride not to speak that tender word and snare her with her own kindness.

'Get out of here before I really do give you a beating,' he growled. 'Lord, didn't your father ever teach you not to throw yourself at a man like that? If I didn't know you to be an innocent...' He ran his hand through his hair. 'It's provocation of the worst sort. Do you not understand? It is asking to be used like the lowest sort of woman!'

The colour slowly drained from Kate's face. She opened her mouth, but the words would not come.

...asking to be used like the lowest sort of woman! He was accusing her of wantonness, she thought despairingly. Blaming her, like all the rest... Throwing herself at a man... *If I didn't know you to be an innocent...* But he didn't know her as well as he thought he did. And what would he think, once he did know her better? That she'd provoked Henri, too? That she'd asked to be a Frenchman's whore?

She would die if Jack ever looked at her the way those men in Lisbon had.

She stared at him numbly. It was true. She had provoked him.

Provoked...the argument. Provoked his anger, that was all.

But Jack had grabbed her first. And he had kissed her when she had no thought of it—well, not much. Oh, yes, she had kissed him back, but he had started it, kissing her in that devastating... And *he* had been the one who had begun to undo her dress! But, like the people in Lisbon, he held her responsible...

Well, if *she* was wanton, then so was *he!*

Suddenly anger bubbled up in her, anger not only for what Jack had said, but for what men had said about her in Portugal and Spain. Blaming her!

Hypocrites!

This time she would not tamely accept the blame for what a man had done to her. She would retrieve her position. And give him the response he deserved!

She stared up at him, her face a white mask. Unconsciously his hand reached out towards her and in a flash she slapped him hard across the face. He stood there stupidly, unmoving, and, in utter silence, she turned and exited, quietly closing the door behind her.

Jack stood staring at the door a long time. After a while his hand came up and rubbed his cheek bemusedly. It was no light slap. His little Kate packed a good wallop. He sat down again and gazed into the fire, his hand still covering the cheek she had slapped, although the sting had long since faded.

How had it got so far out of hand?

Bloody hell, one minute she was driving him crazy, provoking his retaliation—sweeping in like some small avenging angel to wrest his drink out of his hands. He'd been justifiably angry with her then as she danced from chair to chair, flinging insults and bowls of greenery at him—cheeky little imp. Then his anger had started to change. It had become a hunt. And when he'd caught her, felt her small, panting body against his, all his frustrations had come to the fore...

Hell, she needed a lesson, but he'd never intended to hurt her like that. He couldn't get the memory of her eyes out of his mind. For a moment, before she had taken in what he had said, he had glimpsed the shyest, sweetest glow in her eyes as they had blinked up at him, her senses still reeling from the impact of his embrace. Jack would never forget the way that tender glow had died, replaced by anguish and deepest hurt...

She hadn't deserved that. He clenched his fist and slammed it down on the arm of the chair. Hell and damnation, she should have known better than to accost him when he was drunk. But she had felt so sweet in his arms, so sweet and warm and trusting. And he hadn't been able to bear it, knowing that it was impossible. So he had turned nasty to drive her away before it was too late. He groaned again.

He punched the arm of the chair once more, then punched his leg, taking bitter satisfaction in the pain it caused him.

In the sanctuary of her bedchamber, Kate lay across the counterpane, a damp and crumpled handkerchief bearing testimony to bitter tears. She lay, staring at the faded wallpaper, her breath racked by an occasional shudder—all that remained of her terrible weeping bout. She felt oddly calm now, the calm after the storm.

For the best part of the year now she had done her utmost to remain quite aloof from other people, cutting herself off from feeling more than the most superficial day-to-day emotions. The decision, she now realised, had been rooted in fear, fear of being hurt again, fear of being rejected.

And she had been right to fear.

What did you mean about my eyes?

Only that every time I look into them I want to do this—

And his kisses were everything she'd ever dreamed of—and more. For better or worse she was irrevocably in love with Jack Carstairs.

All her resolutions, all her biblical recitations, all her frantic planning to the contrary had been nothing but desperate attempts to deny the truth to herself. She recognised it now. The damage had been done well before she was truly aware of it.

At first, she hadn't seen the danger in him, despite his attractiveness. She'd just felt happy that her skills were needed at Sevenoakes. But his interfering ways had unsettled her—their quarrels had left her exhilarated, infuriated and gloriously alive. But it was more than just physical attraction, she knew. The quarrels were due to his protectiveness. She'd tried to reject it but, for a girl who'd rarely experienced it, protectiveness was a very endearing quality in a man. And when she'd recognised his pain she couldn't help but respond to it despite her resolutions to stay aloof. And by the time she'd realised how deeply entangled with him her emotions had become it was far, far too late.

She had tried...but then he'd kissed her. And with the inevitability of a flower responding to the warmth of the sun she'd opened her heart and let herself feel things for him that she had never felt for another person.

She loved him.

...every time I look into them I want to do this— Jack could not know how much those words had meant to her. When anyone else looked into her eyes, they saw her dead mother—her father, her brothers, Martha. Even Lady Cahill looked at Kate and saw her mother.

But Jack only saw her, living, breathing Kate. And with Jack, only with Jack, her eyes brought her kisses. And in his arms, being kissed, she had offered all that she was and all that she could be...

And he had thrown it back in her face.

It hurt, unbearably badly. She felt utterly crushed.

Chapter Ten

Next morning Kate rose early and went down to the kitchen to prepare breakfast as usual. She had come to several firm decisions in the night. She had allowed herself too much freedom with Jack—she was only his housekeeper. She should not have tried to interfere with his life, no matter how good her intentions. She should never have allowed herself to feel any emotion for him—it was inevitable that she would get hurt. She'd been living in a dream world and it had to stop.

She was *never* going to let anyone—not Jack Carstairs, not anyone—affect her emotions like that again. She would control it all much better in future, rebuild the walls of ice she had made around her heart in Lisbon. She had allowed Jack Carstairs to melt them. This time, she would build them stronger. She had already started the process during the long, sleepless night which had just passed. She could feel the chill of it surrounding her already. Inches thick. It might be cold, but it was also painless.

Kate put the coffee on, then stiffened as she heard unmistakable uneven footsteps coming towards the kitchen door. The door opened. There was a long silence. She could feel his eyes boring into her. Taking a deep breath, she turned to face him.

'I owe you an apology, Miss Farleigh,' said Jack. 'I had no

business saying those things to you. I did not mean them and I regret them very deeply. I also forced myself upon you in the most disgraceful manner. It was unforgivable.' Kate blinked. Damn him, damn him, damn him! He was utterly sincere. She felt a distant sensation of ice melting all around her. Oh, damn him!

He continued, 'I do not ask you to forgive me, but I do hope you will at least accept my humble apologies. I assure you, nothing of that kind will happen again.'

Kate had a lump in her throat. 'Mr Carstairs, it was not entirely your fault. It…it is no business of mine whether you choose to spend your evenings drinking or not.' Her voice grew huskier than ever. 'My interference was unwarranted, so whatever you may have said or done I have only myself to blame.'

Oh, Lord, she thought, why did I do that? She'd had no intention of apologising. It shouldn't matter to her what he thought, said or did. So what was she doing? More apologising, apparently. 'I also said some terrible things to you and I did not mean them…or, at least, I should not have…'

She floundered to a halt. She could feel his warm gaze resting on her. A long, tense moment passed, then the coffee boiled over.

'The coffee! Oh, goodness!' exclaimed Kate, and rushed to rescue it. 'Ouch!' She gasped and flinched, having incautiously grabbed the hot cast-iron handle and burnt her hand. She stepped back from the stove, sucking her hand.

'Let me see.'

'It's nothing,' she said dismissively, cradling her hand protectively nevertheless.

'Here,' he said authoritatively. 'Show it to me.' He gently took her hand in his and bent over it, examining the burn carefully. Kate looked at the dark head bent over her hand and felt herself tremble. She longed so much to place her hand on it and run her fingers through the thick, unruly hair. Ice, she thought. Think ice!

'It's not serious,' she said quietly. 'I've had much worse burns than this.'

'Well, you shouldn't have.'

Kate was astonished at the suppressed anger in his voice.

'You shouldn't be in a position where you keep burning yourself.'

It was that protectiveness again. Unnerved, she tried to pull her hand away. His head came up and he stared into her eyes.

'Oh, damn it all to hell!' he muttered, and pulled her into his arms. His mouth came down on hers, hard, and Kate could feel the passion pouring from him. Ice cracked all around her, turning instantly to steam.

The kiss was over in seconds. Jack pushed her away and left the room, heading outdoors. Kate sagged against the table, the pain of her hand almost forgotten. Moments later he entered again, carrying a bowl of water in which large chunks of ice and snow floated.

'Here you are,' he said gruffly. 'Put your hand in that. Cold is the best thing for burns, the colder the better.'

Her burnt hand seemed utterly irrelevant now. Kate blinked at him, bemused. It was too late—no walls of ice could withstand this man. She loved him. The only ice she could feel were the few chunks in the bowl. Everywhere else around her was warm. Very warm. She glowed.

'Oh, for God's sake, don't look at me like that,' he groaned. 'Put your hand in the damned bowl and forget what just happened. I…I must still be drunk from last night.'

He ran his fingers through his hair. Kate watched them. He saw her watching and swore again.

'I said stop it, damn you, Kate! It was an aberration, a mistake. I'm sorry. It won't happen again. You have my word on it. Just stop looking at me like that, will you?'

'It won't happen again?' Kate whispered. If she couldn't build walls against him, then why resist?

'No, it damned well won't.'

'Then I'm sorry too.'

He clenched his fists, unable to believe what he had just heard. 'Oh, for God's sake!' he muttered. 'I can't take much more of this.' And he limped quietly from the room.

She shouldn't have said it, Kate knew. It was not what a respectable girl should do, but since she wasn't considered respectable any more, then…

And she liked his kisses, more than liked them.

Never had she experienced anything like the emotions she felt whenever Jack Carstairs took her in his arms and lowered his mouth to hers. His kisses left her feeling so devastated, alive, exultant, vulnerable and…most gloriously invaded.

And she wanted more.

'I'm going to write to my grandmother asking her to take you into her house immediately,' Jack announced, entering the library where Kate was busy dusting books.

She whirled from her task. 'But why?' she whispered, her eyes wide with distress.

He could see she'd been working hard; her hair was starting to fall out of its knot, she had a smudge of dust on her chin and a blur of beeswax over her right eyebrow. Lord, was there ever a chit so unsuited to a domestic occupation? She needed to marry a rich man, if only to keep her face clean. He tried to keep the amusement out of his eyes, forcing himself not to soften towards her.

'We can't go on like this.'

'Like what?'

His eyes grew hard. 'Like this morning and the evening before.'

She flushed and clutched the book she had been dusting to her chest. 'Well, I do not wish to go to London to stay with your grandmother.'

'That's beside the point. If you stay here, this will get out of hand.'

Kate's eyes were fixed on him. 'Will it?' she asked softly.

Jack swore under his breath and turned away. Dammit!

Those big grey-green eyes made him lose all resolution. He had to make her understand once and for all.

'God deliver me from naïve virgins!' he growled in frustration.

Kate stiffened, but he didn't notice.

'You don't realise the danger you're in,' he said.

Oh, don't I? Kate thought.

'Men have needs, Miss Farleigh, carnal needs. They are not like women. If the need is upon him, a man will turn to a woman to fulfil those needs. Do you understand me? I said *a* woman, any woman, whichever woman is available to fulfil those carnal needs.'

Kate bit her lip.

Jack cursed again. Dammit, he had no choice but to be as brutal as he could to her, to stop that soft glow that shone in her eyes every time they rested on him. He had no future to offer her. God's truth, but he could not even dance with her, and if anyone was born to dance it was Kate Farleigh, thistledown maiden. He couldn't allow her to bury herself in obscure poverty, especially since she had no idea of what she was missing.

She had never been to London, never danced until the wee small hours at a glittering ball in the arms of a succession of handsome blades, never attended the Opera, Covent Garden, Drury Lane, Almack's. She had seen death, far too much of it, but never experienced the sort of life which London and his grandmother could offer her. She could have a splendid future; if brutal words were what it took to get her to London, then he would speak them.

'I am no exception. I may be a disfigured cripple—' Kate flinched at the raw self-hate in his voice '—but I am still a man, with a man's needs.' He paused to let his words sink in. 'And it has been a long time since I had a woman, Kate. A very long time. And that is what…this is. That's *all* it is. Do you understand me? I would never have touched you, never have kissed you, but I was drunk and it has been too long since I had a woman and I got carried away.' He turned away from her so he wouldn't have to look at her face.

Kate stared at the cloth in her hand and slowly crumpled it. She began to polish the shelf nearest to her. He had to be *drunk* to wish to touch her? That was what he was telling her? She was *any* woman to him? A mere available female? The words were harsh, biting, but, she eventually realised, they hadn't upset her as much as they should have.

Because, deep down, she didn't believe him.

If it was an available female he wanted, then why hadn't he bothered Millie or Florence? Or the barmaid at the tavern he frequented—from all accounts she was no better than she ought to be. No, whatever Jack Carstairs thought of her, it wasn't as any available female. And it wasn't the fault of his drinking either—all that did was exacerbate the problem.

'You will make the preparations necessary to go to London at the end of the week.' His words seemed to come from a long way away.

Kate stopped her mindless polishing. 'No, I won't,' she said over her shoulder. She had no intention of running the gauntlet of London society. Not while she had a choice. And besides, she had made a promise to his grandmother.

He was incredulous. 'Did I hear you say no?'

'You did,' she answered quietly. 'I have no intention of leaving.'

'Have you no sense, woman?' he growled. 'After what I just told you? You intend to stay? And risk being ruined?'

Her lips twisted ironically and she folded the dustcloth into a hard little package. Could one be ruined twice? It was a moot point.

'Didn't you hear what I said, you foolish chit?' He grabbed her shoulder and swung her around to face him. 'You risk losing your virtue by staying here! What the devil is the matter with you?'

She wrenched herself out of his hard grasp and stood there,

smoothing down her skirt like a bird who had just escaped a cat.

His eyes narrowed and his face hardened. 'Perhaps that is your plan.'

'What do you mean?'

'Seduce me and try to trap me into marriage,' he said slowly.

'Seduce you?' she gasped indignantly.

'Isn't that what has been happening here? No doubt my grandmother's cunning claw is somewhere in the plot too.' He laughed harshly. 'Yes, I'm sure it is. No doubt you two planned it nicely between you.'

'How dare you?'

He ignored her and continued. 'Oh, God, what a fool I've been. It's as plain as the nose on my face. My grandmother, concerned I may never marry, now that my betrothal to Julia is at an end, appears out of nowhere. She dumps poor little lost Kate on me, hoping I will conveniently scoop her up and make her mine, thus dealing with two problems at once. Ha!' He glared at her. 'Only it won't work, for I'm wise to your plot. You'll not trap me so easily, Miss Farleigh; I have no intention of wedding you.'

'And I have absolutely *no* intention of wedding you either, Mr Carstairs!' Kate's temper had her firmly in its grip by now. 'I would never, *ever* stoop to such a shabby plot and you have a…a colossal impertinence suggesting such a thing. It's utterly preposterous and I demand an apology at once—for me and for your grandmother too, for I am sure she would never scheme so sordidly!'

'Not sordidly, I agree; incessantly is a far better word.'

Kate ignored his interjection. 'And how dare you accuse me of trying to seduce you? It is *you* who have been grabbing and manhandling me, ever since I got here, plaguing me continually, when all I have tried to do is to get this house in order,' she finished virtuously, if inaccurately.

'Oh, so I've been plaguing and manhandling you, have I?

And who was it who accosted me in my room in the middle of the night?'

Kate stamped her foot. 'I did no such thing! How dare you even suggest it?'

'The upstairs parlour, then. And you came slinking in, knowing I was three sheets to the wind, and proceeded to seduce me.'

'I did not slink! I never slink!' Kate spat. 'And you were not "three sheets to the wind", as you so poetically put it, you were *drunk!* A sot! And if you imagine I was trying to seduce you by removing that poison you were swilling, then you have a very odd idea of what is seductive and no wonder this Julia, whoever she was, jilted you!'

'Leave her out of this,' he snarled.

'Gladly.' Kate tossed her head, wishing she knew more about his erstwhile fiancée.

'And these so-called *manhandling habits* you apparently object to so much—I haven't exactly noticed you valiantly resisting them. And I seem to recall myself calling a halt to proceedings each time, not you.'

Kate, blushing furiously, could think of no adequate reply. Of course she hadn't called a halt to his embraces. He knew perfectly well that his kisses left her with about as much resolution as a blancmange, leaving her with no desire to call a halt to anything. But how…how *scurrilous* of him to taunt her with it. She stood there glowering helplessly.

A slight, knowing smile appeared on his face.

'Oh, you are so infuriating!' she snapped. 'For your information, I have *no* intention of marrying. Not you! Not anyone! Not ever!'

'Rubbish!'

'It is not rubbish, it happens to be true.'

He watched her from under thunderous black brows. It wasn't the first time he'd heard her refer to this nonsense. He could no more imagine Kate Farleigh going through life as a lonely spinster than he could fly.

'And why not, Miss Farleigh? I have heard you assert it, but you have yet to offer one convincing reason. I know what women want—' Jack could not keep the sneer out of his voice '—wealth, a fine home, position, admiration and some poor besotted sap to hand it to them on a platter. There isn't a woman born who doesn't scheme after that.'

Kate winced at his cynical view of marriage. Was he speaking from personal experience? Someone had hurt him; she could see that clearly. Julia? Kate couldn't speak for all women, of course, but, for herself, none of those things mattered—only love. But Henri had stolen Kate's right to be respected; without respect, there could be no love. So she could not marry. Lisbon had taught her that. Lisbon and Harry, her betrothed.

'You are wrong about most women, but I can see you will not listen. All I can do is repeat that I have no intention of marrying. As for my reasons, they are very personal and private. Your grandmother knows and that is why she did not press me to accompany her back to London, why she found me this temporary position as your housekeeper instead.'

He snorted. 'Balderdash! My grandmother only offered you this position because you are too blasted stubborn to know what is good for you. This position was nothing but a temporary sop to your pride. She has every intention of introducing you to society. There is no reason on earth why you cannot marry some rich, respectable fool.'

He stared down at her, his eyes hard and glittering, his mouth compressed with anger. 'You just have to get yourself out of my hair and up to London, flutter those long eyelashes at whichever gentleman meets your requirements, murmur softly in his ear in that smoky soft voice, smile and swish that delectable little body in front of him. Before the poor fool can say "boo" you will be walking up the aisle on his arm and, no doubt, within a year or two you will be dandling his heir damply on your knee.'

His long hard fingers bit into her shoulders and he shook

her as he spoke. Kate's mouth quivered with anguish at his unconscious cruelty. To hear the impossible, put into words like that, painting such a cosy, utterly unattainable picture…

Jack could feel every breath entering and leaving her body, smell the sweet clean fragrance of rosemary in her hair. She quivered under his hands and he took a long, rasping breath.

'And if he proves a touch reluctant in popping the question, then just you look at him like that and the poor idiot won't be able to help himself.' With a groan he planted his mouth on hers and she was swept again into the maelstrom of emotion that was becoming so dear and so wondrously familiar to her.

Eventually he released her mouth and stood looming over her, breathing hard. Kate, her senses still reeling under the impact of his embrace, clutched his shoulders and arms, leaning against his warm, heaving chest for support.

Shakily she gathered together the tattered remains of her self-control and pushed against the powerful chest and arms that enclosed her.

Instantly he released her and stepped back. Kate was conscious of a feeling of isolation so intense that it threatened to shatter her resolution. She wanted to lean back into that hard, wonderful embrace again, but she could not. She retreated to the other side of the room and stood there, gathering her composure.

Kate, with every reason in the world to insist on complete propriety, had failed to do so. If that was what was bothering him, she would ensure that the kisses stopped. She was sure she could manage it, especially if the consequence for failure was for her to be sent away to London. Away from him.

After a few moments she said shakily, 'You are mistaken about a great many things, Mr Carstairs, but you are quite correct about one—this behaviour must stop.' She took a deep breath and continued in a cold little voice, 'I apologise for my part in any impropriety that has taken place. Rest assured, it will not occur again. You will have my full co-operation in that. But I will not go to London.'

Jack stood and watched her, his eyes sombre. He nodded briefly and left, shutting the door quietly behind him.

Kate picked up her dust rag. Tears began to spill from her eyes.

The days passed, but there was no more mention of sending Kate to Lady Cahill. There was little mention of anything at all, for she and Jack rarely spoke unless they couldn't help it.

Christmas came and went as if it were just another day. But it wasn't, not for Kate. After church, she went to some trouble to make an especially good dinner, but Jack did not join them, so it was a very subdued meal with just Martha and Carlos attending. The farm girls had been given the day off, and in any case it was too bitterly cold to do much else but huddle near the fire.

For Kate it was a day of intense, searing loneliness, recalling Christmases past with her brothers playing all sorts of silly tricks and games...

She tried to be strong about it, to tell herself that it wasn't so bad really, that she had food, and shelter, and was better off than many. But this was only the first in a lifetime of solitary Christmases facing her. The realisation seeped into her bones, leaving her feeling chilled and forsaken, despite the roaring fire.

Eventually, at the end of a long, miserable day, she crept into bed, and allowed herself the luxury of crying herself to sleep.

Jack, returning from a day passed in self-imposed isolation at a local tavern, heard the muffled sobbing as he passed her door. He froze, listening. Every fibre of his body urged him to enter her room, to take her into his arms, still the sobbing with his mouth. To hold her, comfort her, lo— But he could not. Even drunk as he was, he knew that to go to her was to ruin her life for ever. He leaned against her door in anguish, each sob reverberating silently in his body, until at last silence fell and he knew she slept.

One morning, well into the new year, as Kate stood taking her customary view out of the window to greet the dawn as it lit the snow-covered landscape, she heard the muffled thunder of hoofs beneath her window. Her heart leapt into her mouth. Would he be thrown again? She flung open the window and leaned out into the chill air, straining to see. The big roan stallion galloped past her, his mane streaming in the breeze. Clinging firmly to his back was Jack Carstairs, riding adequately, if not as stylishly as he once must have done. Kate's hand crept to her cheek, her eyes filling with tears as she realised what he had accomplished.

It was the end of his humiliation. He could ride. Jack Carstairs would once again ride with the Quorn or any other hunt. She watched him as he galloped over the small rise and then slowly she washed and dressed. It was a great day. He would probably not even mention it to her, but she would celebrate the occasion by cooking him an especially delicious breakfast.

Kate was out fetching eggs when she heard the clatter of hoofs on the cobblestones behind her. She whirled and almost dropped the basket of eggs as the roan clattered to a halt in front of her, held firmly in check by a masterful hand. He grinned elatedly down at her, slid off the big horse and grabbed her with eager hands.

'Did you see me, Kate? I can ride again. And it's all thanks to you.' Without warning he swept her up into his arms and whirled her around and around, laughing delightedly. Kate laughed too, wishing she had put down the basket so she could hug him back. Finally he slowed and, still holding her above him, looked up into her face.

'Well, Kate? Shall we call pax? I am too pleased with the world today to continue our armed truce.'

Her heart too full to speak, she blinked back tears.

'What's this?' he said. 'Tears?' The smile died from his

face and he slowly let her slide down to the ground, still holding her hard against his body.

'Oh, no,' she mumbled, putting down the basket and groping for a handkerchief. 'I…I often cry when I'm happy. It…it is the most ridiculous thing.'

He smiled down at her. 'It is, indeed,' he said softly, 'but then, that's Kate, isn't it?'

She looked up, startled at the warmth in his voice.

'Never does anything the commonplace way,' he murmured. 'Here, allow me.' Taking the handkerchief from her unresisting grasp, he proceeded to dry her eyes and cheeks with one hand, the other gently cupping the back of her head.

Kate found she couldn't move. She was overwhelmed by the sensation of his hard, strong body against hers, the warm breath of him on her cheeks, his soft, deep voice murmuring in her ear. She knew she should move away from him. Her inner voice told her so, but she could not bring herself to move. Eventually he finished drying her cheeks and they stood still, unmoving, in silence. Kate found she could not look at him. She was oddly breathless and stared at the buttons on his shirt, totally aware of the warmth and strength of his embrace. Finally he placed a gentle finger under her chin and lifted it until their eyes met.

'Thank you, Kate,' he said softly, and bent his mouth to hers, his tenderness undermining every resolve she had made to push him away. At first his lips were soft and warm and gentle, then, as she opened her mouth beneath the pressure of his, he groaned deep in his throat and the kiss deepened. Kate gave herself up completely to the delicious, disturbing sensation of his tongue seeking, caressing, entwining with hers. She pressed her body hard against his and ran her hands up through his thick dark hair, clutching it in mindless delight. With a groan, he lifted his head and stared down into her face, her eyes dazed with pleasure, his almost black with passion. 'Oh, God,' he muttered, and kissed her again, a hard, long, passionate kiss, which sent shudders of sensation coursing through her body.

Suddenly Kate found herself abruptly released. Dazed, she slowly became aware of voices and footsteps clattering over the cobbles. As Millie and Florence rounded the corner of the house, Jack was collecting the reins of the roan stallion. Kate was still standing where he had left her, trying to collect her wits after the onslaught on her senses.

'Good morning, Miss Kate, Mr Carstairs,' they chorused. 'Father says it be going to snow terrible bad again soon.'

Jack chatted easily with the girls and Kate marvelled at his cool composure. Perhaps he hadn't experienced what she had, she concluded. He couldn't have, if he was able to talk and chat so casually. Lust seemed to do different things to a man than to a woman. But it wasn't only lust on her part—it was love too. Perhaps that was the difference. She forced herself to greet the two girls and then walked with shaky legs to the kitchen, where she sat on the nearest chair and tried to collect her thoughts.

She'd tried so very hard to evict Jack Carstairs from her heart, but it seemed he was embedded there irrevocably and for ever. Nothing seemed to work. She had spent weeks trying to harden her heart against him. And as soon as she felt it was under control he would look at her with those wickedly twinkling blue eyes, and all resolution would melt. Or he would say something in the deep voice that never failed to go straight into her bones. Or he'd carelessly touch her in passing—a light hand on the shoulder, the brush of a thigh against her skirts—the most harmless contact shot sensation through her.

And then there was that kiss just now…

In his joy at being able to ride once more, he was utterly irresistible. In moments like that she was willing to fling all caution, all propriety, everything to the wind and give herself to him for as long as he wanted her. And moments like that occurred all too often.

The only solution she could think of was the one he had

suggested and that she had rejected so strongly—to physically remove herself from his presence—and that she could not bring herself to do. It would happen in a few months anyway, so she would stay close to him while she could...

By the time the girls entered the room, carrying fresh milk from the farm, Kate had herself under control again. She managed to get through the morning without seeing Jack again, except in the distance. For the rest of the day she found excuses to avoid his presence.

But that evening he was in too exuberant a frame of mind to dine alone, insisting on turning their evening meal into a celebration, pouring wine for them all, Millie and Florence included, and talking the most ridiculous nonsense that had them all in stitches. Kate was fascinated, never having seen this side of him before. Carlos, too, was in fine form, a wide grin lightening his dark face as he egged Jack on to further and further extremes of silly banter with the girls and Martha, causing riotous giggles to fill the room.

It appeared that all this time Jack had had Carlos heating oils and making up unguents, continuing Kate's treatment in secret. Some of the stories of the near-misses and narrow escapes from Kate's discovery had them all whooping and shrieking helplessly as Jack mimicked first Carlos, then Kate, then Martha, then the stuffy village apothecary.

He was utterly charming in this mood, Kate thought, wiping tears of laughter from her eyes. She suddenly realised that this was probably how he had been before the war.

This was the Jack that must have been betrothed to Julia, she realised with a sinking feeling—witty, handsome and vital. A man who was at home in the upper reaches of the *ton*. Who would have all the women eating out of his hand, from the lowest born like Millie and Florence and Martha, to the highest like Julia, whoever she was, and his grandmother.

It was clear to Kate now that he was almost well enough in body and spirit to return to the world he had renounced. A world where he would be amongst his peers and in his own element. She wondered dully if he would go back to Julia, now that he seemed to have climbed out of his pit of misery.

She should be happy for him, she told herself. And she was—for him.

Chapter Eleven

One afternoon in late February, in a period of clear weather which signalled the impending demise of winter, a smart curricle drew up at the front door of Sevenoakes. It was followed moments later by another, even smarter than the first, then an elegant travelling phaeton and several grooms leading a string of fine horses. From the sporting style of the vehicles, it was clear that they were driven by young men of substance and fashion. Three gentlemen alighted from the various vehicles and strode up the front steps, shouting merrily for 'Mad Jack' and exchanging good-natured insults concerning each other's driving prowess or lack of it.

Kate opened the front door, and froze. She had not expected visitors, particularly not *tonnish* ones like these. She stood like a statue, barely noticing their hearty exuberance. A short, round-faced man rushed straight past her, tossing her a heavy, many-caped driving coat and a high-brimmed hat as he went. Peering up the stairs, he shouted, 'Hey, Jack! Mad Jack Carstairs! Come out from wherever you're hiding, man, and give us a drink!'

A tall, lanky fellow passed her another many-caped great-coat and a curly-brimmed beaver and, laughing, followed his friend. The last handed her a heavily frogged greatcoat of military cut and said calmly, 'Sir Toby Fenwick, Mr Lennox and Colonel Masterton to see Mr Carstairs.'

Colonel Masterton? A soldier? *From the Peninsula?* Kate tried desperately to bring the panic under control. He could not see her properly—she was almost invisible under three heavy coats. 'Please wait in the drawing-room to your left, sir; I will endeavour to find Mr Carstairs.'

The gentleman raised a quizzing glass to his eye. Kate huddled more firmly behind the coats. Having finished his inspection, he smiled faintly and strolled languidly into the room Kate had indicated. She backed out of the entrance hall, tossed the coats on to a chair and collapsed on top of them, her pulse racing.

She was overreacting, she told herself sternly. There was absolutely no reason to think he might recognise her. Merely because he was a colonel. No doubt hundreds of colonels had never even been to the Peninsula. And hundreds more who'd never even heard of Kate Farleigh. It was ridiculous to expect that this one might have recognised her. She certainly did not recognise him, nor any of the others.

Controlling her anxiety, Kate sent Millie out to fetch Jack while she put out simple refreshments of wine, brandy and bread and butter. She sent Florence into the drawing-room to light the fire. Florence emerged hurriedly, blushing and giggling. Kate's lips thinned. She was being a coward, making the girls put up with that. She would have to face Jack's visitors sometime.

Suddenly she thought of something. She flew upstairs and raced to her room. After rummaging in a large oaken chest she emerged, triumphantly brandishing a white spinster's cap she had noticed some weeks before. She put it on, carefully tucking in every last curl and tying it firmly under her chin with the tapes provided. She looked at herself in the mirror. Perfect. The cap was dreadfully ugly and much too large for her head. It was embellished with lace, knots of ribbon and a frill which hung almost to her eyelashes. In this, she could

face any soldier visitors, secure in the belief that she was unlikely to be recognised. She glanced at her reflection in the
mirror and giggled—she almost didn't recognise herself.

She hurried downstairs, ignored Millie and Florence's looks
of amazement and Martha's gasp of horror, picked up the tray
of refreshments and marched into the drawing-room, her head
held high. It had to be—she could not see from under the frill
otherwise.

'Brandy—this is more like it.' The tallest gentleman leaped
forward from where he had been warming himself at the fire
and lifted the decanter and a glass from her tray.

'Ho, you blackguard!' shouted the chubby young man.
'Don't think you are going to make off with that. Here, pour
some for me!' He too snatched a glass from the tray and pursued his friend. It occurred to Kate that the two were, as her
brothers used to phrase it, a trifle foxed.

The third gentleman sauntered up to her. Kate held her
breath. 'Allow me,' he said, taking the tray from her grasp
and setting it on a nearby table. He glanced briefly at her cap
as he straightened up, then followed her gaze to where the
other two were carelessly filling their glasses, slopping brandy
on to the surface so carefully polished by Kate only that morning.

'You are perfectly right, 'ma'am.' he said, observing her
pursed lips. 'I fear that we stayed a trifle too long at the excellent hostelry a short distance from here. My friends are
indeed a trifle…er…exuberant.'

'So I see,' said Kate dryly.

'And you, ma'am, we have not had the pleasure. Colonel
Francis Masterton, late of the 95th Rifles, at your service.' He
bowed. 'And you are…?' He paused.

'Er…Kate Farleigh,' mumbled Kate. His lightly uttered
words had flustered her badly. The 95th Rifles? He *was* from
the Peninsula. Pray God he knows nothing of me, she thought
frantically. And oh, heavens! Why did I tell him my name? I
should have changed it. Oh, Lord! She held out her hand au-

tomatically, then, remembering, she pulled it back awkwardly. Servants did not shake hands. 'I am the housekeeper here.'

'Indeed?' he said on a long note of surprise. She glanced up at him from under the frill. Heavy-lidded grey eyes regarded her shrewdly. 'You surprise me, ma'am,' he said, and stunned Kate by reaching for her hand and bowing over it politely, carrying it lightly to his lips.

She flushed and pulled her hand away. 'I...I will see if Mr Carstairs is available.' Oh, Lord, what did he mean by kissing her hand? Was he mocking her? Did it mean he knew of her? He certainly thought her no servant. Did he think her Jack's mistress?

'Mr Carstairs is indeed available,' came a deep voice from the doorway. Jack stood there and, by the glint in his vivid blue eyes, Kate knew he had seen the Colonel kiss her hand. She turned to leave. Jack's hand restrained her.

'Don't leave us yet, Miss Farleigh,' he said, frowning at her cap. 'I'd like you to meet my guests, all of whom have recently returned from battling Boney's forces on the Peninsula.'

Oh, Lord, Kate thought—*all* of them? Not just the Colonel? He turned her to face them. Kate was pale and rigid.

Jack spoke with cold formality. 'This is Sir Toby Fenwick and Mr Andrew Lennox, both late of the 14th, the Duchess of York's Own Light Dragoons, and I gather you've just met Colonel Francis Masterton who has, I collect, recently sold out of the 95th Rifles.'

The two younger gentlemen stared at him, surprised.

'Dash it, Jack,' said chubby Sir Toby, 'what's all the formality? Formal introductions to servants now, eh?' He laughed and raised his glass to his lips. 'Introduce me to that other little blonde—'

Kate, mortified, tried to pull away from Jack's hold.

Jack ignored her and spoke with paralysing chill. 'Miss Katherine Farleigh is the ward of my maternal grandmother, Lady Cahill. Miss Farleigh and her companion, Mrs Betts, called here on their way to join my grandmother in London, but they took pity on a poor bachelor and kindly offered to assist me to get this house in order. You will have no idea of the enormous debt of gratitude I owe to this lady and her companion.'

One of Colonel Masterton's mobile brows was raised slightly, but he did not otherwise react. The other two came sheepishly forward under Jack's flinty gaze and held out their hands.

'Sorry, ma'am,' said lanky Andrew Lennox. 'Took you for one of the servants.'

'Er…yes, dam—dashed sorry,' mumbled Sir Toby. 'Er… you'll have to excuse…er…taken rather too much…er… Delighted to meet you, ma'am.' Pink with embarrassment, he took Kate's hand in a damp grip and shook it vigorously.

Kate's fear inflamed her temper. Jack had no right to embarrass her or his guests with this charade, introducing his housekeeper as his grandmother's ward. It was a deliberate ploy to force her into the role she had told him a dozen times she wanted none of. And he'd discomfited his guests on purpose, to declare her off limits.

But he was unwittingly playing with fire. If indeed any of them recognised her later, they would be furious if they thought they had been tricked into apologising to a disgraced woman. And they would blame Jack. They would not know of his ignorance—she must and would repudiate his introduction and clarify her position.

'There is no need to apologise, sir,' she said firmly, 'for Mr Carstairs exaggerates. I am, in fact, the housekeeper, placed here by Lady Cahill, whose ward I am *not*. She was godmother to my late mother, and that is the full extent of the connection.'

'Dammit, woman, don't contradict me. You are my guest!' Jack roared, furious to hear her demean herself like that.

Mr Lennox and Sir Toby recoiled at his tone. They were well acquainted with his temper. Colonel Masterton raised an eyebrow yet again.

'I say, steady on, old chap,' began Mr Lennox, laying a tentative hand on Jack's arm.

Jack ignored him. He shook Kate's arm and glared at her cap. 'You are *not* a servant here, dammit! You are my guest!'

His friends cast wary looks at Kate, as if expecting her to burst into tears at any moment. But Kate was made of stronger stuff. She shook herself free of his hold with an infuriated squeak, and smoothed down her skirt.

'You just bellowed and swore at me, Mr Carstairs,' she said dulcetly. 'No *gentleman* would bellow or swear at a *guest*— particularly in front of other guests. Such behaviour is invariably reserved for mere servants, who are in *no* position to answer back.' She sailed victoriously out of the room, leaving a stunned and breathless audience behind her.

'In no position to answer back!' snorted Jack. 'The little vixen always has the last word.' He turned to face his friends.

Colonel Masterton was convulsed with silent mirth. Mr Lennox was gazing at the closed door, his eyes filled with admiration, and Sir Toby Fenwick stood, his mouth hanging open in stupefaction. He turned to Lennox. 'See what I saw, Lennox, old chap?'

Lennox grinned. 'I saw a female, no bigger than your thumb, give Mad Jack Carstairs the neatest set-down he's had in years.'

Sir Toby nodded vigorously. 'That's what I saw too. Never thought I'd see the day. What an amazin' girl! And the chit's the housekeeper, you say?'

'No, you fool, I told you—oh, to hell with it!' snapped Jack, annoyed. 'What the devil are you doing here in the first place, Tubby?'

Sir Toby looked self-conscious. 'Oh, well…heard a rumour…you'd stuck your spoon in the wall, or close to.'

'So you decided to come up and see whether I was dead or not.'

The others looked vaguely uncomfortable.

'I'm glad you did,' said Jack, surprising himself as he realised that, for the first time in months, the prospect of visitors did not fill him with repugnance. 'Of course,' he added, 'I must warn you, the standard of hospitality here isn't what you've previously enjoyed in my company. Conditions here at Sevenoaks are quite spartan.'

He smiled wryly and looked them up and down. 'In fact, I'm not certain that three such prodigiously elegant sprigs of fashion will be able to bear the lack of amenities at this establishment.'

This brought about a spate of heated denial and much good-natured chaffing.

'Hang it all, man, we've bivouacked with the best of them, in beastly little holes all over the Peninsula, and if you're saying I can't take it any more, then you can dashed well eat your words!' asserted Sir Toby. He peered boskily around the room, taking in the glowing furniture, the roaring fire, the soft, faded colours.

'And besides, this ain't such a bad place as we were led to believe. In fact, dammit, it looks positively cosy. Much more comfortable than that damned cold barracks of a place my ancestors saw fit to build in the dim dark past.' He sank into a chair with a sigh of satisfaction and took a deep draft of his glass.

Kate retired to the kitchen, shaking. She had not intended to draw attention to herself like that. Deny her status as his grandmother's ward—yes. But be drawn into what could only be called a spat with Jack! And in front of his friends! Oh, her wretched, wretched temper! Servants were, by and large, invisible to gentlemen like Jack's friends. That and her cap were her only defences against discovery. But now she'd let her temper ruin everything. No true servant would answer her master back so impudently. Far from being invisible, she'd made herself a source of interest to them. Oh, what a careless fool she was!

All her earlier decisions about seeking employment with

folk not of the gentry came back to her in a mocking I-told-you-so. She would never have behaved in such a way had she taken a position with people who were not of her milieu. She would never have let down her guard enough.

She had let herself become complacent, comfortable, secure.

She'd stopped fearing discovery with every stranger—because she met no strangers. The effects of Jack's self-imposed isolation and the unusually severe winter had ensured that. They had existed, in the months she'd been here, as if in a cocoon, or on an island. And in that cocoon Kate had felt safe.

But now Jack had regained his strength, the spring thaw was coming and the protective isolation had been ripped away. The man whom she could hear now, laughing with his friends, bore little resemblance to the embittered recluse she'd encountered when she'd first arrived at Sevenoakes. The world could come to Jack Carstairs now and he would welcome it. She, however, was exposed to strangers' eyes and dependent on the vagaries of their memories...

There was no use worrying—she should concentrate on preparing dinner out of what she had available. She sent Carlos to kill two more chickens, and prepared a pie from the remains of yesterday's roast beef. It would be a plain but substantial meal. And Carlos would serve it.

After dinner the gentlemen sat over their port.

Kate sat in the adjoining room, her chair pushed as near as was decent to the connecting door. Some sewing lay in her lap, but her fingers weren't moving. She was eavesdropping. She had been unable to endure the strain any longer—she had to know whether any of the men had recognised her. From where she was sitting she could hear every word in the next room.

'Pos'tively cosy li'l place you have here, Jack,' said Sir Toby. 'Good dinner, good wine, roaring fire, good companions—all a man could want, right here. And right smack bang in the middle of some of the best damned hunting country in the world! You're a lucky man, Jack Carstairs.'

At his words an awkward hush fell over the room.

'Oh, God, Jack, I'm a clumsy oaf! I'm sorry. I didn't mean—'

'Just shut up, Tubby!' hissed Andrew Lennox. 'You've said quite enough.'

'I didn't mean…' Sir Toby trailed off miserably.

There was a short silence.

'There's no need to treat me with kid gloves, you know,' said Jack. 'In fact, you don't need to feel sorry for me at all.'

Colonel Masterton leaned forward into the light and stared hard at his friend. 'So…' he said on a long note of discovery.

Jack grinned.'You always were as sharp as a razor, Francis.' He found his hand seized and wrung in a powerful grip.

The other two stared in bewilderment.

'What the devil are you two talking about?' said Andrew Lennox. 'I can only think of one thing…' He stared hard at Jack, read the truth in his eyes, then he too leapt forward and seized Jack's hand, pumping it fervently.

'Will somebody please tell me what's going on?' complained Sir Toby. 'Why is everybody shaking Jack's hand and what are you all being so damned mysterious about? Found an heiress, Jack, have you?'

The others laughed.

'Well, I'd planned to keep it as a surprise for tomorrow, Tubby, but I can ride again. Of course I'm not quite up to hunting yet, but I will be soon.'

Sir Toby stared, dumbfounded, for a moment, then leapt from his chair, spilling his drink, and seized Jack's hand, shaking it until Jack thought it would drop off.

''S marvellous, old man, simply marvellous!' he kept repeating. He glared round at his two friends still seated in their respective chairs. 'Don't you un'erstand, you two idiots? Jack can ride! Ain't you going to congratulate him?'

The others roared with laughter. When the tumult had died

down and a fresh round of drinks had been poured, Francis said to Jack, 'I don't understand. The surgeons swore you'd never ride again, didn't they?'

'They did. Miss Farleigh disagreed.'

'Miss Farleigh?' said Mr Lennox.

In the next room, Kate froze. Oh, no, no, she prayed silently. Do not tell them; please do not.

'Yes, her brother had been cured of a similar sort of injury by some Eastern doctor,' continued Jack. 'She told me her brother regained almost full strength…unfortunately.'

'What?'

Jack explained. 'Miss Farleigh lost her father and both her brothers in the war. Her brothers were in the 83rd, I believe. She is now utterly alone in the world, except for my grandmother, who has become her guardian.'

Kate sagged in her seat. The 83rd. She could not have been more clearly identified. If any of them had heard anything of her, their memories would be well and truly jogged now.

'Yes, that's one point that I must confess quite eludes me. Do, pray, explain, dear boy. I know a little of Miss Farleigh's story…'

Kate leapt from her chair. She stole to the door and leaned against it, breathless with fear. The Colonel *did* know her. He would tell Jack everything. Kate chewed her lip worriedly. She would have to leave. She couldn't bear to see Jack's face when he knew.

'Knew her brothers and met her father on several occasions. In Spain, you understand. And I have met Miss Farleigh once before, though she looked a little different then… But your grandmother's ward? I never heard that you were related to Farleighs, Jack.'

'We're not, of course. No blood relation at all as far as I know. She—my grandmother, I mean—was Miss Farleigh's mother's godmother.'

'Ah,' murmured Francis ironically. 'A close family connection, I see.'

Oh, for goodness' sake, get on with it! thought Kate. The tension was killing her.

Jack shrugged ruefully. 'Well, you all know my grand-mother—if she decides the connection is a close one then nei-ther mortal man nor woman, can shift her.'

'No, indeed,' agreed Andrew. 'Nor the immortals, I'd wa-ger.'

Sir Toby interrupted. 'I don't understand what your grand-mother's got to do with this, Jack. Terrifying old woman! Treats me like a scrubby schoolboy every time I have the misfortune to run into her. As far as I'm concerned, the further she stays out of everything the better.' He paused a moment, then said with deepening suspicion, 'I say! She's not here, is she? Lurkin' upstairs somewhere?'

Kate could have screamed with frustration.

'Oh, shut up, Tubby, you fool!' chuckled Andrew good-naturedly. 'Let Jack finish his story. The oriental doctor, Jack,' he prompted.

'Well, as I said,' continued Jack, 'Miss Farleigh's brother regained full use of his limb, and she told me about it, though, like the fool I was, I wouldn't listen to her... Damn near bit her head off for trying.'

'I can well imagine,' said Sir Toby frankly. 'And, what's more, you can be devilish unpleasant to be around when you're like that, Jack; take my word for it. Wouldn't have come uninvited like this, except Francis made me. Expected to see you snarling round the place like a bad-tempered wolf. Had to stop for a few quick ones on the way. Wasn't going to tackle you sober! So what'd she do? Whisper sweet noth-ings, eh?'

Kate clenched her fists.

Jack chuckled. 'On the contrary, she told me that if I wanted to spend the rest of my life being a cripple and falling off horses, to go right ahead doing what I was doing!'

'She didn't?' gasped Sir Toby.

'She did. Told me to my head I was wallowing in self-pity, too.'

'Good God!' said Francis.

'You didn't hit her, did you, Jack?' said Sir Toby.

'Oh, don't be so stupid, Tubby,' said.Andrew.

'No, Tubby, but she certainly got blasted for her efforts, as I expect you can imagine. But the words stuck in my mind and finally bored their way into what was left of my sanity. So I eventually swallowed my pride, sought her assistance, and to cut a long story short I can ride. It's not a pretty sight, but nevertheless I stay on. I've not ridden to hounds yet, but it won't be long before I'm up to it. So, Tubby, old fellow, you were quite right after all; I am a lucky man—thanks to Miss Farleigh.'

Kate relaxed briefly against the wall. Tears glimmered in her eyes. She'd given him something good to remember her by, at least. When he knew the truth, perhaps his condemnation would be tempered by the memory of her help with his leg.

The men in the next room fell silent for a while, only the occasional clink of a glass or the crackling of the fire could be heard. Then Andrew Lennox spoke, and at his words tension raced through Kate once more.

'You said you'd met Miss Farleigh before, Francis?'

'Indeed, I have,' he affirmed. 'Though it took me a moment or two to place where I'd first seen her.'

'Where was it?' enquired Andrew.

Kate closed her eyes and held her breath.

'At the final siege of Badajoz,' the Colonel announced coolly.

Kate's eyes flew open. *Badajoz?*

'Badajoz? You cannot be serious! Explain yourself, Francis,' demanded Andrew.

'Do you mean to say that that chit was at Badajoz?' spluttered Sir Toby in amazement. 'Not possible, is it? I mean, no women at Badajoz…well…I mean women, yes…that was part of the prob…but not ladies…er…you know what I mean.'

'Indeed there was, Toby, one undoubted lady at least, for which my aunt Charlotte will be eternally grateful,' said Francis.

There was a short stunned silence.

'Your aunt Charlotte? Gammon!' snorted Sir Toby. 'Can't tell me your aunt Charlotte was at Badajoz, for I won't believe it. Stuffiest woman in the world, your aunt! Never been out of the country. Hardly ever been out of London. I'd wager my best hunter on it.'

Francis chuckled softly. 'True, old chap, but whom, above all others, does my aunt value in this world?'

After a short pause Andrew said, 'Er, your cousin Arnold?'

'Exactly—my cousin Arnold,' agreed Francis.

'What the devil are you talking about?' demanded Sir Toby. 'I don't understand why we're talking about everyone's dratted relatives. It was bad enough with Jack's grandmother, but now you must rabbit on about your aunt and your cousin Arnold. I was glad to see the back of him after Badajoz, and I damned well don't ever want to see or talk—'

'What happened to Arnold at Badajoz, Toby?' interrupted Francis sweetly.

'Got shot or wounded in some damned way or other and lost his wits and blethered on and on and on about an angel saving him, or some such nonsense.'

Jack exclaimed aloud at this.

'Quite true, old chap,' explained Sir Toby. 'Drove us all batty with his tales of his angel. By the time he was sent home I for one was ready to finish the work that some damned-fool Frog had obviously botched.'

'Tubby, old son,' said Francis, 'that was no angel—that was Jack's Miss Farleigh.'

Kate's knees almost gave way.

'What?' The exclamation came from three throats in unison.

'Quite true. Miss Farleigh was over there with her father

and made it her practice to venture in, often quite close to the fighting, and tend the wounded. Came across Cousin Arnold with a ruddy great gash in his arm that wouldn't stop bleeding. Tied it up so tight that the blood couldn't get through. Surgeon who finally got to treat him said she'd saved his life. Would have bled to death for certain. Touch-and-go for a while there as it was.'

Kate leaned against the door jamb, her eyes closed. That poor boy was Francis's cousin? In the other room there was a long silence, broken only by the quiet crackling of the logs burning in the hearth.

'She told me her father had confined her to a tent for a week after Badajoz,' growled Jack furiously. 'My God, when I think of the bloody atrocities…'

'I do believe he did,' said Francis. 'After he discovered her saving Arnold.'

There was another long silence.

'Gal's a damned little heroine,' said Toby at last.

'Too true,' agreed Francis quietly. 'And, from what I can make out, Arnold was only one of many she saved.'

In the next room Kate sank silently on to the chair. She felt dizzy with relief. Francis did not know the rest of her story—she was safe for a time. She had been so frightened…but he thought her a heroine! She did not need to hear any more. A *heroine*—he wouldn't say that if he knew about Henri. The relief was overwhelming. She was exhausted. Silently she slipped from the room and went upstairs to bed.

'Arnold's angel, you say? Good Gad!' mumbled Sir Toby. 'Not the sort of thing one expects a lady to…to…'

'No, indeed,' agreed Andrew warmly. 'Most ladies would faint dead away if we even told them one-tenth of the things that could happen in war, let alone…' His voice died away as all four men stared into the fire, recalling how the blood-crazed troops had gone mad after the long siege and storming of Badajoz. The raping, the plundering, the pillaging. It was horrific to imagine Kate in the midst of it all.

After a few moments Andrew raised his voice in a rallying tone.

'And why are we sitting here brooding in such a melancholy fashion? We're all here, alive and well, drinking this excellent port, reunited at last. And Jack, back from the dead, with the best of all possible news.'

'Yes, by Gad!' said Sir Toby. He raised his glass. 'Here's to Mad Jack and the Hunt! Back together at last!'

'Yes, indeed,' agreed Francis. 'Jack and the Hunt, let's drink to it!'

'And to Miss Farleigh,' said Jack quietly, raising his glass. With one accord the others rose to their feet and drank the toast.

'To Miss Farleigh.'

'Arnold's angel.'

Chapter Twelve

Kate yawned as she set the table in the breakfast parlour next morning. She had slept poorly, worrying about what to do. The very idea of leaving Sevenoakes, and Jack, pained her deeply, but she knew she ought to do it. The arrival of his friends had shown her what thin ice she was skating on. All Jack's friends were soldiers; there would be more visitors, more soldiers. They'd come for the hunting as well as Jack's company. And with more visitors there would be more chance of discovery, more chance of denouncement. It was just a matter of time.

But if she wasn't here there would be no reason for any of Jack's visitors to speak of a well-born English girl who'd lived in sin with a French officer. She wanted to stay near him for the rest of her life, but if the price of that was to have him look at her in disgust, then the price was too high. Better by far to leave him in ignorance, thinking well of her.

She stood back, regarding the table setting. As she did so, her hand went to her head, and she flipped at the irritating frill. She probably didn't need to wear her disguise any more, but better safe than sorry. Jack's introduction of her as a guest had given her another reason to wear it. The cap was the sort of thing a spinsterish housekeeper might wear and it, better than anything, would make her position clear.

Finally she heard male voices and footsteps and swiftly began the last-minute preparations needed to serve hot break-
fasts. She had thick home-cured ham and fresh-laid eggs siz-
zling softly in a pan, slices of bread toasting gently, a jug of
ale poured and the tantalising aroma of coffee filling the air
when Jack entered the kitchen.

'What the devil are you doing in that thing again?'

'I have no idea what you are talking about, and if you wish
to converse with me then I warn you that breakfast will be
ruined. I am doing four things at once as it is, and if you
expect me to bandy words with you at the same time, then
you will be disappointed.' Kate was pleased—she was doing
a very good imitation of her previous behaviour; he would not
suspect anything was wrong.

'Please wait in the breakfast parlour and I'll bring everything in to you and your friends directly.' She glanced up at
him. 'I take it they are all downstairs?'

'What the devil are you doing in that abomination?'

Kate stamped her foot. 'I know nothing of abominations; I
haven't got time for them. What I want to know is how many
to serve breakfast to. Are all your friends arisen?'

'Yes,' he snapped. 'Why are you doing all this yourself?
Where are those girls and that good-for-nothing man of mine?
Carlos!' he bellowed.

'Kindly do not deafen me with your shouting.' She whisked
a slice of toast off the grill just in time to stop it burning.
'Carlos and the girls have gone to the village to purchase ad-
ditional supplies needed for your friends' visit.'

'Need they all have gone? Surely one would have been
enough.'

'Mr Carstairs!' Kate whirled around and glared at him, her
resolutions forgotten. 'If you must come in here and pick quarrels with me at this hour, it is your prerogative to do so—but
do not expect to have an edible breakfast at the same time!'

The coffee smelt delicious. The ham and eggs superb. Some

toast was beginning to smoke. It was a tactical retreat, Jack told himself.

The decision had nothing to do with his rumbling stomach. Besides, he had a responsibility to his guests. He would deal with her later.

Breakfast arrived with no further disturbance. Jack's friends instantly hailed Kate as Arnold's angel. Relief swamped her anew. They saw her as a heroine, not a traitor and a whore. A heroine! She couldn't help but laugh. They insisted that Kate join them for breakfast and set themselves to entertain her further.

After a time Kate became very aware of Jack glowering at her cap. She had noticed his friends blink at it each time she brushed the frill from her eyes, but they were all far too well-mannered to comment. Jack, she felt with a sinking heart, was not similarly inclined. She put her chin up stubbornly and continued to ignore his black looks.

Francis's eyes began to glimmer with humour. He'd noticed Jack's foul mood the instant he had returned from the kitchen. He now perceived there was a silent battle of wills taking place across the table. She was not at all the angel his cousin had named her, but a vibrant little minx who gave as good as she got. She was perfect for Jack.

At the conclusion of the meal, Kate rose and gathered up the dishes while the others made plans for the day. Jack murmured his excuses and followed her.

Francis observed Jack's hasty exit. Unless he missed his guess, there was about to be another confrontation between Miss Farleigh and his friend. He had no qualms about following them—it was certain to prove entertaining. Hearing the voices raised in conflict, he slid unobtrusively into the kitchen.

'And now, Miss Farleigh, I will have my answer at last. What the devil is that atrocity on your head?'

'What atrocity?'

'That white thing.' Jack gestured disdainfully.

'It is a cap.'

'I know what it is! What the devil do you mean by wearing it?'

'Is it not obvious?'

'Not to me. That sort of thing is usually worn by dowdy old maids well past their prayers, and then only if they have something to hide. You are still a girl and your hair is too pretty to hide.'

The compliment took Kate by surprise, but she rallied. 'It is kind of you to say so, but I am not a young girl. I am a spinster, and as such I will wear this cap.'

Jack snorted in disgust. 'You are no spinster, so take it off at once and do not let me see the damned thing again.'

'I am indeed a spinster and I have every intention of wearing this cap, whether you like it or not.' Kate glared at Jack, hands on her hips.

'Oh, do you, indeed?'

Francis smiled, recognising the signs—Jack was in a fine temper, but doing his best to hold it back. Jack moved closer. Kate backed away warily, clutching the cap to her head protectively. Francis decided it was time to make his move.

'Pray forgive my interruption—no, no, continue, do. I would hate to spoil your conversation.' He seated himself, clearly with every expectation of being entertained. 'I think you were about to make a dive for Miss Farleigh's cap, old man,' he prompted helpfully.

Kate glanced from Francis's polite expression to Jack's black frown and began to giggle. Francis's smile broadened into a grin. Jack dashed his hand angrily through his hair.

'Damn you, Francis,' he swore, then his sense of humour began to get the better of him. The twitching of his lips, so clearly at odds with his black frown, provoked his observers to further mirth, and finally he too joined in the laughter.

At last Kate stood up, and immediately Francis and Jack rose to their feet. 'Please excuse me,' she said, 'but I have things to do.'

'So do I,' agreed Jack, and before she knew what he was

about he had snatched the offending cap off her head and tossed it into the fire. 'That's better.' He grinned triumphantly.

'Oh! You wretch!' exclaimed Kate.

'It was an abomination and the only thing to do with abominations is to burn them. Don't you agree, Francis?'

Francis bowed towards Kate. 'Forgive my perfidy, Miss Farleigh, but, much as I deplore his crude methods, that cap was indeed an abomination and not, therefore, to be borne by any man with an eye for beauty. Your hair is quite, quite lovely and should never be hidden.'

Kate blushed.

Jack looked at his friend through narrowed eyes. 'Yes, well, I think you have said quite enough, Francis. It is time you took yourself off. Er…isn't that Toby calling you?'

Francis smiled. 'Wonderful hearing you must have, dear boy,' he murmured. 'I didn't hear a thing.'

Jack glowered and thrust him out the door. He turned to Kate, but encountered such a fiery look from the sparkling grey-green eyes that he decided his duty lay with his guests. He followed Francis out to the hall, where they found Mr Lennox.

'Fine morning for a ride, Jack, don't you think?'

'Excellent idea,' Jack agreed, his good mood restored, and, after shouting for Sir Toby to join them, the foursome headed towards the stables.

It was a crisp, sunny morning, ideal for riding. Wisps of fog and remnants of snow lingered in the shadowy hollows, waiting to be burnt up when the bright sun finally discovered them. The horses were in fine fettle and snorted and pranced, eager to be out and moving, but Francis, Sir Toby and Mr Lennox kept their mounts well reined in, unsure of Jack's capabilities and not wanting him to strain his leg. After several minutes of the dreary pace they'd set, Jack became aware of his friends' strategy.

'Come on, you sluggards!' he shouted. 'Race you to the top of that hill.' Recklessly he urged his horse into a gallop. Shout-

ing and laughing, the others followed. It was a mad race and
by the end of it all four of them were flushed and breathing
heavily.

'By Jove, Jack!' exclaimed Sir Toby excitedly. 'I would
never have thought it; stap me if you're not riding damn near
as well as ever you did. S'a marvel, I tell you, a marvel!'

'Not quite as well as I used to, I fear,' responded Jack,
grinning from ear to ear nevertheless. He stretched his bad leg
a little awkwardly and the others became aware of white lines
around his mouth, a sign that he was in some pain.

'I say, Jack, you haven't overdone it, have you?' said Mr
Lennox.

'No, no.' He met his friend's doubting look and grinned
ruefully. 'Well, perhaps a little, but I couldn't have you three
keeping me wrapped in cotton wool, now could I? Such a pace
you'd set, I'd have died of boredom.' The others laughed.
'Now, you all ride on, don't worry about me,' he said. 'I'll
take it a little slower now that my blood's moving again.'

'Yes, go on, you two,' agreed Francis. 'I'll keep Jack company for a bit. My head's still a trifle delicate from last night,
and any more riding like the last episode and I fear the
wretched thing will fall off.' The other two laughed as they
rode away, but Jack turned and regarded his friend sceptically.

'My poor Francis,' he said in mock-sympathy. 'And I always thought you had the hardest head of anyone I knew.'

Francis smiled blandly back at him. 'Ah, well, you have the
advantage of me by several years, you know. I am nigh on
thirty-five.'

They moved forward at a slow canter, chatting as they did
so. After some time, the talk ceased and they walked their
horses in companionable silence, enjoying the morning, each
man absorbed in his own thoughts.

Then Francis chuckled to himself.

Jack turned his head. 'What is it?'

Francis shook his head in amusement. 'Never thought I'd
see you setting up as a milliner.'

'What the hell do you…? Oh, that. Stubble it, will you?' mumbled Jack.

But Francis had no intention of dropping it. 'It was an ugly enough cap, to be sure, and it made that pretty little thing look like a dowdy, but you acted as if she deliberately wore it to annoy you.'

Jack harrumphed. 'She did.'

'Oho…so it's like that, is it?'

Jack glowered. 'Like what? She's my grandmother's ward, that's all.'

'And naturally you must supervise her headgear,' agreed Francis sympathetically.

'She was foisted on me by that meddlesome old witch. I had no choice in the matter.'

'Ahh.' Francis nodded his head wisely.

'Ahh nothing!' snapped Jack. 'You have added two and two and come up with five. The girl means nothing to me. She's a damned nuisance, if you want to know the truth!'

'Mmm,' agreed Francis infuriatingly.

Jack ground his teeth. 'Damn your eyes, Francis.'

His friend chuckled softly. After a few minutes he spoke again. 'Well, dear boy, since you have no interest in little Miss Farleigh, you'll have no objection if I pursue her myself.'

Jack wrenched his horse to a halt, slewed round in the saddle and glared at his friend. 'What the devil do you mean by that? You'll do nothing of the sort. She…she's my grandmother's ward.'

Francis's eyebrows rose extravagantly at his tone. 'I would court her honourably, of course—you could have no objection to that.'

Jack had dozens of objections, but he couldn't think of a single thing to say. It was one thing to urge Kate to take up his grandmother's offer and go to London to find herself a husband. Jack had envisaged some gentle, fatherly soul who would pamper Kate and smother her in luxury. He glanced at his friend and frowned. Not a handsome, worldly, elegant...rake!

'Why the devil would you be wanting to court someone like Kate?' he demanded. 'Dammit, man, you're a notorious rake!'

'A notorious rake?' Francis laughed. 'And what of you, Jack? The man who put all the matchmaking mamas in a flutter to protect their chicks— Ah, no, you settled down, didn't you? The Divine Julia. Whatever happened to her?' He noticed Jack's frown and clucked sympathetically. 'Still carrying a torch, are you? Well, I can see how little Kate, charming as she is, could not compare with the fair Julia.'

'I'm not carrying a torch and I will thank you not to mention Kate's name and hers in the same breath.'

Francis smiled in spurious sympathy. 'Ah, so the goddess is still enshrined in your heart, then?'

'The goddess, as you so mistakenly call her, is nothing but a shallow, self-centred harpy, and if you think for one minute, Francis, that she...she...' Jack was so angry, he was lost for words. 'If you don't know that Julia Davenport is not worth Kate Farleigh's little finger, then...then...I don't know what you are,' he finished lamely.

Francis controlled his urge to grin. Jack was responding beautifully. 'No need to convince me, old man. I was never one of the Davenport's admirers. I am the one, don't forget, who may court little Miss Farleigh with a view to marriage.'

Jack gritted his teeth. His friend's habit of referring to Kate as 'little Miss Farleigh' was starting to annoy him very much. 'Never thought you'd be one for parson's mousetrap. What's brought it on?'

'Oh, well, there comes a time in a chap's life when it's time to settle down. I've been keeping my eyes open for a while now and somehow the idea of one of the schoolgirls on the marriage mart doesn't really appeal. A man wants to settle down with a woman who'll make him comfortable, a woman of sense.'

Jack was revolted by this description of Kate. 'It sounds to me like you are more interested in taking a comfortable old chair to wife,' he said sourly.

Francis chuckled. 'No, indeed. I most certainly don't think of Miss Farleigh as a comfortable old chair. Why, the very notion is offensive.' He paused delicately. 'Ah, perhaps you haven't noticed, old man, but little Miss Farleigh is quite a pretty little thing, with an eminently kissable mouth. Even that smut of flour on her nose this morning looked quite delicious.'

He ignored Jack's growl.

'And have you noticed her dimple? It hardly ever appears, but when it does it's utterly charming. Add to that her extraordinary voice and her delightful laugh, and you have in one small package a very cosy armful indeed, very cosy.'

Jack was appalled at the vision his words conjured up. Kate nestled in Francis's arms. He felt positively sick. 'You know she has not a penny in the world.'

Francis shrugged. 'I'm not hanging out for a rich wife.'

'Are you in love with her, then?' Jack's mouth was dry as he waited for the answer.

'Good heavens, no.' Francis laughed carelessly. 'A chap doesn't have to be in love with his wife to have a happy marriage. As long as she loves him, it will work.'

'And you think she loves you, do you?' Jack growled.

'No, dear boy, not yet.' Francis smiled complacently. 'But the marriage bed has a way of taking care of that, does it not? By the end of the honeymoon she will love me.' He winked. 'I'm told I am rather a good lover, you see. And, besides, I intend to be a kind and indulgent husband. Women like that, you know. And I do believe young Kate has had very little indulgence in her life…'

Observing Jack's face, Francis deemed it prudent to join Sir Toby and Mr Lennox. He reached across and patted Jack's leg. 'You look as if your leg is paining you, dear boy. Why don't you take yourself home and I'll meet you back at the house?' Unable to keep a straight face any longer, Francis galloped away, putting the greatest possible distance between them before his mirth escaped him.

He left Jack staring after him, his face a mixture of fury, chagrin and despair. It was true. Francis would make Kate a fine husband. So why did the thought make him feel so sick inside? It was very confusing. Reason forced him to admit Francis would make someone an excellent husband. Only…not Kate.

Jack entered the house from the side entrance nearest the stables and paused, hearing voices coming from the front parlour: Kate and a man whose voice he did not recognise. He entered the room.

Kate was seated on a lounge sofa, smiling happily at a complete stranger. Jack frowned. The stranger was holding both of Kate's hands in his, and she was making no attempt to remove them from his grasp. She turned and beamed at Jack.

'Oh, Ja— Mr Carstairs, isn't it wonderful? This is Mr Jeremiah Cole.'

Cold blue eyes swept over Mr Cole's person and one eyebrow rose sardonically. His hard stare shifted pointedly from Cole to Kate's hands. Cole immediately released them.

'Forgive me, Miss Farleigh—' Jack's tone was frigid '—but I do not immediately perceive what is so wonderful. Who is this person?' His eyebrow rose again as his gaze swept over the man before him.

To his annoyance, Kate did not even seem to register his arctic reception of her guest. She laughed.

'Oh, I'm sorry. I must confess Mr Cole's unexpected appearance has put me in somewhat of a fluster.' She turned and beamed at the stranger again. 'A very welcome appearance and a very happy fluster, but it has made me forget my manners.'

She rose and immediately the stranger did the same. Jack's eyes grew even flintier as he noted that the Cole fellow was almost as tall as he, solidly built and modishly dressed.

Kate continued, 'Mr Carstairs, I have much pleasure in presenting a distant and until now unknown cousin of mine, Mr Jeremiah Cole. Mr Cole, Mr Jack Carstairs, my…' She hesitated. Mr Cole's eyebrows rose slightly.

Jack instantly recognised her difficulty. 'Miss Farleigh is the ward of my grandmother, Lady Cahill. My grandmother prevailed upon Miss Farleigh and her companion, Mrs Betts, to assist a poor bachelor in setting this house to rights.'

A speculative look came on to Mr Cole's face, so Jack added, 'She will shortly be taking up residence with Lady Cahill and making her entrance to society under her aegis.' That should stop the fellow's suspicious mind, he thought, for what grandmother would sponsor her grandson's mistress into society?

'Delighted to meet you,' said Cole affably. 'I must say, I was bowled over when I found that my little cousin had survived the terrors of war after all. And when I arrived here and discovered what a very charming and delightful little cousin she was too I was bowled over even more thoroughly.' He kissed her hand.

Jack watched balefully as Kate blushed. She was making no attempt to pull her hands out of the fellow's sweaty grasp.

'Tell me, Cole,' he said, 'how did you discover Miss Farleigh's whereabouts? Not many know she is here.'

Cole turned, still retaining Kate's hand. 'I was contacted by Lady Cahill's man, Phillips. My late father was executor of the Delacombe estate, you know, and their property came to him, as closest living male relative. It passed therefore to me on his death two months ago.' He smiled at Kate, an oily smirk to Jack's jaundiced eye. He patted her hand and then grew solemn.

'You can imagine my joy when I discovered that I was not, in fact, all alone in the world, and that my cousin was alive and well—not perished at the hands of the dastardly French along with her father and brothers.' He squeezed Kate's hand sympathetically. 'Naturally I came post-haste to meet her. And of course to make my condolences on the loss of her loved ones.'

'It was very kind of you, Mr Cole,' said Kate softly.

'Please,' he said, 'Mr Cole sounds so formal. I am your only living relative, even if rather distant. Could you not bring yourself to call me Cousin Jeremiah, and allow me to call you Cousin Katherine?'

'Cousin Kate will do nicely, Cousin Jeremiah.' She smiled at him and he kissed her hand again.

Jack stared at the little display, revolted. Could Kate not see the fellow was an oily Cit? He might be well dressed and passably good-looking, if you liked biggish men with sandy hair and regular features, but he was a deal too smooth for Jack's liking, and as for his continual flattery of Kate and that incessant groping and kissing of her hand...

Jack itched to take the impertinent fellow by his elegantly tailored collar and toss him out on his ear, but he knew Kate would never allow it. He regarded her sourly. She was completely taken in. She obviously took the fellow at his word and even seemed to enjoy him pawing and slobbering over her hand. She allowed it at any rate. And smiled.

'So you are the heir.' Jack interrupted before the fellow could kiss Kate's hand for the third time.

'Yes, indeed,' agreed Mr Cole. 'Though it is a melancholy feeling to find oneself enriched by another's demise.' He looked solemn for a moment, then brightened. 'But that reminds me, there is a small bequest for you, Cousin Kate, a peculiarly feminine bequest.'

He smiled at Kate's enquiring look and passed her a flat oblong packet. She looked at it for a moment, puzzled, then opened it and gasped in surprise and pleasure. She looked at Jack, her eyes wide with delight. 'Jewellery.' She turned back to her cousin. 'My grandmother's?'

He nodded. 'Yes, she left one or two pieces to you as a keepsake.'

Jack frowned, remembering his grandmother's belief that

Kate would have been left well provided for. It seemed she was wrong, for there was not much of it—just a string of pearls and one of garnets, some earrings, a ring and a brooch or two.

He suddenly noticed that Kate had gone very silent. She sat, her head bowed, staring at the jewellery on her lap, her hands gently touching the pieces, turning them over, running the pearls slowly through her fingers. Of course, he realised, she must be disappointed that there was nothing there of any value. He could not see her face, but he knew how she must be feeling. Frustration and anger grew in him as he noticed a tear roll down her cheek. She must have hoped for the sort of things other women wanted, and which she deserved to have more than any of them—diamonds, emeralds, rubies. He silently called a curse on the heads of all her thoughtless relatives.

She looked up. Her eyes were filled with tears, but her smile was radiant. 'Thank you, Cousin Jeremiah, thank you. You don't know how much it means to me that my grandmother left these to me,' she said in a soft, husky voice that told Jack she was very moved. Mr Cole shifted uncomfortably in his seat. She stood up abruptly and smiled mistily at the two men. 'If you don't mind, I would like to look at my grandmother's bequest in my chamber. Will you excuse me, please?' She held out her hand to her cousin. 'Will I see you again, Cousin Jeremiah?'

'Of course.' He smiled, bending over her hand again. 'You don't think I will go away again, just when I have discovered a charming little cousin all of my very own? I will seek accommodation in the nearest town and with your permission, Cousin, will call again tomorrow.'

She nodded happily and left the room, cradling the packet to her bosom. Jack stood staring after her, flabbergasted. To see her face, one would have thought she had been given the Crown Jewels, not a small collection of trumpery beads. The girl never failed to amaze him. She was like no other female he had known. He turned and looked at Mr Cole. He was smiling to himself in a very satisfied manner. Damn the man. Jack didn't like him one little bit.

'The front door is this way, Cole.'

'It has been a pleasure to meet you, Mr Carstairs,' said Mr Cole politely, disregarding the glowering look his host was giving him. 'I look forward to furthering our acquaintance. I collect you are one of our gallant heroes from the Peninsula. I would be delighted to discuss it with you at some future time.'

The gallant hero, nauseated by the description, managed not to throw Kate's cousin down the steps and contented himself with slamming the door instead.

Jack needed a drink, so he went into the library and stopped dead. Kate was sitting in a wing chair. She looked up. 'Millie is washing the floor in my room,' she said by way of explanation of her presence in the library.

He nodded. 'That fellow has left.'

'It was very good of him to come all this way,' Kate said quietly. 'He could have just sent these to me by mail.'

Jack watched the way her hands stroked the packet that still lay in her lap. There was a long silence.

'You seemed pleased to see him,' he said at last.

Kate sighed. 'Yes, it is so wonderful to discover that I am not utterly alone in the world, after all.'

'You are not alone at all.'

'But I am, Jack,' she said softly. 'Or at least I was.'

'You have my grandmother—' he began. *And me.*

'Oh, Lady Cahill is a dear,' she interrupted, 'but in truth she is no kin of mine. I am a charitable project she has taken on for the sake of my mother's memory, that is all. She has been very kind and generous, and I am grateful to her for it, but you must see that I have no real claim on her. It is different to know that someone is part of your family, that you belong to them.'

Jack objected to that in the strongest terms. 'You do not belong to that overfed, overdressed, fawning puffbag!'

'Mr Carstairs,' Kate reproved him coldly, 'I will thank you to speak politely of Cousin Jeremiah in my presence. He is well built, not overfed in the least and I find his taste in clothes impeccable.' The look she cast on Jack's stained buckskins was not lost on him. 'Moreover, he has a kind heart and he came all the way here from Leeds only to meet me and to give me my grandmother's jewellery.'

'Trumpery beads,' he snorted.

Kate bridled at his tone. 'They may be trumpery beads to you, but they are all the jewellery I possess, and they belonged to my grandmother, whom I never met.'

She clutched the small packet of jewellery to her breast.

'My mother died when I was born and I never knew her. All I had of her were her pearls and her eyes. The pearls I had to sell, to pay our debts.' *And her eyes cost me my father's love.* 'You cannot understand what it means to me to know that my grandmother remembered me, for my father fell out with my grandparents before I was born and they never contacted us as far as I know.' Her eyes shimmered with unshed tears.

The bequest was far greater than its size or monetary value. Kate had only known her mother through others' eyes—and the image had been tarnished with her own guilt. But now Kate had something tangible, from a grandmother who'd thought of her with love instead of blame. Who'd cared enough to send her a keepsake—one which was not tainted by her father's resentment of Kate's existence.

'You call them trumpery beads, but my mother may have worn these as a girl, don't you see?' Her voice broke and she turned and fled upstairs.

Jack swore under his breath and ran his hand angrily through his hair. Damn him, did he always have to speak before he thought? He hadn't meant to sneer at her pathetic little collection of jewellery; it had just been too much for him. First

Francis had put him in a temper, with his damnably impertinent plans for Kate's future, and then to come home and find Kate beaming with delight on some oily Cit…it was too much! And besides which, his leg was hurting him. It was his own fault too, showing off before his friends. He would have to have it massaged again before it stiffened up on him any more.

'Carlos!' he bellowed. 'Carlos!' He stumped his way morosely upstairs.

Chapter Thirteen

'Damn it all, Francis,' Jack exploded. 'At least Tubby and Drew had the decency not to outstay their welcome. Haven't you got anything better to do than to hang around here for weeks on end, eating me out of house and home?'

Francis chuckled. 'Not the least, dear boy. I like it here. The fresh air, the scenery…' he raised his eyebrows significantly in the direction of the terrace, where Kate was strolling with her cousin '…the charming company.'

He took another sip of port and added ironically, 'Oh, and of course you are a superlative host, Jack, old man. Make a chap feel so welcome.'

Jack growled under his breath. 'A man can't take a step in any direction without tripping over you or that damned Cole fellow.' He glared at a hapless vase of flowers. 'And the place is so cluttered up with these stinking weeds! Haven't either of you anything better to waste your blunt on? I don't know which of you is worse—that blasted Cit bleating platitudes all over Kate and kissing her hand until it must be quite soggy—or you, mouthing flowery compliments at her like a blasted poet.'

'I do pride myself on my poetic talents, and little Kate seems to enjoy them too.'

'Little Kate? Miss Farleigh to you! I'll thank you not to treat my grandmother's ward with such familiarity, Francis.'

Francis's grin broadened. 'She asked me to call her Kate, dear boy, and I hate to refuse a lady's request.'

Jack muttered something unintelligible and stomped out of the library, leaving Francis chuckling. Jack had been acting like a bear with a sore head for several weeks now, snapping and snarling at his guests for no good reason. Or no reason he could be brought to admit to.

Francis's gaze sharpened on the pair on the terrace. His own so-called courtship posed no danger to Jack, but that Cole fellow was a serious contender. He had visited Kate morning and afternoon for the past three weeks, bringing her flowers, books and sweetmeats, though where he found the flowers at this time of year, and in the countryside, was more than Francis could guess. The man was obviously very plump in the pocket.

Francis frowned. He liked the fellow no better than Jack, though not for the same reasons. There was a pushiness about him that Francis disliked. Cole had pursued Kate from the moment they met with a single-mindedness and determination that to Francis's eye smacked of the calculating, rather than the lover-like. His possessive attitude towards his 'charming little cousin' was increasing daily, and Francis suspected that Kate was finding it uncomfortable.

However, Jack's open hostility to the man made it difficult for Kate to repel her cousin's over-familiarity, for they all knew Jack was just itching for any excuse to toss Cole out on his ear and forbid him the house. Cole was Kate's cousin, after all, and her only living relative, and she wanted to be able to see him, even if she might not relish his possessive attitude towards her. Francis sighed and poured himself another drink.

'My dearest cousin,' Jeremiah Cole began.

Kate felt her stomach sinking. She'd known for some time that this was coming, and no amount of hinting had managed to dent her cousin's obvious determination. Perhaps it was better to allow him to speak, and then it would be over. He took her hands in a moist grip.

'Perhaps you have been aware these last weeks of my desire, my very ardent desire, to make this relationship of ours a closer one.'

'Cousin Jeremiah, I am very happy to have you as my cousin—'

'But *I* am not,' he interrupted. 'You must know, Kate, how I feel about you.' He pressed her hands against his broad chest. Kate tried to pull them away, but he only held them more tightly. 'I am in love with you, Kate—madly, desperately—and I want you for my wife.'

'Cousin Jeremiah,' she said gently, 'it is very kind—'

'Kind! It is not kindness I feel for you, my beloved. It is love! I want you to be mine. You are all alone in the world. Allow me to care for you, to protect you, to love you for the rest of your life. Only give me your hand, sweet Kate.'

Despite the seriousness of the moment, Kate's sense of humour got the better of her. 'Indeed, Cousin Jeremiah, you seem to have taken it whether I will or not,' she said, tugging to release her hands from his grip. He did not let go, but smiled, almost angrily, at her.

She said more firmly, 'Please let me go, Cousin Jeremiah. You are hurting me.'

'And you are hurting me, Kate, by not answering. I asked you a question, one of the most important questions you will ever be asked in your life. Will you be my wife?'

'No, Cousin Jeremiah,' she said gently. 'I am sorry.'

He frowned at her disbelievingly. 'I don't believe it!' he said, releasing her hands only to take her shoulder in a tight grip. 'I don't believe it!' he repeated, shaking her quite hard. 'I love you and I am sure that you love me.' His tone softened. 'That is it, isn't it, Kate? You are teasing me.' He pulled her hard against him and though Kate tried to push him away he was far too strong.

'Naughty girl to tease your Jeremiah like that,' he crooned, and before Kate realised what he was about he had planted his lips firmly over hers and was kissing her with a wet determination that filled her with revulsion. She struggled in vain as his hands stroked down her body and his thick tongue probed to enter her mouth.

Suddenly she found herself released. She staggered back against the balustrade as Jack thrust himself between her and her cousin.

'You filthy swine, keep your paws off her!' he roared, and let swing a punch that sent Cousin Jeremiah sprawling inelegantly on the flagstones. Jack stood over him, rolling up his sleeves, the light of battle fairly blazing from his eyes.

'How dare you maul a decent girl, you cowardly scum?'

Cousin Jeremiah scuttled backwards.

'Come on, you scurvy blighter. It's one thing to bully a helpless female, and another to stand up to a man, isn't it? Subject an innocent girl to your filthy lust, will you? Not on my property, you won't. I'll teach you a lesson in how to treat a lady—one you'll never forget.'

Jack stepped forward, murder in his eyes, oblivious to Kate's frantic jerking on his sleeve.

'Jack, stop it! You mustn't. He didn't hurt me. *Jack!*' she cried, but he was determined on his course. He moved purposefully towards Cousin Jeremiah, his fists bunched, blue eyes glittering with rage.

'Jack, he asked me to marry him!' screamed Kate in his ear.

At that Jack came to a dead halt. He swung around and stared at her in shock. The angry colour died from his face, leaving it a bleached grey.

'He what?' he croaked at last.

'He asked me to marry him,' repeated Kate quietly, belatedly realising she'd given Jack the wrong impression, but seeing no immediate way out—except violence. She'd seen enough violence.

'So that's why...' Jack choked. He wrenched his eyes from

her face and turned away. 'I…see,' he muttered. Without looking at either of them, he left.

Kate gazed after him, biting her lip. There had been pain in his eyes. Because he thought she was to marry Cousin Jeremiah? She wanted to run after him and tell him she'd refused, but she was afraid that if she did Jack would return to his former rage and do Jeremiah a grave injury. And now that Jack had stopped her cousin she felt she could handle things herself. She might be angry with Jeremiah for the way he had forced his embraces on her, but much could be forgiven a man rejected in love, and he was still her cousin, after all.

She turned. 'I think you'd better leave, Cousin Jeremiah. I'm sorry it had to come to this.'

He had struggled to his feet by now. His fright had passed, and was fast turning to indignation at the way he had been treated. 'I must tell you, Cousin Kate, that I am deeply offended by that man's treatment of me. I have a good mind to report him to the nearest magistrate. He is clearly a dangerous lunatic.'

Kate's temper finally exploded. 'How dare you say such a thing? If you must know, I think you got off lightly, for if I were a man I would have knocked you down much sooner. How dare he? How dare *you?* To force your kisses on me, and think to overcome my refusal by brute force! Report him to a magistrate if you dare, Cousin Jeremiah, and you will find yourself reported for assault—on me!'

Cousin Jeremiah blanched and calmed down immediately. 'Now, now, Kate, my dear, I did not mean it. I…I was upset. I think you must allow me the right to feel angry at being attacked so violently, but of course if it will upset you I will take no injudicious steps to have the matter followed up.'

Kate was mollified. She spoke more softly. 'I am sorry it had to come to this, Cousin Jeremiah. If you please, we will never speak of this matter again.'

'No, no, of course not,' he agreed eagerly. 'But now, my

dear, I would like to have the matter of our marriage settled
as soon as possible.'

Kate stared at him incredulously. Was the man utterly impervious? 'Cousin Jeremiah,' she said firmly, 'all this happened because you refused to listen to me the first time. I am
sorry, but I will *not* marry you.'

'But I love you,' he insisted.

'Then I am sorry for you, but I do not return your love.'

'Love can grow after marriage,' he persisted.

'Not in this case,' said Kate bluntly. She had endured
enough of his florid compliments and hand-kissing to last a
lifetime.

'I do not mind if you don't love me; I will marry you anyway,' he declared nobly.

Kate gritted her teeth and began to wish that she had let
Jack give him a thrashing after all.

'But I do not wish to marry you.'

He took several steps towards her, and she backed away.
Good God, he was going to try to embrace her again.

'Cousin Jeremiah, I am *not* being missish!' she almost
shrieked in her frustration. 'I said I will not marry you and I
meant it. *Nothing* will make me change my mind.'

'How sweetly shy you are,' began Cousin Jeremiah, advancing on her, a determined smile on his face.

'*I am not shy!*'

'I think you'd better listen to the lady,' said a quiet voice
from behind them. 'My friend Mr Carstairs has already introduced you to the rather crude fighting methods of the Coldstream Guards. I would like to demonstrate the techniques favoured by gentlemen of the 95th Rifles.' Francis began to roll
up his sleeves, then paused. 'That is, unless you apologise to
the lady and leave before I finish rolling up my sleeves.' He
continued rolling them back, very deliberately and precisely.

Cousin Jeremiah eyed the sinewy forearms that were emerging. He already had a massive headache and a cracked jaw
from just one frightful punch from Carstairs. He began to mut-

ter indignantly about violence being offered to a man whose only crime was to woo a lady too ardently, when he caught Colonel Masterton's glittering eye. It bore a disturbing similarity to the look that he had seen in Mr Carstair's eye a few moments before. Hastily Cole gabbled an apology to Kate and left, almost running across the lawn in his desire to be quit of the place.

Despite the comical sight he made, Kate had no desire to laugh. She felt like a wrung-out rag. Nor did she feel up to discussing it with Francis.

'Thank you, Francis,' she said quietly, and turned to leave.

'Are you all right?' he said.

'Oh, I'll be as right as a trivet,' she said, attempting a cheerful smile that failed miserably. 'I just need to rest for a while, I think.' She turned and ran upstairs to her room.

Later that evening she went downstairs to supervise the preparation of dinner. Jack had taken himself off somewhere. The tavern, no doubt. Kate didn't feel up to dining with Francis, so she ate in the kitchen with the servants. It was too ironic, really. Here she was, a girl who knew herself unable to marry, being courted by two gentlemen, neither of whom she wanted…

Kate sighed. For a short while, her life had been so pleasant. Now it was all changed. She still felt Jack's eyes on her a hundred times a day, but instead of protectiveness and a lurking tenderness there was suspicion and brooding disapproval in his gaze. Whatever she did, he seemed to be furious with her. It was confusing, hurtful—and more than a little annoying.

She had no idea what his intentions or feelings towards her were. There was no denying that his kisses moved her like nothing she had ever experienced, but it was a feeling she knew she ought to fight. Even if by some wondrous chance he came to feel something deeper than lust for her, an alliance between them would not be possible. Anyone with a grain of sense would realise that in his position Jack would have to marry money.

Kate wondered what sort of a man his father had been to disinherit his son so callously. Had he not been playing cards the day he died, and won the deed to this property, Jack would be living…heaven knew where. At any rate, if he was to make anything further of his life, Jack would have to find himself an heiress, a well-born heiress—not a poor clergyman's daughter with nothing but a tawdry scandal for her dowry…

'Miss Kate.' Florence interrupted Kate's train of thought. 'Are we goin' to have the next bit o' that story soon?'

Kate smiled. While cleaning the library a few weeks before, she had discovered some of Mrs Radcliffe's novels. The vicar's daughter had been utterly forbidden 'rubbishy novels', so naturally Kate had become addicted to them. Now, each evening, while Martha and the girls sewed and mended they also gasped with horror and delight as Kate read the heroine's adventures aloud.

And Kate's audience had grown. The girls' sisters and brother, hearing each thrilling episode of *The Mysteries of Udolpho* retold at the farm, had soon decided that Millie and Florence needed to be escorted home. Each evening, the six Cotter siblings, Martha, Carlos, Francis's groom, and even his very superior valet, 'accidentally' arrived in the kitchen in time for the next episode.

Glancing around, Kate saw that her audience had assembled already. She hadn't realised it was so late. She took out the book, sat down near the fire and began to read. An hour later, she closed the book, to the sighs and protests of her audience.

'Eh, Miss Kate,' said Millie's brother, Tom. 'That Sinner Montoni, 'e's a proper villain, ain't 'e? Our Dad allus says you can't trust foreigners.' He tossed a dark look at Carlos.

'*Sí,*' said Carlos immediately. 'Me, I never trust Italians…never! That Signor Montoni is a bad man. Poor Miss Emily.'

There was a chorus of agreement. The girls shuddered eloquently and chattered about the story as they filed out.

'Coming up to bed now, dearie?' asked Martha.

'No, not yet.' Kate wasn't at all tired, after her earlier sleep. 'I think I'll just sit here for a bit in front of the fire, Martha. You go up, though.' They exchanged their goodnights and Kate was soon left alone with her thoughts.

'How many more hidden talents do you have, I wonder?' The deep voice coming out of the shadows made her leap in fright. She turned and perceived Jack leaning casually against the scullery wall, half hidden by the gloom.

'How long have you been there?' she gasped.

He moved forward out of the darkness. 'Twenty minutes or so. They were all so entranced by your reading that no one noticed when I came looking for you, so I decided not to disturb things. You read well, li'l Kate.' His voice was mocking and he stumbled over a chair.

Kate's stomach clenched. He was drunk.

'Quite the li'l actress, aren't you?' He loomed over her. Kate pressed back in her chair as far as she could. He reached out a long finger and brushed her nose lightly. 'Spot o' flour. Damned if I ever saw a woman so inclined to messiness.'

Kate jerked her head away from his hand. She did have a tendency to splash things around when she was working, and despite all her best efforts to remain neat she usually found a splatter of flour or a smear of dust on her face or hands when she went to have her usual nightly wash. But she was sure it was not nearly as bad as he implied. She rubbed her nose vigorously with her sleeve, watching him swaying gently on his feet.

'You're foxed,' she said bluntly.

'And what if I am? 'Tis none of your business what I do.'

Kate frowned. 'Where is Francis?' she asked.

'So it's Francis now, is it?' he sneered. 'Very familiar you are with my friends.'

Kate did not reply. There was no point in arguing with him when he was in this state.

'Have you told him yet of your little arrangement with that greasy Cit?'

Kate had no doubt of whom he was speaking. 'Please do not call Cousin Jeremiah rude names. I know you do not like him, but he is my only living relative, however distant.'

'And soon to become even closer, eh?' he jeered. 'So much for all your pious talk of not marrying! All it takes is a wealthy Cit to smother you with flowers and greasy compliments, and all your res'lutions go down the drain.' He snorted in contempt. 'Women! You're just like all the rest of them. Let some fellow dangle his moneybags in front of you, and you're all sweetness and compliance.'

He imitated her voice mockingly. 'Oh, Cousin Jeremiah, I would be delighted. Dear Cousin Jeremiah, you wish to kiss me? Please do. Oh, yes, Cousin Jeremiah, I will wed you, will allow you to put your greasy paws all over me, to plant your disgusting fishy lips on mine!' He was enraged by now. 'How you can have the stomach to consider wedding such a loathsome upstart is beyond me.'

Kate glared at him. She had initially opened her mouth to inform him she had refused her cousin's proposal, but by the time he had paused for breath, and she had an opening, she was so incensed that all thoughts of telling him had flown from her head. His close proximity was rather overwhelming, though, so she wriggled out of the chair and faced him across the kitchen table.

'How dare you speak to me in this way?' she spat. 'It is no concern of yours what I do, Mr Carstairs, no concern at all. If I wish to see my cousin I will, if I wish to embrace him I will, and if I wish to marry him I will! It is nothing whatsoever to do with you!'

She stamped her foot on the hard flagstones and continued. 'And how dare you impugn my honour in that way? A person's wealth or lack of it has nothing—*nothing*—to do with my attitude to them, and it's outrageous of you to suggest otherwise. It is quite irrelevant to me whether Cousin Jeremiah is wealthy or not. I have not the slightest interest in a person's financial standing, and only a completely vulgar person would think it could ever be important.'

'If the cap fits...' he began.

'Then *you* must wear it,' she snapped, 'for such considerations have never been mine!'

'You cannot mean you love that contemptible creature.' His voice was scornful, but his body was tense as he waited for her answer.

She tossed her head at him. 'That, Mr Carstairs, is none of your business!'

'It damned well is!'

'Why?' she demanded, her mouth dry.

They glowered at each other, then he moved with unexpected speed, dragging her against him. He stared down at her for a moment, then crushed his mouth on to hers.

It was a stormy kiss, full of passion and desperation and anger. He gripped her hard, and if she had been aware of his grip she might have told him he was hurting her. But Kate too was lost in the roiling waves of passion and she returned his kiss with equal anguished desperation, clutching him fiercely, returning his every caress with interest.

Eventually they separated and stood there staring into each other's eyes, breathing heavily. Kate's lips were bruised, but she was oblivious of anything except him. She swallowed, trying to recover her poise. He watched her silently. Eventually the silence became too much for her.

'What did you mean by that?' she said in a low voice. She wondered if he could hear her heart thudding, it sounded so loud to her.

Jack stood, breathing heavily, slowly gathering his wits. He'd given her the chance to repudiate Cole and she hadn't. Nothing was changed. She was still betrothed to her wealthy Cit. He'd be damned if he exposed himself to gratify a woman's vanity. He had done quite enough of that already. He looked down into her eyes. He could see her waiting, willing him to say the words, so she could throw them back in his teeth, no doubt. She was no different from any other woman.

'What did it mean?' he said. 'What did it mean? Why, nothing, my dear Kate. A pleasant interlude, that's all.' He licked his lips suggestively. 'I did say you are talented, did I not?'

Kate felt her throat close as the eyes, which had been blazing with fiery passion a moment before, iced over.

'You beast!' she whispered. His words were a timely reminder. It was the old story of the dog in the manger. But it had been a long, exhausting day, and for once Kate didn't have the energy to deal with the hostility and the anger she saw in his eyes. She was feeling so miserable herself that all she wanted to do was to throw herself against his chest and sob her heart out. Only the mood he was in, he would probably rip it out of her chest and devour it. Or had he done that already?

He laughed harshly. 'Haven't you heard, my dear girl? I would have thought a parson's daughter would have been warned many a time that all men are beasts. That's why you like us so much.'

'On the contrary, my father taught me to love all mankind, as he did,' said Kate dully. *My father, who loved all mankind—except me.*

Jack took her unconscious expression of pain to be caused by his words. He recoiled and his hand reached out to her half pleadingly, but she did not notice.

Kate did not look at him again. She quietly left the room, and went upstairs to bed. She was just blowing out her candle when she realised she hadn't made it clear to Jack that she was not going to marry her cousin. If only he would get it into his head that she would never marry! Stubborn, wretched man! And why was he drinking again? Surely not because he thought she had accepted her cousin? No—why would he, when he had been urging her to go to London and find a husband there?

Oh, well, it was cold, she was tired, and she certainly had no intention of seeking him out when he was in the state he was in, and she in her nightrobe. He would probably kiss her again, and she was feeling so lonely and miserable tonight that she would probably do absolutely nothing to prevent it, and that would be fatal.

She'd had enough accusations of impropriety in her life— she needed no more.

'Have you seen Kate today?' Francis asked Jack.

'No,' Jack mumbled. He continued reading a newspaper that had been sent by a friend. He did not even want to think about Kate. It was too distressing, imagining her wedded to Cole, forever out of sight, out of touch. It was no concern of his what she might be doing. He didn't care. He was reading the news instead.

The paper was out of date, but it contained a detailed description of the army's retreat from Spain back to Portugal. Both Jack and Francis had found the news very depressing, containing, as it did, news of dreadful casualties. Jack was particularly affected by the horrendous losses suffered by Anson's brigade. They had fought together at Salamanca, and Anson and many of his officers were friends of Jack's.

The paper criticised Wellington for allowing it to happen. The press were fair-weather friends to Old Hookey, Jack decided. He was a hero when he was winning, and a bungling fool when things were difficult. Disgusted, he tossed the paper aside. After a few moments, he recalled Francis's question about Kate. He hadn't seen her at all that day. No doubt she was avoiding him again, after their clash in the kitchen the previous night.

'She's probably in the kitchen.' He got up to pour himself a glass of madeira, but was annoyed to discover the decanter empty. 'Carlos!' he bellowed.

Carlos arrived and was dispatched to fetch a new bottle. As he was leaving Francis spoke. 'Carlos, have you seen Miss Kate?'

'No *señor,* she went off for a drive with Señor Cole this morning.'

Both men frowned. 'But it is now well into the afternoon. Are you sure she has not returned?' asked Francis.

Carlos nodded lugubriously. '*Sí, señor,* for Mrs Martha and the girls have been waiting for her to come back all afternoon.'

The two gentlemen exchanged glances. Jack sullenly shrugged, endeavouring to conceal his concern. 'If she wants to spend all day with her betrothed, then it is her concern. She clearly has no concern for her reputation.'

'Her betrothed?' said Francis. 'She is not betrothed.'

Jack shrugged again. 'She neglected to inform you? That greasy Cit had the confounded impudence to propose to her yesterday and the stupid chit accepted him.'

Francis frowned. 'When exactly was this?'

'Yesterday, on the terrace. I caught him with his greasy paws all over her, kissing her. Gave him a leveller.' He clenched his fists. 'Wish I'd knocked his teeth clear out the back of his head. I would have too, but the wretched girl hung off my arm, screeching that they were to be married, so then there was nothing left for me to do but go away and leave the happy couple to plan the wedding.'

Francis's brow cleared, and he tried to hide his twitching lips. His friend was trying very hard to sound indifferent, with scant success. He took pity on him. 'She didn't accept him, you know.'

'Yes, she did.'

'No, she did not. I was here, in the library, when you knocked him down.' Francis chuckled. 'I was just about to go out and intervene, but you beat me to it, for she was no willing participant in that embrace, I can assure you.'

Jack looked doubtful. 'Well, she must have changed her mind later.'

Francis shook his head. 'Not a chance, old boy. After you left, the fellow had the infernal cheek to persist with his suit. I heard Kate refuse him in no uncertain terms, several times. He would have forced himself upon her again if I had not intervened and sent him to the rightabout with the offer of a little of my own home-brewed.' He grinned reflectively. 'You should have seen him scuttling off across the lawn. I expect his coachman caught up with him by the time he reached the front gate.'

Both men burst out laughing at the thought.

Then Jack sobered abruptly. 'Then why the devil did she go driving with him this morning?' Their glances met. 'And why has she not returned by now?' He ran his hand through his hair.

'I have to tell you, Francis, that I taxed her with it last night and she never denied that she and Cole were betrothed.'

'I suppose you did it in your usual tactful manner, didn't you?' said Francis.

Jack grimaced.

'In a filthy temper, were you?' said Francis. 'Doing your level best to pick a quarrel?' He shook his head. 'The best way to make a woman do the opposite of what you want is to try and bully her. Especially a woman as spirited as Kate. She probably told you she was betrothed to her cousin to pay you back for your impudence.'

He met his friend's eye. 'Depend on it, Jack, it was all a hum. If yesterday was anything to go by, the little Farleigh has nothing but dutiful family feeling in her heart for that fellow, and it was pretty strained at that, after the way he tried to push her into marrying him.'

'So where the devil is she?' Jack headed for the kitchen, shouting for Carlos, Martha and the two girls. He questioned them as to why Kate had gone for a drive with her cousin when they had not parted on good terms the day before.

''E came around this morning,' said Martha, 'with an 'an-gdog look on 'is face and a bunch of flowers. Said 'e were sorry and would she forgive 'im and let 'im take 'er for a drive.' She wrung her hands in her apron. 'But that were hours and hours ago, sir, and it ain't like Miss Kate to stay out so long, 'specially with a gentleman.'

'Did she take anything with her, Martha?'

Martha looked puzzled. 'What do you mean, sir?'

'A portmanteau, a bandbox, something like that.'

Martha shook her head firmly. 'No, sir, nothing like that.' She peered suspiciously at him. 'You bain't be thinkin' as Miss Kate's run away, sir? Not Miss Kate. She wouldn't worry us all like that.'

She caught his look of doubt and shook her head again. 'I've known that girl since she was a tiny babe, Mr Jack, and it's simply not in 'er to sneak off behind people's backs.'

He looked sceptical, but Martha would have none of it. For once her beloved Mr Jack was wrong, and she, Martha, would put him right. 'Oh, I admit, she 'as a temper, when it's roused, sir, but to do somethin' like that—never! I'm worried, Mr Jack, summat awful, and I don't like 'er cousin, not one little bit. She shoulda been home long since.' Her old face crumpled with concern, and she clutched Jack's coatsleeve.

'Find 'er, Mr Jack. Find 'er and bring 'er 'ome.'

'Carlos, saddle my horse,' snapped Jack.

'Perhaps the curricle would be better, Jack. Your leg wouldn't stand up to riding for hours, would it?' said Francis.

'Damn my leg. A horse is faster than a curricle. Saddle the roan, Carlos.'

'And my chestnut,' added Francis.

'Does anyone know which direction they were headed in?'

'Sir, I saw the carriage turn at the gate and head north,' said Florence.

'North?' Jack turned and looked at Francis grimly. 'Are you thinking what I am thinking?'

Francis nodded slowly. 'He was damned persistent yesterday. Seemed almost desperate when she refused him so adamantly. But would he force her?'

Jack swore. 'If that bastard lays as much as a finger on her, I'll kill him!'

Chapter Fourteen

Darkness was falling rapidly as the two men neared the out-skirts of a village. Francis deliberately reined in his mount and after a moment Jack, too, slowed his horse, with obvious reluctance. He'd set a killing pace. Their horses were nearing exhaustion. As the pace slowed, his tension increased—this village was probably their last chance.

Jack's shoulders slumped. His face was grey with pain and anxiety. He'd expected to catch Cole long before now. The longer the search, the less chance they had of catching up. The consequences of that were too appalling to even think of. And of course he could think of nothing else. They must be on the right track; they had to be!

Enquiries had revealed that Cole had exchanged his gig for a hired closed carriage and was heading north. Informants had further disclosed that Cole had his sick sister with him and was conveying her home. Armed with a description of the carriage, Jack and Francis had ridden furiously onwards, enquiring at every village.

The moon rose; its pale beams silvered the countryside. Francis cast a worried look at Jack. It was perfectly obvious that Jack was almost at the end of his tether, and in a great deal of pain. 'We should rest up for a short time, old chap. Give the horses a break, you know.'

'And leave her a moment longer than necessary in the hands of that fiend?' Jack's tone brooked no argument. 'He has kidnapped her to force a wedding. He cannot possibly reach the border in less than two nights. That means he intends to force her, Francis. Tonight. Do you think I can rest, even for a short while, while she is in the hands of that madman?'

'Ah, don't torture yourself, Jack. I agree, the direction seems to indicate he is making for Gretna, but he has no reason to know he is pursued. He has no reason to force her tonight.'

Jack opened his mouth to reply when something caught his eye. He wrenched his horse to a halt, backed up and peered down a narrow lane. 'Do you see what I see?'

Down the lane, silhouetted against the silver sheen of a small pond, was a shape which could have been that of a travelling carriage. Beside it was a small cottage. Exchanging silent glances, the men quietly walked their steeds down the lane.

The cottage was old and run-down. It was clear from the weeds that surrounded it that no one had lived there for years. They dismounted and crept closer. A figure moved inside, illuminated by a candle. It was Cole, bending over a motionless shape on a pallet on the floor.

The door crashed open. Cole swung round in fright. The high colour drained from his face and his lips began to writhe in a ghastly attempt at a smile as he perceived the face of the large black shape in the doorway. 'Er…ah…'

'Get away from her,' said Jack in a soft voice that chilled Cole's bones to the marrow.

Cole scuttled sideways as far as he could.

'If you have touched so much as a hair on her head, you're a dead man,' Jack said in that same chilling tone, moving towards the pallet. He laid a gentle hand on Kate's cheek, smoothing the hair back from her forehead. Her eyelids fluttered and she moaned.

'What the devil have you done to her, you blackguard?'

'Nothing, nothing on my life, I swear it!' gabbled Cole. 'She is not hurt, only drugged.'

'Drugged!' said Francis from the open doorway.

Cole started and turned towards the door. 'Only a little laudanum, I swear it...it was just that she strugg—' He found himself grabbed by his collar and flung against the wall.

'Struggled, did she, you filthy swine?' snarled Jack. 'And do I have to ask why she felt the need to struggle?' A rocklike fist slammed into Cole's stomach, and he doubled over, gasping for breath. Another one crashed into his jaw with a resounding crack. Then he was ruthlessly dragged up by the hair and shaken like a rat. Blazing blue eyes met his.

'I'll teach you to abduct innocent girls!'

Two more punches smashed into Cole, almost simultaneously. His nose felt as if it had exploded. Cole collapsed.

'Get up, you blackguard,' roared Mad Jack Carstairs. 'I haven't finished with you yet! Not by a long shot!' He reached down and grabbed the blubbering Cole by the throat. He smiled, a peculiarly sinister smile which sent the blood draining from Cole's face, and said softly, 'I'm going to kill you, you know that?'

Cole had always thought himself a big man, but now he found himself dangling by the throat, being slowly choked to death by an enraged madman. He struggled, but it was as if he was a rabbit in the grip of an eagle. His face began to turn purple and his eyes bulged as the powerful hands tightened their relentless grip around his throat.

'Jack...?' The faint, wavering voice came from the pallet.

Cole was tossed aside like a bundle of rags. He lay on the floor, gasping for breath like a beached and battered fish. Jack bent solicitously over Kate, his arms lifting her off the dirty pallet until she lay cradled against his chest.

'Are you all right, sweetheart?' A gentle hand smoothed back her tangled curls with infinite tenderness.

'Oh, Jack, I feel so strange,' she murmured, trying to sit up.

'No, no, don't try to move, sweetheart. It's all right. You're safe now.' He pulled her more closely against him. His arms were hard around her, holding her protectively, whilst he crooned soothing nonsense in her ear, interposing it with small kisses on her hair, her ears, whatever he could reach.

Kate, bewildered, ill and dizzy from the effects of the drug, burrowed into his chest and lay there, clutching him, understanding nothing except that Jack was there, holding her, and that everything was therefore perfect.

Francis watched them, a soft look in his eyes, then a movement to his left caught his attention, and his gaze hardened as he took in the sorry sight of Cousin Jeremiah. Blood was oozing from cuts over his eye, and gushing from his nose and lips. His jaw was beginning to swell and both eyes were puffing up.

Francis's lip curled contemptuously as he took in the snuffling, sobbing creature. Silently he opened the door, and curtly jerked his head. Casting fearful glances towards Jack, who was still wholly absorbed with Kate, Cole lurched to his feet and tottered out. Francis followed.

'Not the carriage, I think,' he said softly as Cole headed towards it. 'We will need that to convey Miss Farleigh home.'

'But how will I get home myself?' Cole whimpered. It was a freezing night.

'I have not the least notion,' said Francis coldly, 'but once my friend realises you are out here I have no doubt that you will return home snug and cosy enough—in a coffin.'

Cole gasped in terror and set off down the rough track towards the main road, stumbling and crashing, casting frequent fearful glances behind him. Francis watched until he was out of sight, and out of earshot, then quietly re-entered the ruined house.

Kate was curled up almost in a ball, cradled in Jack's lap, nestled against his chest like a child. She seemed to be asleep. The eyes of the two men met. Francis's eyebrow rose in a silent question and Jack nodded imperceptibly. Francis heaved a sigh of relief. She was all right, then. Cole had drugged her, but no violence had been done.

He glanced at the pair on the pallet and sighed. Neither of them were in any condition to move tonight. Kate was exhausted by her ordeal and still partly drugged; as for Jack, he might have had enough strength to give Cole a thrashing while his body had been functioning on rage, but now that his anger had died away Francis would hazard a guess that Jack would barely be able to walk.

'I'll see to the horses,' he said quietly, and left the room. Jack did not appear to hear him. All his attention was on Kate. She murmured something in her sleep and his hold on her tightened.

Over her head Jack stared blankly at the wall. What a fool he'd been. He'd thought he could give her up, convinced himself that she would be better off without him, that the best thing he could do for her was to send her to his grandmother…

He didn't want to send her anywhere. He wanted to hold her like this for the rest of his life. He shifted slightly and winced as his bad leg reminded him of his uncomfortable position. Well, not exactly like this. Not on a grubby pallet on a hard cold floor in a squalid little tumbledown cottage.

Kate shifted and wriggled against him, and despite his discomfort he felt his body respond to her. No, he didn't want to hold her like this for the rest of his life. Hold her, yes. In his bed. Caressing her and loving her and introducing her to the delights of passion. Oh, yes, she had passion in her, his little Kate. He felt his body tighten just thinking about it as it had so many times recently. Too many times. He had barely been able to control himself. The slightest look or movement of hers had been enough to force him to battle with his body's response.

She shivered and moved against him again. Damn his stupidity, she was cold, he realised. Blasted fool that he was, thinking of himself when all the time the girl was cold. It was his body warmth she wanted, not his body. Selfish, bloody, stupid, insensitive fool! Gently, trying not to disturb her, Jack shrugged himself out of his greatcoat and wrapped it snugly around her.

'Mmm, nice,' she muttered, and he grinned wryly, realising that she had indeed been cold. Carefully he moved, gritting his teeth at the jarring pain, tenderly manipulating her until he was lying half on his side, half on his back, with her small body tucked into the warm curve of his. He opened his jacket and shirt to pull them more closely around her and give her more of his body warmth. Instantly she snuggled her arms around his bare torso and moved closer on top of him, nuzzling her mouth against his throat.

Steadfastly ignoring his body's tumultuous response, he closed his shirt and jacket over her and tucked the greatcoat carefully around her. She would be warmer now, with his body and his coat sheltering her from all possible draughts. He could feel his pulse thundering. His body throbbed for release. He was torn between savouring her closeness, the feel and scent and touch of her, and battling the demands of his body to further that closeness. An electric jolt passed through him as she wriggled again. He swore silently and gritted his teeth, willing his body into obedience.

Damn it all! He was little better than Cole, he thought. She was drugged. She didn't know what she was doing. He should be protecting her, not lusting after her like a mindless beast! She had just come through a dreadful ordeal and all he could think of was how desperately he wanted to make love to her. He stared at the stained and sagging ceiling and tried desperately to think of other things.

He was failing miserably at this task when Francis re-entered the cottage, staggering under a load of wood. Swiftly he cleared the grate and soon had a fire crackling briskly. From his position on the pallet Jack grinned approvingly. Francis left again, and soon returned with several rugs.

'Found 'em in the carriage.' He tossed one over Jack and

Kate. 'Brought you something else, too.' Grinning, he produced from his pocket a substantial flask of brandy.

'Good man!' whispered Jack, and reached out. He took a long pull on the flask and sighed, feeling the liquor burn a cosy trail through his body. 'Ah, that's better.'

'Leg paining you much?'

'Not too bad.'

Francis grunted. 'Always were a shocking bad liar, old man. Have another drink. It's going to be a long, uncomfortable night for you. She's all right?'

Jack nodded. 'Just cold and the after-effects of the drug—filthy swine. I gather you let the bastard go.'

'Couldn't have you clapped up for murder, old thing. You gave him a good enough hiding and I sent him out into the night. Bloody cold at that. Might not survive. If not, no bad thing. If he does, well, he's still been punished.'

'Not enough.'

'Try and get some sleep, old man. Or worry about young Kate if you must, not Cole. I'll sleep in the carriage, keep an eye on the horses.'

The cottage fell silent, the only sound the occasional crackling of the fire and the blowing of the wind in the trees outside.

Kate was the first to waken next morning. She came slowly to consciousness, her mind still fuzzy from the drug she had been given. Despite a slight headache and a stomach that was insisting it be fed, she was aware of a tremendous feeling of rightness. Still with her eyes closed, she inhaled slowly, moving her cheek sensuously against its pillow. She stopped. Her pillow felt…odd.

She opened one eye. Her pillow was a naked male chest, lightly sprinkled with dark hair. Good God! Cautiously she lifted her head and looked at the owner of the chest. Jack? She had slept with Jack? Swiftly, with a minimum of movement, she glanced around the room. She had never seen this place in her life.

The last time she had wakened with no recollection of the previous day she had found herself in the hands of the French. But Jack was here. Grimly she forced her mind to recall its last memory. Arguing with Cousin Jeremiah…and drinking that bitter coffee. Had she been drugged? Or had she passed out for some other reason? It was no use. She couldn't answer. She would have to wait until Jack woke.

She looked down at Jack as he lay sound asleep and her mouth curved in a tender smile. He looked so young and boy-ish and handsome, the harsh bitterness wiped away in sleep. Gently she stroked the lines of his face, smoothed the tousled thick dark hair. Unable to help herself, she touched her lips to his in the lightest of kisses. She froze as he stirred, then re-laxed as his breathing returned to its previous regularity.

She watched the broad chest moving up and down with each breath and marvelled that she had slept all night on it without realising it. She bent and kissed the warm, slightly salty skin. She feathered tiny damp kisses up his chest, over his throat, along his jaw and back to his lips. She spent long moments tasting and caressing him, all in the lightest of gossamer touches so as not to disturb his sleep, revelling in the contrast of texture of his darkly rugged jaw, scraping her soft lips against its harsh texture, then placing her mouth gently against his soft, relaxed lips. Greatly daring, she touched his lips with her tongue, just to know again the taste of him. He moaned and shifted slightly and she froze again, watching him, but he was still asleep, and she returned to her illicit explorations.

Kate's heart was pounding. She knew she should not be doing this, lying so with a man, exploring his unconscious body like a thief in the night. It went against every principle she had been raised by, every tenet of the proper behaviour for a lady—but she couldn't help herself. She would never have this opportunity again. This was not simply a man—it was Jack, the man she longed for with every fibre of her being, the man she loved but could never have. Surely God would forgive her this once.

She gazed at his sleeping face, her body tingling all over. Oh, but he was a beautiful man. Gently she ran her hand over his naked torso, marvelling at the smoothness of his skin, the contained power in the relaxed muscles of his chest. Delicately she ran her fingers through the soft curls of his chest hair. His flat brown nipples were ringed with whorls of dark hair. She kissed them and he shuddered under her touch.

She lifted her head, waiting for signs of him awakening. Her eyes ran over his face, his dear battered cheek, his long aquiline nose, the deep grooves that ran from nose to mouth. Her gaze stopped on his open mouth and slowly she lowered her mouth to his, seeking that incredible, wonderful sensation she had experienced before, when her tongue had touched his.

Jack silently groaned as he felt her mouth come down on his again. He couldn't take much more of this without responding. His body was aflame with the desire to hold her, return her sweet, tentative caresses, to take her and bring them both to glorious crescendo. But he couldn't, not here, not now, not in silence and stealth, for he was too aware of their situation: the filthy cottage, the sagging ceiling, the hard floor. And Francis could walk in at any moment. No, it would be too sordid.

When he took Kate and made her his, he wanted it to be utterly perfect. But for now he would take what he could. And what he had was the most exquisite torture he had ever experienced.

He had come awake almost instantly, as soon as he had felt her stir, but had not moved, allowing her to escape from their embarrassingly intimate position if she wished to. He had waited for her to move away from him, feeling the cold rush of air as she lifted her body away from his, feigning sleep to make it easier for her to leave him.

He'd been unprepared for the shock of the first feathery caress on his skin. So light, he had almost not believed it was happening, but it had been followed by another and then another, and it had taken all his will-power just to lie there instead of gathering her hard against him in a passionate embrace. Such a thing had never happened to Jack Carstairs before. To lie still, and to all intents placid and unaware, while the little creature that had wound herself around his heart planted the tiniest, most delicately moist kisses all over him.

His pulse pounded with the effort of remaining relaxed under her innocently questing sensual onslaught. He had no choice. He had to lie here in tormented bliss, treasuring each tentative, seductive caress, as if he had no more feeling than a block of wood. It was that or lose the precious moment to sordid reality. No choice at all.

God, but she was sweet. Oh, Lord, she was kissing him on the mouth again. He braced himself for the ravaging temptation as her small pink tongue reached in and delicately touched his. The jolt of sensation swamped him, and with silent anguish he felt his tongue responding, curling around hers. He felt her alarmed withdrawal but he could not help himself and his tongue followed hers. She jerked away in panic. Gently but firmly his hand cupped the back of her head and, blue eyes blazing into hers, he pulled her mouth back to his.

The kiss was long, sweet and intensely passionate.

Outside the cottage, Jack could hear Francis getting the horses ready. He released Kate and after a moment she drew back, a dazed, bemused expression on her face. Jack yearned to pull her back into his arms and kiss her arousal into passion. Instead he smiled, an odd, twisted, tender smile.

'Morning, sweetheart,' he whispered. 'That's the nicest awakening I think I've ever had.'

Kate blinked, then blushed rosily. Good God, she was lying full length on top of Jack Carstairs in the most immodest position, legs entwined, her breasts resting on his naked chest and his…his manhood pressing into her. And he was awake!

Hurriedly she scrambled off Jack and stood, tugging frantically at her clothes, desperately attempting to achieve some semblance of decency and composure. Heavens! How long had Jack been awake? Had he known all that she had done?

Deeply embarrassed, she busied herself with tidying her clothes and her hair, unable even to look in his direction, let alone meet his gaze. She wanted to break the fraught silence with words, but could think of nothing to say. Behind her she could hear Jack moving; presumably he was closing his shirt, buttoning his waistcoat, shrugging himself back into the coat she had found herself wrapped in…

'Morning, all. Sleep well?' Francis entered the cottage with a stamping of boots. 'Brrr, it's cold out there. I think we should try to get moving as soon as possible. Kate, how are you, m'dear?'

Kate murmured something unintelligible and slipped outside the cottage, her face flaming. Francis here as well? Who else knew of her shame? Bad enough that she had allowed herself to be kidnapped by her cousin, but to have two witnesses to it—and then to have behaved in that manner with Jack! What must he think of her, to have touched him that way…with Francis somewhere about too? It was all too mortifying.

She went in search of water in which to wash. She could find no well, nor any pump or stream. The night had been a bitter one and the small pond beside the cottage was frozen over. Kate tried to smash through the ice with a rock, but it would not break. She rubbed some icicles over her skin until they melted and dried her tingling face on her petticoat. She tore a ribbon of lace off her petticoat and tied her hair back as neatly as she could. Then she returned to the cottage, shivering in the morning chill.

By the time she returned, both Francis and Jack looked presentable, if not their usual immaculate selves. She avoided Jack's eyes and knew her face was flaming, but hoped it would be put down, by Francis at least, to the nip of the frigid air outside.

'Good morning, gentlemen,' she said brightly, smiling impartially at a space somewhere between the two of them. 'Anything to eat? I'm utterly ravenous.'

Francis chuckled. 'The lady is hungry, old man. We can't

have that. Shall we adjourn to the nearest hostelry and obtain some breakfast? I fancy there is an inn in the next village which can accommodate our needs tolerably well.'

'Oh, yes, let's,' said Kate immediately, beaming at him. She still could not look at Jack.

'In that case, ma'am, I shall fetch your carriage at once!' said Francis, bowing like a flunkey. Kate giggled as he left the cottage, bowing repeatedly like a Cit facing royalty.

She turned to find Jack leaning against the wall, glowering at her. 'Must you flirt with him so early in the morning?'

Kate flushed and looked away. She felt his gaze scorching her.

'I wasn't flirting.' Her heart plummeted.

Jack grunted disbelievingly.

Kate turned her back on him and walked to the open door and looked out. There was nothing she could do. He would think whatever he wished to. She could not change his mind. She shivered in the bitter cold and folded her arms against her chest then jumped as a heavy coat was dropped over her shoulders from behind.

'Here,' he said curtly. 'Wrap this around you.'

The coat was still warm and smelled faintly of him. Kate didn't move. She felt his hands coming over her shoulders, tugging the coat more firmly around her. She tried to shrug it off. 'No, no. I don't need—'

'Don't be so stupid,' he growled. Strong hands came down on her shoulders and turned her around. She looked up at him, but he concentrated on buttoning the coat firmly over her.

'Thank you,' she said softly.

He glanced at her briefly, a hard, unreadable look, muttered something under his breath, then pushed past her and went to help Francis with the horses.

He was limping heavily, she realised with dismay—his leg must be paining him dreadfully. White lines of pain were back around his mouth, deeper than they had been for months—he had hurt himself rescuing her. She wanted to run after him, do something, but she knew she could not. Hadn't she done enough? He was clearly embarrassed by that morning kiss, and angry with her because of it, or why would he be so cross with her for responding to Francis's nonsense? Although pain did nothing for anyone's temper.

The carriage arrived. Francis acted as driver, and the two horses he and Jack had ridden were tied behind. Kate got in and waited while Jack and Francis had a brief altercation about who was to drive. Eventually Jack conceded, but said in a surly manner that he would sit up with Francis.

'Don't be ridiculous, man,' said Francis acerbically. 'Your leg is in no condition to be climbing up here and, in any case, you haven't got a coat and you'll freeze in this weather. Now shut up and get into the carriage before Kate thinks you have conceived a distaste for her company.'

Kate swallowed. Francis had been joking, but he had inadvertently hit the nail on the head. Jack didn't want to be in the carriage with her. It was obvious.

Jack climbed into the carriage. Kate gazed out of the window.

Wordlessly he seated himself and stared moodily out of the opposite one.

They travelled the short distance to the next village in silence and pulled up before a small, neat inn. The innkeeper looked them over with a practised eye, taking in their crumpled clothing, the men's unshaven chins, Kate's loosely tied-back hair, and a knowing look crept over his ruddy features.

'Two chambers, landlord, if you would be so good,' drawled Francis. 'One for myself and my friend and the other for…my sister.'

Kate flushed at the landlord's glance. He clearly disbelieved the tale and took her for quite another sort of female. She put her chin up proudly, defying him to judge her.

Jack had noted the exchange. 'My *wife* will want hot water and a maid to assist her,' he snapped. 'Her maid and our coachman were injured in the accident we had last night. We have no time to delay, landlord. Shall we say breakfast in forty minutes? Oh, and hot water for my friend and myself as well and shaving implements.'

The landlord responded to the haughty tone of command and leapt to obey, calling his wife to come and help the young lady, a look of deepest obsequiousness replacing the sleazy gleam.

Kate blinked. *His wife?* She sighed. Sister, wife—it was all the same—a tale fabricated to protect her non-existent reputation. She followed the landlord's wife upstairs in silence.

After a hearty, though not exactly jolly breakfast, during which Francis and Kate chatted while Jack ate in morose silence, they set off again. Mile after mile passed in uncomfortable silence, both passengers brooding and thoughtful. The impasse continued until the countryside began to look familiar.

Kate finally spoke. 'You didn't need to tell that man that I was your wife, you know. Francis's sister would have been quite sufficient.'

'That's all you know,' snapped Jack. So she would rather appear as Francis's sister than as Jack's wife, would she? Had this morning meant nothing, then? Women! He would never understand them.

'What do you mean?' asked Kate.

'Well, after last night, you'll have to marry one of us, and as you slept in my arms the whole night it might as well be me,' he snarled ungraciously. Oh, God, he thought. I've botched it. I hadn't meant to put it like that. Oh, you fool, fool, fool!

Kate went white. So that was why he was in such a furious temper. It wasn't his leg or her so-called flirting with Francis at all. He thought she had trapped him into marriage.

'I don't see that there is any need to marry you at all,' she said. 'After all, nothing happened.'

A blazing blue glare forced her to drop her eyes. What did he mean by that look? He had kissed her before and not felt compelled to offer marriage.

Jack's fingers itched to grab the little hussy and shake her until her teeth rattled. So nothing had happened, had it? How dare she lie to him like that? He could still feel the tiny moist kisses travelling slowly and delicately over his naked skin, leaving behind them a trail of fire.

'The fact remains that you were known to have been abducted by one man, and then spent the night in the company of two others, neither of whom was related to you. You have no choice. If you can't stomach the thought of marrying me, then Francis will oblige, as I am sure you are well aware. He is a much better catch—we both know that.' His bitter sarcasm flayed her.

'There is no need to be so horrid,' she said with quiet dignity. 'And there is no need to marry either of you. I have no intention of wedding anyone, as I have told you before, only you are so stupid you refuse to believe me,' she concluded, her temper getting the better of her. How dared he speak to her like that? As if she would care two hoots whether or not a man was a good 'catch', as long as she loved him! Stupid, stupid man! Did he know her so little?

'Your so-called intentions have no relevance any longer, my dear,' Jack said in a withering voice. Call him stupid, would she? 'The fact remains that your reputation is now in shreds, and you have no choice but to marry one of us. I, at least, know the ways of the world, even if you do not.'

'Well, you know nothing at all!' she flashed. 'My reputation cannot be destroyed by the events of last night.'

He snorted in mocking disbelief.

'You cannot destroy something that was in shreds months ago!' she snapped. 'And believe me, Mr Carstairs, my reputation was utterly destroyed long before last night.'

'Don't be ridiculous. You had my grandmother's maid and then Martha with you the whole time. It may have been a trifle unorthodox, but you were well and truly chaperoned the entire time—my grandmother made sure of that!'

Kate gestured impatiently. 'The damage was done long before I even met your grandmother.' Her voice broke.

She felt sick to her stomach. She had hoped never to have to tell this story ever again in her life, and now here she was, obliged to tell the one man in all the world she wished not to tell.

But he could not be allowed to sacrifice himself for the sake of her non-existent reputation. He needed to marry well, she knew. Some girl with no dark shadows in her past, who would bring her innocence to her marriage. Innocence, an untainted name, and wealth—wealth so that he could rebuild his shattered life. Kate had none of these to offer him, nothing but herself and her heart—small, pathetic offerings at best.

Innate chivalry, despite his gruff manner of expressing it, was forcing him to offer her the protection of his name. It would be rank cowardice for her to put off the inevitable...

Kate shivered. She felt like some small sea creature which had had its shell ruthlessly peeled from it and was now open and vulnerable to every hurt. The sensation was devastating.

'I will explain, Ja— Mr Carstairs, but before I do I must ask you not to say anything, either while I am explaining or afterwards, particularly afterwards. It...it is very difficult for me to tell you this, but I know I have no choice, and...if you look at me or touch me or say anything to me at all...it will destr— Well...you must promise me you will not.'

Jack stared at her, puzzled. Deep foreboding filled him— she was in deadly earnest. 'And if I do not promise?'

Kate looked despairingly at him. 'Well, if you do not, I suppose I must tell you anyway...but it will be much worse, much more painful for me.'

'Then I promise,' he said quietly.

Kate took a deep breath and looked resolutely out of the window, staring unseeingly at the countryside flashing past. She turned her face away, hunched his big warm coat around her and in a hard little voice related the events of her last few months in Spain and Portugal, leaving nothing out, making no excuses, making it totally clear why she had no reputation to destroy and why she could marry no one.

Jack was oblivious to the jolting of the coach and the pain of his leg. He moved not an inch towards her, but his eyes dwelt on her averted profile with passionate intensity. He regretted nothing more than that last promise he had made her, wanted desperately to pull her into his arms and kiss her grief and pain away. But he could not. He had given her his promise.

His eyes were sombre and his throat filled as he realised the desperate courage that had made her lay her life bare for his edification. His eyes were soft and heavy as they took in the brave tilt of her chin, the resolute carriage of her slender frame as she destroyed herself in his eyes. Or so she thought, his little love. Did she not know how wonderful she was, how brave and gallant and beautiful?

She finished just as the carriage was drawing in to Sevenoakes. The carriage pulled up. She gave a shaky little laugh and said, 'So there is no need for you—or Francis or anyone— to put yourself out to save my reputation or defend my honour. You cannot save what has already been destroyed, nor protect what was lost long ago.'

He made an inarticulate sound of repudiation deep in his throat and reached out a hand to her, but she flinched away from him. Francis, unaware of the drama which had taken place inside, jumped down, shouting for brandy and hot food. He threw open the carriage door; Kate scrambled out and fled blindly into the house. Francis looked after her, frowning, then turned and saw the haggard face of his friend.

'Come on, old chap,' he said softly. 'I'll give you a hand.'

As Jack limped slowly up the front steps of the house, a vehicle swung in through the front gates. It was a smart travelling carriage. Jack recognised it. It bore his grandmother's crest. It drew to a halt and an unknown man alighted and walked briskly towards the two waiting men.

'Mr Carstairs?' he said.

'Yes,' said Jack.

'My name is Phillips. I have the honour to be Lady Cahill's man of business. I have come with important news for Miss Farleigh, whom I understand to be staying here.' He beamed at the two men, then faltered at the look on Jack's face. 'She is here, is she not?'

Jack frowned. 'Yes, she is here, but I am afraid she will not be able to see you immediately. She…she is indisposed.' With an effort he gathered his composure and said wearily, 'Please come inside and I will have some refreshment brought to you. I'm sure you'll need it after your journey.'

Chapter Fifteen

'She's an heiress, isn't she?' Jack could restrain himself no longer. Already he'd had to wait until he and Francis had changed and refreshments served to Mr Phillips.

The elderly lawyer looked momentarily shocked at his bluntness, but after a moment seemed to come to a decision. He allowed a discreet smile to transform his face.

'Yes, sir, you have guessed correctly, although I must say no more until I have informed Miss Farleigh of the whole. But it is wonderful news indeed.'

Jack turned to Francis. 'According to my grandmother, Kate's Delacombe grandparents were extremely wealthy. Undoubtedly they have left her a legacy,' he said, feeling unaccountably low.

'That should please Kate. Girl deserves a bit of good fortune,' Francis said.

'Wait a minute…' said Jack slowly. 'I thought all the money went to that cousin of hers.'

'That's right,' said Francis, sitting up.

'What cousin is that?' said Mr Phillips, frowning. 'I investigated the matter very thoroughly, and to the best of my knowledge there is no living cousin.'

'Fellow called Cole.'

'Cole!' snorted Phillips rudely. 'He is no cousin of hers. I've sent Bow Street Runners after him!'

'What?' Both men leaned forward, riveted.

'Well, if it is the same man—Jeremiah Cole, big fellow with sandy hair?' They nodded. 'He's the rascally solicitor that I caught with his hands in the honeypot, so to speak. He slipped out of my hands a few weeks ago and disappeared.'

'Good God!'

'Fellow has been discreetly helping himself to funds from the Delacombe estate for some time since his father, the previous trustee, died.'

'Good God!' exclaimed Francis again.

'Do you mean to say that swine was embezzling Kate's money? And that he's no relation at all to her?'

Phillips nodded. 'Yes, indeed. But how do you know of him?'

Jack exchanged a long look with Francis. The motive for Cole's abduction of Kate was perfectly clear now. Had he forced Kate to marry him, her entire inheritance would have legally belonged to him. But there was no need to let Phillips know of the abduction attempt.

'He was here,' said Jack grimly. 'Posing as Miss Farleigh's cousin and attempting to get her to marry him.'

Mr Phillips gasped in amazement. Jack glanced at Francis. 'You should have let me kill him, you know,' he murmured.

'The Runners will get him, old man. He'll hang, or be transported at the very least.'

'If they catch him.'

'Oh, they'll catch him, no fear of that,' said Mr Phillips confidently. 'I have no doubt at all. None at all.'

'They'd better,' growled Jack.

'I don't suppose he got his greasy paws on too much of Miss Farleigh's inheritance?' asked Francis diffidently.

Jack shot a look at him. Francis had no need of a rich wife.

'No, no. Fortunately the great majority of her inheritance is tied up so he could not touch it, and the whole is of such a

size that it makes Cole's depredations almost negligible, a fact
I expect he was counting on, should the heirs ever have been
discovered,' said Mr Phillips, rendered indiscreet by the generous quantity of brandy his host had pressed upon him.

Jack's heart sank. She was rich, immensely so, from what
Phillips had inadvertently revealed. She would not stay here
long, in that case. With a fortune she would have need of
nothing, nobody.

'I gather there's some significance to your arrival in my
grandmother's carriage,' he said heavily.

'Yes, so very kind of her ladyship,' agreed Mr Phillips. 'I
am to convey Miss Farleigh to London as soon as may be
convenient. Lady Cahill has great plans for her, I believe, great
plans.'

'I'll wager she has,' muttered Jack sourly.

'Perhaps Miss Farleigh will have her own ideas about that,'
suggested Francis. 'She may not wish to leave here.'

'Not wish to leave here!' Mr Phillips was astonished. He
glanced around the shabby room. 'Not wish to live in a fine
London house, to go to balls and routs? Why would she not?'

'Why not, indeed?' murmured Jack. 'If you will excuse me,
I must go upstairs and have my man see to this curst leg.'

He stumped wearily upstairs, almost relishing the distraction
of the pain of his leg. He stopped at the door to Kate's room
and stood there for several minutes. There was something to
be said for purely physical pain, after all. An hour or so of
massage, a half-bottle of brandy and it was cured.

Neither of those remedies would help the other sort of pain.
In fact, they only served to intensify it; massage invariably
conjured up the memory of the time when Kate first laid her
small, strong hands on his leg, kneading, stroking, caressing…
And as for brandy—there was neither pleasure nor forgetful-
ness for him in getting drunk now, for the very scent of alcohol recalled that night when she had stormed into his sanctuary like a small avenging angel, smashing all his decanters
and bottles. He would never forget the look on her face that

night…nor what occurred afterwards…the pleasure, the madness, the bitterness.

He had to let her go. She had no future with him. Not now. Not since she had become a rich woman. She might have agreed to take him on in exchange for a home, shabby as it was, for security, for his protection for the rest of her life. He hadn't dared to speak of love. That would have remained his secret. But a home—that might have been enough for a girl who had lost everything. That and the promise of a family. To an orphan, the promise of a family might have been appealing.

None of those things held any significance now. She didn't need to marry now—she could choose. She would go up to London and choose. He would never ask her now—he would not have her think him a fortune hunter. He cursed the Delacombe inheritance. He cursed Mr Phillips. Had the man not arrived when he did, Jack might have had her agreement to wed him already. And he would have wasted no time, would have had her to the village church the very next day.

He glanced up and down the corridor, then leaned his ear against her door and listened. Nothing. He could smell the beeswax she had used to polish the timber panelling. Beeswax. Another reminder of Kate. Reluctantly he brought his cheek away from her door, and headed towards his room. There were flowers on a side table in the corridor, small, insignificant blue things in a mass of green spiky stuff. He bent down to smell them, closing his eyes in anguish. They smelt of Kate's hair. This must be rosemary, then. He pulled out a sprig, crushed it in his long, strong fingers, and inhaled the fragrance.

'Carlos.' He absent-mindedly tucked the sprig of rosemary into his shirt.

'*Sí señor.*'

'Do something about this blasted leg, will you?'

'At once, *señor.*'

As Carlos clattered downstairs to heat the massage oils, Jack began to shrug off his coat. He paused for a moment, then stepped back into the hallway. He gazed down at the vase of fragrant greenery. Carefully he picked it up, carried it into his room and set it down beside his bed, where the morning sun would catch it.

'No, it is very kind of Lady Cahill, but now that I am able to support myself there is no need for me to go to London.'

'But Lady Cahill was most insistent—' The elderly lawyer tried to keep the frustration out of his voice. The heiress was being extremely difficult. He had tried every persuasion, painted pictures of the marvellous things she would see and do, of the shops, theatres, concerts and balls, of the cultural wonders, the famous places and people she would see. Nothing had the slightest effect.

Mr Phillips cast a tense look at Mr Carstairs. Her ladyship's grandson had observed the entire argument, arms folded, looking sardonic and bad-tempered. He had said not a word so far.

Mr Phillips felt very put out. Having a romantic soul underneath his dull exterior, he had envisaged himself as a kind of knight, who would escort the lost princess back to her rightful milieu. Only the princess was unaccountably resistant and unfemininely sharp of tongue and wit, and nothing he said could move her.

And, what was more, he thought, with a growing sense of injustice, when he had told her of the immense fortune which was at her sole disposal she had reacted quite as if she had other things on her mind. When he had repeated himself, thinking she was too overcome to take it in, she had replied, 'Yes, yes, I heard you the first time. It is very nice, thank you.'

Nice! Mr Phillips might be a mere solicitor, but there was something downright insulting about referring to such a huge fortune as 'nice'. He began yet another attempt to persuade her, but his remarks were cut across by the harsh, deep voice of his client's grandson.

'I've had quite enough of all this nonsense. Kate, you are

going to London and no argument. Carlos!' he called, moving to the door.

'*Sí,* Major Jack?'

'Tell Martha to have Miss Kate's things in that carriage within the hour. She and Mr Phillips will accompany Miss Kate to London, to my grandmother's house.'

'She will do no such thing!' snapped Kate, meeting his eyes for the first time.

He looked back at her, his expression unreadable. 'No, you are right, of course. Carlos, tell Martha to pack only what she and Miss Kate will need for the journey. They will be purchasing all new clothes and what-have-you in London.' He ignored Kate's gasp of indignation. 'Oh…Carlos, have the girls pack some food and refreshments in a basket in case Miss Kate gets hungry on the way.'

'Do no such thing, Carlos!' said Kate in a voice ringing with indignation.

Carlos met her gaze sheepishly. 'I am sorry, *señorita,* but I must obey Major Jack.'

Jack laughed at her infuriated exclamation, a harsh, humourless laugh. 'I see I am still master in my own house,' he said dryly.

'Yes, but you are not my master and I refuse to do your bidding!'

'I'm not asking you to do my bidding,' said Jack coldly.

'I…I don't underst—'

'I'm telling you. This is my house and I choose who I have in it. You know perfectly well I was reluctant to have you here in the first place. Well, now there is no reason for you to stay on any longer. You're going to my grandmother, all right, and will leave here today—if I have to toss you in the carriage myself.' He snapped out the orders crisply, every inch the military officer. 'Do you understand me, Miss Farleigh?'

Kate flinched, then turned away, hiding her distress.

Only Jack saw the expression on her face. He ran his hands through his hair in frustration. Damn it, he couldn't bear that wounded look on her face. What the devil did she think his grandmother was going to do to her? Torture her? It was the opportunity every young woman dreamed of. She didn't know what she was turning down. Oh, he knew what was stopping her, all right. But his grandmother would soon set her straight.

A scandalous accident in the past would mean nothing in the face of her huge inheritance. She would find she had the pick of the eligible bachelors—only the stuffiest would quibble at her lost virginity. It wasn't as if she had done anything wrong, after all. Kate Farleigh was honourable to her finger-tips; any fool could see that. The biggest problem she was likely to face was fortune hunters, and he could rely on his grandmother to deal with those.

Best to have it over with quickly. He hated long goodbyes. And he did not know how much longer he could stand that look on her face without hauling her into his arms. But the last thing Kate needed was to be tied to an embittered cripple. With this fortune she had a glittering future ahead of her, a future he would have no part in.

'Then shall we all agree to meet in the front hall in, say, half an hour to make our farewells? Good.' He nodded to the astounded observers and left the room.

'What a splendid fellow!' said Mr Phillips after a moment. 'Such decision, so masterful! I'm sure he was an excellent officer. He is more like his grandmother than I realised.'

The travelling chaise jolted and bounced along the road; Mr Phillips had bespoken rooms at an inn in readiness for the return journey and he was anxious to reach their destination before dark. Kate hung on to a strap, staring out of the window, oblivious of the passing scenery, the state of the road and her companions in the vehicle. She felt utterly wretched, desolate, shattered. Tears dripped unheeded from her eyes.

When Harry had abandoned her, she'd thought she could never be hurt so terribly again. She was wrong. This was a thousand times more painful. Harry she had loved with a schoolgirl's light-heartedness—Jack she loved with all of a woman's heart and body and soul.

It was her own stupid fault—she had allowed herself to care, to hope, to dream, and now, as she had told herself a thousand times would happen, all was in ashes.

He despised her. The man she loved despised her.

She'd gathered up her courage, told him all about Henri, about Lisbon, hoping against hope that it wouldn't matter to him. Oh, she hadn't expected him to renew his offer to marry her, not really—though her foolish heart had hoped a little. No, she knew it was impossible. The most she had hoped for was that he would finally understand why she didn't wish to go to London with his grandmother, why she would never be on the marriage mart. She'd hoped he would let her stay, let her live in his house as long as she could…

But he'd heard her story and the very next morning he'd ordered her belongings to be packed.

He hadn't been able to rid himself of her polluted presence quickly enough, had bundled her into the coach without so much as a by-your-leave, had given his farewells as if she were a complete stranger. He hadn't even looked her in the eye then, but had murmured goodbye in a voice devoid of emotion.

Kate bit her lip, tasting blood as she recalled the way he had taken her hand in the lightest of touches, fingers barely meeting as if he couldn't even bear to touch her. Francis at least had bowed over her hand, kissing it lightly, as he had that first day—he, apparently, still thought her a lady. Kate supposed that Jack had not yet enlightened him.

It was almost impossible to reconcile herself to the change in Jack. Only twenty-four hours previously she had woken in his arms. Even sleeping, his powerful arms had held her possessively, cradled her gently. She savoured the memory: the taste of his skin, the rough delight of his stubbled cheek against hers, the tremulous excitement of her body spread full length on his. The glory and the wonder of that secret, stolen kiss, the tentative tasting that had blazed into passion. And then, when he'd opened his eyes, those blue, blue eyes, and smiled that wonderful, crooked smile of his— 'Morning sweetheart'—it had been one of the most beautiful moments of her life.

At that moment she'd known—had believed—in the deepest part of her heart and soul that she loved him and that, miracle of miracles, he loved her in return. Her lonely, battered heart had at last found safe harbour. She had allowed herself the momentary dream that this was how she would wake up every morning for the rest of her life… 'Morning sweetheart.'

Oh, how she wished it could be so…but wishing was futile, racking her body with empty, echoing pain. It was not to be. She'd known it, deep down; she'd never believed otherwise. Like a hungry child, knowing herself doomed to a life of starvation, she had risked all to snatch at a morsel, knowing she'd never taste such nectar again.

Was it that which had made him reject her now? Her behaviour in the cottage? Did he think that the Lisbon gossips were right about her? What irony. She had never in her life felt wanton except with Jack Carstairs. But how was he to know that?

Being kidnapped once could be seen to be an accident. But twice? First Henri, then Jeremiah. A half-hysterical giggle rose in her throat—thrice—even his grandmother had kidnapped her. She clearly attracted such attention. Of course he would blame her.

The cruelty of his denial burnt into her heart now like acid into flesh…but she could not yet regret her moment of foolishness, her taste of bliss. Would it have been easier in the long run had she never known his embrace? she wondered. Perhaps. But now her dreams had substance to sustain themselves through the long grey years ahead.

The past was an ocean of pain; the future lay before her. Kate contemplated the thought. One day at a time; that was the way to go. First she must endure the rigours of 'the Season'.

Endure? No, she decided. There would be endurance enough to come; if there was pleasure to be had, she would have it while she could. She would make the most of her opportunities, experience the best that society could offer her. Sooner or later her secret would be out and she would have to leave town in disgrace, but it could not hurt her if she did not let it. Forewarned was forearmed, after all.

She would make no friendships here that she could not bear to be severed. She could build that much ice around her at least. She would not allow herself to think of this as anything other than a temporary treat. That way, when the time came to leave, she should be able to do so, if not without regrets, then without pain.

She could never be hurt as badly again. By the time she reached London, Kate silently vowed, her armour would be well and truly in place. When the time came, she would disappear quietly, none the worse, to take up her life elsewhere. At least this time, with a substantial income at her disposal, she would not starve.

Not for food, anyway.

She focused back on the scenery flashing by, becoming aware that her hands were very cold. Fishing around in her small travelling bag, she pulled out a pair of gloves. Kate looked at them. They were a very large pair of gloves, well-made leather, worn and soft, fur-lined. A gentleman's gloves. Only yesterday Jack had noticed how cold her hands were and had given her his gloves to wear. She must have forgotten to give them back to him.

Small frozen hands slipped into the big furry gloves, taking comfort from the size, the scent, the warmth of them. She rested her cheek in one gloved hand; the other was cupped against her heart. She leaned against the hard corner of the travelling chaise and closed her eyes. Finally, cradled in Jack Carstairs's gloves, Kate slept.

* * *

'Quiet, ain't it?' murmured Francis. He glanced across at his companion. Kate had left almost a week before, her face white and set, her eyes tragic. Since that day, Jack had spent his time furiously riding about the countryside, pushing himself to the absolute limit, galloping recklessly as if invisible demons were pursuing him. And in the evenings he got silently, determinedly drunk.

Francis had accompanied him in all things, understanding Jack's need to purge himself of the excess energy, to tire himself out, to blot a certain woebegone little face out of his memory, to try to drown his guilt. For a time at least.

'Got something to say to you, old man. Don't think you'll like it. Going to say it anyway.' Francis drained his glass.

Jack glanced at his friend in disgust. 'You're foxed.'

Francis nodded. 'Probably. So are you,' he said. 'Still going to say it.'

'Well, for God's sake just spit it out, then, instead of rambling on.'

'All right, then. Think you did the wrong thing. Shouldn't have forced her to go.'

Jack swallowed the contents of his own glass and slammed it down on the table at his elbow. 'Oh, God, not you too. As if it isn't bad enough, the whole household looking at me as if I'd taken the girl out, slung a brick around her neck and drowned her in the river. Damn it all!' he exclaimed. 'It's for her own good! Not a blasted Cheltenham tragedy… Anyone would think I'd sent her off to her own execution!'

'Well, you just might have, old man,' said Francis, after a pause.

Jack swung round in his chair. 'What the devil do you mean by that?'

Francis didn't answer immediately. He got up and poured another measure of brandy into both glasses. He caught Jack's eye. 'Planning to get us both stinking drunk,' he said. 'Tell you something in strictest confidence, old chap. Delicate matter. Concerns Kate.'

Jack frowned. 'If you mean what happened to her on the Peninsula, I know about it.'

Francis nodded thoughtfully. 'Told you in the carriage, didn't she? Thought that was it when I saw your faces that day.'

'So full marks for observation,' muttered Jack sourly.

'Brave little soul. Very painful to bring that sort of thing up again.' Francis added, 'Probably frightened that you'd despise her, too.'

'Despise her? *Despise her?*' Jack's voice was angry. How could anyone despise Kate? 'What the devil do you mean?'

'Not saying *I* do,' interjected Francis pacifically. 'Not saying anyone should. On the contr'ry. I'm talkin' about what *she* thinks. Thing is, it damned well looked like you couldn't wait to get rid of her. Less than twenty-four hours after you find out she's been…sullied…by a Frenchman, you bundle her out of the house. Girl probably thinks you *do* despise her. What else is she to think?'

Jack whitened. 'She wouldn't…she couldn't…'

'Nothing to indicate she don't,' said Francis quietly. 'Didn't exactly make it clear to her, did you? Threw her out, not to put too fine a point on it.'

'But I…'

'Oh, yes, *I* know what you were about, but did *she?*'

Jack groaned and clutched his hair in anguish.

'Expects to be despised, you see. Happened before. Lost her betrothed for that reason. Not saying that was a bad thing, mind you—chap wasn't good enough for her. He'd known her all her life, childhood sweetheart sort of thing. Didn't stop him despising her after the scandal. Fellow called off the wedding on account of it. And most people thought he did the right thing.'

Jack groaned again. 'I didn't know…didn't think…'

'Thing is, the story got out and all the cats got stuck into her in the most appalling fashion.'

'My God.'

'Things some of them said to her would make your hair curl. Ha! The gentler sex! Bitches carved young Kate up in the most vicious and cold-blooded fashion, and all the time with the sweetest smiles on their faces. Held her to be a traitor because she nursed wounded French soldiers. Claimed she went with them willingly. Called her a whore behind her back…and a few said it to her face. And all with such smiling politeness and seeming sweetness… I tell you, Jack, it almost put me off women for life. The gentler sex.' He shuddered.

The beautiful, hypocritical face of Julia Davenport appeared in Jack's mind. 'I know just what you mean,' he muttered grimly. The two men sipped their brandy. The flames danced in the grate.

'Thing is, same thing could happen in London. Some of the tabbies in Lisbon last year are bound to be in London now. Even if they aren't, you know what women are like for writing letters. Bound to be someone who knows the story. Come out sooner or later, I'd say—just a matter of time.'

Jack was too appalled to speak. He felt as if his stomach had dropped out of his body. Oh, God, no wonder she'd looked as if she was going to an execution; she would have an axe suspended over her head the whole time she was in London, and it was only a matter of time before it would fall.

Jack groaned and clenched his fist. There was a snap as his glass shattered in his hand. Francis sat up, exclaiming at the blood dripping from Jack's fingers. Jack waved him aside impatiently.

'Going to London,' he said. 'Can't leave her to think that— Oh, shut up, Francis, what's a damned scratch? I'm off to London in the morning. Are you coming with me or not?'

'Oh, absolutely, old man, absolutely.'

Chapter Sixteen

'Your young protégée seems to be doin' rather well, Maudie.'

'Thank you, Gussie,' replied Lady Cahill. 'I couldn't be more pleased with her if she was my own daughter.'

Lady Cahill and several of her cronies were doing what they called 'taking tea and cakes'. The tea trolley was laden with dainty cakes and elegant little savouries. Steam curled languidly from the spout of the teapot, and each lady sipped delicately from a fine eggshell-thin teacup. The sherry decanter was half empty.

'Charmin' gel, quite charmin'.' The speaker, wearing an enormous feathered turban, reached for a fourth crab-and-asparagus patty.

Lady Cahill beamed. Kate had taken to her new life like a duck to water, hadn't put a foot wrong. Lady Cahill had, at first, been rather anxious lest Kate reveal herself as a true scholar's daughter—it would be fatal for her to gain a reputation as a bluestocking.

However, to Lady Cahill's pleased surprise, Kate had proved to be almost as delightfully ignorant as any anxious sponsor would wish her protégée to be. She seemed to take more pleasure in a visit to the Pantheon Bazaar or Astley's Amphitheatre than she did in an afternoon at the British Museum or a viewing of the archaeological sensation, Lord Elgin's Marbles. She knew nothing of famous thinkers, writers or philosophers. Her conversation was not weighted with dull pronouncements from weighty tomes, and she was in no danger of frightening gentlemen by spouting screeds of poetry at them. It seemed that the only topics on which Kate was knowledgeable were horses and the Peninsular War—and since the *ton* was full of horse-mad military gentlemen that was not held to be a disadvantage.

Lady Cahill basked in her protégée's praise.

'A sensible, well-bred, pretty-behaved gel, Maudie. Poor Maria would have been delighted to see how charmingly her daughter has turned out.'

The others nodded.

Kate's success was only to be expected, Lady Cahill told herself complacently. Kate was a sociable girl, and a sympathetic listener. Moreover, a life of ordering her father's household and her experience of having had to adapt to extraordinary conditions had given her an indefinable air of assurance, taken by many to be a sign of good breeding.

And, from having spent most of her life in male company from all walks of life, she was neither shy nor coy nor odiously missish with the London gentlemen she met. She seemed to listen as happily to the dull military pronouncements of an elderly general as to the stammering confidences of a young man in his first season or the practised compliments of a rake.

Lady Cahill's granddaughter, Amelia, had introduced Kate to her more dashing set, made up largely of young fashionable matrons. They had noted her elegant, modish appearance, her mischievous sense of humour, her quick wit and her complete lack of interest in their husbands, and pronounced her to be a sweet and charming girl.

'*Very* popular with the soldier laddies,' said one elderly lady waspishly, holding out her teacup to be refilled.

'And you know why, Ginny Holton, so you need not sneer!'

snapped Lady Courtney. 'You know perfectly well what that dear sweet girl did for my Gilbert.'

The others nodded. Lady Courtney's grandson, Gilbert, had barely set a foot outside his home, until Miss Farleigh had teased him into going about in society with her, apparently oblivious of the awkwardness of his missing arm and the ominous black eyepatch.

'Told him he looked like a wonderfully sinister pirate and that it would help protect her from unwanted attention.' Lady Courtney wiped her eyes.

'And *then* she told him that he must not blame her if they were mobbed by young ladies because he looked quite disgustingly romantic, and, while *she* knew him to be odiously stuffy, other girls were not as discriminating as she... And he laughed—my boy actually laughed—and consented to take her out. He hasn't looked back since.'

'Yes, shame on you, Ginny,' agreed another elderly lady. 'If Maudie's Kate is popular with military gentlemen, it is not to be wondered at. You are only being uncharitable because your Chloë is without even a sniff of an offer! A pity to be sure, but no reason to snipe at others!'

It was true. Kate's unselfconscious attention to the wounded had done her no disservice in the eyes of the more fortunate of the military. The polite world soon noted that little Miss Farleigh had a court of large, protective gentlemen, led by Mr Lennox, and Sir Toby Fenwick and other military types, who seemed equally delighted to fetch her a glass of ratafia, escort her to the opera, take her driving in Hyde Park at the fashionable hour or depress the pretensions of any too assiduous suitors.

There were many of these, as word of her inheritance had leaked out. She was being courted by several gazetted fortune hunters, as well as men of substance and position.

Lady Cahill sat back in her chair as the talk turned to more general topics. She was almost satisfied. One factor, however, was missing from the equation. She hoped he would bestir himself soon and get himself to London before Kate was snapped up by some fashionable fribble who didn't deserve her.

'What do you think of this, miss?' The maid held an elegant spray of artificial flowers to Kate's hair and looked enquiringly at her new mistress in the mirror.

Kate stared. She almost didn't recognise herself. Her hair had been cropped in the latest style and feathered curls clustered round her face, doing amazing things to her appearance, things Kate would never have dreamed possible. For the first time in her life, she felt elegant, and, though the Reverend Mr Farleigh's daughter knew it to be an immodest thought, almost pretty. The new face and hairstyle were enhanced by the gown she was wearing—a soft shade of green that brought out the colour in her eyes and minimised the slight unfashionable golden tone of her skin, brought about by too much time outdoors.

Lady Cahill and Amelia had subjected Kate to a rigorous regime of crushed strawberries—to refine and clarify the skin—buttermilk baths—to soften it—and, for general toning and nourishing, slices of raw veal laid on her skin for hours at a time while Amelia read to her. In addition there were twice-daily applications of distilled pineapple water—for clarity and beauty and to erase wrinkles—egg and lemon face packs—to fade that dreadful tan and nourish the skin—and oatmeal masks—to brighten and refine the skin.

Kate laughed, complained they made her feel rather like the main ingredient in a strange and exotic stew, and admitted her complexion had improved under their ministrations. But it was still a terrible waste of good food.

And then there had been the shopping, a positively sinful orgy of it, in Kate's eyes, but 'the merest necessities' as far as her female mentors were concerned. Kate tried to remain sensible and practical, but the fizzing excitement that rose in her at the sight of the exquisite, dashing outfits that Lady Cahill and Amelia had bullied her into purchasing was irresistible to a girl who had had very little opportunity to indulge in fashionable feminine frivolity.

Kate's head had been spinning at the end of that first day, which had begun at the silk warehouses. Delicate and lovely fabrics were draped, compared, contrasted, swathed, discussed, discarded and selected, mostly without reference to Kate, who was far too easily pleased, according to her companions. Then it was off to see Amelia's modiste, Madame Fanchôt, who, well primed as to the state of *mademoiselle*'s finances, went into professional Gallic raptures about *mademoiselle*'s face, her figure, her air of *je ne c'est quoi,* then flew into genuine raptures when Kate responded to her in fluent French. Then there were hours spent poring over issues of *La Belle Assemblée* and *Ackerman's Repository,* with dozens and dozens of plates, all of the most elegant outfits.

In the end Kate had spinelessly allowed Madame Fanchôt, Amelia and Lady Cahill to decide everything and left to them the meticulous planning and endless discussion which went into every choice. For her part, Kate could not have cared less whether, for instance, the lemon muslin was cut to drape *so,* enhancing the lovely line of *mademoiselle*'s shoulders and neckline, or like *so,* to enhance her bustline, or like *so,* to give her height. Her only contribution to that discussion had been to suggest that perhaps the neckline was rather too low, a suggestion that was ignored by all three ladies as too nonsensical even to warrant a response.

So now Kate stared at her reflection, exposing more of her chest than she had ever done in her life. She became aware of her maid still holding out the artificial flowers, awaiting her response, and smiled apologetically.

'I think not, Dora. To be quite honest, I am terrified that it would fall out of my hair.' The maid bridled, assuring her that such a thing was quite impossible.

Kate interrupted the flow. 'It is just that my head feels so strange and light since my new crop, and I cannot but feel that something is missing, so although I am sure you would place the flowers most securely you do understand how I feel, don't you?'

Dora relented after a moment and said that of course she did, and miss looked very elegant and lovely and would be sure to be a success again tonight.

Kate wrinkled her nose. Yes, of course, 'success' was what was important. How could she have forgotten? She had tried not to let herself think of other things, or wonder what might be happening at Sevenoakes. That was one benefit of such hectic socialising—one didn't have time to brood. Tonight, for example, she was going to a ball and it would be surprising if she had time to think of Jack even once.

Jack leant against an elegant column, arms folded, a black frown on his face, staring, glaring, unable to tear himself away. It had been Francis's idea to come to this ball on the evening of their arrival in London and Jack had regretted it the moment he'd arrived and clapped eyes on Kate, utterly transformed from the shabby little starveling he had first met. She was dancing, her head thrown back, mischievously laughing up into the eyes of a fellow Jack had been to school with, and knew to be titled, rich and eligible.

'Blast it!' he exclaimed to Francis. 'What the devil is she doing dancing with that fellow Fenchurch? And in such a dress!' Jack could hardly take his eyes off the creamy curves revealed by the fashionable low-cut neckline of Kate's dress, and neither, he noticed, could Kate's partner. Nor a number of other so-called gentlemen.

Francis glanced from his friend's black frown to Kate's laughing visage and back again. He controlled his twitching mouth and said innocently, 'Nice chap, Fenchurch. Kate would do well to encourage his advances. Couldn't do better, in fact.'

'Fellow's a complete bounder!' snarled Jack.

'Good heavens, is he?' said Francis placidly. 'How very

shocking. News to me, I must say. Always thought he was a friend of yours, old man. A bounder? Well, well. I must say, I am surprised. Still, he's a dashing-looking chap, and there is the title. I dare say that accounts for his popularity with the ladies.'

Jack grunted. There was nothing particularly dashing that he could see in the tall Viscount's regular even features, thickly curling blond hair and tall, muscular physique. Fellow was addicted to sports, that was all. Damn it, what the deuce was he saying to make her blush like that? Jack found he was clenching his fists and thrust them into his pockets to hide the fact.

'Stand up straight, boy, and stop lounging all over the wall like a looby! How many times have I told you to get your hands out of your pockets? Not that I can see how on earth you can have pockets in such indecently tight garments.'

Jack sighed. 'Good evening, Grandmama.' He turned to face her. He bowed, and she ran her eyes over him assessingly. A marked improvement from the last time she'd seen him.

'Have you seen my little protégée?' she said, grinning.

Jack grunted.

'Looks charming, doesn't she? Gel's done me proud. I wish her mother could see her.' She raised her lorgnette and peered short-sightedly at the dancers. 'Who's she dancing with now? Eh, Jack?'

'Fenchurch.'

Lady Cahill smiled. He hadn't even turned to look. And what was more, she thought delightedly, he was so taken up with Kate's activities that he had forgotten to be sensitive about his altered appearance, his shattered cheek and his limp.

'Fenchurch? Ah, yes, fine, big, handsome chap, ain't he? Not that that signifies. All her beaux seem to be. Gel's mighty popular—her dance card was full before she'd been here ten minutes. I doubt she could give you even a country dance, Jack. You could ask her, though.'

He snorted.

Lady Cahill smothered a chuckle and continued. 'Oh, look, the dance is finished and see how they rush to procure her a chair and refreshments. Can't leave the girl for a moment but she's surrounded by admirers. Taken very well, Maria's girl. But, there Jack, you're not interested in an old woman's ramblings. Tell me, what has brought my favourite grandson to London?'

Her favourite grandson mumbled something inaudible and stumped away, scowling. Kate was undoubtedly a social success. And he was unaccountably infuriated. He'd rushed up to London in a state of high anxiety, ready to rescue a poor little waif from social ostracism and humiliation. He'd found her apparently in the highest of spirits, with any number of fellows underfoot, making complete cakes of themselves over her! Her dance card too full to allow him even a country dance! He snorted again. He had no intention of joining the ranks of her admirers, begging for a moment of her attention! He retreated behind another pillar and scowled at her from there.

Kate saw him arrive. For a moment her heart seemed to stop. He looked worn and tired and the broad shoulders of his plain dark coat glittered from the hundreds of candles that lit the ballroom. He had come in the rain. His hair too was damp and clung to his brow in dark wild curls. She longed to run across the room and fling herself into his arms. She longed for him to stride out across the ballroom floor and sweep her into his embrace. She longed to kiss him.

She continued through the cotillion mechanically, finding in the performance of the stately measure the control she needed. Her heart was ablaze with excitement. Why had he come? How long would it be before he noticed her? Would he like the way she looked now? Would he ask her to dance? Oh, how she had missed him!

She forced herself not to look at him, not trusting herself to do so. She responded to Viscount Fenchurch's sallies, laughing and smiling automatically, having no idea of what he was saying. The dance would finish soon and then Jack would come over to her. Unable to restrain herself any longer, she used the movement of the dance to dart another quick shy glance at him.

And froze. He was staring right at her. His gaze scorched her…and she froze. There was nothing but the strongest condemnation in his face. He was staring right at her as if he despised her. Her steps and smile faltered, and as she stumbled her partner gathered her smoothly up, concern in his handsome face. Kate recovered herself and continued.

The dance felt like the longest one in history. Somehow she got through it, smiling blindly at her partner whenever his face swam into view. She had thought she had come to terms with the pain of Jack's condemnation, but the sight of him had been so unexpected, her response so joyful, that his obvious disgust had slid through her icy armour like a hot knife through butter, straight into her heart. Again.

The dance finished, but before she could excuse herself and seek solitude in which to deal with her desolation the band struck up again and she found herself being whisked back on to the floor. Pride alone carried her through it, and if her partner found her to be a little inattentive and *distraite* he found nothing amiss with the dazzling smiles she flashed him.

By the time the second dance drew to a close, Kate's temper was rising. Jack had continued to prop himself against the wall, glaring at her throughout the dance, black fury and total disapproval on his face.

How *dared* he follow her here and stand there sneering at her? It was *his* fault she was here in the first place. She hadn't wanted to come to London. And if she had made her entrée to society under false colours, as he obviously believed, then it was his grandmother who'd made her do it. And *he* had delivered her to *his* grandmother, so *he* was as much at fault as anyone. How *dared* he look at her like that?

Kate's anger enabled her to sweep through the next dance in glittering style and to parry the flirtatious compliments of her small court of admirers with wit and panache. For the next hour she danced, flirted, smilingly declined an offer of marriage and added a dozen new members to her circle of male admirers, all in the most furious of tempers and under the scorching long-distance glare of Mr Jack Carstairs.

Jack forced himself to stay for an hour or so longer, seeking out all the most beautiful women. She would not think he had no female admirers! Look at her—responding to the gallantries of the biggest collection of rakes and downright gudgeons he had ever seen—and they called themselves his friends!

Finally, unable to stand the sight any more, Jack left, turning abruptly from the sight of her, pushing his way through the glittering throngs of people.

Kate watched as he disappeared out into the night. He hadn't even looked at her for the last half-hour. Suddenly she realised she had the vilest headache. She sought out Lady Cahill and asked to be taken home.

'Mr Carstairs called again this morning, Lady Cahill,' announced the butler, an edge of disapproval in his voice.

The old lady frowned. 'And I gather from your tone, Fitcher, that Miss Farleigh was "out" to him again.'

Fitcher assented with a dignified half-bow.

'The foolish child! I suppose I will have to talk to her about it. Ask her to step down for a moment, will you?'

'Now, missy, I'd like to know why my grandson has been haunting this house for the last week or so but not, apparently, finding anyone home, and I do not refer to myself.'

Kate flushed. 'I've been so busy...' Her voice trailed off under Lady Cahill's sardonic gaze. 'Well, if you must know, I have no wish to speak to him.'

A well-plucked eyebrow rose.

Kate's voice warmed in indignation. 'Well, and why should I subject myself to more of his tyranny?'

'Tyranny?'

'Yes, ma'am. As if it is not impossible enough having him glaring and glowering—and gnashing his teeth at me from across every room I enter, whether it is at Almack's, or a concert or a private ball. He is making me—and himself— ridiculous. I wish he would return to Leicestershire and leave me alone. He has nothing to say to me that I have not heard before…or, if he has, I do not wish to hear it, for I know what it will be.'

'You think so, eh?'

'Yes, ma'am.' *He despises me.*

'As I understand it, you have barely spoken with my grandson since leaving Leicestershire.'

Kate flushed again. 'There has been no need,' she said in a low voice. 'He made it perfectly clear then what he thought of me. And his behaviour since then only reinforces it.'

Jack's behaviour made a horrid kind of sense to Kate—he thought she was some sort of immoral lightskirt, and he was there to prevent her from disgracing his grandmother. That was why he glared at her every time she so much as looked or smiled at a man, no matter who the man. He didn't trust her an inch, that was obvious!

The old lady observed the tense way her young protégée fiddled with the fringe of her shawl.

'And there is no possibility that you could be mistaken? Young men, and young women too, often say foolish things that they do not mean, especially when they are in love.'

'In love! No, indeed, ma'am, you are quite, quite mistaken there!' The fringe tore in Kate's fingers. Unaware, she moved restlessly around the room.

Lady Cahill heaved herself off the sofa. 'My dear, foolish child, when you are as old as I am, you will learn that young men, particularly young men of my grandson's cut, do not generally make cakes of themselves following a young lady around only to glare at them from a distance, unless their emotions are *very* strongly engaged. And only one emotion prompts that sort of behaviour.'

She held up a hand to forestall Kate's reply. 'No, that's quite enough. The subject is becoming tedious and fatiguing. I beg you will think about what I have said, but we will speak no more of it now. I intend to repose myself for a few hours before I ready myself for the ball tonight.'

She paused at the doorway and looked back. 'I expect you will find that my grandson will be present at the ball tonight— Wellington is guest of honour. It is to be his last social appearance before returning to the Peninsula.'

Chapter Seventeen

'Good God, how has *that* young woman managed to insinuate herself amongst decent people? Do our host and hostess not know she is a traitress and a whore?'

The penetrating voice was overheard by dozens in the tightly packed ballroom. As one, heads turned.

'Who do I mean? Why, that Farleigh chit, of course. Look at her, dancing as if she had not a care in the world, the shameless hussy. And at a ball in honour of our brave and gallant Marquis of Wellington; the gall of the woman!'

The voice lowered itself slightly, and continued to a gathering crowd, avid for gossip.

'That little tart betrayed our brave soldiers to the French, lived with a Frenchman *as his mistress!* I know, for my husband was one of the officers that captured her. Her father would be turning in his grave—he was a man of the cloth, you know. Mind you, I always wondered why he never looked at her—he must have known…'

The crowd pressed closer.

Something was wrong. Kate knew it. So many looks, sideways glances, whispered comments followed by significant stares.

'Miss Farleigh, our dance, I believe.' An elegant young frib-ble bowed over her hand and led her into the next set.

'Have you heard, Miss Farleigh? 'Tis monstrous exciting. Apparently some little whore has been passing herself off as a lady, when all the time she played spy for old Boney and whored for his officers. *And she's here tonight!*' Her partner glanced around the room, speculating.

Kate glanced away, a sick feeling in her stomach. Let me just finish this dance, she prayed silently, then I can leave inconspicuously.

But it was not to be. As they moved through the stately steps of the cotillion she noticed her partner eagerly whisper-ing his news to the others in the set. At one point he faltered, stopped and stared at Kate, aghast. He turned back to his source, whispered something and resumed the steps.

Only now he would not look her in the eye. His fingers did not so much touch hers as gesture disdainfully in her direction. The dance continued. Kate felt the ice surround her. No one looked at her. No one touched her. No one spoke to her.

Bitterness rose in Kate like bile. She had known how it would be. *This* was the reason she had never wanted to appear in society ever again. Had she been allowed to go her own way, she would not be experiencing this. Again.

'Ceddy, please escort me to my mama. I cannot think she would wish me to associate with a traitress!' Nose held high, a young lady abandoned the set in mid-movement.

In seconds, the ordered progress of the dance collapsed, as each of the ladies in Kate's set marched righteously off the dance floor, escorted by their partner. Kate looked at her part-ner in mute appeal. If he would only escort her from the floor, she would be able to leave with a shred of dignity.

His face twisted in contempt. 'My brother was injured at Salamanca!' he snarled, and stalked away.

Kate stood in the middle of the dance floor, frozen. She knew she had to move, to get away from all of the eyes, from the whispering and pointing. From the hate. The loathing. The avid speculation. But she couldn't move.

Around her she felt the rest of the dancers faltering, the rising hum of gossip and conjecture. The music petered out in mid-tune as the last of the couples left the floor. It had the effect of focusing all attention on Kate. She felt the crowd gathering into a dense barrier, the seething, greedy stares of bored aristocrats, eager for sensation to alleviate their safe, pampered, dull lives.

Lions and Christians.

The thought gave Kate the strength she needed to move. She turned, seeking Lady Cahill with her eyes, but there was no sign of her. Kate moved slowly towards the circle of watchers, trying to ignore the barrage of eyes upon her, probing, malicious, scornful.

She had nothing to be ashamed of. She would not give them the satisfaction. She stiffened her spine. The way before her parted reluctantly. Ladies, who only hours before had claimed friendship, turned their faces coldly away. No one would meet her eye; a hundred eyes bored into her.

'Little better than a camp follower!'

'The cheek—to try to pass herself off like that in decent company!'

And one, less elliptical than the others. 'Traitorous whore!'

Her body began to shake. She could do nothing. There was no standing up to insubstantial whispers from people who would not even look her in the face. She forced herself to keep walking, desperately hoping the trembling of her body was not visible to the observers.

Was there ever a room so long? Only four more steps. Three…two…

A powerful black-clad arm snaked out of the dense crowd and pulled her into the centre of the circle again.

'What—?'

'I think you must have forgotten me, Miss Farleigh,' said Jack. His normal tone of voice carried in the watching hush.

Kate blinked up at him.

'My dance, I believe. Did you forget it?' He smiled down at her bewildered face, his casual manner belied by the implacable grip on her arm.

'But…' With everyone listening, Kate couldn't say it. She *hadn't* promised him a dance. He didn't dance. Not since he was wounded, anyway. He only leaned against walls and columns, glaring at her. So why would he seek her out now? Now, when the world was turning against her again and she wanted nothing more than escape. Kate tried to pull away, but his hold on her was too powerful.

Ignoring Kate's glance of pathetic entreaty, Jack moved steadily back through the crowd, towing her beside him, greeting acquaintances in a cheery tone as he went, for all the world as if they were not in the very heart of a major scandal, their every movement watched by hundreds.

His uneven footsteps echoed as he led her out on to the deserted dance floor. He finally released her arm, but took her hand instead. Bowing, he kissed it lightly. Kate stared at him in a daze. He grinned at her, a wicked, tender grin.

'Courage, love,' he whispered as he straightened up. 'Let's show them that an old cripple and a gallant war heroine are not beaten by a paltry bit of gossip.'

He nodded to the band. Kate followed his glance. Sir Toby was standing over the band in a very determined manner. He smiled and waved, then turned back to the band. The music started.

Kate's eyes misted as she looked up into the handsome face bent over her. She had been prepared to withstand anything— scorn, mockery, disgust, revilement. His kindness had undone her.

Jack determinedly stumped his way through the intricate steps, his bad leg making a clumsy mockery of the movements. Kate gracefully performed her part, making adjustments for his limp where she could.

Jack's eyes never left her face. Her head was held high, but she danced blindly. No one in the audience could see the tears which trickled down her cheeks unheeded. Jack wished he could take her in his arms, wished that strait-laced English society would bend their rules sufficiently to adopt the scandalous Viennese dance which was all the rage in Europe. Jack smiled at her tenderly. Yes, it would be wonderful to hold Kate in his arms for a waltz.

The ballroom might have been deserted, the audience silent ghosts. Only the strains of the band playing, the clumping of Jack's shoes and the faint shuffle of Kate's tiny satin slippers could be heard at first, then the murmuring started again.

The dance ended, but under Tubby's supervision the next one started almost immediately. As the second dance drew to a close, Jack bent over her hand again and murmured, 'Two dances are my limit, I'm afraid. A third and people will begin to think you are fast.'

Kate stared at him, stupefied. She was being pilloried as a whore and a traitress, and he was concerned that three dances with the same partner would label her *fast!* A bubble of hysteria rose in her throat. The music started again.

'My dance, I believe, Miss Farleigh. Off with you now, Carstairs. This lady is promised to me.' The whole room heard him, but without waiting for a reply Francis swung Kate into a country dance.

There was still no one else on the dance floor.

'Miss Farleigh, would you do me the honour of partnering me in the next dance?' A young man bowed over Kate's nerveless fingers. He was dressed in immaculate evening attire, one empty sleeve pinned neatly back. Kate stared at him dumbly.

'You may not remember me, Miss Farleigh, but we met at Badajoz. Arnold Bentham at your service. Francis's cousin.'

Kate glanced at his empty sleeve. The young man smiled. 'No, Miss Farleigh, that arm I lost at Salamanca. You saved the other one at Badajoz, and I offer it now at your disposal.

Shall we?' With his one remaining arm, Arnold Bentham swept Kate into the next dance.

Two other couples joined them on the dance floor—Francis and Andrew Lennox and their partners. There was no sign of Jack.

'Miss Farleigh, may I present my son as a desirable partner? He…he is a little out of practice, but I'm sure you will not mind that.' The well-modulated voice broke.

Kate turned, then stopped dead. Her prospective partner stood very still, smiling in her general direction, his hand resting on the arm of a middle-aged woman.

Kate's face crumpled. It was too much. All this unexpected kindness. All this support. And now this.

It was Oliver Greenwood. Oliver Greenwood, whom she had first met as a terrified young lieutenant at Torres Vedras, with blood gushing all over his face. She had visited him several times since she had come to London, but he was the last person she'd expected to see at a ball. Oliver Greenwood was blind.

'Miss Farleigh, I would be most honoured if you would stand up with me,' said Oliver Greenwood, bowing in her direction.

Kate glanced at Mrs Greenwood. His mother's face was working with emotion. She nodded at Kate, her eyes filled with tears.

Kate curtseyed. 'The honour would be all mine,' she whispered through a mist of tears, and took her place.

Immediately they were surrounded as others joined the set. Francis, Tubby, Andrew Lennox and others, unknown to Kate, some whose faces were vaguely familiar to her, others who were clearly friends of Oliver Greenwood. And their partners, girls for the most part unknown to Kate, girls who smiled encouragingly at her and nodded their heads.

Somehow they got through the dance, Oliver being gently

steered in the right direction by his fellow officers, and Kate too, for by this time she was completely blinded by her tears.

And by the time it finished she was not the only person with wet eyes.

'May I escort you to your guardian, Miss Farleigh?' said Oliver Greenwood.

'Not yet, young Greenwood,' a bluff voice boomed heartily from behind them. 'I want to talk to this young lady.'

'Sir!' All the young officers snapped instantly to attention, Oliver Greenwood included.

Kate turned. Jack and a man in a plain, neat, dark blue coat were approaching her—a smallish, thin man, whose blue eyes twinkled at her from over one of the most famous noses in all Europe.

'My Lord!' she gasped, and sank into a curtsey.

'So it's little Kate Farleigh who's got my officers in knots, is it?' said the Marquis of Wellington. He smiled again at Kate, bowed and kissed her hand. A gasp ran round the room.

'Knew your father, m'dear. Very fine man he was. Sorry to hear about his death. Your brothers, too. Brave boys, brave boys. Know they would be proud of you.'

He took her hand and tucked it into his arm. 'Shall we take a turn about the room?' Without waiting for a reply, he moved off, lowering his voice so that only she could hear.

'Young Carstairs filled me in. Pack of worthless gabble-mongers. But we'll fix them. Face 'em down, what? Show 'em for the cowards they are, eh?'

Wellington moved slowly towards the crowd which pressed forward, eager to speak with the great man. As he did so, he introduced Kate, mentioning to this person that he was a friend of her family, to that person that she was a gallant young heroine, to another that she was a brave little lady, one of England's finest.

They were soon joined by a group of older ladies, one of whom linked arms with Kate, clearly declaring her support. Kate blinked at her. The woman was a complete stranger.

She bent towards Kate. 'Lady Charlotte, my dear. I'm so terribly sorry this happened. If I'd known...but we were all in the card room, I'm afraid, and only just heard what was happening.' She indicated the rest of her party. Kate recognised Lady Courtney and several others, but this glittering matron was a complete stranger.

Seeing Kate's continuing puzzlement, the lady added, 'I'm Arnold Bentham's mother—you know my nephew, Francis.' As Kate suddenly nodded in comprehension, the lady continued, 'You saved my Arnold's life, Miss Farleigh. For that, you have my undying friendship and support, and that of these other ladies too.'

Kate slowly circled the room; on one side of her, the Marquis of Wellington, on the other, a collection of society's most formidable matrons. She was dazed by the turn in her fortunes, unable to comprehend quite what was happening. She nodded, curtseyed and smiled, oblivious of whom she was meeting, who was shaking her hand.

Jack was there, a pace or two behind her, hovering protectively. She could feel his presence, sense his strength. She wanted to touch him, but she couldn't. She turned to look at him over her shoulder. Their eyes met, caressed, clung, but she was moved forward inexorably, and they were separated by the crowd, pressing closer, eager to meet the Great Man and his protégée.

Kate could hardly believe it. She had been snatched from her worst nightmare, and now was engaged in an almost triumphal procession on the arm of England's greatest living hero. But it was Jack who'd saved her. He had risked social ostracism, had stood up with her in the most public of places, had declared his support of her for all the world to see. Jack, who'd been a recluse, hiding his wounds from the world— he'd come out and danced with her, when no one else would even look her in the eye.

And it was Jack whose arm she wanted to be on, whose arms she wanted to be in.

Kate glanced back. He was no longer there. Her eyes scanned the room anxiously. Where was he? She could see him nowhere. He had stood up for her in her hour of need. Surely he wouldn't desert her in her moment of triumph? Didn't he know it would mean nothing to her if he was not with her?

She caught Francis's eye across a dozen heads and asked him the silent question. He returned a sombre look, then shrugged and shook his head hopelessly. Kate's face dropped. Jack had left. But why?

With a leaden heart, Kate returned to the hollow greetings of well-wishers and sycophants.

'What do you mean, she's gone? Gone where? She hasn't been seen since that blasted ball, and let me tell you, Grandmama, nothing could be more ill-judged. She needs to be out there, circulating, seeing people, showing them she's nothing to hide. We've scotched the worst of it, but if she's hiding herself away…'

'I said she's *gone,* Jack. Gone away. Left.'

'Left where? What do you mean?' Suddenly Jack turned white. He sat down in a rush. 'You mean gone? She's left London?'

Lady Cahill looked at him in some compassion, then hardened her heart. He'd been acting like a fool.

'Gone where?'

'Back to that village I found her in.'

'Good God, how could you let her do something so…? What is there for her anyway? Why would she do such a thing?' He rose to his feet again and paced about, raking his fingers through wildly disordered locks. Suddenly he looked up sharply.

'Who is escorting her? How is she travelling? And who is to meet her?'

His grandmother shrugged.

'You mean you let her go alone!' he roared.

'I was not exactly consulted, Jack, and do not take that tone with me. I'm as worried about the dratted girl as you are!' snapped his grandmother. 'The foolish child slipped away at dawn.'

'So how is she travelling?'

'I don't know, Jack, the Mail or stage, I presume!'

'Good God! Mail or stage! Rubbing shoulders with God knows who! Doesn't she know the dangers? Footpads, highwaymen! Doesn't she know how often accidents happen? Pray God she took the Mail; at least they have a guard!' Swearing, he rushed from the room.

Lady Cahill sat back, a satisfied grin on her face.

'What the *devil* do you think you're doing?'

The roar, which seemed to echo from the heavens, almost startled Kate into dropping her basket. It was, however, a very familiar roar. She looked around. There, on a horse flecked with foam, its sides heaving, legs trembling, sat Jack Carstairs, glaring at her yet again.

He looked dreadful. Covered with mud, his jaw unshaven, his neckcloth all awry. Her eyes softened. She glanced around. The narrow country laneway in which she'd been walking was by no means deserted; several farm workers were within earshot. She smiled up at him for the benefit of their observers.

'Good afternoon, Mr Carstairs,' she said in a clear calm voice. 'As you see, I'm just off to the village.'

'Just off to the village, are you? And with no thought for how others might be worried about you?'

She looked up at him in silence. Why would he be worried? And why so angry?

'How the hell did you get here anyway?'

'I hired a chaise and outriders.'

'A chaise and outriders? A chaise and outriders!' He seemed

outraged by the notion. He was breathing heavily, his eyes positively crackling with blue rage.

'Well, and what is so wrong with that?'

'Only that I stopped every bloody stage and Mail coach between here and London, searching for you!'

'Oh, no. You didn't, did you?' Kate looked up at him, her eyes wide, imagining the scene. She giggled.

As far as Jack was concerned, it was the giggle that did it. With a groan of fury he leaned down, grabbed her under the armpits and dragged her up on to his horse. Ignoring her outraged squeaks, he clamped her to his chest and moved off. Kate struggled, but as the horse moved faster she clung to Jack to save herself from falling. The farm labourers came closer, several of them carrying sticks and cudgels.

In a trice Jack clamped his mouth over hers. Kate's struggles suddenly ceased as the familiar magic of his kiss washed over her. She was, after all, where she most desired in the world to be. One hand slid around his neck, her fingers tangling in his wild, damp hair. The other hand gently stroked his rough, unshaven jaw. Abandoning all defences, she opened her heart and allowed herself to simply love him.

By the time the kiss had finished, they had left the grinning farm workers long behind. Kate sighed, nuzzling her face against the underside of his jaw. She leaned against him, relishing the taste of him on her lips, the strong embrace of his muscular arms around her.

'There was no need to run away, you know,' he said after a time. 'We had everything under control. You will be completely accepted in society, no shadow of a doubt. There was no need to hide here.'

'Run away?' she said quietly. 'Did Lady Cahill not tell you?'

'Oh, she told me all right. How else do you think I knew where to look?' He swung her round to face him, eyes blazing, hands gripping her hard. He shook her. 'What is there here for you? A small dirty village? A falling-down cottage? The company of rustics? You cannot possibly prefer this to London!'

Her eyes clung to his. 'Everything I want in the world is right here,' she said slowly. 'Nothing I want or need is in London.' She leaned back into the curve of his body.

He turned ashen. His hands loosened their hard grip. He looked away, staring blankly across the top of her head. 'Nothing?' he said at last.

'Nothing in London. Everything I want in the world is right here,' she repeated.

He sagged in the saddle. 'So be it.'

Defeated, he turned his horse back towards the village. They rode in silence, the only sound the twittering of birds and the slow clip-clopping of the horse's hoofs. Kate lay back against his chest, rocking against his hard, warm body in rhythm to the horse's gait. She could say no more. How could she, not knowing how he felt? She had told him as much as she dared.

Why had he come after her? Had his grandmother sent him? Was it duty? Or a constitutional dislike of being crossed? He'd saved her reputation, but then made it clear that he wanted nothing further to do with her. Oh, he desired her all right, but she wanted more than that.

They drew closer and closer to the village until at last the cross on the spire of the tiny stone church was clearly visible. The horse stopped.

'Damned if I do, damned if I don't, so I bloody well will and damn the consequences!' Jack suddenly growled. He wrenched the horse around and started to gallop in the opposite direction. Kate clung on for dear life.

'Where are we going? This is not the way to the village,' she shrieked. His only response was to clamp her more tightly against his chest and spur the horse onwards.

'The cottage is in the other direction!' she shouted, bouncing up and down.

The horse galloped on. Jack said not a word. Kate thumped at his chest in frustration. 'Jack! Where are we going?'

His arms tightened around her. 'I'm kidnapping you.'

Kate was stunned. *Kidnapping her?*

'Everybody else does, so why not me?' he shouted into her ear.

'Oh, Jack, no. Not you, Jack, please, not you,' she cried tremulously. She began to weep.

Appalled, he wrenched the horse to a halt. Awkwardly he slid off it and lifted Kate to the ground. Her legs buckled under her and she crumpled on to the grass. He followed her, gathering her into his arms. 'No, Kate, don't, please don't,' he said brokenly. 'Don't cry, please.'

He pulled out a large handkerchief and clumsily started blotting her cheeks with it. 'Don't cry, sweetheart. I can't bear it if you cry.'

Kate just sobbed harder.

He held her against him, rocking her gently. Finally her sobs shuddered to a halt. He continued to hold her in his lap, her face pressed against his chest, stroking her tumbled hair with a gentle hand.

After a time she pulled away. 'Why?' she whispered.

He took a deep breath and shook his head despairingly. 'I…I just thought that if you really had decided to live in rural obscurity…'

'Go on,' she prompted.

He looked deeply uncomfortable. 'Well…I thought…you might…'

'Might what?' she prompted again.

Suddenly he exploded. 'Well, if you must know, I thought that if you wanted to bury yourself in obscurity the least you could do is do it with me! There, now you have it! I am a despicable rogue, am I not? An arrogant fool, who thought you might consent…'

'Consent to what?' Her heart was thudding uncontrollably. This was the crux of the matter. What had he thought she might be willing to do? Consent to be kidnapped? To be his mistress? His doxy? Consent to have her heart broken?

There was a long silence. Finally he reached into an inner pocket of his coat and drew out a folded document. He stared at it a moment, his mouth twisting ruefully, then tossed it on the grass between them.

'See for yourself. There it is, documentary evidence of what an arrogant, desperate fool I am. Go on, open it, see for yourself. Just don't laugh in my face.'

With shaking fingers Kate reached out and picked up the parchment. Opening it, she read it several times, her mind struggling to come to terms with the meaning of his having obtained this document.

'It is a special licence,' she said at last. 'And not so very new, either.' He'd obtained it before she'd been kidnapped by Jeremiah Cole, Kate realised, with a thrill.

'Yes, fool that I am, I thought I could get you to marry me.' He laughed, a harsh, dry laugh that ended abruptly.

'Why did you not simply ask me?' she said softly.

'Ask you?' His voice was bitter. 'Why ask when there's no possibility of acceptance? What woman would consent to marriage with a fellow like me, a cripple, and a bad-tempered, ugly one to boot? And with barely a penny to my name. What sort of a bargain is that for a woman?'

'Some women might think it a very good bargain.'

He looked at her then. 'Perhaps…if the woman had lost everything—her family, her home, her…her good name. Such a woman might have thought it sufficient. She would have had no other options.'

And yet he'd lent her his family, given her a home and saved her good name. Kate felt a spurt of anger grow inside her. How dared he think himself such a poor bargain? And herself so mercenary!

'But a woman who had been left a fortune?' she said. 'A woman whose good name had been retrieved by a bad-tempered, poverty-stricken cripple—such a woman must needs be tricked, kidnapped, coerced?'

He looked stricken. 'Only because you ran away. You didn't seem to want the London life, so I thought…'

'I came down here to redeem the things I sold when I had no money. Some of my mother's jewellery, my father's books, things like that. Lady Cahill knew that very well. She expects me back on Tuesday. I wasn't running away from anyone or anything. You should know me better than that!'

'I didn't think…' He shrugged despairingly.

'No, you didn't think!' raged Kate. She moved closer and thumped him on the arm. 'You *are* bad-tempered and poor, and also quite stupid! You great brainless clod! You don't talk to me for weeks and weeks—'

'But you wouldn't—'

'—and you glare and spit blue fire at me across crowded dance floors—'

'What do you mean, blue fire?'

Kate ignored that. If he didn't know the power of his beautiful blue eyes, then she wasn't going to enlighten him. She thumped him again, this time on the chest.

'And then you must drag me up on to your poor, smelly…'

'Smelly?' One arm went around her.

'Smelly, exhausted horse in front of men who I've known since I was a child, and then, with not a shred of shame about you, you must kiss me in front of—'

'It seemed to me you were doing a bit of kissing of your own,' he said, catching one small fist as it sailed perilously close to his jaw.

'And then, you great lout, as if that isn't enough, you must bounce me over miles and miles of countryside—'

'And very beautifully you bounce, too,' he interjected wickedly.

'And *then* you decide I don't even deserve the courtesy of a proposal! When I'd already told you I loved you!' She collapsed furiously against his chest with a final thump.

He snatched her away from him and stared into her face.

'You what? You did no such thing!'

She blushed. 'I did too.'

'When?'

She blushed a deeper, rosy pink. 'When I told you I had everything here I wanted.'

He stared at her, dumbfounded. Then his eyes started to twinkle. 'And I was supposed to understand from that that you love me?'

She nodded, embarrassed.

Suddenly he laughed, a joyous ringing laugh. 'Oh, what a clod I am indeed! So clear you made it, and, stupid great lout that I am, I didn't understand!'

'I did kiss you back,' she mumbled, aggrieved.

He stopped laughing and she could feel the warmth of his smile as he leaned close and gathered her back in his arms. Kate wouldn't look at him. 'Yes, you did, didn't you? And very nice it was too.' He bent his head towards her, seeking her lips.

Kate pouted. 'I'm not kissing any horrid kidnapper.'

He laughed and rolled back on to the grass, pulling her down on top of him. 'Then, my little spitfire, will you kindly consent to kiss a man who is utterly mad for love of you? A man who has nothing but his heart and a run-down but very clean house to offer you. And, though he does not deserve you, he asks you most humbly and desperately to be his wife.'

She stared down at him for a moment and Jack was horrified to see tears welling in her beautiful eyes again. 'Oh, no, my love, I'm sorry. Whatever I said or did wrong, I'm sorry. Oh, God, I'm such a clumsy fool, but I love you so much. Oh, Kate, darling, please don't cry.'

The tears dripped harder, landing on his face. He kissed her wet cheeks, her wet eyes, her wet mouth. 'Don't cry, my little love. I can't bear it.'

She looked at him through the shimmering veil of tears. 'I'm sorry…'

His heart contracted unbearably.

'Sorry, Jack, darling… It's just that I'm so happy…' she wailed.

It was so wonderful to be held like this, safe and warm in his arms, her cheek resting against his heart, her head tucked beneath his chin. She rubbed her cheek softly against the rough bristles along his jawline, and sighed with pleasure. She looked up and met his eyes, and the tenderness she saw in them warmed her clear down to her toes. After some time Kate forced herself to push him away. Reluctantly he allowed it. She sat up and straightened her dress. He lay there watching her, a tender, proud smile on his face.

'I've just thought of another reason for you to marry me,' he drawled.

'Hmm?'

'Valet service. I never knew a woman who was so good at getting into a mess,' he chuckled, picking pieces of grass out of her hair. She slapped his hands away and pushed him back on to the ground. Her hands rested on his chest, partly to ensure he kept his distance, partly so she would not lose the contact with his body.

Her face grew serious and her eyes darkened with anxiety. 'I have to ask this, Jack. Do you truly not mind about what happened to me, in Spain?'

His eyes softened. 'On the contrary, I mind it a great deal…but not for the reasons you're worrying about, my love.' He pulled her down into the curve of his body. 'I mind that you were hurt, that you were frightened and abused, that you were hungry and in danger and that you were alone with no one to protect you. I mind that you did not get the support and assistance you needed, that you were subjected to gossip, cruel impertinence and worse. I mind that you came home to nothing and no one, facing destitution, and I mind that to earn a living you had to scrub my floors and put up with my vile temper…'

His voice came to a shaky halt and he held her tight, trembling with emotion. After a time, he stopped shaking, his grip altered and his mouth came down over hers, infinitely gentle, infinitely loving. 'I give you my word, Kate, that you will never again suffer hunger, fear, pain or loneliness, not while I am alive to prevent it. And I vow to dedicate the rest of my life to loving and protecting you.'

She was weak with relief and joy. 'And I to you, my love,' she whispered. It was all she had time to say before his mouth came down over hers again.

After a long, tender interval, he added, 'Besides which, it is my firm belief—' he moved against her in an unmistakably erotic fashion, his face coming alive with wicked humour '—my very firm belief, that virginity has absolutely no place in marriage.'

Distracted by the feelings engendered by his movement, Kate was a little slow in realising his meaning, but gradually she became aware of his wickedly quizzing look, the laughter, and deep, passionate love and acceptance in his eyes. In relief she began to giggle, and his lazy chuckle joined hers as he swept her into his arms and hugged her tightly against him.

After a time, Kate pulled his chin down so she could look him in the eye. There was a hint of mischief in the loving look she gave him. 'So you promise to love and protect me always…'

'Always, sweetheart.'

'And to make sure I never go hungry again?'

'Of course.'

'And kill spiders for me.'

'As many as you want.'

'And never make me scrub your floors.'

'Baggage!' He flicked her nose teasingly. 'If you recall, it was not my idea in the first place.'

She nodded wisely. 'Oh, yes. I recall now. You prefer your floors dirty.'

A low mock-growl and a swift, hard kiss was her only answer.

'And you promise I will never have to put up with your

"vile temper" again?' She reached up and curled a lock of dark hair around and around her finger until it was held tight. She gave it a little tug to make her point.

A baleful look from glittering blue eyes made her giggle.

'That depends,' he said sternly.

'On what, dearest?' she murmured, fluttering her lashes innocently.

'Oh, on such things as whether coffee pots and vases remain on tables or come flying through the air.'

She dimpled. 'Oh, I do not know if I can possibly promise such a thing. Coffee pots are so unpredictable, you know.'

'Mmm,' he agreed dryly. 'I see it will take me at least twenty or thirty years to understand the ways of coffee pots.'

'Oh, no,' she said dulcetly.

He looked quizzically down at her. His heart thudded at the blatant adoration that poured from her eyes.

'Much longer than that, my darling, much, much longer,' she murmured, reaching up and pulling his mouth down to hers.

Epilogue

'Oh, mind you do not drop me, you wretch!'

'Silence, baggage! And stop that infernal wriggling or I will!'

Laughing, Kate was carried over the threshold. Jack kissed her long and hard, and set her on her feet, smiling down at her. His bride of three weeks looked radiant. So radiant, in fact, that he found he had to kiss her again. And then again.

Carlos, Martha, Millie and Florence looked on, beaming. Eventually Kate became aware of their audience. Blushing, she tugged Jack's sleeve and pointed. Immediately they were surrounded by well-wishers.

Refreshments were brought in, congratulations were exchanged and the girls clustered round, admiring Kate's frock. After a time, Martha came forward with a bulky letter, an apologetic look on her face.

'I'm that sorry to interrupt everything, Mr Jack, but this letter has been here for a couple of weeks now and it's been worrying me. It's from London and looks very important.'

Jack took it and turned it over in his hands, frowning.

'From *lawyers!*' said Martha darkly. 'Never any good news from lawyers. Sorry, sir.' She left, ushering the other servants out of the room.

Jack opened it and began to read through the papers. After

a moment he sat down, an odd look on his face. Kate, worried, ran to him.

'What is it, Jack? Is it bad news? It's not your grandmother, is it?'

'No. Not bad news,' said Jack in a strange voice. 'Here, read it for yourself.'

Kate took the sheaf of papers. The first was a letter from a solicitor, saying he had instructions to forward this letter when certain conditions had been met. Kate frowned. It was very puzzling. She turned to the next letter and glanced at the opening.

'Jack!' she gasped.

'Read it out, love,' he said. 'I'm not sure I believe it myself yet.'

Kate read:

Jack, my beloved son,

When you receive this letter, either my lawyers have been convinced that you have finally and irrevocably broken with Julia Davenport, or it is a year and a day since I have died. I hope it is the former.

Either way, you will inherit everything you ever expected to. I never intended you to be poor. My will was a dying man's ploy to free you from That Woman.

My doctors tell me I shall be dead in a matter of weeks, so I have done what I can to give you the best chance of happiness. I know my actions will cause you pain, my son, and I am sorry for it. But I believe it is for the best.

Julia Davenport is a Harpy, Jack, and a Faithless, Greedy Harpy at that. I am counting on her to abandon you when she discovers you inherit nothing. I hope it does not hurt you too badly, my boy.

I hope also that you can forgive my apparent rejection. It is cruel, I know, for you have always been a loving son, even when we quarrelled. But I want so much to see you happy, Jack. There is nothing as important as true

*love—your mother and I were so very happy and my
heart went with her when she died. You are the image of
her, my beloved son, and I know she would never forgive
me if I did not make a push to secure your happiness.*

*Find another woman to love, Jack—one with a true and
loving heart, who will love you for yourself—not for your
fortune or your position. And when you find her, Jack,
marry her at once and never let her go.*

*I will carry five hundred pounds and this damned deed
to Sevenoakes wherever I go from now until my death,
so that you will not find yourself entirely destitute. And I
know your grandmother and sister will look after you.
You are much beloved, my son.*

*I hope you can find it in your heart to forgive a father's
meddling. May God protect you.*

Your loving father...

'Oh, Jack, he did love you after all...' Kate was in tears.

Jack could not reply; he just reached out and gathered her
into his arms. After a long moment he said in a cracked voice,
'I found my true and loving heart, Father. Here she is...'

* * * * *

MR TRELAWNEY'S PROPOSAL
by
Mary Brendan

Mary Brendan was born in North London and lived there for nineteen years before marrying and migrating north into Hertfordshire. She was grammar-school educated and has been at various times in her working life a personnel secretary for an international oil company, a property developer and a landlady. Presently working part-time in a local library, she dedicates hard-won leisure time to antiques browsing, curries and keeping up with two lively sons.

Also by Mary Brendan
in Mills & Boon Historical Romance®

A KIND AND DECENT MAN
THE SILVER SQUIRE
A ROGUISH GENTLEMAN
WEDDING NIGHT REVENGE

Chapter One

1814

'So you are travelling back from visiting your sister in London, Miss Nash,' remarked that unpleasantly soft voice for the second time in five minutes.

'Indeed, yes, I am,' Rebecca Nash agreed, struggling to keep impatience from her voice and revulsion from her eyes as she again raised them from her teacup to glance at the slightly built man sitting opposite her. Having redrawn her attention to himself, Rupert Mayhew lounged his wiry frame back into the battered leather wing-chair.

Rebecca forced a polite smile and tried to prevent her eyes from fixing too obviously on the arrangement of lank, greying strands of hair which threaded across the man's balding pate. At one time he must have had a thatch of gingery-fair hair, she guessed, judging by what remained. The colour would have been similar to those beastly yellow eyes that leeched on to her every movement.

During the twenty minutes or so since she had arrived, whenever she had shifted slightly on the ancient hide wing-chair, a pair with the one in which he was ensconced, his

feline eyes had stared boldly as though anticipating something interesting might be revealed.

Rupert Mayhew slid his scrawny frame forward on his
seat, enquiring solicitiously of the beautiful young woman
opposite, 'And how is your dear sister? And the new babe?
Well, I trust?'

'Thank you, yes,' Rebecca replied civilly, suppressing
the urge to shrink back as he leaned towards her.

'My own dear wife is in the same delicate condition…as
I believe I mentioned in my last letter to you,' he reminded
her with a sly smirk.

This time Rebecca was unable to prevent a tremor of
revulsion, clinking her delicate china cup against its saucer.

'Had she not been indisposed, Caroline would, of course,
have been happy to meet with you today,' Rupert Mayhew
informed her smoothly. 'But we are about to be blessed
with our infant at any time now, so Dr Willis informs me.
So my lady wife is staying with her dear sister in Shoreham
for her confinement.' Yellow eyes slid from Rebecca's face
to craftily linger on the closely buttoned bodice of her
sprigged cotton gown.

The ensuing lengthy silence seemed to be metered by the
sonorous tick of the heavy oaken grandmother clock positioned behind Rupert Mayhew's chair. Rebecca felt her
spine stiffen and her flesh creep. Desperate for casual conversation to distract his hooded, wolfish gaze, she remarked
lightly, 'You must be glad of your stepdaughters' company
while your wife is away. Lucy is fifteen, is she not, and the
younger, Mary…?' She hesitated, expecting him to advise
her of the younger girl's age.

His only response was to mutter on a grunting laugh, 'At
times they have their uses.' His manner and words heightened her uneasiness.

Rebecca replaced her pretty china cup and saucer on a

low table close by. 'I am most grateful for the refreshment, sir, but I really need to be back on the road to Graveley, without delay,' she informed him with a busy, professional tone. 'Perhaps you would discover whether your stepdaughter is now ready to depart. I'm sure you're aware this unseasonable heat makes travelling after noon quite unbearable.'

As though to reinforce her anxieties about the climate, Rebecca dragged her eyes from Rupert Mayhew's sparsely covered head, where they had once again drifted, and stared through the casement window to one side of her.

On this late September morning. the atmosphere glowed bright and lucid, threatening another blazing, sultry afternoon. Her intention to be directly abroad had as much to do with the valid reason voiced as with the desperation to escape this odious man's presence.

Rupert Mayhew's thin visage pinched further. He straightened himself in the chair and leaned stiffly back into it. Bony fingers steepled together and he regarded Rebecca imperiously across them and the hooked bridge of his nose. He obviously had no intention of acceding to her courteous request and wanted her to be aware of it.

It was hard to determine what about him was the most repellent, Rebecca realised: his puny build, his ugly countenance or his objectionable manner. Thank goodness all prior contact had been carried out by letter. Had she previously been subjected to his obnoxious presence, she might well have turned down his application to send his stepdaughter, Lucy, to board at her school. The notion that she could afford to reject custom, however unwelcome, caused a wry smile to escape her.

Misinterpreting this melancholy humour as cordiality, Rupert Mayhew's arrogant bearing relaxed. One blackened tooth was displayed centrally in an otherwise surprisingly clean set as he smiled widely. His eyes narrowed to gleaming yellow dots as he purred insinuatingly, 'You barely look old enough, Miss Nash, to have acquired the teaching experience to which you lay claim.' His unpleasant smile was back as he noticed her reaction.

An attractive blush immediately rimmed Rebecca's high cheekbones, accentuating the sculpted contours of her ivory-skinned oval face. Her youthful looks were a constant source of embarrassment to her. But her chin tilted defensively.

Rupert Mayhew's avid appraisal continued, his beastly eyes targeting full, shapely lips that hinted at a promise of sensuality. A small straight nose was skipped past as he examined a pair of wide, lustrous eyes of the most extraordinary and exquisite colour. He stared into glossy turquoise depths, lushly fringed with lengthy dusky lashes before his voracious interest roved on to her thick dark-gold hair. Loosely wound ringlets dropped to curl like honeyed silk against the crisp sprigged cotton of her serviceable travelling dress.

But for Rupert Mayhew, the most outstanding feature of this delectable young woman was that she chose to earn her living by running a young ladies' academy situated in the backwoods of a small Sussex coastal hamlet. He had travelled widely and visited the fashionable spa towns of Bath and Harrogate, yet he was hard pressed now to recall a face as classically beautiful. Her figure was too slender for his profligate taste. Yet even so, he knew of skinnier wenches who had procured wealthy protectors and opulent lifestyles only dreamed of by most young women in straitened circumstances.

He regretted now not having taken the time to visit her and her poky establishment at Graveley. He knew from the meagre fees she charged that the business she ran must be struggling to survive and had accordingly negotiated even more favourable terms through their correspondence. Rupert Mayhew knew himself for nothing if not an astute businessman.

And he'd imagined her to be some spinsterish bluestocking! Undoubtedly she kept herself hidden away in that wooded copse, for Graveley was little more than that as he recalled from passing through. Or did she? he reflected with quickening pulse, his tongue flicking out to moisten thin lips. She resided on the Ramsden estate. Robin Ramsden was her landlord. He could have hardly overlooked her.

'Wily Old Ram', as he was nicknamed, was reputed to exercise his *droit de seigneur* at every opportunity. The last laundry maid he had impregnated had been ejected from Ramsden Manor and bundled off into a labourer's cottage as second wife and mother to that widower and his brood. Bawdy jesting had abounded amongst Rupert Mayhew and his cronies, especially when gossip had it that the newly wed girl had been sneaked back into the house for a repeat performance. The labourer now, by all accounts, had two brats undeniably resembling the lord of the manor.

His darting, foxy eyes pounced on a glimpse of ankle as Rebecca shifted on her chair. She seemed a haughty chit, though. Perhaps increasing her prospects by lowering her principles—and certain items of clothing, he inwardly smirked—was beneath her. How he'd like her beneath—

'I am twenty-five years old, Mr Mayhew, as I believe I mentioned to you in our earliest correspondence,' Rebecca cut coldly into his lecherous musings, having conquered her indignation. 'I believe my qualifications also met with your approval at that time.'

'My dear Miss Nash, don't feel you have to be defensive with me,' he smugly dismissed, waving a bloodless hand. 'You come most highly recommended. I contacted Mr

Freeman as you suggested I might. He continually regaled me with the successes his daughter has enjoyed since leaving your establishment two summers ago. She has bagged a Viscount as fiancé, no less. Mr Freeman was generous enough to credit your establishment with helping them snare the quarry.'

'I'm pleased to hear—'

Rebecca's mild approval was cut short as Rupert Mayhew interjected bitterly, 'Should you be able to achieve anything similar with the lazy, sullen minx skulking upstairs, I shall be above contentment.'

At the mention of her prospective new pupil, Rebecca stood up with a purposeful finality. A hint of genuine amusement hovered about her full, soft mouth as she was abruptly made aware of two things. Firstly, that her ex-pupil, Alexandra Freeman, a girl of little talent and even less to recommend her in the way of either looks or personality, had done so well for herself. Secondly, that the odious little man, who now rose from his chair to stand over-close to her, had little liking for his eldest stepdaughter. Rebecca sensed an immediate empathy with the fifteen-year-old girl she had yet to meet. Judging by the barely concealed envy in Rupert Mayhew's tone as he recounted Alexandra Freeman's excellent prospects, he was now anticipating some similar good fortune to befall the Mayhews.

'Well, the sooner your stepdaughter and I are able to set upon the road, the nearer we come to achieving your ambitions,' Rebecca announced, striving to banish mockery from her tone.

Rupert Mayhew's ochre eyes were on a level with her own and she was certainly not regarded as tall for her sex. Yet she had misjudged in thinking him perhaps frail. There was a wiry strength about him which was now apparent close up. A squat, corded neck and thick expanse of collar bone were exposed by his open-necked linen shirt. The same sparse greying hair that streaked his scalp poked from the unbuttoned collar.

The weather recently had been uncommonly hot for late September, but even so, she wished he had made some effort to dress in the manner as befitted a wealthy gentlemen farmer in the presence of a lady caller. Perhaps he classed her as just an employee and unworthy of any special considerations. Well, she was just such, she supposed, and the sooner he settled his account for Lucy's board and lessons and the sooner they were on their way to Graveley, the happier she would be.

Rebecca tore her offended gaze away from the coarse hairs sprouting from his throat and distanced herself from him by wandering to the large casement window. She gazed out. Heat was beginning to shimmer across the meadow just glimpsed beyond the formal gardens of Rupert Mayhew's house. A splendid house it was too, she realised, rather forlornly, because its solid graceful character was so at variance with that of its master.

When she had alighted from the London post here in the village of Crosby some forty-five minutes ago, the house's classical porticoed façade set in mellow stonework had seemed welcoming and auspicious. At that time, she had imagined cordial introductions between herself and her new pupil, perhaps an opportunity to discuss with Lucy's fond parents any matters of special interest concerning their daughter's ultimate refinement before she was launched into society. And then they would travel on to the Summer House Lodge, her home for the past five years.

She remembered Rupert Mayhew informing her of his wife's delicate condition. But nothing in any of his correspondence had prepared her for the vile man she had met today. From his letters, she had guessed him to be perhaps a little pompous. And she recalled thinking it a trifle odd that the girl's parents had not taken it upon themselves to visit her establishment to assess its suitability for their daughter. The hamlet of Graveley and the village of Crosby were, after all, barely fourteen miles apart along the coast road. Rupert Mayhew had obviously been content to settle his stepdaughter's future on the strength of his neighbour's success. Rebecca couldn't grumble at that: such recommendations were what kept her small, thriftily run establishment in business. No doubt the low fees she charged had also been a consideration. Rupert Mayhew didn't seem a man generous in spirit or coin.

An abrupt noise from behind splintered Rebecca's musing, jerking her attention from the tranquil garden scene into the spartanly furnished parlour. Rupert Mayhew was overlooked as Rebecca gazed towards the polished mahogany door which now gaped wide on its hinges.

The auburn-haired young lady who slouched in its opening was quite lovely, despite the aggressive glower, the sulky, slanted mouth and the livid purple bruising which shadowed one sapphire eye.

Luke Trelawney's dark head fell forward to momentarily rest in his cupped hands before long, blunt fingers threaded through thick, raven hair, drawing it away from his damp forehead. He jerked himself back against the uncomfortable squabs of the hired travelling coach and swore. An irritated flick of a glance took in the sun-yellowed grassy banks along the road side as a dark hand moved to release yet more mother-of-pearl buttons, hidden among the snowy ruffles of his lawn shirt.

'If you're intending supping at the Red Lion naked to the waist, don't expect me to protect your honour,' Ross Trelawney remarked with a grin from the opposite side of the coach. He nevertheless followed his handsome older brother's lead and loosened his upper torso from the clinging confines of a perspiration-soaked shirt.

'Infernal weather,' Luke Trelawney growled. 'That damned fool of a coachman must have taken a wrong turn. He promised us this Red Lion inn was within spitting distance some ten miles back. If we're not upon it soon, I'm out and walking.' Another black glance took in the arid scenery, scorched by a lengthy summer parched of rain, before he relented and half-smiled at his younger brother. 'I told you we should have used one of my coaches...at least we could have roasted in comfort. The springs in this contraption are more out of the seat than in it.'

Ross grimaced a wry apology at his older sibling, aware of his exasperation and the reason for it.

Luke Trelawney was one of the largest landowners in Cornwall. He owned Melrose, a magnificent house set in parkland. He owned an impressive fleet of traders sailing from the port of Bristol and mining interests closer to home in Cornwall. Today, however, the most piquant irony was derived from the fact that the coach house at Melrose was filled with every type of conveyance any gentleman was ever likely to need. The estate also boasted stables full of thoroughbred horseflesh the equal of any aristocrat's equine collection. And it had been Ross who had persuaded Luke to hire a coach for this journey...just for the hell of it, he had said. And hell it had been...complete with furnace. For himself, though, ever seeking just another untasted experience, he rather enjoyed the beggarly novelty of it all.

He looked across at his brother, scowling at passing scenery again, irritation distorting his narrow yet sensuously curved mouth.

Luke had strived to provide himself with the very best. As the oldest son of Jago and Demelza Trelawney he had, on their father's death, taken that gentleman's sizable bequest and increased it a thousandfold. He now had wealth and reputation that no other Cornish landowner could match. There were other things they would certainly never equal, Ross realised wryly: his astounding dark good looks; his eligibility, which had every hopeful mama, trailing nubile daughters, visiting their mother and sister under any ridiculous pretext they could deviously devise. And all to no avail for, at thirty-two, Luke had resisted all temptations, threats and ludicrously transparent plots to hook him.

Ross dwelt on Wenna Kendall, with some relish and not a little envy. The voluptuous dark-haired mistress Luke had installed in fine style in Penzance obviously satisfied him physically, but emotionally...? He gazed at the side of Luke's lean, tanned face, still idly turned towards the uninspiring passing scenery. Emotions were not something often associated with his older brother. They were kept tightly reined, as controlled as every other aspect of his life. Their father's death some eleven years ago was the last time he could recall witnessing Luke in distress. Apart from that, family problems, business pressures, all were dealt with in the same calm, disciplined way.

But he knew how to enjoy himself...as all Trelawney males did. Roistering bouts of drinking and wenching were a regular part of life, so long as business never suffered. And dependable Luke was always there to ensure it certainly never did. Status and wealth were Luke's motivation and priority.

An urgent solicitor's letter, hand-delivered from Bath, had set Luke on the road, unwillingly and with many a curse, but it had moved him as Ross had known it would. For Luke never shirked his responsibilities, even those that disturbed memories of generation-old family rifts. But that estrangement was of little consequence to the present Tre-lawney clan.

Ross had decided to go along for the ride and to alleviate the insatiable restlessness that dogged him. Melrose had been left in the capable hands of their imperturbable brother Tristan who, at thirty, happily married and living on the Trelawney estate, was the most sensible choice. Being second eldest also made him natural deputy, Ross always thought, when justifying his need to slope off, courting fresh excitement.

Besides, Luke had made it clear the matter was to be dealt with as expediently as possible with a quick return to Cornwall. Luke had neither the time nor inclination to linger in rural Brighton once business was satisfactorily settled.

Luke relaxed back into the battered squabs. He withdrew a half-sovereign from a pocket and tossed it in his palm a few times. The pair of nags doing their best to convey the ancient coach towards Brighton was increasing pace: a sure sign that, having travelled the route many times, they recognised water and sustenance were soon to be had. 'A half-sovereign says we reach this dive within five minutes,' he challenged his younger brother, stretching long, muscular legs out in front of him and flexing powerful shoulders in an attempt to ease niggling cramps.

'Three minutes,' countered Ross, as aware as Luke of the horses' renewed efforts. They were fairly bowling along now.

Five minutes later the rickety coach swung abruptly left and into the dusty courtyard of the Red Lion inn.

'Order up whatever they've got that's long, cool…' Luke hesitated, noting the direction of Ross's gaze, which had, on alighting, immediately been drawn to a titian-haired tavern wench '…and comes in a tankard,' he finished drily.

'See what sort of food they've got about the place too,' he said but with little enthusiasm, as cynical peat-brown eyes roved the dirty, whitewashed building.

The seedy-looking Jacobean hostelry was nevertheless a hive of activity. Well situated along the coastal road to refresh those travelling from the west country towards the fashionable gathering place of Brighton, it attracted the patronage of both farmer and gentleman alike.

Luke glanced around in cursory fashion. A coach, displaying an Earl's coat of arms, protected its glossy paintwork beneath the shade of a massive spreading oak on the perimeter of the courtyard.

Two young ladies, elegantly and coolly dressed in pastel muslin, sat, with parasols twirling, beneath the shielding canopy of boughs on a spread tartan travelling rug. Their coy attention was with Ross and himself. Aware of his observation, their daintily coiffured heads collided as they chattered and giggled, parasols whirling faster. He glanced away, feeling unaccountably irritated. The fact that Ross was now torn between giving them or the flame-haired serving girl the benefit of his hazel-eyed silent charm irked him further.

Not that he was unused to female interest: all Trelawney males had the tall, dark good looks women seemed to find hard to resist. He knew without particular conceit or satisfaction that due to his superior height, and the classical set of his features, framed by a mass of thick, jet-black hair, he, more than any, was most sought after. His looks, coupled with his status and wealth, ensured a limitless supply of eager women. Thus the need for charm or seduction was rarely required for amorous conquests. When the mood or need took him, therefore, he seldom bothered with either, exploiting his attractiveness and willing partners to the full. Occasionally, acknowledging this callousness made him uneasy. Why the sight of two simpering debutantes at a strange tavern on a blazing afternoon should induce one of those conscience-ridden moments he had no idea, and it only served to needle him further.

He kicked at the parched, powdery gravel beneath one dusty Hessian boot and looked down the two or more inches at the top of Ross's sun-glossed chestnut head. He smiled slowly, consciously lightening his exasperation which he knew had much to do with the unwanted responsibility that brought him to this neck of the woods. He inwardly cursed all the Ramsdens to perdition as his businessman's brain sorted through all he'd left in abeyance at Melrose and all that awaited him at Brighton. He clicked his fingers in front of Ross's line of vision, redrawing his brother's attention to himself.

'I'll visit the stables and see what sort of horseflesh they've got on offer. I'd sooner ride a farm hack the remaining miles to Westbrook than set foot back in that boneshaking contraption.'

'If she dunt wanta move then she dunt and she wunt,' the old man announced morosely, nodding sagely, yet eying the horse with what seemed to Rebecca like any amount of satisfaction.

'Can't you coax her a bit?' Rebecca suggested with a wheedling smile at the squint-eyed old groom, as her lacy scrap of handkerchief again found its way to her perspiring brow.

'Just beat the stupid animal,' was Lucy Mayhew's heartless instruction to the granite-faced old retainer, who served as a stablehand for her stepfather now that advancing years had numbered his farm-labouring days. Bert Morris stared straight ahead not deigning to react at all to this outrageous proposal of treatment for his old Bessy. He fished in his shirt pocket, removed a clay pipe and began to stuff the bowl of it with some foul-looking dried grass extracted from the same source.

Rebecca alighted nimbly from the one-axle carriage and immediately flexed her cramped limbs. The worn benchseat was barely wide enough for two people travelling in comfort. For three packed close together in this stifling early afternoon heat, it was unbearable. The fact that Bert Morris smelled as though he not only groomed but slept amongst his treasured horses had largely added to the discomfort.

Rebecca bestowed a sympathetic look on the exhausted elderly mare who refused to travel up the steep wooded incline towards the Summer House Lodge in the hamlet of Graveley. As though aware of observation, the animal swayed her head round. Such solemn, apologetic eyes, Rebecca thought, before she lifted her face towards the breeze, closed her eyes and, momentarily, savoured the wonderfully refreshing sensation. Soft cooling air disturbed honeygold hair clinging in damp tendrils to her slender, graceful neck. Then she gazed up into the carriage where the old man smoked stoically, apparently undisturbed either by circumstances or the heat. Lucy Mayhew returned her a sullen look, swiping a careless hand across her forehead to remove beading perspiration.

'We can walk from here,' Rebecca encouraged her with a smile. 'It's barely a quarter of a mile and mostly through woodland. The shade will be delightfully cool and most welcome.' She anticipated objection but Lucy had gathered up her cotton floral gown in eager hands and jumped from the carriage in a trice.

Rebecca reached up behind the benchseat, grasping her own and Lucy's travelling carpet bags. Old Bert Morris stirred himself enough then to aid her attempts at unwedging them, dropping them carelessly to the dusty ground.

'You will ensure that the trunks are delivered as soon as possible?' Rebecca enquired of the old man. He grunted some unintelligible noise past the pipe clenched in stained teeth which she took to be an affirmative.

Rupert Mayhew had testily decreed that a carpet bag of essentials must suffice today and the trunks be forwarded later in the week. Had they travelled in a sturdier carriage pulled by an energetic pair they could have brought all with them and would now be alighting at the familiar white-boarded doorway of her Summer House Lodge.

Without another word, Bert Morris clicked encouragement at the tired mare to back step along the narrow path. The animal did so with amazing briskness, considering its previous lethargy. Soon the small trap had turned in the clearing and was making good progress back towards the village of Crosby.

With a smile at her new charge, Rebecca directed brightly, 'Now you take one of the handles to your bag, Lucy, and I shall take the other. Thus we can share the load as we walk, for the woodland path is a little on an incline.'

'What of your bag?' Lucy asked doubtfully. 'Will you manage that too?'

'There's little in it,' Rebecca reassured her with a smile, surprised and heartened by the girl's concern. Lucy had hitherto on the hour-long journey from Crosby displayed nothing apart from a scowling profile and a great reluctance to be drawn into any light conversation. Uncomfortable silence had been the prevailing feature of the journey: the blistering heat and her travelling companions equally to blame.

Rebecca stole a quick glance at her new pupil, trying to ascertain her mood. Lucy's small hand was fastened on the crown of her poke bonnet, shielding her face from the sun's fierce rays as she dragged her bag across shrivelled yellow grass. Rebecca took the same sensible precaution, settling her own straw headgear firmly on her golden head.

With an encouraging smile, Rebecca lead the way towards the cool, inviting wooded pathway.

Rebecca sensed that the girl now might chat, but her attention was sidetracked by the painful-looking bruising shadowing one of Lucy's eyes. An aged yellowing could be glimpsed amongst the fresh purple and Rebecca's heart went out to the young girl.

Lucy informed her abruptly, 'He did it…but you know that, don't you.'

'I guessed…yes, that your stepfather must have chastised you.'

'Chastised me?' Lucy repeated with a sneer coarsening her voice. 'I don't mind it when he hits me,' she muttered vehemently before changing the subject abruptly. 'Do you always collect your new pupils from their homes? I would have imagined you to be too busy. Where are the other pupils? Who's looking after them?' she ran on, barely pausing for breath.

'Well,' Rebecca began, troubled by Lucy's attitude to her stepfather but glad she displayed an interest in her fellow pupils, 'to answer the first part of your question: No, I rarely collect my pupils from their homes. They are usually delivered to the Summer House by their parents. But while my school has been closed for the summer months… There,' she interrupted herself, 'I have answered the second part of your question first. The school has been closed since July and the boarders now gone. I have only a very small school premises and board only one or, at the most, two girls at a time. You will be boarding alone. But there are day pupils too,' Rebecca hastily added, keen to let Lucy know she would have company and perhaps make friends. 'I have spent two months in London, visiting my elder sister. Elizabeth has recently been blessed with her first-born son and invited me to stay with her for company while she was confined.' And a little fetching and carrying, Rebecca could have added but didn't and felt uncharitable for even thinking it. 'Since I was travelling back through Crosby today, I informed your stepfather that it would be no hardship to break my journey and collect you.'

Lucy was gazing around at tangled undergrowth during this explanation. She abruptly threw back her brunette head, scouring the canopy of shivering greenery entwined above them. 'It's very quiet,' she breathed conspiratorially.

'And very refreshing after the heat on the road,' Rebecca commented.

A magpie flew with a raucous cry between treetops, contradicting Lucy's words. Within seconds its colourful mate joined it in the whispering foliage.

'That's an auspicious sign. Sighting a pair of magpies signifies good fortune, Lucy. You shall obviously enjoy great success at the Summer House,' Rebecca said lightly with no thought for her own future. Her aqua eyes fixed on the birds as she recited softly, 'One for sorrow, two for joy...'

Rebecca's vague smile faded as she noticed the poignancy on her young companion's face: a wistful mingling of misery and hope.

Aware of observation, Lucy became petulant. 'I've never been superstitious,' she sneered, pointedly turning her face away from Rebecca. The bag held between them swung savagely before Lucy dropped her side to the ground. She stalked off and started exploring the perimeter of matted undergrowth.

'I'm hot and thirsty,' she flung back over her floral cotton shoulder. Yanking at the ribbons beneath her chin, she carelessly flung her bonnet down on to peaty ground. Plump fingers raked through her thick, auburn hair, lifting it away from her neck. Then she swirled around, holding the skirt of her pretty, summer dress away from her warm legs.

The two bags Rebecca held slid to the ground and she sighed. It was still hot and sticky, even within this shielding woodland, and she had to admit that she too was thirsty.

'We can have a short rest, if you like.' Following Lucy's example, she undid the ribbons on her own straw hat. Golden tendrils of hair were loosened from her moist neck by a pale hand. 'There's a pretty pond close by, to your left a bit. We could sit there a while.

It was a sizable pond too. Fed from a spring as well as from the tinkling stream that ran through the gully from the hamlet of Graveley, it retained depth and clarity, despite the recent hot, dry weather. 'Not that you can slake your thirst there, of course,' Rebecca cautioned with a smile. 'I've seen all manner of creatures in the water.'

Lucy managed a weak grin at this. She wordlessly demonstrated her agreement by catching hold of the handle of her bag.

'I shall tell you a bit about Lord Ramsden, our landlord, while we rest.' Rebecca offered conversationally. 'He resides at Ramsden Manor in the village of Westbrook, which adjoins Graveley. The Summer House Lodge is part of his estate. A very good and kind landlord he is too,' she praised him unreservedly, as she led the way off the main track.

They threaded their way gingerly through creeping undergrowth. 'Take care your gown doesn't snag. There are some brambles concealed amongst the ferns,' Rebecca cautioned Lucy.

A musical sound of running water became audible. Rebecca pushed aside the last of the pliant branches that barred their way and they stood in a picturesque rough-grassed glade, a large pond situated centrally.

A small sound of delight burst from Lucy. She immediately relinquished her side of the bag again, but before she rushed away Rebecca received an apologetic smile. Reaching the bank of the pond on fleet feet she called back, 'Look, a toad, there on the water lilies.'

Rebecca nodded and smiled, repressing a shudder at the sight of the enormous speckled creature. She knew all manner of wildlife took refuge in this quiet oasis. She had often sought its soothing sanctuary herself in the past when needing privacy and solitude.

Lucy slipped her soft shoes off and Rebecca enjoyed a pleasant, relaxed moment before it dawned on her that the girl was, incredibly, intending to wade out to fetch the creature. No doubt that sort of slimy beast was preferable to the one Lucy was obliged to share a home with, Rebecca surmised with a sigh.

'Lucy…come back at once,' Rebecca admonished, threat and plea mingling in her voice as the girl eagerly hitched up her skirt and inched forward into the still green depths of the pond.

Lucy's high-pitched giggle was all the response Rebecca received. Anxiously watching Lucy's painstaking progress towards the glossy flat-leaved lilies was nerve-racking. Foreboding was taking hold of her with a vengeance. The uneasiness that she had experienced earlier that day with Rupert Mayhew returned to haunt Rebecca. She was becoming certain she would have fared better without this family's patronage. She was an accomplished tutor and took pride in what she achieved with her students, but so far Lucy's moods had been totally unfathomable and unpredictable. At times her conduct and attitude seemed completely inappropriate. Disciplining her might prove impossible.

Sensing danger, the toad dived into the still surface of the pond.

'Come back now, Lucy,' Rebecca ordered firmly, an icy prickling stalking her spine, as she noticed the girl's dress dragging in the water.

In response, Lucy ducked herself down in the water, submerging up to the shoulders. She twirled about, and gaily coaxed, 'Come in…it's so cool.'

'Come back here this minute, Lucy,' Rebecca bit out through clenched teeth, her heart now in her mouth. She knew the pond was quite deep towards the centre. Her worst fears were realised when Lucy suddenly shrieked and slipped backwards, thrashing her arms.

Without further conscious thought, yet inwardly cursing, Rebecca sped to the pond and began wading, skirt gripped high about her thighs, towards the struggling girl. As she approached, Lucy surfaced, giggling. 'See…I told you it was refreshing. It's better than the spa at Bath. It's better than sea bathing at Brighton. Have you swum in the sea at Brighton?' she demanded gaily, splashing water at Rebecca's still relatively dry figure.

Rebecca gathered her skirts into a clenched hand. The other covered her face, clearing pond water and shielding the raging fury and utter disbelief contorting her delicate features. Had Lucy been within reach, she would have shaken her until her teeth rattled and her stupid, selfish head fell off.

'Well, what have we here?' came a sardonic male voice. 'Water sprites? Woodland elves? A welcome diversion?'

Chapter Two

The ironic well-modulated voice had Rebecca swirling unsteadily around.

Two strangers were watching their antics from the pond bank mere yards away. Rebecca felt her heart pumping painfully as she hurriedly smeared filming pond residue from her vision. Then she stared, horrified.

One man sat astride a grey farm horse, the other was lounging comfortably against the bole of a centuries-old oak, and was the most handsome man she had ever before seen in her life. His long, thick hair appeared jet-black beneath the shading oak. His narrow mouth was curved a little with the same mocking humour that had tinged his words, for she knew instinctively that it was he who had spoken. Peat-dark eyes were heavy-lidded and fixed on her with the same intensity that she watched him. In one hand he idly held the reins of a second rather mangy-looking horse, placidly cropping the rough grass. As his lazy gaze lowered to slowly survey her drenched form, her fists abruptly opened, dropping her thigh-high skirts into the water.

Rebecca closed her gritty, stinging eyes momentarily in utter despair. Why did disasters invariably always cluster together? Why would they never spread themselves out a bit in her life? This was too much for one day! Thank heavens five years had lapsed since she had last endured times such as this, crammed with alarm and anxiety.

The stranger astride the horse, who had fairer colouring and looked to be younger by some years, laughed down at his broad-shouldered companion and exchanged a few quiet words. Earthy eyes skimmed to her sodden bodice and aquamarine eyes lowered there too. The thin wet cotton was almost transparent and clung to her bosom like a second skin. As her breasts hardened with shame and her nipples stung she instinctively closed screening arms about herself.

She remembered Lucy, positioned somewhere behind her. Her pupil's safety and well being were now her responsibility. Through the girl's stupid recklessness they now found themselves stranded in soaked clothes that served only to display every feminine contour they were designed to cover. They were in the densest part of the wood, still a good way from home, with two complete strangers witnessing their discomfort.

She had never seen either of them before. She would have remembered if she had. Both were memorably good looking but the powerfully built, darker man was quite ridiculously so. She was acquainted with most people in the small communities of Graveley, Westbrook and the immediate surrounding areas. These two were probably just passing through. They might be miscreants…

The disturbing possibility possessed her abruptly, monopolising every thought. Why were they off the main track and in private woodland? Why were they dressed in finely tailored black breeches and white lawn shirts but, confusingly, in possession of horses that looked little better than tired farm hacks? She had heard fearsome gossip about young village women being mistreated by bored gentlemen out looking for diversion. Even as she thought the word, she recalled him uttering it, and her temples hammered as blood surged through her veins.

The hideous danger in their predicament forced itself mercilessly upon her and she twisted towards Lucy, wanting to reassure the girl. The expression on her young pupil's face was the most daunting aspect of the whole nightmare situation. Excited interest was darkening and widening Lucy's blue eyes as she ignored Rebecca and stared at the strangers on the bank.

'Who are you? Why are you trespassing?' Rebecca demanded tremulously of the man who still relentlessly watched her. Before he could reply she swivelled away, aware of Lucy approaching her through the water. She believed the girl to be seeking her closenesss for safety, but Lucy made to glide straight past. Catching at one of Lucy's wet arms she attempted to detain her in the pond. Should the need arise for physical protection it would be far better to be close together. Lucy impatiently slipped her arm through Rebecca's cold, stiff fingers and swayed herself forward. As she approached dry land, her plump arms raised and the movement caused her precociously curvaceous body to be quite deliberately outlined as she slowly wrung out her dripping dark hair.

Rebecca watched in horrified embarrassment as Lucy brushed closely past the tall, athletic figure leaning against the tree. A slight deepening of the cynical smile curving his mouth was the only reaction. His eyes remained with Rebecca. She watched anxiously as the younger man dismounted, his eyes following Lucy's hip-swinging progress.

Fury and humiliation engulfed her. It made her wrap her arms tighter about herself and snap out, albeit it tremulously, 'I asked you who you are and what you are doing here.'

The raven-haired man shoved himself away from the ancient oak then and walked the few paces to the pond. 'Are you intending to stay in there?' That deep, sardonic voice caused Rebecca to involuntarily shiver and take a step back. She attempted to dart a glance past him, desperate to see Lucy's continuing safety from his companion.

'I asked you who you are.' She challenged in a fierce shaky whisper.

Her simultaneous fear and courage erased his amusement. 'Well, why don't you come here and perhaps I'll tell you,' he cut soothingly into her unsteady speech. He extended a lean, tanned hand towards her. When she still didn't move but merely stared at it, he beckoned peremptorily.

Remaining there like a fool to defy him was, she knew, ridiculous. She forced her boneless legs forward but chose to ignore his offer of aid. She scrambled up the bank, slithering a little as her sodden skirt hampered her, and belatedly, gratefully, sought his hand, preventing herself sliding back.

A warm, firm grip pulled her to within a few inches of his tall, spare body and she could feel the heat of him warming her chilled form. Without meeting his eyes, she quickly disengaged her hand, mumbled her thanks and then felt churlish and cowardly. Besides, she wanted so much to look at him more closely. She drew a silent, steeling breath and forced herself to slowly raise her damp gold head in a semblance of pride and confidence.

Turquoise eyes fused with dark brown for a timeless moment. She wasn't mistaken. He was as exceptionally handsome as she had thought. No warts, moles or pockmarks to mar the lightly bronzed angular planes of his face. His hair was as glossy and pitch black as it had seemed when he lounged beneath the shading oak. A small crescent-shaped

scar by one thick dark brow was an imperfection yet it only
served to enhance the beautifully piratical air about him.

'Thank you for your aid, sir,' she said, striving to casually modulate her tone. But she knew she had failed miserably when one side of his sculpted, narrow mouth lifted
in a vestige of returning amusement.

'Do you often wade fully clothed into woodland ponds?
Is it a local custom of sorts?' he teased, the humour in his
eyes strengthening as they roved her damp and tousled dark
honey hair.

Rebecca raised an impulsive hand to her unruly locks,
realising just what a fright she must look. She stepped away
from him hurriedly, aware that his outstanding attractiveness made her feel even more bedraggled than she probably
was. She averted her crimsoning face from sepia-coloured
eyes knowing she could do nothing to conceal her accen-
tuated silhouette from his heavy-lidded scrutiny. She hastened towards Lucy who stood idly sliding bold glances at
his companion from beneath moisture-spiky lashes.

Rebecca hastily grabbed up Lucy's carpet bag from the
ground and with shaking fingers pulled the clasp apart. She
grabbed at the dry garments within and brusquely shook
them out. She thrust a plain lemon day dress at Lucy, snapping in a vehement undertone, 'Hold this in front of you.'
The undiluted anger in Rebecca's voice and the icy sparks
in her turquoise eyes made Lucy wordlessly do as she was
bid. Removing a dress in the same way from her own carpet
bag, Rebecca finally spun back towards the two men. She
gulped another calming breath and even managed a wavering smile.

'Thank you once more for your aid. But if you would
now be so kind…my pupil and I need to dry ourselves after
our mishap. I'm sure you wouldn't want either of us to take
a chill…' Her voice trailed off as she watched a tanned,

squarish jaw set as he realised he was being summarily dismissed.

'I thought you were keen to know who I am,' he drily reminded her.

'It matters little,' Rebecca rebuffed him, nevertheless managing a small, conciliatory smile. She was quite astonishing herself, accomplishing this sham composure. It disintegrated with equally astounding ease as he commenced strolling towards them. She spontaneously stepped protectively in front of Lucy, and her dress, gripped in white-knuckled hands, was raised a little.

He hesitated and seemed momentarily undecided before changing direction, gathering the reins of his grazing horse, and mounting the beast in a swift athletic movement. He sat thoughtfully considering her before suggesting soothingly, 'Perhaps you'd care to tell me who you are then, as you appear to have lost interest in my identity…Miss…?'

'Certainly, sir,' Rebecca agreed, compelling herself to sound polite and confident. 'My name is Nash…Rebecca Nash. And this is Miss Mayhew…a pupil from my school at the Summer House Lodge. We are returning there directly. It is barely a few minutes' walk away,' she lied for good measure, 'on Lord Ramsden's estate.'

His eyes narrowed instantly at this information and she caught the younger man darting a swift, searching look at him.

'I should warn you,' Rebecca informed helpfully, when he made no move to depart, 'that Lord Ramsden prosecutes all trespassers. He has a reputation for dealing harshly with all such. You really should leave now before his gamekeeper happens upon you.' She seized upon the idea at once, a relieved breath breaking from between her bloodless, trembling lips. 'The gamekeeper…keepers, for there are several,' she lied again, 'scour these woods ceaselessly for poachers…'

His spontaneous smile at this local news made her blush hotly. She was sure he was about to call her bluff.

'You think I'm a poacher?' he enquired softly. 'Do I look like a poacher?'

'It matters not how you look,' she countered sharply. 'Williams is apt to shoot first and examine you later.'

'Williams?' he mildly queried.

'Lord Ramsden's gamekeeper,' she explained. 'Please, sir. If you and your companion would be so kind…' She snatched a searching glance at Lucy who was shivering and now looking as though one of her dejected moods was taking a grip. 'My pupil needs to dry herself and you should make haste to depart. Believe me when I say if you are discovered you will be prosecuted.'

'And what do you suppose…' he paused '…Lord Ramsden's reaction is to you trespassing in his pond?' he persisted silkily, as he controlled his restless mount with a cursory flick of the hand.

Rebecca gave a short, dismissive laugh. 'Lord Ramsden and I are well acquainted,' she informed him with a deal of satisfaction. 'I have no fears on that score.'

This confident declaration drew an amused snort from the younger man. He appeared about to speak but a swift, silencing gesture from his darker companion made him simply shake his head disbelievingly and examine the leaves that sighed above him.

'Lord Ramsden doesn't frighten you?' the dark man suggested with a half-smile as he nudged the horse slowly forward.

'Not at all,' Rebecca confirmed, shifting slowly to keep him in sight and Lucy positioned behind her, as he approached. She sensed a new, disturbing undercurrent to their exchange.

'Good,' was his brief, dulcet response as he reined in close and looked down at her in the same thoughtfully amused way.

He extended a dark hand towards her in the gesture of one wishing to shake hands before departing. Clutching her shielding garment in front of her in one, she politely offered her other pale, slender hand to him.

'Luke Trelawney and my brother Ross…at your service,' he introduced them both as his warm fingers retained her cool ones in his firm grip. A dark thumb traced the delicate skin of her palm in a careful, camouflaged caress as he reluctantly relinquished it.

'Mr. Trelawney…' Rebecca courteously acknowledged, with a small dip of her head, as his horse passed her. She nodded civilly to Ross also as he followed Luke.

Rebecca's eyes stayed unwaveringly with them until they had disappeared from view, when they closed in utter thankfulness.

As the two cart horses started an ambling trot down the grassy bank towards the track that lead to Westbrook, Ross grunted a low, lascivious laugh. 'I'm most definitely at her service. Servicing that wench would be no hardship—'

Luke pulled his horse up sharp and swung about in the saddle. His perfect features were savage as he ground out, 'Touch her and I'll—' The fierce caution ceased mid-flow. He was as aware as Ross of what he had astonishingly been about to threaten.

'—be most put out,' he remedied, relaxing a little. But a wry grimace was the closest he got to apology…or to analysing his aggression, before he urged his lumbering nag into something approaching a canter.

*   *   *

Rebecca gently disengaged herself from the grey-haired woman's firm embrace. 'It's good to be home, Martha,' she greeted her with a sweet smile as the woman dabbed at her eyes with her grubby starched apron. 'Hush,' Rebecca soothed. 'I've only been gone just four weeks. I'll wager you've hardly missed me at all,' she teased. She contentedly surveyed the familiar pristine interior of her kitchen at the Summer House. Everything looked as meticulously ordered as it always did when Martha Turner was in attendance.

Martha and her husband Gregory lived in a tiny spartan dwelling, on the perimeter of the woodland Rebecca and Lucy had just traversed. Their cottage was situated barely a stone's throw from the Summer House, easily within walking distance for the elderly couple who made the journey each day.

While Martha prepared meals and cleaned, generally helping Rebecca run the household, her husband coaxed the sizeable vegetable patch situated along the western flank wall into providing Rebecca and her boarding pupils with fresh produce. Gregory Turner also tended the few chickens and geese they kept with the same natural diligence, ensuring his wife always had fresh eggs and poultry available to prepare nourishing fare.

The Turners' property, which had been settled on them by Robin Ramsden on their retirement from his service, had very little tillable land surrounding it. Woodland predominated on three sides, rendering it picturesque but poorly self-sufficient. In a way this unfortunate situation had benefited Rebecca and she often felt ashamed acknowledging it. She was well aware that she would never have been able to pay this dear couple for their aid. But she could offer an arrangement whereby, in return for housekeeping and gardening services, the Turners helped themselves to whatever surplus eggs, poultry and fresh fruit and vegetables the Summer House gardens produced.

Approaching the large floury patch on the scrubbed pine table, Rebecca idly dusted her arms free of pastry traces from Martha's welcoming hands. She peered at the mouth-watering sweet and savoury ingredients assembled for supper. As her stomach gurgled a little, she realised just how hungry she was. She had eaten nothing since departing from the King's Head hostelry early that morning at Guildford, when setting out on the last leg of her journey home.

Martha's silver-bright eyes were crinkle-cornered as she regarded Lucy, standing subdued and quiet by the open kitchen door. Her smile faltered a little and Rebecca knew Martha was focussing on the bruising about Lucy's eye. As she noted Martha's troubled reaction to the injury, she finally relented and gave Lucy a small smile.

It was the first token of friendship she had felt capable of bestowing on the girl following the fiasco at the woodland pool. She was still in equal parts furious and bewildered by Lucy's behaviour.

Having both changed hastily into dry dresses, their final trek through the woods had passed in strained, chilly silence. Rebecca had decided that until her anger was again under control, it was best to keep quiet and keep walking lest she say or do something she might regret. But every speedy step taken had been filled with an inner wrangling about whether to contact Lucy's stepfather to ask him to fetch her. The fact that her meagre income would be again reduced, leaving her in severe financial difficulties, had been the only consideration in the girl's favour. As she looked at Lucy now and met those injured blue eyes, Rebecca sensed a niggling sympathy. Lucy seemed resigned to being rejected.

'This is Lucy…Lucy Mayhew, who is going to be joining us for a while,' Rebecca introduced her, with a strengthening smile for Lucy. 'Lucy, Martha and her husband Gregory have been giving me invaluable help here at the Summer House over the past five years.' Trying to lighten their moods, she indicated Martha's laden table. 'Martha's cooking is delicious, Lucy, it is very easy to over-indulge.' Lucy gave the cook a shy smile before perching demurely on a kitchen chair and gazing interestedly about.

Such a picture of youthful innocence, Rebecca couldn't help ironically surmising. But she cheered herself with again acknowledging just how fortunate she had been since the double tragedy of her parents' and fiancé's deaths some five years ago. At that time, circumstances had conspired to make a future in harsh employment or marriage to the first man to offer for her seem the only avenues. Instead, she now had a kind and generous landlord, friendship and aid from the Turners and also from dear friends who lived close by. But, most of all, she had this small, pretty Summer House, providing her with home and employment. She sighed her contentment, acknowledging that she would persevere with Lucy's education.

Martha fetched a stone jug from the dark pantry and set about filling two glasses with aromatic lemonade. Rebecca smiled her thanks, determined not to let this afternoon's humiliating episode spoil her pleasure at being home. Consciously recalling the incident allowed raven hair and earthy dark eyes to once more dominate her thoughts, but only momentarily before she determinedly banished them.

Luke Trelawney disturbed her by fascinating her far too much. But he had now gone and she would never again see him or his brother Ross. The strange bittersweet pang tightening her chest at that certainty made her fingers instinctively seek the large silver locket she wore. She could feel its warm, solid shape beneath her cotton dress. Her fingers smoothed its oval silhouette as she held on to the dear memory of David, her mourned fiancé.

'I knew you'd be wanting some lemonade. I made that fresh this morning.' Martha broke into her wistful reverie, arms crossing contentedly as she watched the two young women draining their tumblers. 'I knew you'd be along and hot and thirsty,' she emphasised with a wag of the head. 'Mind you,' she cautioned, rolling her sleeves back to her elbows before expertly pummelling the dough on the table. 'Mind you...' she repeated for good measure '...Gregory reckons that rain is on the way at last and you know he's rarely wrong.' Her head bobbed again as deft hands rolled the pastry into a ball. 'His legs have been playing up bad again...a sure sign o' wet on the way...biscuits are nearly done,' she tacked incongrously on the end. 'I can smell them coming along nicely.' She smiled at Lucy. 'I reckon a healthy young lady like you can polish off quite a few before her dinner.'

Lucy nodded, settling expectantly back into her chair like a biddable child. Watching her, Rebecca wondered how she could veer so rapidly between wanton sophistication and childlike innocence. But if what Gregory predicted was true and rain was on its way, she had pressing matters to attend to. She replaced her tumbler on the table.

'Has John fixed the roof while I've been away, Martha?' she enquired anxiously, remembering Robin Ramsden's promise that he would send his young carpenter to repair some summer storm damage.

'No...we've seen not hide nor hair of that young man. Gregory was going to attempt it hisself...but his affliction in the knees meant he could barely rise up three rungs of the ladder.'

'Is Lord Ramsden returned yet from Bath?' Rebecca quickly interrogated.

'Well, he wasn't at the manor five days ago when Gregory fetched the provisions but Miles was expecting him at any time. I reckon he must be at home now. If you chase that John up he'll be over and fix that roof quick as can be before his lordship finds out he's been idling again while he was away.'

'How many staff remain?' Luke asked the sombrely dressed elderly man standing stiff and quiet behind him, as he idly surveyed the weed-strewn gravel driveway. The chippings were piled high at the perimeter of the circular carriage sweep, testament to how long it had been since it was tended or raked. Numerous coach wheels were quite visibly imprinted in the dusty grit.

Both dark hands were raised, bracing against the framework of the large casement window he stood by. He gazed out, far into the wooded distance, his mind still deep in that quiet sanctuary with a girl with turquoise eyes.

'Eight,' came the terse response from behind.

Luke's eyes narrowed, his jaw setting as he recognised the barely concealed insolence in the elderly butler's tone. He swung away from the large square-paned window and faced him across the mellow yew desk.

Edward Miles must have been seventy if he was a day, and in a way Luke could understand his belligerence. What he could not comprehend was the man's stupidity. Had he any sense at all, he would take great pains to appear pleasant and obliging. His livelihood was now at great risk. For an aged butler of three score years and ten, employment was scarce. Employment without a reference would be impossible, as would keeping a roof over his sparsely covered head in his twilight years.

Luke knew he was tired, he knew he was thirsty but mostly, he knew, today he had been frustrated and that irritated him. Meeting the first woman in an age who had tried to rid herself of his presence at the earliest opportunity was quite a novelty and one he now realised he could have done without. Rejection came hard. And the more he dwelt on it, the more he knew it was ridiculous to allow it to matter. He forced himself to concentrate on Edward Miles. A rheumy-eyed gaze challenged him unwaveringly.

'Is there some brandy about this place?' Luke demanded testily, determining to leave matters for an hour or so whilst Ross and he refreshed themselves. They had been travelling solidly for almost two days with barely an overnight stop.

A slow, satisfied shake of the head met this request.

'Some wine of some sort?' Luke persisted, his patience with the butler's aloof attitude nearly at an end.

'Judith might have made some lemonade,' the old man advised dolefully. 'I can ascertain, if you wish.'

Luke stared at him, wondering if he was being deliberately facetious. But Edward Miles returned his black-eyed stare phlegmatically.

'Fine,' Luke agreed, knowing it wasn't fine at all, and wondering how he was going to break the news to Ross. And where the hell was Ross? Since they had arrived in the village of Westbrook an hour ago he had been off exploring. Luke allowed himself a rueful smile; at times his twenty-five-year-old brother was a fitting playmate for his young nephew of five. Thinking of that little lad brought Tristan to mind. His brother Tristan had his own wife and family to look after and couldn't be left to cope alone for too long, sensible and dependable as he was. He needed to deal speedily with this matter and set on the road home to Cornwall

'I'll meet with the staff in the main hallway in an hour. Assemble them there at three o'clock...and bring some sort of refreshment to this study, if you please,' Luke dictated steadily to Miles. The elderly man gave a creaky, insolent bow and quit the wood-panelled study with Luke close on his heels.

Miles ambled slowly towards the kitchens on stiff joints. He slid a recalcitrant glower up at Luke's handsome face as he passed him with one long, easy pace.

Luke descended the stone steps and strode around the side of the house towards the outbuildings, hoping that Ross's lengthy absence didn't mean he'd found a distracting servant girl to seduce. The notion made the throbbing in his own loins increase, and he cursed as he pushed open the barn door and walked in. He wished to God he'd never seen her. If they'd stayed on the main track instead of seeking shelter from the sun in those woods, he damned well never would have. Since the moment she had spun, dripping, to face him in that pond, he had been uncomfortably aware of the impact she'd had on him.

'Mr Trelawney!' Rebecca breathed out the name in utter astonishment as she shielded her eyes from the dusty sunlight streaming in through the open barn door.

Chapter Three

They stared at each other in stunned silence for a moment before Luke removed his hand from the planked door and it swung shut, obliterating most of the light. He approached Rebecca slowly, cautiously, sure she must be a tormenting figment of his lustful imagination. Sun streaking in through windows set high in the barn wall behind him burnished her honey hair with golden tints and made her squint those beautiful eyes. She stepped back, re-positioning herself close to stacked hay bales, so she had an unimpeded view of him.

'What are you doing here?' she demanded, but with an ingenuous, welcoming smile. It was impossible for her to hide her pleasure at seeing him again. She had believed him to be long gone from the neighbourhood. 'Oh, no! Did Williams catch you trespassing after all?' she softly exclaimed. 'Where is your brother?' The tumbling queries didn't halt his slow, purposeful pursuit. She backed off instinctively, angling away from him, still attempting to keep the fierce sunbeams from impairing her vision.

'Are you in trouble…with Lord Ramsden?' His continuing silence started to unnerve her a little so she offered breathlessly, 'I could speak to him for you…tell him how you assisted…' Warmth suffused her cheeks. She hadn't intended reminding him or herself of the sight she had presented when he had hauled her out of the pond. Her tongue tip came out to moisten her dry lips. The closer he came, the taller and broader he appeared. She felt infinitely small and fragile…and vulnerable. She attempted to peer past him and the piled hay to the exit. Why wouldn't he talk to her? Why wouldn't he say something…anything? Just hello would suffice.

Making to slide past his obstructing body, so near hers now, she announced nervously, 'I'm sure I could persuade him. I'll go and look for him.'

A muscular arm shot out to brace itself against the rough brick wall, blocking her intended flight to the door. 'You've found him,' he said softly. 'How are you going to persuade me?'

Rebecca placed a tentative hand on his linen-clad arm, feeling rock-like sinewed muscle flex at her feeble attempt to move him. She looked up into his dark intense features, struck again by how unbelievably handsome he was.

'That's not funny,' she mildly rebuked him, managing a small, sweet smile even though she didn't understand his sense of humour. 'Robin Ramsden can be very… understanding. I've found him so,' she falteringly explained, as she carefully removed her hand from his lawn shirt-sleeve and unobtrusively retreated, giving herself room to detour to the exit.

Luke watched her back off, his black-pupilled eyes heavy-lidded as they discreetly surveyed her from head to foot. Dried off, wearing a plain cotton dress, she was as beautiful and desirable as she'd been with her clothes plastered to her slender curves and damp tendrils of honey hair clinging to her delicate face. Perhaps not quite so erotic…

His tormenting reminiscence tailed off. Her turquoise

eyes were watchful, a blend of caution and courage again coalescing in their glossy depths. He recognised it from their last encounter. Then it had been enough to make him reluctantly leave. She was intending to go this time. He had frightened her again. He could tell from the way her eyes slid furtively past him that she was within a hair's-breadth of making a dash for the door.

He didn't want that. If she ran he would stop her and if he touched her that way… No woman yet had caused him to lose self-control, he wryly reminded himself. Nevertheless, he dropped his arm and walked away a yard or so but still casually blocking any escape route.

'Are you often to be found in Lord Ramsden's barn, Rebecca?' he asked mildly, with a charming, boyish smile. His calculated ploy worked. Rebecca visibly relaxed.

'Only when I'm looking for John,' she said, returning his smile and feeling unaccountably pleased he had remembered her name.

'John?' he echoed with deceptive softness, as his smile thinned and he became furiously certain he had just interrupted a lovers' tryst. She didn't look in the least chagrined at having been thus discovered. Perhaps he should have let her try to escape after all, he thought cynically. If she'd been abandoned by some spineless rustic swain, he was sure he would prove a more than satisfactory substitute.

'Lord Ramsden's carpenter…well, he is an apprentice, really,' Rebecca pleasantly interrupted his savage supposition. 'But he's quite capable of repairing my roof.' She gazed about then as though she might spy the lad lurking somewhere. 'He's usually to be found in here, sleeping away hot afternoons…when he thinks he can get away with it.'

Silence between them lengthened and Rebecca became uneasily aware of dark eyes fixed unwaveringly on her.

'For it is about to rain, you know,' she said distractedly.
'Gregory Turner…oh, he and his wife help me at the Summer House…well, Gregory is quite sure that rain is finally due. He's rarely proved wrong. I wouldn't be at all surprised if…'

She trailed off, aware that Luke had approached her again while she had been nervously chatting. He now rested against a hay bale within a foot of her, a disturbing sleepiness in his velvet-brown eyes. '…it rains tonight,' she breathlessly finished, her aquamarine eyes wide and entrapped by his.

A slow hand moved unthreateningly to her face, cupping her fragile jaw. She remained entranced as a dark thumb traced the curve of her lower lip with featherlight softness. Either he wasn't as tall as she had at first thought or… He was bending to kiss her, she realised wildly as his face neared hers. Their eyes were still inextricably merged and when the leisurely descent of his narrow mouth brought their faces within inches of touching, Rebecca breathed out, 'What are you doing here?' She watched him frown and slowly, frustratedly, close his eyes as she shattered the spell he'd been casting.

'Were you discovered by Williams trespassing?' she asked, reverting to her initial line of questioning, stepping away again.

'No,' was the extent of his terse response and she sensed his irritation. He threw his head back and gazed up at the fanlight windows set high in the barn wall. He sighed, knowing explanations were long overdue. But then, so was easing the tantalising ache in his loins she had provoked hours before, and was now innocently boosting. Tumbling her in a sultry barn in the middle of the afternoon…it was hardly the time or place.

Besides, he knew he wasn't going to be that lucky. He

almost laughed at his arrogance. Getting close enough for a kiss was proving one hell of a job. What was it he had mourned earlier today? The lack of necessary charm and seduction in his life? He had an unshakeable notion that he was about to dredge up every skill he had ever mastered in those areas. He gazed back at her, momentarily undecided, then said softly, 'Come.'

Approaching the barn door, he stretched out a hand behind him, beckoning for her to follow. She did so, ducking under his arm to gain the dry heat of the afternoon as he held the door open for her.

'Miss Rebecca!' Rebecca twisted about and then hurried the few paces towards Edward Miles as he hobbled across parched grass towards the barn.

'Miles,' she greeted him, for no one who knew him well ever used his given name. Miles was always just Miles. She gave the elderly man an affectionate peck on the cheek, as always, aware of his pleasure at seeing her. His faint watery eyes peered past her to the tall, dark man who impassively watched the scene.

'So you've met the new master, Miss Rebecca,' Miles bitterly muttered.

Rebecca's welcoming smile faded. She frowned her bemusement. 'What do you mean?'

Miles glared purposefully past her. She turned then to watch as Luke Trelawney approached them, aware, oddly for the first time, of overwhelming authority and power in his manner and bearing. Her mind raced back to his puzzling statement in the barn when she had offered to seek out Lord Ramsden. 'You've found him…' he had said and she had believed him to be joking; had wondered at his odd sense of humour. Her eyes sought Miles quickly, pleading for immediate explanations before Luke reached them. But the butler's attention was with his employer.

'The servants are assembled in the hall as you wished, *my lord,*' he informed with a certain disrespectful emphasis on the title which didn't pass unnoticed either by Luke or Rebecca.

Mingling horror, disbelief and recrimination strained and whitened Rebecca's face. She whispered, 'Why didn't you…?'

'I did,' Luke reminded her curtly. 'You weren't listening.'

'In the woods…you could have told me hours ago in the woods. You let me make a fool of myself. Where is Robin Ramsden? You let me warn you needlessly earlier today…about prosecution…about the gamekeeper…' The disjointed accusations and queries jumbled together in her distress.

'As I recall,' he mentioned silkily, 'you seemed to lose all interest in who I was. You were more concerned with ridding yourself of my presence at the earliest opportunity.' He caught proprietorially at her arm as he made for the oaken entrance to Ramsden Manor, intending to take her with him. Rebecca immediately shook him off, her feverish mind foraging for information.

'Where is Robin Ramsden?' she demanded shakily of her new landlord.

He returned her stare impassively. 'Well, come inside the house and I'll tell you,' he coolly answered. 'The staff are assembled.' He cursed inwardly as he realised he had made it sound as though he classed her amongst them. But Rebecca deliberately shunned him, turning to Miles. As Luke alone walked ahead, a solitary thick tear trickled from the corner of one turquoise eye.

Ross weaved down the steps of the Manor, just as Luke was about to ascend them. Luke swore softly, wondering if the day could yet get worse. He grabbed at his younger brother's arm, turning him and making him mount the steps with him and enter the hallway. Ross waved the bottle he grasped under Luke's nose and slurred conspiratorially, 'Found the wine store, big brother.'

'So I see…' Luke replied drily, at one and the same time relieved and exasperated by knowing the reason for his brother's lengthy absence. He was beginning to wish to God he'd made this trip alone. Ross was becoming just another burden he had to deal with. Heaven only knew what he might get up to next. He supposed he ought to be grateful he hadn't discovered Ross naked with one of the female servants he was about to sack.

Two elderly, and three young, women scrambled to stand in a straight line as Luke entered the dim, cool hallway. They shuffled uneasily until they had the courage to look up. All were then instantly still with riveted attention.

Rebecca entered with Miles, and Gregory who had brought her over to the manor in the small trap. She noted the women's unwavering interest and being female knew the reason for it. As mouths dropped open and heads angled back to gaze at perfect features, she realised dully her estimation of his outstanding looks was being openly endorsed.

Cathy, Joan and Sally, the three young women who worked below stairs at the Manor, stared with unabashed amazement. There then began a chain reaction of clandestine rib digging, Joan forgetting herself enough to actually nudge the middle-aged housekeeper in the same way.

Judith instinctively slapped at her for this insubordination before freezing to attention as her new employer's smouldering dark eyes settled on her. She nervously jangled the keys at her waist and then gripped her hands behind her back.

Ross walked with intoxicated precision to the sweeping

ebonized stairway, and leaning on the newel post, allowed himself to swing around and sit on a stair. He smiled amiably at everyone, his eyes lingering on the three homely young servants who, aware of his inspection, all blushed furiously and recommended discreet elbowing.

Luke collected a black superfine tailcoat from a mahogany hall chair. He shrugged casually into it before strolling to stand centrally in front of them and then turned to look at Rebecca. She and Gregory hovered by the open doorway, although Miles paced resolutely forward on arthritic joints to merge with the paltry line of servants awaiting their new master's oratory. Luke stepped back from the people ranged in front of him so that Rebecca was kept in his line of vision. He shot a penetrating look at the elderly man with her, wondering who he was, wondering too why the whole place didn't seem to have an able-bodied man about it. Remembering Rebecca talk of a carpenter's apprentice, and a gamekeeper, he enquired, 'Is there anyone else?'

'Only young John, and Williams the gamekeeper,' Miles informed him stiffly. 'I can't find them anywhere.'

Luke moved a dismissing hand, signalling he wasn't about to wait longer. He looked at the sorry assortment in front of him. At Melrose he had more staff than this working in the gardens and three times as many working in the house. In fact, he was barely aware any more of just how many servants he did have. His mother and sister dealt with such matters for him.

'I should like to introduce myself to you,' he began in a firm baritone, without preamble, 'and tell you of the circumstances surrounding my inheritance of the Ramsden estate and title. I am Luke Trelawney of Pendrake in Cornwall and this is my brother, Ross. We are here because the fifth baron, your late master, has tragically and unexpectedly died of a heart complaint while away from the estate in Bath. He will be buried, in accordance with his wishes, in Bath, beside his wife in the Granger family crypt.'

He paused as a ripple of dismay from the amassed servants swelled in volume. Sally and Joan raised their white pinafores to dab at damp eyes and shake their heads in disbelief. Luke turned his head and stared at Rebecca, his eyes narrowed as they searched her tense white face. Solemn, sparkling aquamarine eyes unblinkingly returned his gaze. He started to speak again, his head still turned in her direction, which made the others in the hallway dart curious looks at her.

'I am sixth Baron Ramsden,' he stressed quietly, 'and have inherited this house and the entire estate and buildings upon it. The estate and title is remaindered to heirs male which means it has passed to me through my great-grandmother Charlotte Ramsden. She left this area and settled in Cornwall more than a hundred years ago,' was the extent of his terse explanation. 'As you know, Robin Ramsden was a widower and on his late wife's death there were no legitimate heirs of the union.'

Another wave of murmuring and coughing interrupted his speech. All were aware of two estate children who bore striking resemblance to their late master. 'Daughters in any case,' was heard to be whispered in a sibilant female voice.

Luke paced restlessly to where Ross sat, speaking to him while waiting for the muttering to quieten. It did almost immediately. He planted a dusty boot on the first step and addressed them from the foot of the imposing stairway.

'You should know that I have no intention of leaving Cornwall or the estates I have there to settle in Sussex.' A renewed buzzing met this information but now he spoke clearly over it, keen to get matters finalised. 'I therefore propose to sell this estate in its entirety.' This time only stunned silence reverberated about the great hall.

'I will honour all back wages due and furnish each of you with references. I will do whatever is in my power to obtain alternative employment for those who wish it.' Luke's eyes tracked Rebecca as he noticed her gliding back to the open doorway. He started to move forward, passing the line of silent, shocked servants, as he stated quickly, 'There will also be a generous severance payment commensurate with length of service…'

He quit the hall and descended the stone steps two at a time and caught up with her just as she was about to flee towards the waiting trap.

He caught at her arm and she half-turned, but seeing it wasn't old Gregory after all, she swung away again trying to break free. He crowded close to her, forcing her back against the mellow brickwork of the house, an open palm braced either side of her golden head.

'Listen…' he soothed but she jerked her white, tear-streaked face away from his.

'Rebecca…listen,' he ordered, authority abrading his tone this time.

Glossy sea-green eyes met earth-brown eyes then and he slowly moved a hand from the wall towards her stained face. She ducked, trying to evade him, but his open palm was flat against the brick before she'd caught her breath enough to bolt. Her abrupt movement brought her cheek up hard against his black superfine shoulder and he moved closer so that she had nowhere left to go apart from him.

Strong arms closed around her as though it was the most natural thing in the world for him to offer her comfort now he had shattered her world. He could feel the thundering of her heart against his chest and smell the scent of lavender in her golden hair. His head dipped, and a lingering sigh escaped him as his mouth sought its perfumed softness and he knew with utter certainty, and quiet amazement, that he was going nowhere without her. He'd known her not yet a full day but nevertheless would take her with him.

Rebecca closed her hot eyes. They stung with unshed tears but she was determined not to cry any more. She would never cry in front of him. At home…at the Summer House, perhaps. She had no home…that was the whole point. She no longer had a home or a business premises. She had nothing other than the paltry few pounds Rupert Mayhew had paid her for Lucy's board and tuition. And now she would have to return it…and Lucy. For she had nowhere to board her or teach her. She didn't know whether to laugh or wail at the irony that she had been uncertain whether to send Lucy home. The decision had now been made for her and she was desolate.

'I only came here to find John…to repair the roof before the rain comes,' she mentioned in a low, flat tone as though merely talking to herself. 'I no longer have a roof to repair…'

He pushed her back away from him to look at her. She met his gaze quite candidly, aquamarine eyes wide and sheeny. Small white teeth clenched on her unsteady bottom lip, making him aware how poignantly hard she strove for control.

'Come back inside…I want to talk to you,' he stated softly, yet in the tone of voice that brooked no refusal. She swallowed as though about to speak, then gazed past him.

'Here's Gregory,' she announced quietly as the elderly man slowly rounded the corner of the manor on his bowing legs. 'Gregory and his wife Martha have helped me at the Summer House for five years,' she tremulously informed him, while persistently plucking his restraining hands from her arms. At her third attempt he slipped his hands deftly about so that they gripped hers rather than the reverse. But she pulled backwards, twisting her fingers to free them until he finally relinquished her.

Rebecca walked slowly towards Gregory and took the man's arm, partly in affection and partly to aid his progress.

Luke leaned back against the warm mellow brickwork of the Manor and watched her slowly pass him without another glance. He didn't move from the wall until the trap was screened from view by poplars at the end of his drive.

Driving rain streamed in endless rivulets down the wide window pane, capturing Luke's mesmerised attention.

'Brandy?' he offered Victor Willoughby, holding his half-full glass of amber liquid out indicatively, although his dark eyes were still with the wet afternoon. He swivelled the leather chair about, his long fingers purposefully rifling through papers on the leather-topped desk, as he gave Robin Ramsden's man of business a cursory glance.

'Thank you…no,' the fair-haired forty-year-old man declined, but licked his lips a little ruefully, as though reluctantly denying himself. 'We should plough on, I'm afraid, my lord. There are several other matters yet, besides those we have covered.'

Luke nodded and decided not to mention yet again that he had no wish to be addressed so formally. He gave Willoughby his full attention as he replaced his crystal tumbler on the desk and then pushed it away. 'Tea?' he suggested, feeling inhospitable drinking alone.

'Why, yes, thank you,' Willoughby accepted with a smile.

Luke glanced over at his brother, ensconced close to the bookshelves in a comfortable brocade armchair with an open newspaper across him. 'Ross, find Judith and arrange for some tea to be brought to the study. Three cups…' he advised his brother meaningfully. Ross delivered a pained look at the prospect of light refreshment but got up good-naturedly and strolled from the room to find the house-keeper.

Luke knew he could have rung for service but a response was erratic. Not that the servants were hostile now; far from it. They were more likely to be beavering away in some odd corner of this Gothic pile.

In the three days since he had been in residence at Ramsden Manor, having found the household provisions sadly lacking, he had immediately replenished all stock cupboards. The lack of alcohol had been his and Ross's first consideration. Old Edward Miles hadn't been lying when he had denied any knowledge of brandy about the place. And the wine store Ross had found was down to its last dozen dusty bottles. So he had made good in buying in both alcohol and foodstuffs and taken care of various other shortcomings at the Manor. That, together with the promise that back wages and severance bonuses would be paid when the estate was sold, had combined to make him increasingly popular.

'Due to the rather dilapidated state of the property, I wouldn't like to estimate how long it might take to achieve a sale,' Victor Willoughby mentioned, drawing Luke's thoughts back to business, as he leafed through documents in front of him. 'Perhaps if I were to arrange for minor work to be carried out…neaten the gardens, a little redecorating, for example…'

Luke cut in quietly. 'I haven't the time or inclination to tarry here. I would be willing to accept offers for the freehold which reflect its state of disrepair. Renovation is necessary, I agree. But the building is solid and free from any rot as far as I can detect.'

'Indeed, my lord, I'm sure. I only meant…'

Luke interrupted him mildly. 'I know what you meant

and I thank you for your concern. The highest price possible isn't my main consideration. Returning to Cornwall is, at the earliest opportunity.' He gave the slightly disconcerted man a brief, conciliatory smile. 'Shall I leave it to you to arrange for the sale of the freehold? And to deal with staff remuneration?'

'Indeed, my lord,' Victor Willoughby assured the preoccupied man who was again gazing through the rain-spattered glass into the drizzly-grey distance. 'It may mean that several of my clerks will be working on your behalf, my lord.' He coughed delicately. 'Will payment for my firm's services be taken from the proceeds of the estate sale, or will an earlier…?'

A small, cynical smile escaped Luke but he didn't turn away from surveying the sodden landscape as he informed Willoughby levelly, 'You will receive interim payments. I want the estate dealt with as a matter of urgency and will pay for that service accordingly. Your fees will not be dependent upon the actual sale. Should the matter be closed in record time, however, a bonus might…' He allowed the enticement to hang between them for a moment. 'I shall be travelling back to Cornwall next week and would like to leave in the sure knowledge that everything possible is being done to expedite matters. And that it is all in capable hands.'

'Of course, my lord,' Victor Willoughby assured him, but sensing that somehow he had just received a subtle reprimand.

A light tapping at the door heralded the arrival of Judith with a laden tea tray. She smiled at Luke, informing him pleasantly, 'I've brought you some treacle biscuits, my lord. You remember, those you liked yesterday.'

'Thank you, Judith,' Luke said graciously, with a small smile for her. She blushed happily, pouring tea into wafer-thin china cups. Once this was accomplished and tea distributed she loitered, shifting uneasily from one foot to the other.

Luke raised querying brows at her, wordlessly inviting her to speak if something was troubling her.

'It's nothing really, my lord…'

'Mr Trelawney, Judith…I thought we had agreed you would use that,' he reminded mildly, hoping that Victor Willoughby was also taking due note.

'Yes, sir, I mean, Mr Trelawney. Well, sir, it's nothing really, as I said, it's just your brother…' Judith tailed off and shuffled uncomfortably again.

Luke sighed out, 'Yes, what now? Is he sliding down the banisters? Rolling drunk in the drawing room?'

'No, sir. He's…er…rolling dice with Joan and Sally…in the hallway. If you want dinner tonight, Mr Trelawney, he had best leave the girls be so I can get them to the vegetables.' She rubbed appreciative hands together as she expounded, 'It's to be smoked trout and roast guinea fowl with roast potatoes and fruit tarts with cream and…'

'And as you pass him in the hallway, Judith, tell him I want him, would you?' Luke cut into her menu, a slow hand spanning his forehead, soothing his temples.

Judith bobbed a quick curtsy before bustling busily from the study.

Poking professionally about in his cavernous document case, Mr Willoughby seemed deaf to the unusual discourse. But he ruined his nonchalance by admitting with doleful sympathy, 'I have a younger brother…'

Luke nodded acceptance of the man's tacit condolences before getting back to business. 'The Summer House Lodge…where is the lease for that building? I haven't found it among any of the documents in this study. Do you hold it?'

'The Summer House?' Mr Willoughby repeated, a trifle surprised. 'Oh, you won't find any lease for that; there is none.'

Luke frowned enquiry across the desk at him. 'Are you sure? The building is presently used as a small school, by Miss Rebecca Nash. She rents the premises on a lease, I would have thought.'

As Ross sauntered back into the room, Luke glanced up idly, scowling a little at his brother's impenitent smile. Picking up the newspaper he had previously been reading, Ross strolled across to the window by Luke's desk, as though enjoying better light there to study it.

'Well, yes, she does reside there. But there is no lease,' Willoughby confirmed as his pale eyes darted from one brother to the other.

'Why not?' Luke asked a little too quietly.

Willoughby noisily cleared his throat and slid nervous fingers between his stiff collar and his warming neck as he sensed an atmosphere fomenting. 'There was never any need of one,' he quickly advised Luke. 'Robin Ramsden and Miss Nash appeared to have…an agreement. She just resides and works there and he—' He broke off, desperately seeking the right words, aware of two sets of brown eyes watching him now. The silence strained interminably.

'And he…?' Luke finally prompted him, in a voice that was silky with danger, while his eyes relentlessly pinned down the weak blue ones seeking to evade him.

'And he allowed her to,' Mr Willoughby concluded quickly, pleased with his innocuous phrasing. It didn't have the desired effect of diverting Luke Trelawney's piercing gaze.

'Possibly he took pity on her…because of the tragedy which occurred some five years ago,' Willoughby suggested hastily. 'It would have been about the same time she took up residence at the Summer House. Yes, that must have been it.' He nodded, sure he had now satisfactorily managed a delicate situation.

'Tragedy…?'

Just one soft word coupled with a penetrating, fierce stare and Victor Willoughby readily explained. 'Miss Nash lost both her parents in a carriage accident in the winter snows. Within the same week she learned of the death of her fiancé in the Peninsula…er…he was a captain in the Hussars, I believe. Then her brother disappeared, too. That I believe was, financially, the crux of the matter. For her brother held the purse strings on her father's death. He was charged with administering her small inheritance for her but no one could find him. I believe they still can't.' He licked dry lips and glanced warily at Luke Trelawney, noting his narrow-eyed thoughtfulness.

'And Robin Ramsden..?' Luke interrogated him calmly.

'And Robin Ramsden appeared to take her under his protection…er…I mean to say, he looked after her, so to speak,' Mr Willoughby flustered, unwilling to imply too much of what he had never been certain. He had his own theories but he was not going to voice them. Definitely not to this man who had become rather daunting in the past few minutes.

Miss Nash was a lovely woman…he had seen her once or twice and had drawn the only logical conclusion he could for his late client's continuing aid and protection. This new lord of the manor seemed also to have taken an immediate personal interest in her. It was no concern of his…but she was very beautiful…

Luke shoved back in his chair and stood up. He walked to the window and stared out, appearing oblivious to his brother barely a yard away, even though Ross's anxious hazel eyes followed his movements. But Luke was peripherally aware of Willoughby behind him, gathering together his papers and stuffing them abruptly into his case in readiness to depart.

A hard, humourless smile curved Luke's mouth as he finally allowed himself to concentrate fully on Rebecca. It was all beginning to fall into place. What a gullible fool he'd been and that rankled. Everyone knew him for a cynic. No wonder she had been prepared to speak to Robin Ramsden on his behalf when believing he'd been discovered trespassing. Using charm and influence on the lord of this Manor was, by all accounts, nothing new for her. Well, that would suit him damn fine. There was no need for that to change.

Whatever Robin Ramsden had provided for her over the years, he knew he could improve on…a thousandfold. And he'd believed her to be some chaste provincial maid he would need to proposition with utmost care. She'd cried on learning of Robin Ramsden's death. Was it the man or the meal ticket she mourned? he wondered. Perhaps it was the prospect of losing her home…the schoolbuilding. What was she teaching there, in any case? If provocative Miss Mayhew, the young temptress he recalled from the woodland pond, was an untried schoolgirl, then…Ross was teetotal.

What did it matter? Rebecca had obviously fallen on hard times five years ago and had survived in any way she could. It was a commonplace tale.

He had already decided to take her with him and this changed nothing. Logically it made things easier, he acknowledged with a callous smile. He could now proposition her without risking having her outraged or hysterical. Even enthusiastic virgins were damn hard to tutor and sometimes barely worth the trouble. By the time they were adaptable

and accomplished he was usually bored and looking elsewhere.

He thought of Wenna, something he hadn't done for a
week or more. He was bored and looking elsewhere, he
acknowledged sourly, yet she had always been the perfect
mistress. Passionate, obliging, skilful, discreet, faith-
ful…the list was endless. One of his large, dark hands
curled into a fist. She'd suited him fine until he'd come
here.

Chapter Four

'Lucy!' Rebecca's low disciplined voice carried easily in the quiet room and brought the girl's brunette head directly around. Rebecca pointed indicatively at the book in front of her on the pine desk and mouthed, 'Read!'

Once Lucy's attention was once more with her work, Rebecca glared at John. The young carpenter shifted from the open doorway where he had been loitering under the pretext of examining its battered wooden framework.

Rebecca quietly left her own desk and, passing the few younger day girls who were chalking on small blackboards, entered the kitchen. John was kneeling on the floor, replacing. tools in a canvas holdall.

'The work must be finished now, John, surely?' she asked the fair-haired youth. He scrambled up then, reddening, and she realised that he hadn't heard her approach. He tugged at a lock of sun-bleached hair hanging low over one eye.

'Yes, m'm…' he mumbled. 'Just a few more rafters to look at under them slates…once rain eases off a bit.'

He had turned up, totally unexpectedly, within hours of Rebecca learning of Robin Ramsden's death. The new master had sent him, John had shyly explained and he had set to work. Rebecca was grateful he had arrived so speedily too, for by dusk the first fat drops of rain were staining the dusty ground around the Summer House.

John had been back each of the three days since, awaiting a break in the showers to carry out repairs. That was the problem. While he innocently surveyed the internal structure of the Summer House for chores to occupy him until he could get back on the roof, Lucy was purposefully surveying him. He was now watching her back, Rebecca realised with alarm. Her small parlour-cum-schoolroom often now found him lurking in its vicinity.

'You still here, young man?' Martha greeted John jovially as she entered the kitchen with a basket of washing beneath one capable arm. 'Just about got this lot dry between showers,' she informed Rebecca in the next breath. 'Waiting for them biscuits to get out the oven, I suppose,' she again addressed the blond youth.

'Well, I wouldn't say no, Martha.' He dodged her playful swipe at him.

'You'd best get yourself up on that roof then and earn some. Rain's eased off a bit now.'

He sauntered from the kitchen, cradling his prized tools beneath one arm.

'Never going to rid ourselves of him now, are we?' Martha mentioned with a shrewd meaningful look towards the parlour door.

Rebecca sighed, approached the open kitchen door, and surveyed the dripping landscape. 'I'll have to speak to Lucy again. She distracts him…'

'Distracts him?' Martha echoed with a derisive snort. 'That young miss is a bundle of trouble, if you ask me. Why, even my old Gregory has had eyes made at him. Not that I'm worried…or he's capable,' she added with a good-natured smile. 'But that young John…now there's a different matter,' she warned with a sage wagging of her grey head.

'I know she tends to flirt,' Rebecca admitted, biting anxiously at her bottom lip.

'You're looking a bit brighter today, if I may say so, Miss Becky,' Martha changed the subject abruptly.

'I do feel a little less anxious, Martha,' she said quietly. 'The shock of hearing of Robin's death made me a little illogical. But since then I have been thinking…perhaps things aren't quite so black. Now I have had time to consider…' She sighed, reflecting that 'consider' hardly began to do justice to the sleepless, fretful nights she had endured since first learning of this tragedy. 'I certainly can't honestly blame Mr Trelawney for wanting to return to Cornwall or to the home and estates he has there. Nor could I have complained had he wanted to take up residence at Ramsden Manor and charge me rent for using this building. It is his property, after all, to do with as he wishes. Because Robin was so good to me I tend to forget that I am just here on sufferance. But Mr Trelawney has sent John to repair the roof, so with all things considered, he has been quite kind…quite nice…'

'Gregory says he thinks the young master be quite taken with you too,' Martha mentioned with an astute narrowed look at Rebecca, as she deftly folded laundry. 'He says last time he laid eyes on his lordship, he were watching you walk away from him as though…'

'He feels sorry for me,' Rebecca cut in quietly. 'He realises that I shall be dispossessed and is good enough to sympathise. But I shall manage. I believe it will be some months yet before the matter of the estate is settled. I must use that time to again search for Simon. And I must now succeed,' she announced vehemently, concentrating on memories of her twenty-four-year-old brother and her in-heritance, held within his grasp.

It wasn't a great fortune. But her five thousand pounds was the dividing line between poverty and self-respect. It would have her dowry on her marriage to David. It was hers by right and she now needed to invest it for her future; to keep her free of soul-destroying drudgery as a provincial governess or companion. For she was aware that very little else awaited her once her rent-free tenancy of the Summer House was terminated. She was a spinster of almost twenty-six now and meeting someone to love and marry was increasingly remote.

She rarely socialised. Even when in London with Eliz-abeth they had visited the theatre on only one occasion due to Elizabeth's recent confinement.

There was always the chance that a widower with chil-dren might take her on and provide her with a reasonable life. She sighed wistfully, for the notion of a loveless, con-venience marriage for respectability and shelter was dispir-iting. Since David no one had attracted or excited her... Her meandering thoughts circled back to Luke Trelawney. Her heart rate increased and a spontaneous rush of blood stained her cheeks at what would have been her next thought. She abandoned it immediately.

Her fingers sought automatic comfort from her silver locket, and she thought of dear David. She concentrated on his fine straw-coloured hair, his rounded face and the light freckling that dusted his nose and cheeks. It was so unfair. He had loved her dearly, although his parents had been keen for him to make a match with a young woman of better family. A middle-class merchant's youngest daughter was certainly not what they had in mind. The fact that all the Nash children had been well educated and had good connections mattered little.

David's father, Sir Paul Barton, was a baronet with a certain social standing and he had hoped his eldest son would improve the family's status and finances on marriage. There had been no celebration and only a small announcement in the paper, which David had insisted upon. Her sapphire betrothal ring was safely wrapped in tissue in her bedroom. She hoped she would never be forced to sell it to survive.

But David had been strong and loyal and had firmly declared his intention to marry her as soon as his commission terminated. It would have been three years ago, Rebecca realised. She would have been a happily married woman for three years, perhaps with children of her own. And a neat villa in Brighton. It was what she and David had discussed during their nine-month courtship. He had always treated her with such respect…such affection…

Her poignant memories were interrupted by a gravelly voice. 'You be best off forgetting about that brother of yours, Miss Becky,' Gregory sternly noted as he laid pungent, freshly dug leeks on the scrubbed pine table. Martha shot him a warning frown. 'She be best to know,' Gregory insisted. 'It was just a shame your poor late pa didn't know what his son was getting into. If he hada known, he woulda left you your money in safer hands, I reckon.'

'Gregory!' Rebecca admonished him, shocked by his temerity. He always had tended to speak his mind, but as he aged he was becoming a little too blunt.

'You know I speak truth, Miss Becky,' he placated her softly, seeing the distress in her lovely face. 'But I'm sorry fer upsetting you. Just know this. Jake Blacker's been seen in Brighton again recently, so I heard. And that means only one thing. Contraband is coming ashore again.'

'My brother was never involved in smuggling, Gregory,' Rebecca stated stiffly as she occupied her nervous hands by folding laundry with Martha. She noted the anxious look that passed between the couple. 'I know Simon had dealings with that ruffian,' she admitted, trying to ease the atmosphere. 'I challenged him about Jake Blacker disturbing Mama at home once when Simon and I were in town. He swore Blacker was only looking for him because he lost to him at cards. You know how he was always gambling in taverns. But Simon swore to Papa that he had repaid him and that he would avoid mixing with any of those reprobates in the future.'

'Where's he been all this time, then, Miss Becky?' Martha asked quietly. 'Why hasn't he been by to see how you are coping alone? It's a terrible thing for a brother to leave his sister so alone to fend for herself.'

'He obviously knows very well that Robin assists me....' She broke off, realising then just what worried this dear couple. Robin Ramsden was no longer able to do so. 'Besides,' she hurriedly said, 'he knows that I see Elizabeth also. My sister may be married and in London, but we keep in touch.'

A derisive snort met this information and Rebecca knew the reason for it. In all the six years Elizabeth had been married to James Bartholomew, a London lawyer, Rebecca had never once received an offer of help, financial or otherwise. She gave the Turners a conciliatory smile. They were only concerned for her welfare, she knew that. She also knew that without them she would never have been able to cope with running this small establishment.

She had always known that once Robin Ramsden and his patronage were gone she would be alone and vulnerable. She now felt foolish for not having prepared better for that day.

But she had always believed Simon to be alive. She knew sometimes with quite frightening certainty that her hell-raising brother was ridiculously close to her. Just as she was sure that he had used her inheritance as his own and was striving to replace it before he returned with a plausible tale for his absence. Finding Simon and extracting her money from him was now crucial.

Gazing, preoccupied, through the doorway into the damp afternoon, it was a moment before Rebecca noticed the couple strolling down the pathway towards the Summer House. As her eyes alighted on them, her soft mouth immediately curved into a delighted smile. 'Oh, Kay and Adam are visiting us,' she advised the Turners with a backward flick of a glance.

'Best check them biscuits,' Martha noted briskly. 'Be baking another batch, more'n like, what with the girls, young John and vicar 'n wife on the way.'

As Rebecca greeted the new arrivals, ushering them into the kitchen with cordial complaints about the abrupt change in the weather, Gregory mentioned casually, 'You'd best add his lordship to that list, Martha. I heard from Judith that he's pertickler to a biscuit.'

As Kay and Adam Abbott crowded into the small kitchen, accepting the invitation to be seated and partake of a little light refreshment, the bustle prevented Rebecca clearly understanding Gregory's cryptic remark. Noting his weatherbeaten countenance still turned to the window, she doubtfully approached the doorway.

Ross was standing, hands on hips, chestnut head thrown back, staring assessingly up at her roof. He shouted something up at John and pointed. Rebecca walked immediately out into the humid afternoon to greet him. She had an odd liking for this good-looking man she barely knew.

'He considers himself a bit of a carpenter,' explained a sardonic well-remembered voice that had her twisting immediately about.

Luke Trelawney was behind her and just to one side of the building as though he had walked around it. He held the reins of a magnificent pitch-black stallion in one hand. Rebecca's eyes were drawn immediately to the fine animal, such a contrast to the farm hack she had seen him with by the pond.

'Handsome brute, don't you think?' Luke stated ironically, noting her interest.

Rebecca raised thick-lashed luminous eyes to search his, noting the glitter in their dark depths. The description was as fitting for the rider as the horse and he was well aware of it.

She gave him a small smile, trying to calm that sudden increased pulse that his imposing presence always seemed to raise. She turned quickly on her heel, attempting to hide the colour she could feel staining her cheeks.

'Thank you for sending John so quickly,' she said distractedly, gazing up at the roof where the young carpenter was still receiving advice from Ross below. 'I was right about the rain, you see. Or rather, Gregory was. We've only had a little leaking. I'm very grateful.' Confident she had regained her composure, she faced him again, biting her lip a little at the expression in his eyes. They were narrowed and intent, as always. But the amused assessment had a harder edge that disturbed her. She realised he probably no longer found her rustic gaucheness quite so entertaining.

'You knew I'd send him, didn't you?' he remarked mildly, as his eyes followed John's careful descent from the roof's summit. 'It's what the lord of the Manor does for you, isn't it? Looks after you?'

Rebecca moistened her lips, feeling her agitation increasing as dark eyes swooped back to pitilessly pounce on her.

'I want to talk to you. I told you that last time I saw

you,' he said a touch irascibly. 'You disappeared before I had a chance to discuss future arrangements…'

Rebecca managed a smile, a coiling and fluttering in the pit of her stomach at the memory of how he had comforted her that day. His arms had felt so welcome…so strong and protective. She sensed another wave of colour about to suffuse her skin and steeled herself desperately against it.

'Well, come in…please. And Ross,' she pleasantly offered. 'Reverend Abbott and his wife are here, too. We are just having tea. Please do come in,' she urged sincerely, a hand extending towards the Summer House. 'I'm sure they would both like to meet you before you return to Cornwall. Have you any idea how long you intend to remain in Sussex, Mr Trelawney?' she asked conversationally.

'I shall be leaving next week,' he brusquely informed her.

This information had Rebecca's golden head angling immediately up to him. 'Next week?' she breathed, her face whitening now, enhancing aquamarine eyes to jewel richness. 'Have you found a purchaser so soon?' she demanded a little boldly in her agitation. She recalled her brave words with Martha barely fifteen minutes ago…how she would cope with arranging her future and her search for Simon in the time it would take to find a new landlord.

'The matter will be left to a man of business…' he tersely supplied, while inwardly cursing that he had managed to turn up to proposition her at the very same time the damned vicar arrived to take tea. He gazed about impatiently and Rebecca falteringly invited, 'Well…would you like to come in and—?'

'Not really, Rebecca.' He bluntly cut across her words, aware how boorish he must sound. But seeing her again, trying to reconcile the role of paramour to Robin Ramsden with this fawn-like beautiful young woman who hesitated nervously before him, was excrutiating. Robin Ramsden had been fifty-two and a renowned lecher. Luke had since learned Robin had suffered with a heart complaint for some years. Instead of expiring atop some harlot in a Bath brothel it could just as easily have been here at this Summer House. God, he wished he'd never seen her. He could have come and gone from this place within a week, attended to business, spent a pleasant few nights roistering with Ross in Brighton, then returned to his life of luxurious contentment in Cornwall.

As his granite-jawed silence became protracted, comprehension dawned on Rebecca. He had come to tell her to leave. He was returning to Cornwall next week and wanted to evict her before he went. He was irritated because he was unsure how to broach the matter now she had company. She had sensed he had something to say. Her pale face lifted to his, her chin tilting in pride. She wasn't about to beg for time or anything else. She had little in the way of possessions. She could probably be packed and out in less than a week.

'When would you like me to leave, Mr Trelawney?' she asked coolly. 'I should have liked a little more notice, but I realise I have no rights in the matter. I would appreciate it if you would at least allow me to get a message to Miss Mayhew's family, so they can arrange to collect her. Thankfully, she is the only boarder at present...' Feeling a lump thickening in her throat and tears spearing her eyes, she swiftly turned and walked away.

She hastened blindly through the crowded kitchen, noting Ross leaning nonchalantly against a wall, a mug of tea in one hand and a large aromatic biscuit in the other. She managed a quiet cordial response to his greeting, and even to swap a few bright words with Kay as she made her way to the parlour and her pupils. She felt guilty now at having abandoned them for so long.

Lucy and John were standing close, chatting quietly by the girl's desk; as they saw Rebecca, they sprang apart. The three younger girls had abandoned their alphabets to chalk pictures on their blackboards.

'That's all for today. You're a little later leaving than usual so hurry home,' Rebecca emphasised as she dismissed them. 'Martha has made some refreshment. Perhaps you'd care for something before you leave, John,' she offered the loitering youth.

'Thank you, m'm,' John gruffly mumbled as he and Lucy quit the room.

Alone in the parlour, Rebecca momentarily bowed her head in despair before abruptly raising it. She would not be cowed by this. She had survived the loss of her beloved parents and her fiancé five years ago—she would surely survive the loss of this building. She glanced about the small parlour, at the whitewashed walls hung with a few pictures from her late parents' home, at the polished pianoforte from their parlour. She sighed. It was an enchanting building, filled with fine memories, and she would miss it dreadfully.

With head held high she walked back to the kitchen and forced a smile as she entered. There was little need; apart from Martha the hot room, redolent of cinnamon, was empty.

'All gone out to look at the horseflesh,' Martha advised, on taking in Rebecca's bewilderment. 'Gregory never did say just how handsome a man he is. Nor did you for that matter,' she added with a sideways look. 'Charming as can be, too. Came in and introduced hisself and his brother...such a pair of good lookers as I never did see.'

Rebecca was aware that Adam Abbott was a keen horseman who owned a particularly fine grey gelding himself. The beautiful black stallion she had seen was sure to interest him. And Kay took an interest in whatever pleased her husband.

As Rebecca peeked discreetly through the kitchen window, she noticed Adam mount the magnificent ebony horse and enthusiastically trot it around in a large circle in front of the Summer House. He called something out to Luke who nodded, while casually surveying the scene. Kay and Ross were chatting idly; Kay petting the neck of a chestnut mare that Rebecca had not seen before, obviously Ross's. Gregory leaned against the house, smilingly watching the pastoral scene, while Lucy and John seemed content to observe each other.

After a moment, Luke stepped back a pace or so and then turned and strode purposefully towards the house. Rebecca felt her stomach knot and sat abruptly down at the kitchen table. She had no intention of hiding from him.

She sensed his presence in the doorway long before he actually spoke to her. Martha started to hum tunelessly, busying herself with tidying every crockery item she could lay her plump hands on.

'I want to talk to you, Rebecca. Will you come for a walk with me?'

'You can say anything you need to in front of Martha,' Rebecca calmly replied without turning towards him.

'I think you'd rather I said this in private,' was his steely, quiet response. 'Now…' he smoothly added when she made no move to obey.

She knew it was senseless to defy him. She needed to know when he expected her to move out.

Strolling in tense silence was unbearable. Rebecca realised she would rather be disappointed straight away. She abruptly halted on the perimeter of the woodland close to the Turners' small cottage, and leaned back against the solid trunk of an elm. She crossed her arms around her middle, holding her warm, black-fringed shawl tight about her. It was nearly dusk now and although the rain was holding off, a light breeze was strengthening. Its cool caress fanned wisps of honey hair softly across her features. She shook her head to clear them, removing the stragglers with slender, white fingers.

'Is this private enough? Can you talk to me now?' she queried with tremulous sarcasm and then felt immediately wretched for stooping to it.

He walked back slowly towards her and stood close, so close that Rebecca sensed his warmth through her chill.

'When I leave here next week I want you to come with me to Cornwall,' he stated with quiet candour. He watched her golden head jerk back and her eyes searched his as though she was unsure she had heard correctly.

His narrow mouth twisted in a hard smile. 'I should perhaps explain my worthy circumstances first. I have a large estate in Cornwall…very large. I have considerable wealth and status. It's one of the reasons I have no use for Ramsden Manor or the title. I have various other properties…not only in Cornwall, but a smaller estate in Bath and a house in Mayfair.' He halted as though bored with the details he was recounting. 'I have a lot to offer you, Rebecca. You will want for nothing. I know moving away from here and people you know will be difficult but I will care for you, protect you…'

Rebecca gazed at him in utter awe, unable to credit what she was hearing and equally startled by the spontaneous warm relief that drenched her. She had heard similar promises before…so long ago…when David had proposed and declared how well he would provide for her.

'Why would you want to marry me?' she queried in a

husky whisper. 'If what you say about your circumstances is true, you could make a very successful match. You now have a title…'

Luke stared at her, sure she was jesting. He searched her face for guile but there was nothing; no sarcasm, no humour, just glossy-eyed gravity and a heart-wrenching sweet expression on her face. God, she was going to accept him. She thought he'd proposed marriage and she was going to accept.

'You will want time to consider. Think over what I'm offering you,' he stressed slowly and quietly. 'Think it over carefully, Rebecca. But know this…I want you with me. I want you very much and I promise you will never regret allowing me to take care of you in Cornwall.'

A soft, dewy-eyed smile met this affirmation before turquoise and sepia eyes locked. She couldn't believe this was happening to her. Only an hour or so earlier she had been lamenting the likelihood of remaining a spinster her life through or marrying simply from convenience and now… Luke Trelawney was proposing to wed her and the idea of it was simultaneously terrifying and exhilirating.

Conscious of her submission, her allure, but mostly the insistent pulsing tightening his groin, he leaned slowly towards her. Now was as good a time as any, he realised cynically, to find out just what she could do. If she was compliant, screening woodland was barely a pace away. A dark hand was placed deliberately against the tree trunk at the side of her golden hair while the other leisurely moved to her face.

Rebecca allowed her lids to droop, shielding shining eyes as she raised her face a little to meet his kiss. David had kissed her after he had proposed. The first proper kiss she had ever known.

But not like this, she thought, panic-stricken, as a warm,

hard mouth slid against hers and firm fingers at her jaw skilfully manoeuvered her lips apart. Her hands slid immediately up between them, to purchase space and try to weaken his hold. His palm moved abruptly from the tree trunk and curled about her soft nape, urging her forward while controlling her head and keeping her close. Dark fingers laced up into her silky hair, intentionally loosening honey tendrils to drape her neck and face. At the first thrust of his tongue into her mouth, Rebecca jerked back so violently that the knuckles of the hand cradling her head, scraped against tree bark.

Heavy-lidded black eyes merged with skittering turquoise. He gave a small sardonic smile. So she still expected to be wooed, even believing that he had proposed marriage to her. He had been right in estimating that seduction would be a requirement with this one. But he was prepared to indulge coy role-playing up to a point. A modest maiden might be briefly diverting. He dropped his head back to hers abruptly, before she had a chance to properly evade him.

Rebecca reflexively bunched her fists against the solid expanse of his torso. But there was no need this time. A gentle moist caress soothed her bruised lips with subtle art. As her fingers uncurled to lay against his muscled chest she instinctively leaned into him, raising up on tiptoe to protract the contact as she sensed him moving away. She felt the smile against her mouth and he deepened the kiss just enough to startle her before he let her go.

'I have to go back now,' Rebecca stated breathlessly, sliding sideways and away from him. She felt utterly confused. He had proposed marriage to her, promised to care for her, and yet there was something in his eyes…in his manner, that made her uncertain he liked her. There was something in the way he had kissed her, too, that had both

excited and repelled her: an odd mix of anger and tenderness. 'The Turners will be waiting to leave. They won't go
home until I get back.' She pointed distractedly towards the
small cottage close by, attempting to lighten the mood between them with bland chatter. 'That's their home just over
there. It has very little land about it, unfortunately…' She
glanced at him, leaning back against the tree with his arms
folded across his broad chest, watching her with that same
thoughtful amusement.

Perhaps he expected her to flirt a little with him. She had
very little experience of flirting; could hardly remember any
of the coy techniques that she and Elizabeth had employed
when in their teens attending local assemblies and balls.
She had met David at such a gathering. If she recalled
anything, it had most to do with the artful use of eyelashes
and a fan. A small inward smile thankfully acknowledged
that the fan was definitely out of the question.

A poignant curling tightened the pit of her stomach as
she was again struck by how incredibly handsome he was.
A thick lock of black hair fell heavily across his forehead,
nearly into narrowed eyes. There was something disquieting about him too, she abruptly recognised, apart from the
arrogance and authority that privilege and wealth had
honed. There was an air of menace, something dangerous
dissembling behind his sophisticated manner and quiet
speech. Through the mounting dusk, she glimpsed the
mockery in the slant of his mouth. He was acknowledging
her fixed interest in him, she realised. She shivered a little,
wrapping her shawl tightly about her, but returned him a
small, sweet smile, before turning in the direction of the
Summer House.

It was an opportunity too good to miss. She might not
catch him alone again. He and his brother seemed insepa-

rable at times. And there was so much she needed to know…to find out about this man who was to become her husband; for she had quietly accepted they would marry.

She had returned to the Summer House some half an hour ago to find Kay and Adam had left. She felt guilty at having been so ill-mannered as to have abandoned them when they had come to visit her. Kay and she were good friends, yet they had barely exchanged a dozen inconsequential words. She wondered how Martha had explained away her absence and that of the new Lord Ramsden.

Martha and Gregory had made their slow progress home, hoping to avoid showers threatening in the lowering sky in the north. Only John and Ross remained, standing at the foot of the rough-hewn wooden ladder, inspecting various carpentry tools with great debate and attention.

Luke had immediately returned to the Manor with barely a parting word either for her or his brother. His mood as they walked back to the Summer House had been unusually solemn and preoccupied. He had merely looked long and hard at her and told her he would call in a day or two to speak to her again. Before he did, she needed to speak to someone. And there was only Ross. She needed to know more.

Lucy was safely in her room, indulging in a quiet hour of sewing before dinner. Rebecca watched Ross stride towards his chestnut horse, tethered to a nearby branch. Without conscious decision she lightly ran over the slippery grass towards him.

Hearing her approach, he swung about and gave her a friendly smile. 'That young lad knows what he's about. His father has taught him well. He's spliced a piece of rafter—'

'May I talk to you, Ross, before you leave?' Rebecca breathlessly interrupted his praise. 'Just for a moment. I won't keep you long.'

'Of course,' Ross agreed but Rebecca noted his slightly bemused look. She was sure then that he knew nothing of Luke's proposal.

A silence developed as Rebecca strived to formulate a way of extracting information about his brother which didn't seem prying or audacious.

She blurted quickly, 'Luke wants me to go to Cornwall with him when he leaves here. I know so very little about him, Ross. It's such a great step to take. I realise what he's offering is a great honour but...'

Ross cut in mildly, 'Ah, I see. Well, I can't say I'm surprised he has approached you, Rebecca. He has been...umm...' he laughed and looked at her '...quite enchanted by you since he first saw you floundering about in that pond.' As Rebecca flushed, he added, 'It's natural you should be...er...cautious. But whatever he's told you about his ability to provide for you is no exaggeration.' He glanced at the top of Rebecca's golden head. She was amazingly beautiful and desirable and yet what astounded him most was that she wanted to quiz him like this.

Obviously she was more worldly wise than he had imagined. Old man Ramsden had indeed been lucky in finding such a sophisticate hidden away in this backwater. It took quite a bold and confident paramour to investigate a prospective lover's financial standing through his brother. The usual method, as far as he knew, was to discreetly check on how recent cast-offs fared. Not an option in her case, he had to admit. Cornwall was a long way to go to get a reference. So he could afford to be obliging. After all, she had such an engaging way about her, he understood why Luke was so smitten. If he didn't value his health quite so much, he'd be tempted to show an interest himself.

'Luke is well known for his extreme generosity,' he kindly explained. 'He has a reputation for discretion, too.

So if, by chance…er…he found that you didn't suit him, after all…' Noting an odd frown and her face whitening, he hastily added, 'Or you were homesick and wanted to return to Sussex, of course; well, he would, undoubtedly, secure your comfortable future and your reputation…' He tailed off, noting that his reassurances seemed to have had the opposite effect. Her lustrous, unblinking eyes gazed into his and she suddenly bit down hard on her full bottom lip. She still stared at him but those incredible blue-green eyes were vacant, her mind far away. 'What I mean to say, Rebecca,' he expounded helpfully, 'is that with Luke… because of his consideration and generosity…umm… *chères amies* remain *chères amies*…'

'Even when they become less expensive, you mean,' Rebecca said in a strangling whisper.

Ross looked at her and laughed, relieved that she had at last spoken and wittily. 'That's very good…dear friends become less expensive. Very true, too,' he wryly reflected with another chuckle.

Rebecca joined him. A laugh jerked out of her with such force that she moved a shaking hand to shield her face, while twisting away from Ross. She regained composure within a moment and her arms wrapped tightly, comfortingly about her body. Ross watched her, enchanted by the way her golden hair draped in fetching tendrils about her slender neck. She appeared to be cold because her white fingers rubbed ceaselessly against her arms.

'You didn't mind me mentioning…?' Ross posed uneasily, unsure why but sensing something was amiss.

Rebecca slowly faced him. She fussed busily at her hair, attempting to shove golden strands back into pins. 'No, of course not. I'm just so glad I managed to have this talk with you, Ross. Thank you,' she murmured graciously, with a small dip of her head.

'So, what have you decided then?' he persisted.

Rebecca swallowed hard. 'Well, I have definitely decided that we ought to keep this conversation just between ourselves. You won't say anything to Luke, will you, Ross?'

Ross couldn't have been more relieved by the request. He was certain he had been more than complimentary about his brother, yet Rebecca had seemed happier before his praise. And how Luke was going to react to that he didn't dare contemplate. 'I promise not to say a word,' he agreed conspiratorially.

Aware of his steady gaze on her, Rebecca smiled and peered up, through the dusk at her roof. 'You're quite right about John, you know. He is certainly a fine carpenter. I hope the next landlord recognises just what an asset he is...' Words failed her then and she swung away, calling huskily over her shoulder, 'Well, goodnight, Ross. It was nice to see you again today.'

She could wait to see him in a few days when he visited the Summer House or she could go tomorrow to Ramsden Manor and seek him out. She could pretend continuing ignorance of his true intentions or she could immediately challenge him. Perhaps it might be interesting watching him squirm off the hook if she persisted with the belief that he wanted to marry her. Or perhaps it would just be unbearably degrading for her to hear him laugh and say he thought she would by now have had sense enough to interpret his proposition.

He couldn't have made it more plain. 'Think over what I'm offering you,' he had said. Not once but twice and still she had not. It had taken Ross to clear her mind. Ross to bring woundingly home to her just what penniless, unprotected spinsters could expect from life and wealthy men. And once the shock of it had dulled, she had indeed almost considered the benefits of what he was prepared to offer her.

When had he once mentioned marriage? He hadn't mentioned love either, but then she hadn't expected him to. They barely knew each other. But she had recognised the instant mutual attraction. It was something to build on. He had been kind to her…comforting, and she had mistaken disguised lust for respect and affection. She had taken David's honest qualities and applied them to this man. Rebecca closed her eyes and leaned her hot forehead against the cool glass of her bedroom window pane. She couldn't help her inexperience. She couldn't help her naivety. But Heaven knew how she regretted them both now. And how she hated Simon—he had taken her small inheritance and left her so bereft that she was obliged to consider sordid propositions from a stranger.

Whichever way she approached it, whichever course of action she took, she knew she had to steel herself against the utter humiliation which threatened to choke what remained of her confidence and self-respect.

Chapter Five

Rebecca walked briskly, swinging her straw bonnet in one hand, concentrating on the pleasant warmth of the October sun on her head. She could now see the Manor—it was barely another five minutes' walk away—but still she curbed her apprehension, attributing the increased thudding of her heart to the brisk pace she was setting herself.

She already had set in her mind what she would say. She had rehearsed the coming interview countless times through the sleepless night. She would not now give it further thought until the actual encounter.

The weather was fine again she impressed upon herself, as she lifted her wan face to the sun, but without the oppressive sultriness of previous weeks. She was determined to do her utmost to urgently seek out Simon and investigate suitable employment. She had Martha and Gregory as companions. She had Kay and Adam as friends, and although neither couple was in a position to help her financially, she knew they would support her in other ways. She had a lot to be grateful for. She would not allow an arrogant, immoral stranger to blight her future. Once the mortification of the next hour or so was behind her, she would be ready to continue with her life.

She lightly ascended the stone steps of Ramsden Manor and immediately rapped the knocker on the sturdy black-oak door. Her palms were clammy and she automatically dried them on her silver-grey cotton skirts. That edginess apart, she looked quietly about at the sunny scene, noticing how the recent rain had brought a little verdure back into the landscape.

'Miss Rebecca…!' Miles greeted her, a smile creasing his lined countenance.

'Hello, Miles,' Rebecca returned in a cordial but wavering tone. 'Is Mr Trelawney at home? I should like to speak to him.'

'Big or little?' Miles asked with a mischievious grin.

Rebecca looked searchingly at him and then said, 'Oh…I see.' She managed a small laugh. 'I mean Lord Ramsden. Is he at home, Miles?'

'Well, come in…come in,' Miles prompted, realising they stood by the door conversing. He ushered Rebecca into the cool, marble-floored hallway. 'I believe he went to the stables. I'll go and check. You make yourself comfortable,' he said as he hobbled down the stone steps. He called casually back to her, 'Judith is about in the kitchens somewhere. She'll be pleased to see you.'

Rebecca stood alone in the vast hallway. A week ago she would have done as Miles prompted and wandered off to find Judith. She had always felt relaxed and at home in this house. Now she glanced about at familiar ebonized panelling and the elegant sweeping stairwell, feeling unwelcome and intrusive. An unsteady hand went to her hair, checking and tidying stray tendrils, loosened by her brisk walk. She moved to one of the high-backed hall chairs and sat down and waited.

Partial obliteration of the sunbeams streaking the floor was the first indication of his arrival and despite her absolute resolution that she would not panic, her fingers tightened convulsively about the velvet chair seat. As heavy, ringing footsteps neared her, she stood up carefully and then turned towards him.

He was closer than she had imagined and she stepped back from him before raising her eyes to his. He was dressed in plain black breeches and an open-necked white shirt, sleeves rolled back from solid tanned forearms, and his overwhelming virility nearly made her seek the chair again. Instead she greeted him coolly.

'Good morning, Mr Trelawney. I'm sorry to arrive uninvited. Might I have a few minutes of your time? I should like to speak to you.'

Luke's eyes and mouth narrowed assessingly. He had been suspicious as soon as Miles told him she had arrived. He was certain even the keenest fiancée would allow her suitor slightly longer to reappear. It was barely fifteen hours since last he'd seen her. A thin smile touched his lips. But he'd known new mistresses take less time before soliciting. When he had left her yesterday she had been subdued but tranquil. Strangely, so had he.

But there was no such serenity about her now. Probing dark eyes slowly surveyed her alabaster face. She was finding it hard to meet his eyes and to cease chewing at her bottom lip. He waited, allowing a brief silence to develop between them, attempting to gauge her mood and intention. But she had prepared well and merely stood before him with a polite, neutral expression fixed on a spot slightly to his right.

He held out a hand, indicating she should walk in front of him. 'Come along to the study. It's a fine day,' he added conversationally.

'Indeed, yes, it is,' Rebecca agreed, forcing herself to

adopt his bland tone as she entered the door he held open for her.

'Sit down, Rebecca,' he ordered quietly as he closed it.

She immediately did so, in the comfortable wing-chair across from the one he used behind the large, leather-topped desk. 'How did you get here? Did Gregory bring you? I didn't see the trap in the drive.'

'I walked,' Rebecca calmly informed him. 'I often walk…I often used to walk between here and the Summer House. It isn't that far.' She halted abruptly. She hadn't come here to chat and the sooner she could get through this, the more likely she was to leave with a vestige of pride intact. She drew a steadying breath, about to speak.

'Would you like some tea? Judith will fetch some,' he said at the same time.

'Thank you, no. I have simply come to apologise and then will be leaving.'

He knew then; she was going to reject him because she'd done as he had stupidly hinted she should and thought too long and hard. He had done the same through an endless night until towards dawn he no longer knew which of them was right. The irony was, now he did. And he wasn't prepared for it. His jaw gritted and his lids drooped as he leaned back into the chair.

Rebecca, noting his disquieting change in attitude, launched immediately into her studied speech. 'I have come to apologise, Mr Trelawney, for misinterpreting your proposition yesterday. I am conscious that in doing so I have embarrassed both you and myself. I can only offer my naïvety in mitigation but can assure you that as far as I am concerned the matter is now finished and will never again be mentioned. Good day to you, sir.' She stood up as she murmured this last, and was halfway to the door when he spoke.

'And I can assure you, Rebecca, that the matter is no-where near finished,' he informed her remorselessly.

She swung back to him then, but continued stepping backwards towards the door. She breathed deeply, desper-ate to maintain her icy composure. She had been doing so well. Better than she had dared imagine. 'I can categorically state, sir, that nothing could be further from the truth,' she tremulously declared.

He shoved his chair back then and started towards her, making her speed backwards even faster towards the door. She twisted to open it at the same time as his hand jammed across her shoulder, slamming it shut.

She flung herself round to glare up into his tense, dark face. 'You will allow me to leave this instant. Remove your hand,' she commanded icily, spearmint sparks glittering in her eyes.

'No,' he denied her with equal chill and greater authority. He didn't bother elaborating and merely stared down into her white, strained face.

She was losing control. She knew she was. The protec-tive shell of frigid civility was cracking and she could feel hurt and humiliation welling up, waiting to seep out. She lowered her face immediately and studied the mother-of-pearl buttons in the lawn folds of his shirt. Her eyes were inexorably drawn to the expanse of dark, muscled chest exposed by the gaping material so she closed them and bit down on her lip as she felt its first tremor. It was so unfair. She had so nearly made it. Two more paces…and she would have been out, into the meadow, on her way home.

The injustice of it made a final burst of courage hearten her and she clung desperately to it. She shook back her golden head to meet his eyes squarely. 'If you please, sir, I should like to leave. My pupils are awaiting my return. I told Martha I would be but an hour. It is more than that now,' he was glacially informed.

'I thought about you all through last night, Rebecca,' he said softly, ignoring her plea. 'I've thought about you every night…every day, since the first moment I saw you.'

Rebecca hurriedly dropped her eyes from a burning pitch-dark gaze that slowly roamed her set features.

'Do you know what else I was thinking about, Rebecca?' He moved a hand towards her face as though to make her look at him. But then he changed his mind and merely carried it on to lean that against the door too, so she rested within an untouching embrace. 'I was thinking of children…daughters with molten-honey hair and eyes the colour of foreign seas.'

A pained, bitter laugh erupted from Rebecca. 'How poetic, Mr Trelawney…and there was I believing you an insensitive barbarian. Fortunately, you will not need to worry further about bastards. Leastways, none that resemble me.'

A swift, dark hand relinquished the door and curled about her nape, forcing her head up to his. 'You believed I wanted to marry you yesterday. What would have been your answer?'

She swallowed and her tongue swiftly moistened her dry lips. 'No,' she answered hoarsely.

'Liar,' he rejected on a satisfied smile. 'So you were prepared to be my wife but not my mistress. Which makes me wonder what it was that Robin Ramsden gave you that you think I cannot.' His eyes and tone hardened as he spoke and he abruptly swung her about, walking her backwards with him towards the chair she had vacated.

'Perhaps you would like to tell me, Rebecca,' he suggested quietly. 'Or is it simply that you don't want to leave Sussex?'

She pulled herself out of his grasp and to escape him

walked about the desk and stood close to the chair he had sat in. She gripped the leather back of it with white-knuckled fingers. 'What is it Robin Ramsden gave me?' she choked on a small bitter laugh. 'He gave me everything. In the last five years he gave me a roof over my head, food to eat, a way of earning my living…he gave me my self-respect.'

'You think I won't care for you…give you all of that and more?' he asked softly.

'I have no wish to earn my living with you. By profession I am a teacher.'

'I'm not judging you, Rebecca,' he said gently. 'I know you have endured a lot of tragedy in your life. You must have been very young when you lost your parents and your fiancé. How old were you, sixteen…seventeen?'

'I have no need of your pity and it is somewhat misplaced as I was almost twenty-one at that time,' she informed him with a strange mix of triumph and regret at letting him know her age.

Sepia-dark eyes narrowed on her and he queried, 'Twenty-one?' He barely paused before calculating, 'You're nearly twenty-six?'

The unalloyed surprise in his voice was simultaneously wounding and satisfying. 'Yes, Mr Trelawney, I am very nearly twenty-six,' Rebecca confirmed, tilting her chin. 'I'm sorry to disappoint you with my advanced years. Perhaps they will now permit me to leave.'

'You haven't disappointed me, Rebecca,' he said with a smile. 'Just surprised me somewhat.' And she had, he had to admit. She looked a good deal younger but, that apart, it also showed Ramsden in a more ethical light. Bringing a poverty-stricken woman of twenty-one under one's protection was infinitely more acceptable than ruining a child of sixteen.

In the brief silence, words hovering and nudging on the edge of Rebecca's mind surged in. She froze and stared, not daring to believe it true. She concentrated on them as they ran back and forth through her head. *What was it Robin Ramsden gave you that you think I cannot?* She moistened her dry lips, unwilling to countenance his meaning or that she had been so incredibly unworldly again. She had just admitted to being a woman of nearly twenty-six years old, yet what he had naturally assumed had prompted Robin's help and protection had never once occurred to her.

'You believe that Robin…you think that…you believe he would have used me in the disgusting way you wish to?'

Her hands gripped so hard on the chair back that it started to tip backwards and she abruptly let it go. It clattered back, castors skidding against the polished wood floor.

'You are quite despicable. I wish my uncle were alive. I wish so much he were alive. He would kill you for insulting me so…' In her fury and agitation, she rounded the desk to confront him, barely noticing the change in his demeanour.

'What did you say?' he grated, as she approached with violence in her eyes.

'I said he would kill you…he would kill you,' she cried, the sheen in her eyes threatening to spill.

'What else…you said something else,' he uttered hoarsely, catching at her forearms to hold her away from him as he guessed her intention.

Rebecca was instantly still. She swallowed hard and shook straggling honey curls back from her flushed face. 'I said that my uncle would kill you. But he can't and I wish I could.'

Luke slowly relaxed his grip on her but didn't let her go.

'What is this "uncle" you term him. Some coy epithet for lover?'

A hand immediately attempted to fly up towards his face. It was as instinctive as the struggle to free herself. She fought him silently and savagely until he swung her about and forced her spine back against his torso. A brown arm banded her tight against him until her thrashing calmed. It did almost immediately. She held herself rigid against his tense, hard body, steeling herself to ignore the heat and mingling male scent of leather and citrus soap enveloping her. He released her tentatively, as though believing she might turn and swing at him. But she didn't. As soon as possible she pulled far away and then faced him.

'No,' she finally answered him, as though there had been no break in their conversation. 'It's more a coy epithet for my father's brother. Half-brother, actually. Not a fact that was well known, for they hated each other. My grandmother, Grace Markham, was mother to them both. She married into the Ramsden family. She married Saul, the fourth baron, I believe he was. On his death she married Granville Nash,' she recounted remotely, as her wobbly fingers attempted to straighten her hair and her dress. 'But Robin liked me.' She gave a shaky laugh. 'I should say he liked us all, for no doubt you will again suspect him of singular depravity. He was fond of Simon, Elizabeth and me. Perhaps because he and his wife had no children of their own they were good to their nephew and nieces. He would let us play in the Summer House as children. For that's what it was then: a children's summer house.'

She continued to neaten her appearance as she neared the door, quite collected now. 'So now you know, Mr Trelawney, a little bit of Ramsden history. Not many people do. But then it was none of their concern. Just as it was none of yours.'

She turned at the door to look at him. 'I'm glad that you have decided you're too grand and sophisticated to join us in Sussex. It's comforting to know that you will be relinquishing this property and title to return elsewhere. The Ramsden estate...the people here...the Summer House...all have been dear to me for five years or more, and knowing you despise them only endorses their worth for me.

'So there is something else you should know, Mr Trelawney. I will not give up any of it lightly. I have no intention of quitting the home my uncle gave to me. If you wish me out of the Summer House, you will have to get the bailiffs to forcibly eject me.' She barely paused for breath. 'Good day to you, sir,' she quietly, politely directed to the expanse of broad back positioned by the large window.

'The nights are getting colder, my lord. I'll stoke this up a bit for you,' Miles offered helpfully, as he poked at the already blazing pile of logs in the grate. Luke murmured something inaudible without looking away from the open newspaper across him. He leaned one side of his face in a broad palm and flicked the page over.

Miles slid him a look from the fireplace. He had again been assigned by the rest of the servants to try and winkle out when this unexpected benefactor might be withdrawing his person and purse from the Manor to return to Cornwall. Severance pay and references were all very well but didn't compare with retaining the present status quo.

This sixth baron had inherited just two weeks ago, yet in Miles's fifty years of service at this noble residence, he had never known such open handedness. There was ample food in the stock cupboards, candles enough to light a ballroom, fuel for every fire. A new groom had been hired to

care for the two magnificent horses ensconced in the stables, even though, by all accounts, they would soon be
gone. Miles had only mentioned once, in passing, that another kitchen servant would benefit and he had been given
notice to hire one.

But each one of the servants dejectedly knew it was not
to last. This Baron had told them at the outset that the
Ramsden estate and title found no favour with him. Yet the
week of departure had come and gone…but the Trelawneys
had not…not yet.

Miles creased his already furrowed brow thoughtfully at
the darkly handsome man who seemed engrossed in three-
day-old newspapers. He glanced at the crystal tumbler at
one side of him. It was empty…again. He creaked across
on his painful joints, collecting the decanter on the way.
He carefully replenished the glass, a stiff bow acknowledging the grunt which he now recognised as gratitude. He
replaced the decanter on a mahogany side table. Then
picked it up again and moved it to another. He scuffled
wearily to the mantelpiece and moved a candlestick…then
moved it back again. He girded his courage.

'You'll be soon away back to Cornwall then, my lord?'
Miles croaked out.

Luke glanced up at him, then down at the paper. He
pushed himself irritably back into the brocade sofa and one
black-booted foot came up to rest on the opposite knee. He
rustled the paper open again and stared at the print without
answering.

Miles crept about the room, tinkering with various pot-
tery, cushions and stray books. Luke looked up impatiently
at his furtive ministrations, about to dismiss him, when he
heard the gravel crunch outside the window. He turned his
dark head towards the black night, seeing the blur of the
carriage light as it passed.

Miles saw it, too, and ambled slowly across the Aubusson carpet towards the window. 'Can't be Master Ross, he's gone to Brighton…too early for him,' he mumbled to himself. 'Perhaps it's Gregory come over at last.'

He glanced casually at his master as he passed him, and noted that he had somehow just gained his full, black-eyed attention. So he explained. 'Gregory Turner. I've been expecting him all week. Thought he must have been ailing…'

'Why is that?' Luke questioned evenly.

'Afflicted like me…in the knees,' Miles readily explained.

'Why have you been expecting him all week?' Luke spelled out through lightly gritting teeth.

'Well, no one's come to collect the provisions. I thought if Gregory was poorly perhaps Miss Rebecca would come herself. She can drive that trap good as any man. I've seen her. And they must be low on everything. Shouldn't think they've a pound of flour left. Can't think why they've not been…'

Luke could, and a low oath ground out of him as he sprang up and strode to the window. 'It's not the trap. I thought I told you that the Summer House was to be maintained.'

'Oh, yes. But Gregory always collects the provisions. Miss Rebecca's uncle…that was Robin Ramsden, you know, because not many people do. Only the old 'uns like me and the Turners…'

A harsh bark of laughter made Miles start and cease his rambling dialogue. Luke glowered, thin-lipped, at the ornate plaster work on the drawing room ceiling before piercingly at the old man. 'Yes, I do know now and I would have been obliged had someone thought to mention it sooner.'

Miles squinted uncertainly at him, wondering what had

prompted this abrupt passion to overtake his master's previous apathy. 'Well, Lord Ramsden as was, said how Gregory should collect once a week,' he testily explained.

'Well, Lord Ramsden as is…' Luke informed silkily, '…says make very sure that whatever they are lacking is delivered at first light tomorrow. Do I make myself clear?'

Miles peered myopically at him. 'Indeed, my lord. I'll send John,' he warily agreed, before continuing his lopsided gait to the window.

'It's your brother, my lord. And some of his friends by the look of things.' Miles shuffled away from the window, a smile rejuvenating his ancient features. Young Mister Trelawney always livened the place up a bit. This one tended to stamp about, surly and uncommunicative, especially in the last week or so. A wealthy young man like he should be out, roistering with other young blades, Miles deemed, wagging his head to himself as he hobbled towards the door.

He could only recollect him going to Brighton a half-dozen times with his brother and then he never came back in a better mood than he went. He hardly left the house in the evening…which was a great pity, for the servants could frolic a little themselves with no master in residence.

Luke dropped back into the red brocade sofa. His dark head leaned back against the comfortable cushions. He closed his eyes and allowed himself to think of Rebecca. He'd managed not to think about her for practically the whole day. Now he'd worry the night through that she was hungry. Why the hell hadn't the stupid old fool said she was out of food? He'd made it plain enough that every consideration given to the Summer House by Robin Ramsden was to continue. But he should have realised she would choose to starve rather than accept any aid from him.

A hand went to the paper and he idly flicked the pages

before carefully folding it and dropping it back on to the seat beside him. He gazed at the intricate ceiling, he stared at the glowing fire and then out into the moonless night. He looked back at the newspaper for a second before he hurled it viciously across the room. He grabbed at the tumbler by his side, downed the brandy in one swallow, and replaced it heavily. He could seduce her, he could coerce her, he could do anything he damn well pleased. He could make her homeless right now…this minute. He could be back in Cornwall in two days with her permanently in his bed. She couldn't deny or fight him.

But he knew he wouldn't. He wouldn't even go over and see her after eight days.

But she'd had the courage to come to him. And politely apologise with grace and dignity for her lack of sophistication. No tearful recriminations, veiled threats or fits of hysteria. She would have come and gone within five minutes had he let her. What wounded him most was that she now genuinely regretted her innocence. Just as he genuinely regretted causing her such hurt and humiliation. She might be naïve…more innocent than she had any right to be at her age, but her intuition was strong. She had recognised instantly what had taken him fifteen hours longer: that they were each other's destiny. It was the source of the quiet serenity that had radiated from her and enveloped him before they parted.

He had arrived at the Summer House to proposition her in irritation; kissed her in lustful selfishness and still she had believed in him. She would have accepted being his wife. He knew it as surely as he knew she would now do her utmost to reject him. Whether it was a sack of flour or marriage he offered, she would spurn him and he would not accept that he had let something so infinitely precious slip through his fingers.

He jerked himself up out of the chair in self-disgust. God, he was behaving like some maudlin callow youth, bemoaning the loss of his first maid.

The drawing-room door was flung open with a flourish. 'Brought you a present back from town,' Ross said on a laugh, sending alcoholic fumes towards Luke.

Luke enquiringly raised bored dark brows and reseated himself on the brocade settee. The voice that then reached him actually had him back up and crossing the carpet.

'George!' He clasped the sandy-haired man warmly by the hand and shoulder and ushered him in. 'Have a drink. Have a seat. What are you doing about these parts?' he demanded, in one breath, of George Dellon, his Cornish neighbour.

'John's here and brought some flour by the look of things,' Martha said, the relief in her voice plain.

'Thank God for that,' Gregory muttered beneath his breath with a sliding peek at Rebecca as she sat breakfasting abstemiously at the kitchen table.

Rebecca sipped slowly at her mug of tea, her attention on the hot beverage resting between her palms.

Martha repeated for her benefit, 'John's here, Miss Becky. It looks as though he's brought over the provisions.'

Rebecca stared, then rose and moved quickly to the kitchen window. She watched the fair-haired youth drop a sack of flour to the ground from the cart and turn to haul the next to the edge to drop.

She rushed purposefully to the kitchen door but Martha's low caution made her halt with her hand on the doorknob.

'If you enjoyed that tea you were just supping you'd best leave him be for there's no more. There's no more flour either or sugar or spice or…'

Rebecca looked at Martha with pained apology. She

knew she could never provide the Turners with the amount of food that they had received from the Manor. The provisions had always been sent to the Summer House, but the Turners also benefitted. What Rebecca could afford to pay for food would barely cover what she and Lucy would use. But she would reject it and try to deal with the consequences later.

Martha and Gregory exchanged looks of worry and disbelief as Rebecca walked towards the laden cart.

'Good morning, John. What are you doing?'

John bobbed his yellow head in greeting. 'Miles told me to bring you your provisions, Miss Rebecca, as no one has been by to collect them,' he explained with a shy smile, letting another large sack hit the ground.

'Please reload and return it all to the Manor. There has been an unfortunate mistake. I'm sorry you have had your time wasted.'

John squinted against the hazy yellow orb gilding the eastern horizon. 'Are you sure, miss?'

'Quite sure. Please return everything.'

John twisted about and surveyed the laden cart: spices, sugar, tea, dried fruit. Who in their right mind would turn it down, even if it was a duplicate load? He gave Rebecca a conspiratorial wink. 'Perhaps you could store it, miss…'

Rebecca gave him a weak smile but looked away from his amiable features. 'I don't want it.'

John stared at her pale, strained face for no more than a few seconds before jumping lightly from the cart and shouldering a sack of flour. It was tipped back on to the cart, the next speedily following it, but John's perplexed gaze tracked Rebecca as she re-entered the Summer House kitchen.

Aware of both Martha and Gregory watching her, Rebecca reminded them quickly and forcefully, 'I have said I will provide us all with what we need and I will. The Jennings' farm flour is a good price and next time Gregory is in Westbrook he can purchase tea. I have money. I have said I will pay…'

Gregory's derisive snort brought her quiet placation to an end. 'You are willing to pay money you can ill afford for what has always been provided free? And still is?'

'Hush,' Martha advised him, with a pointed look for him to remove himself. He did so, but impatiently muttered beneath his breath as he quit the kitchen for the garden.

Aware that a lecture was imminent, Rebecca tried to distract Martha. 'The children will be here soon. I need to prepare for the lessons.'

'You need to prepare for a lot more than that. This won't be the end of it…you mark my words. Just because he's stayed away for a week, doesn't mean he won't be back. That cartload of victuals was his calling card.'

Rebecca swung around at once, her tense face blanching. 'What do you mean by that, Martha?' she demanded, although she knew very well. She had mentioned nothing to the Turners about what had passed between Luke Trelawney and herself. They knew nothing of his proposition or her naïve misinterpretation of it.

But Martha's canny silver eyes and sharp perception missed very little. Would they want her to acquiesce to their landlord's lechery just to keep bread and tea on their tables? She glanced reproachfully at Martha. Recognising the mix of compassion and comprehension in the woman's eyes, she regretted even thinking it.

'I will provide for us, Martha. Not nearly as much or as often, but we will manage, I promise. Once I find Simon and extract my inheritance from him we will never again have these worries.'

Martha walked slowly towards her and enveloped her in

a warm hug. The spontaneous comfort choked an involuntary sob from Rebecca. She buried her face in the woman's fleshy shoulder for a moment before regaining composure.

'There…don't be fretting so,' Martha cooed at her as she laid a plump hand on Rebecca's silky hair. 'It'll all turn out right. You'll see. Lord Ramsden's a fine gentleman…I know he is.'

A bubble of hysterical laughter burst from Rebecca at that. An unsteady hand smeared moisture away from her eyes. 'How much flour and tea have we left?' she asked in a businesslike way.

'There is just about enough flour left for one loaf. None for pastry or biscuits. Enough tea for one brew of the pot.'

Rebecca nodded in mild acceptance of this alarming information and then made for the parlour.

Luke lead the coal-black stallion out of his stall and ran a large dark hand along the animal's sleek flank. He would make a welcome addition to his stables at Melrose. The horse fair at Brighton had been an enjoyable well-spent day. He wished there would be another soon. He needed something interesting to divert him from the monotony of his time here. He liked to think he knew a bit about horseflesh and that he could drive a hard bargain. This beautiful animal and the fine chestnut he had bought for Ross were… His pleasant musing tailed off as his eyes followed the lumbering cart making slow progress back towards Ramsden Manor.

He swung up easily into the saddle and was, within a minute, alongside the loaded vehicle.

'What are you doing with this?' Luke asked evenly.

'I'm sorry, my lord. Miss Rebecca said to bring it back. She says she doesn't want any of it.'

Instead of the ire John had been expecting, his master gave a grunt of resigned laughter. The black stallion pawed restlessly at the ground and he expertly controlled the animal, reining it in as it circled skittishly. 'That's what she said, did she,' he muttered to himself.

To John, he ordered, 'Take it back…and tell Miss Rebecca from me that if it comes back here again I'll burn all of it.'

John stared at him as though he must have taken leave of his senses. There was enough food on the cart he drove to see a family through to the new year. Lost in shock, he sat unresponsive until a steely soft voice queried, 'Do you want me to repeat the message?'

John shook his corn-coloured head. 'No, my lord. No.'

'Good. Do it now.' A flick of a jet-black head indicating west sent John back the way he had come.

'You'd better come and look at this.'

'Continue with your numbers,' Rebecca called out to the four young girls scribbling on blackboards. She quit the parlour and curiously followed Martha into the kitchen.

Martha indicated outside with a sideways nod of her grey head.

Rebecca walked apprehensively to the window. John was once more unloading sacks of flour from his cart. Swinging furiously away, she sped to the door.

'I believe I told you earlier, John, that I don't want any of this.'

'I know what you said, Miss Rebecca, but Lord Ramsden…' He tailed off as though finding explanations beyond him.

'Take it away, John,' Rebecca ordered quietly, fiercely. 'Take it away this minute, no matter what he threatens.'

'If I take it back again, he says he will set light to it,'

John advised dolefully. 'He said to tell you that he's going to burn it all.'

Rebecca stared, horrified, at him. The thought of precious sustenance being so wantonly destroyed was quite obscene. She felt it, John felt it and so would the Turners. So would every peasant family in this village…every village in the land. Yet Luke Trelawney would carelessly do it because he knew nothing of being hungry, nothing of hardship.

All he knew was that he could blackmail, threaten and bribe in order to get his own way… 'The matter is nowhere near finished,' he had assured her. He was obviously smugly confident she would submit to his lust. Rebecca was sure she had never hated anyone more.

'Lord Ramsden said he would burn all this food?' she echoed in a whisper.

John's wretched nodding signalled he could not believe it either.

Without another word Rebecca turned and walked towards the Summer House. She called calmly over her shoulder, 'Just wait a moment, John, if you please.' She entered the kitchen and made for the cooking range. Having selected the longest and sturdiest of the spills from the hearth she went back outside. 'Give this to Lord Ramsden, please, John. Tell him I hope it assists with the blaze.'

John stared at her, open-mouthed. But she thrust the sliver of timber into his hand and immediately turned and walked away.

John examined the clouding sky, the timbered horizon, the sturdy mellow brickwork of Ramsden Manor, anything but his lordship's black expression. Relaying her message this time had not prompted his master to chuckle…or smile…even weakly. As the stony silence lengthened John slid a peek from the corner of a blue eye. His lordship's face could have been hewn from granite, his mouth thrust forward in hard sardonic contemplation of the spill he held between the thumb and forefinger of one dark hand. Black eyes regarded it thoughtfully, then just those two digits abruptly snapped and discarded it.

John glanced at him, spontaneously rubbing nervously at the bridge of his nose. Trouble was brewing, he could tell.

'You must be excited at the prospect of seeing your new baby brother,' Rebecca remarked conversationally as she turned the pages of the music.

Lucy looked up at her with a scowling grimace, immediately lost her place and plinked to a discordant halt on the piano. 'I don't want to see any of them,' she rejected in a low voice. 'Only Mary. I'd like to see my sister Mary. I do miss her.'

'I'm sorry, Lucy, I shouldn't have interrupted you. You've lost concentration now and you were doing so well. Start again.' Rebecca flicked the pages back to the start of the piece. Lucy obediently alternatively squinted at the music and at her fingers.

The instrument had a good tone but Lucy was never going to be an accomplished musician, although her singing voice was quite sweet. A lingering sallowness about Lucy's eyebrow drew Rebecca's eyes.

The girl never mentioned her stepfather or her mother or the new baby, although she had received a letter from her mother advising her of the birth. No one had yet visited Lucy at the school and she seemed untroubled by her parents' lack of concern.

Rebecca's slender fingers turned the page and as Lucy faltered, she pointed to the sheet to indicate her place. Lucy wasn't keen on her music lessons and Rebecca knew that her obedience and attention would soon waver and probably give rise to an irritable tantrum. She still found it difficult to control her moods and would sometimes sulk or cry or giggle helplessly with the slightest provocation. She could also be spiteful with the younger girls who came as day pupils and would think nothing of delivering a sly pinch here or a light cuff there when she thought Rebecca was not watching.

Lucy abruptly sighed and shrugged in exasperation. She flung herself around on the piano stool, began to complain and then gawped, straight past her tutor.

Rebecca murmured, her eyes with the music, 'Come along…you were doing so well. Just finish it. There is barely half a page to go.' Lucy's continuing silence made the hair at the back of Rebecca's neck prickle and she instinctively touched the turquoise ribbon, loosely confining her honey hair in a thick, flowing wave that reached to the middle of her back. The disturbing sensation intensified and she pivoted slowly, holding her breath.

'I did knock…the kitchen door was open so I let myself in.' Luke Trelawney excused himself quietly from the doorway.

Rebecca stared, facing him fully, feeling her colour fading and her pulse strengthening. 'Mr Trelawney…' she murmured weakly, partly greeting and partly identifying him.

Chapter Six

He moved slowly away from the door like a large, drifting black shadow in the small, dim parlour. It was barely six o'clock yet the cloudy sky had darkened the day to dusk. The small brass candelabra burning atop the piano was scant flame enough to read the music Lucy had been playing, let alone brighten the room.

Aware of Lucy watching her with a small, knowing smile, Rebecca hastily dismissed her. 'That will do now, Lucy. You can have your quiet hour sewing in your room and then we will dine.'

Lucy approached Luke with a bold, upturned face and an arch smile. 'Lord Ramsden,' she greeted him with an exaggerated, dipping curtsy and a flick of her floral skirt.

He returned her a brief nod and watched her leave before his black eyes returned to the piano and Rebecca.

'Why is the kitchen door not locked?' This unexpected interrogation left her momentarily speechless. 'You should keep it locked…you never know who may be about, up to no good in the neighbourhood.'

'Indeed…' Rebecca breathed with studied irony.

A thin, acerbic smile acknowledged the subtle insult. 'I

mean someone who might really intend you harm, Rebecca. Keep the door locked at all times.'

'I do usually,' she returned quickly, compelled to defend her routine vigilance. 'Martha and Gregory have only just left for home. I usually lock and bolt directly they have gone.'

He nodded acceptance of this explanation.

A silence between them lengthened and tautened. Merely to occupy herself, Rebecca turned to the piano to close the lid. The highly polished wood slipped straight through her nervous fingers, crashing shut. She suppressed a small scream at the abrupt vibrating din and closed her eyes, crossing her arms about her waist to still their trembling.

'What do you want, Mr Trelawney?' she demanded in a low voice, aware she could hardly order him from the house. It was his. The land was his, the building was his.

'A mug of tea and a biscuit,' he informed her softly as he approached. He halted just a foot away, steeling himself not to touch her. But a hooded look caressed her fragile, ivory cheekbones curtained by thick swathes of honey hair.

Rebecca shook clinging tendrils back from her face and forced herself to look up at him. The candle behind her was reflected in his eyes, firing them to onyx stars.

'I'm afraid…I have no tea and I believe the biscuits are finished too,' she stated proudly, understanding exactly why he wanted them.

'I know,' he said with a slow smile. 'That's why I brought my own.'

'Are they charcoal biscuits?' she taunted with sweet sarcasm. The immediate humour in his eyes as he impenitently acknowledged his threats of arson, made her blurt out, 'You can take them away with you.' Gathering her skirts in shaking fingers, she made to walk quickly around him.

Two dark hands fastened on her arms, keeping her in

front of him. She instantly attempted to pull back but muscular, black-sleeved arms folded her tightly against him.

'Don't fight me, Rebecca,' he pleaded hoarsely.

She held herself rigid in his embrace, her heart tattooing crazily, while her eyelids drooped languidly as she indeed did fight…but against her own need to lean her head against him and slip her arms about him.

She felt his long fingers spanning her back, sliding up to stroke the sides of her neck and spear into thick golden tresses. The turquoise ribbon slid from her satin hair as firm, dark fingers tilted her head back to look at him. She averted her face, unable to meet his eyes but he was relentless. Tanned thumbs brushed enticingly against ivory skin as he insisted, 'Look at me, Rebecca.' She did so then, sepia and aquamarine eyes fusing.

'This is no way for a fiancée to behave. The servants are beginning to talk,' he gently rebuked her.

Rebecca stared at him, feeling a painful lump thickening in her throat. She forced herself to speak huskily through it. 'I should be obliged if you would leave now, I find your sense of humour distasteful.'

'I'm not joking, Rebecca. The servants *are* beginning to talk and I expect my betrothed to support and respect my decision to provide for her.'

'I am not your betrothed…I am not your fiancée…I am not your *chère amie* or any other fancy name you care to put on it. Now go away and leave me,' Rebecca choked, desperately trying to free herself from his grip.

He twisted her rejecting hands behind her, bringing her closer to his hard body. His mouth lowered to her hair and a sighing warm breath stirred its lavender-scented silkiness.

'You agreed to marry me, Rebecca. You're my future wife…my one choice. And I intend to hold you to that and make public our engagement. A notice needs to be put in *The Times.*'

'I did not agree… When did I?' Rebecca breathed, looking up at him in wonder. He appeared sane and serious.

'After I asked you to share my life. You told me when you looked at me…when you kissed me back…when you put up with my vile mood and still accepted me as your husband. All that was lacking was the word.' He suddenly gave a low grunt of unamused laughter. 'You've been talking to Ross, haven't you? *Chère amie,*' he scathingly sneered. He moved her back a little from him and studied her evasive face. 'You wouldn't have known, would you?' A dark hand relinquished one of hers and moved to her face, cupping it tenderly. 'You would never have realised. Ross told you, didn't he?'

Rebecca felt blood flood her face as she remembered her promise to his brother. 'Ross and I haven't spoken,' she denied quickly, lowering her eyes.

'Don't lie to me, Rebecca,' he said quietly. 'Only Ross uses that ridiculous term for a harlot…apart from the harlots themselves.'

'Would I have used it, do you think?' Rebecca challenged bitterly, unwittingly acknowledging just how susceptible she had always been to his coercion.

Luke lifted her so that her face was level with his and then placed her gently back to sit on top of the piano. He braced an arm either side of her and leaned close. 'You were never going to be anyone's harlot, Rebecca. Least of all mine.' His mouth moved slowly towards hers and she watched it come. Her lips parted before they touched, her eyes closed and her head tilted. He paused to survey her serene beauty; an innate sensuality increasing her breathing to a shallow pant, straining her small rounded breasts enticingly against her bodice.

He recalled the spirited water nymph in the pond who had first enchanted him, her dress tantalisingly stuck to her body, and found her mouth rather too fiercely. A sturdy palm supported her head to prevent her jerking away, but this time she didn't. She accepted his ardour with a yielding sweetness that made him check and pull her forward to the very edge of the piano top and hold her reassuringly close against him.

His mouth slid hot and moist back and forth against hers with slow, calculated eroticism, tasting and caressing every inch of sensitive skin, until she was mindlessly gasping and her thighs intuitively parted to accommodate his body between them. His tongue-tip flicked against her lower lip, making her mouth reflexively widen and her back arch. Biting kisses trailed along the satin-skinned pearly column of the throat curving provocatively to meet him.

'Rebecca,' he murmured her name reverently; then with anguished humour, on hearing her low whimper of dismay as he moved away. Large hands gently enclosed her face to make her look at him.

'Rebecca,' he huskily repeated with strengthening authority.

She raised weighty lids, her dilated turquoise gaze engulfed by smouldering coal-black eyes. He touched his mouth tentatively to her swollen lips, pulling reluctantly back as they spontaneously clung and parted. 'I think I'd better put the notice in *The Times* this week,' he said on a gruff laugh. 'We'll be married at the end of next week, here in Sussex, so you can be amongst friends. Then we'll travel to Cornwall. We'll honeymoon there. For as long as you like,' he said with a slow, sensuous smile as his eyes travelled her beautiful flushed face and lingered on her slick mouth. Long blunt fingers threaded into her silken hair.

'What do you say?' he demanded on a soft, satisfied

laugh, noting the sensual torpor that still drugged her. God, how easy it would have been to seduce her. One captivating kiss… And the knowledge made him simultaneously arrogant and ashamed; predatory and protective.

'Will you marry me, Rebecca?' he asked in an aching whisper against her unbearably sensitive mouth.

'Yes.'

One word, it was all the energy she could summon but her lips curved in a smile against his, deliberately tempting. He kissed her gently, lifted her from the piano and placed her close beside him.

'Make me a cup of tea,' he requested with a tenderly amused smile as she immediately swayed against him. 'I can wait for the biscuit until tomorrow, when Martha does her baking.'

Rebecca knew she mustn't panic. Girls liked to wander. She had been the same at that age. It was part of growing up, she remembered, to have quiet times to oneself. Nevertheless, she ran the remaining yards to the Turners' cottage and her rap on the door was loud and urgent.

It was opened cautiously within a few seconds and Martha's rotund face appeared at the crack.

'Why, Miss Becky. What on earth are you doing here at this time of the night?'

'Have you seen Lucy, Martha? I can't find her anywhere about the Summer House. She's not in the coach house or in with the chickens. I don't know where else to look.'

Martha opened the door fully as Rebecca was speaking and ushered her in. She plonked her hands on ample hips and said plainly, 'Have you thought to look at the Manor?'

Rebecca whitened. Martha's initial thought had been the first horrifying possibility that had occurred to her too on discovering her pupil missing. 'You think she may have gone to find John?'

'I'm saying nothing, Miss Becky. But you and I both knows how smitten she is. If she's nowhere to be seen, she's probably up to no good in the hay somewhere.' She nodded her head in emphasis. 'I'd get Gregory to drive you over there, but he and Jeremy Watson have gone to the White Horse supping tonight. He had a bit of luck on cards.' She muttered about her husband's wastrel ways as she stalked off to sit back down by her small fire. The spotless room was spartan but cosy: a kettle hissed steam over the flickering glow and there was a redolence of chicken stew.

'You think she will be at the Manor?'

'I lay a pound to a penny that if young carpenter is there, that is definitely where she is. And doing what she shouldn't. Leave her be. Get yourself home and safe and leave her be. She's a woman grown…however old she is,' Martha advised sagely.

Rebecca put a shaking hand to her forehead. 'Whatever will her stepfather think? She's in my care and I've let her—'

'You've let her nothing. You can't watch that one every minute of the day. If you did, she'd still slope off. It's her way.' She looked at Rebecca sympathetically.. 'You get yourself home. John will look after her…bring her back. He's a good lad.'

Rebecca shoved a shaking hand through her loose, golden hair. After a moment's indecision, she simply bade quietly, 'Goodnight, Martha,' and closed the ill-fitting cottage door behind her.

She stepped hurriedly away, back into the moonless night. She wrapped her shawl tight about her shivering body and hugged the perimeter of the woodland to avoid the worst of the stiffening breeze.

She had felt so joyous barely an hour ago. Luke had been with her then. He had sat with her in the kitchen and taken tea…eventually. Her fingers instinctively sought her tender, swollen mouth and an ache stirred deep within her as she concentrated on him. His kisses had been brief and gentle, lengthy and passionate and every delectable nuance in between. It had been the aroma of her dinner, bubbling slowly away to nothing on the cooking range, that had finally brought her to her senses.

She and Lucy had still not eaten and the hour by then was getting late. Aware just how unbelievably shameless her behaviour had been, especially believing Lucy to be sewing upstairs in her room, she had finally jumped, mortified, off Luke's lap, and begun attending belatedly to saving their stew while Luke drank his cold tea. He had then unloaded the cart of its provisions while she set about tidying her appearance and setting the dinner table.

She should have looked for Lucy earlier, she realised, while Luke was still with her. She had been too bewitched by him and the untasted, glorious feelings he aroused to relinquish him for a minute. Yet she recognised the peril in this wonderful new emotion, for it greatly undermined her logic and self-control.

Rebecca felt her face ice, then burn with embarrassment. She had behaved appallingly. She had allowed Luke too many liberties. One kiss would have been enough to seal their betrothal. Earlier today she had felt she hated him. Now he meant so much, it was as though she possessed no will when he touched her. She wouldn't allow it to happen again. She would show more composure.

Did he think her wanton? He did, she groaned to herself. It was the source of that warm amusement in his eyes when he looked at her. Well, it was his fault if she was. She knew he deliberately made her feel that way. It empowered him and made her weak. But he wanted to marry her.

He had said so and she believed and trusted him now. He had no reason to lie; he was well aware just how defenceless and beholden to him she was. If only he had said…but he hadn't said the words…nor had she. But they sang mantra-like through her head now as she sped back towards the Summer House.

The glow of light from the lamp she had left burning in her pantry window became visible and she lightly ran across the grass towards the kitchen door.

Deliberately hiding to frighten her was the sort of antic Lucy would find vastly amusing. There were only five rooms in all, including the kitchen and she again searched each. A gust of tepid wind slammed the kitchen door back on its hinges. Rebecca ran through the dusk to the rickety small coach house where the trap was kept, although she knew it was fruitless double-checking. Dorcas, Gregory's old cart horse, whinnied softly at this second intrusion in one evening before dipping her head back to her feed.

'Lucy!' Rebecca called, fear and panic making her voice high and strident. There was nothing. No sound apart from the soughing of the wind in the trees and the dry swirling of early fallen leaves.

She would have to go the Manor. She would have to go to find Luke and ask him to help her look for Lucy. She didn't like to dwell on it…but she wouldn't be at all surprised if, in the barn she knew John favoured for lazy afternoons, she also found Lucy reclining there this evening.

The first sound had her frozen to the spot and she backed against the closest tree, her hands gripping behind her at scraping bark. She held her breath, straining to listen but could hear nothing apart from the increased pumping of her own blood. She threw her head back and looked at the rustling canopy of leaves swaying above her. An owl called somewhere nearby, making her start and then a white blur broke cover, swooping low and close.

Rebecca closed her eyes, unsure whether to laugh or cry at her terror. An owl! She pushed herself away from the sturdy bole of the tree and had skirted another few yards of woodland when she saw the light. It bobbed intermittent yellow flashes into the pitch of the night. When it was joined by another and then another and three pinprick lamps undulated through woodland, she stepped back rigidly, her hands frantically exploring behind again for another shielding tree.

Voices were audible now too, although actual words were indistinct. She heard a gruff masculine laugh, then another, higher-pitched, in response and heavy twig-cracking footsteps.

Rebecca froze, petrified, to the spot. She glanced quickly down at her clothing. Trembling fingers swiftly gathered her black silk shawl up high about her throat, obliterating any sight of her white lawn bodice. She heard the men pass within yards of her, their laughter and conversation so muted, it was obviously intentionally muffled.

She twisted silently against the tree trunk as they made their way out of the wood towards Westbrook village. She watched them go. There were four of them, walking fast…or as fast as they were able with the hampering barrels hoisted about their shoulders. Each man carried two over each of his shoulders. Their identity was now obvious and chilled her to the marrow.

They were smugglers…the tub men, probably carrying spirits or tea. She remembered Simon telling her how tea was smuggled ashore in kegs. Tea! She might have sent

Gregory to Westbrook to unwittingly purchase some. The irony almost made a hysterical giggle escape. She stuffed a shaking fist to her mouth.

Simon had also told her terrifying tales of bodies found on the beaches of people who had been in the wrong place at the wrong time when contraband came ashore. People murdered because they could identify the miscreants who brought illegal goods into the country past the Revenue men. Revenue men too were often found lifeless on the shore.

Rebecca closed her eyes tight, waiting, barely breathing, in case another party of free-traders was trekking up from the coast through this wood. She hardly dared consider just how lucky she had been. Had she left the Summer House a few minutes earlier in her dash to the Manor, their paths would undoubtedly have crossed.

She recalled what Gregory had told her just a week ago: that Jake Blacker had been seen locally, and a sob stifled in her throat. That blackguard was renowned throughout the area for his cruelty and corruption. But he had managed to evade detection and arrest. He had moved away, so they had heard, because there were richer pickings to be had in Kent for he and his cronies.

That had been years previously but now he was back. And Rebecca had missed confronting him or his associates by minutes. Where was Simon? Please don't let Simon be involved with them, she prayed to the whispering leaves above her head.

Gathering her shawl tightly about her, she slipped silently forward, keeping within the screening woodland and fled towards Ramsden Manor, her heart and mind calling out to Luke Trelawney for love and protection.

'Evening, Miles,' Luke amiably greeted his butler as he entered the Manor and strode towards his study. He changed his mind and started towards the stairs instead, realising he was ravenous.

'What's for dinner?' he called over his shoulder to the old retainer who was doing his uneven best to keep up with his master's speedy pace across the wide hall.

'Stew?' Luke suggested. 'I feel quite partial to a nice stew,' he informed the butler, savouring the memory of the rich aroma of the Summer House kitchen.

'Stew?' Miles mouthed at his back, wrinkle-nosed and pinched-mouthed. '*Stew?*' he repeated aloud in a disparaging tone. He wore the expression of someone recently assaulted with a dead fish as he related, 'I believe Judith has done a *nice* roast leg of lamb with roast vegetables and a redcurrant jelly, my lord, with a *nice* crème brulée to follow.'

Luke shrugged and continued towards the carved black-oak stairway. 'Oh, sounds good,' he said, but lacking enthusiasm. He started to hum, then whistle as he disappeared up the stairs two at a time. 'Arrange hot water for a bath, Miles,' he called back, just before he rounded the corner of the landing which lead towards his rooms.

Luke seated himself at the glossed mahogany table and picked up the paper which lay, neatly folded, for his attention. He absently ruffled his damp dark hair to aid its drying, before casually sleeking it back.

Miles eyed him warily. Something was amiss. He was far too cheerful, the elderly man deemed. Something of moment had happened. He must have been out till late arranging his travel back to Cornwall, he guessed. That was it. He was finally leaving Sussex, Miles was sure, and his slack, ancient features drooped further.

'Has my brother been back from town?' Luke gregariously enquired as he set about his evening meal with gusto.

'No, my lord. I haven't seen anything of that young man since five of the clock. Perhaps he won't be back to dine,' Miles suggested dolefully. He watched gloomily as his master cheerfully polished off his dinner then turned his attention to the brandy decanter.

Luke relaxed back in his chair and smiled. He felt content. He felt elated. He felt in... He hastily checked what he had been about to give conscious thought to and straightened in the Chippendale dining chair. He threw the remaining inch of amber liquid to the back of his throat, then stood up and wandered to the square-paned window. He immediately stared off to the west, just making out the fringe of woodland that shielded the Summer House.

He would leave it half an hour and then go back and see her. He didn't like the idea of her being out there on her own in any case. She was his now. It was official between them and he had an obligation to look after her. He should go back and see her. Make sure she was comfortable. Not in need of anything....like a goodnight kiss.

His narrow mouth curved in sheer satisfaction even though he was aware that these kissing sessions were torturing his highly sensitive body. The straining, bulging discomfort that had tormented him since he had first seen her was still inadequately relieved. And without conscious thought he flexed and rotated his hand. What he desperately needed was a lot more than another tantalising kiss.

He walked back and refilled his glass from the decanter, smiling reflectively into space. His features softened and his dark eyes glazed as he realised that the ache that consumed him when he thought of her now wasn't just confined to his loins. Within a fortnight she would be his bride...in his bed...that beautiful hair spread across snowy sheets...limpid turquoise eyes fiery with passion...

'Young Mr Trelawney's back, my lord.' Miles finally broke into Luke's fevered imaginings with a dry cough to gain his attention. Rheumy eyes now squinted anxiously at his handsome young master. Something was without doubt seriously awry. He had spoken twice. Once from the window, when gazing out at the new arrivals, and then again on approaching the dining table. Yet still glittering black eyes gazed off into space as though the man were in the presence of angels.

Perhaps he'd got religion, Miles brooded. Then proceeded to shake his head to himself. No, it couldn't be. He was from Cornwall, and Miles had it on good authority that the Cornish were heathen reprobates, every one. As long as they were as generous as these two appeared to be, Miles was happy to mingle amongst friends.

He shambled to the dining-room door, peered out, and then turned back to address Luke before disappearing.

'Your brother's brought some of his nice friends to visit again, my lord.'

Luke grunted a non-committal response to this and, collecting his paper from the table, sat down in a comfortable chair to read for ten minutes.

'Brought you a present from town,' Ross bestowed on his brother a tipsy grin.

Luke returned an indulgent smile, wondering which neighbour or old acquaintance he had managed to find in Brighton this time. He had been quite amazed by the varied assortment of people who had turned up at Ramsden Manor over the past fortnight. 'Well, bring him in. You're probably just in time for dinner.'

Ross laughed and swung the door wider. 'George is here,

too. Met him again at the Bull and Mouth. He hadn't yet
left for Cornwall.'

Luke gave a brief blow of annoyance. He had been under
the impression that George Dellon was on his way back to
his wife and sons in Cornwall. He had accordingly entrusted him with a letter to deliver to Tristan with important
business instructions concerning the mines. He had managed to deal with his shipping interests at Bristol quite easily from here and sent hand-delivered messages to the port
every other day.

But he would allow nothing to dampen his good humour.
He dropped the paper to the floor wondering why Ross had
left the visitors out in the hall. Deciding to investigate, he
strolled into the hallway and immediately stopped dead. He
looked at Miles placing gloves neatly on the hall table,
before his eyes returned to the three young women, two
brunettes and one silver-blonde and none of them much
older than twenty.

A puzzled look was aimed at George Dellon, lounging
by the stairs. The man gave him an uncertain smile and
shifted uneasily before his lascivious eyes again assaulted
the dazzling women. Luke pivoted slowly on his heel to
stare disbelievingly at Ross.

'You've brought three whores to my house?' he enquired
quietly. 'You've actually brought them *here*…to this
house?'

Ross's smile faltered a little. 'Well, it won't be yours
much longer. We'll be leaving soon…returning to Cornwall. Anyway—' he gave a backward nod of his head to
indicate Miles '—I told him they're George's sisters, and
the servants can have the night off.' He snorted an infectious laugh and George joined him after a second, trying to
camouflage his amusement with a coughing fit. Ross con-

tinued in a choke, 'The poor old cove must be practically blind…'

'He's not blind,' Luke informed with exceeding calm. 'He's unsuspecting. If you said they're George's sisters, then that's what he believes them to be.'

Ross approached his older brother and placed an arm about his shoulders. 'The blonde is for you,' he whispered magnanimously.

The young blonde woman must have been straining to listen because she launched a triumphant, territorial gloat at her colleagues, then provocatively swayed herself forward. She shimmered beneath the hall candles like a silver and lilac moth and with her movement Luke caught a waft of the cloying perfume Wenna used. They were costly whores, then.

As the woman undulated closer he could tell that the quality of her dress was fine, her coiffure elaborate and her face artfully rouged. Nothing too dramatic that would immediately brand her a courtesan. He wondered abstractedly if Ross was expecting him to pay for them all.

Aware of Luke's impassive attention as she glided forward, Molly Parker wet her reddened mouth with a sly pink tongue. 'Struth, but he was handsome. She had thought the other dark one, that cheeky Ross, a looker and more than welcome, but this one… She gave him a dimpling smile, archly lowering sooty lashes, desperate to please and anticipate what he would want from her: brash doxy or shy flirt. Professional technique or passive obedience.

Luke stood stock still; enraged yet stunned and unwilling to give up his joy and contentment of ten minutes ago. So he was unsure whether to laugh dementedly or swing around and punch his brother straight in the mouth.

'I know you've been hankering after a blonde…' Ross said and the gruff concern in his voice did it for Luke. He laughed, just as Molly reached him and slid possessive, perfumed arms about his neck.

And just as Miles attended the door again, muttering cheerfully about a busy evening, and greeted Rebecca.

Chapter Seven

She stared and actually glided into the hallway a bit as she uncertainly murmured, 'Luke?'

His name was little more than a doubtful sigh yet he heard it.

The shock of finding harlots littering Ramsden Manor was nothing to the devastation which now ripped into him. The one that cluttered his person was shoved ungently back from him and straight at Ross.

Rebecca momentarily froze. She hadn't been mistaken. She understood perfectly this time. What she was witnessing was exactly what it seemed: three men being entertained at home by three harlots.

She was physically exhausted from her run through the woods; she was mentally fatigued from her fears about Lucy and the smugglers she had evaded by yards, yet she turned and fled down the steps of Ramsden Manor as though the hounds of hell snapped at her heels.

She flew into the dark night and instinctively towards the barn, the duty to find Lucy still fast in her mind, even as a hand covered her mouth to stifle her heartbroken sobs. The night was so pitch black and her eyes so awash that she could barely see a yard in front of her but she knew the direction of the barn from the house and sped towards it.

Luke hadn't the vaguest idea which way she had headed. Guessing she might have instinctively sought home, he ran the wrong way. Within a vain minute he halted and re-tracked to the Manor where the only light was to be had.

'Rebecca!' He thundered her name with such command and pain in his voice that she actually stopped dead and swung about.

It was enough. Her trailing shawl revealed the white flag of her bodice and he walked slowly, purposefully towards her. Rebecca stood shaking on the spot, watching him advance with the amber glow of light from the Manor outlining his silhouette. By sheer willpower he was holding her unmoving, unresisting. She knew it, but acknowledging that he could made her jerk about again and run.

She reached the barn, knowing he was within a second of catching her, so she swirled to face him, warding him off with unsteady, outstretched hands. 'Don't touch me. Please, don't touch me,' she begged and threatened in one tone.

He slowed his relentless progress towards her until he walked the final steps and towered over her shivering form.

'I'm sorry,' she blurted on a sharp, hysterical laugh. 'I arrived unexpectedly…uninvited again. But I had to come. It…I…' She trailed off, unable to force any further words past the aching blockage in her throat.

One black-sleeved arm slowly raised to lean against the barn wall. His head lowered to meet it and rested there. 'Tell me what you think you just saw, Rebecca,' he demanded hoarsely.

'Nothing…' she whispered.

'You saw nothing?' A grunt of mirthless laughter issued from the crook of his arm. He wearily raised his head to gaze down at her. 'You didn't see three whores loitering in my hallway?'

Rebecca swallowed painfully. She looked feverishly about her, anywhere but at him.

Luke moved a testing hand towards her and she reflexively slapped it away. 'I said don't touch me,' she immediately hissed at him.

'Ah…so you did see something. Tell me what you think you saw,' he insisted in a raw voice.

Rebecca slid surreptitiously along the brick barn, the opposite way from the barrier of rock-like arm, striving for composure. She rested her head back, feeling her soft, thick hair catch against the gritty brickwork. A trembling hand went to her face, clearing tearstains and honey tendrils wisping about her neck with every gusting breeze. She concentrated on finding Lucy. She allowed no other thought.

'I'm sorry to intrude,' she said quietly. 'But I must find Lucy. I've searched everywhere for her. This was the last place to look. I think she may be with John. I suppose you haven't seen them?' Had that really been her remote voice? she dully wondered.

He was denied the need to reply. The barn door opened not three yards from where they stood and John's bright head became quite visible through the dusk. Lucy's muted giggling and then whispering was just audible. The intimate way their heads angled towards each other made it clear they were oblivious to anyone but each other.

Luke twisted on the hand braced against the brickwork and glared over his arm at the young couple. He thrust himself in a deliberate, savage jerk away from the barn wall and approached them. Sensing the latent exasperation in him, yet to be vented, Rebecca hastened past him.

'Lucy!' she exclaimed in a voice mingling relief and chastisement. 'I've hunted everywhere for you. What in heaven's name have you been doing here?' The simple query was the first ingenuous phrase that formed in her numb brain.

The young couple jumped apart and Lucy muttered an involuntary exclamation of dismay. Within a few seconds she had regained confidence and her full mouth took on its customary sullen droop. Her eyes scanned from Rebecca to Luke and then back to Rebecca.

'What have I been doing here?' she repeated nastily. 'Why don't you ask his lordship what I've been doing here? He knows. It's something he'd just love to be doing here with you.'

Intolerable humiliation prompted a rash and spontaneous reaction; Rebecca's hand arced up to slap the girl's coarsely smiling face. But it was arrested in mid-air and gripped hard as Luke pulled her close to his side. The silence that followed was broken only by the wind catching the barn door and creaking it back and forth.

'You will apologise, Lucy,' Rebecca eventually breathed in a trembling rush. 'Apologise to Lord Ramsden this minute for that disgraceful outburst.'

'Why? It's true!' Lucy spat back, but warily, her eyes hovering on his lordship's inscrutable dark features.

Luke stepped towards the couple then and they, as one, stepped back against the barn wall. 'Take Lucy back to the Manor,' he ordered John in a voice of silken steel. Then, as he remembered that the place already housed three trollops and another might crowd the place enough to give even credulous old Miles pause for thought, a dry grunt of a laugh escaped. 'No, forget that. Get the carriage out and put her in it…alone. But wait with her until you have my further instructions.'

'Yes, my lord,' John mumbled in a strange croak, rubbing furiously at the bridge of his nose. But neither John nor Lucy made a move or uttered another word. They appeared entranced and rooted to the spot.

Luke stared off back towards the Manor, waiting. A muscle started to jerk in his jaw. He looked down at his booted feet. He kicked the toe of one into damp earth. He roared, *'Go!'*

Rebecca started violently, making the hand that still grasped hers tighten and a slow thumb soothe her chilled skin. Lucy began noisily blubbing, her outrageous impertinence totally expired. John grabbed at the girl's arm and started solicitiously steering her towards the house.

'Don't ever again tell me not to touch you,' Luke ground out, as his hands fastened on the tops of Rebecca's arms and she was pulled close.

The strength in the movement knocked the breath out of Rebecca. But she was determined this time not to yield to the immediate lure and rest against his solid body for warmth and comfort. He could beguile her so easily. He had done so scarcely two hours ago; her mouth still pulsed from that subtle assault. Yet he must surely have already had business arranged with these women when he was kissing her. This wounding conclusion broke a small sob of denial from her aching throat and her forehead ground involuntarily against him, back and forth. He immediately folded her closer, soothing and restricting her feeble attempts to break free, as he groaned her name.

But her hurt and fury were no longer containable. 'You must surely hold the Ramsden name and all of our small community in such contempt to bring those...' she strived for the vulgarity to flail him with the word but failed '...women...here to my uncle's home. It is a despicable thing to do.'

Luke moved her back and his glittering eyes scanned her

face. 'Your memory is improving, is it, Rebecca? You remember something now, do you?'

Her turquoise eyes were as icy as her voice. 'Yes, I remember. I remember you asked me to marry you earlier today. I remember agreeing to do so. But I have forgotten why. I have forgotten why I would do such a ridiculous thing when I know what sort of degenerate you are.' She shook herself to try and escape him but his fingers tightened to painful vices on her arms.

'Go on,' he urged, deceptively softly. 'What else do you remember about my proposal earlier? Or perhaps I should remind you why you agreed to marry me, Rebecca.' He moved her closer. When she resisted, digging into the rain-wet earth, he lifted her a few inches away from it and slammed her hard against him.

'Shall I remind you, Rebecca?' he taunted softly, as black-fire eyes roved her face, lingering on her soft mouth. She turned her head swiftly away, her heartbeat so fast and strong it seemed to knock her yet closer to him. His warmth and familiar verbena scent enveloped her and her eyelids drooped. Recognising at once the sweet ache which coaxed capitulation, she cleaved to the vision that tormented her.

'I remember you embracing a harlot and laughing with her why you did so. That's what I remember. She was wearing a lilac dress…she was blonde and pretty…' Her voice cracked as she was about to add that she looked very young. Instead she whispered, 'Let me go now. I have to take Lucy home. It is getting very late.'

'Well, now you've admitted what you saw, perhaps I should tell you how it came about,' he stated, ignoring her request to leave. 'If I say that what I recount is the truth, will you believe me?' Her answering silence made him bitterly mutter, 'Well, I shall tell you anyway.'

'Ross brought me a present home from Brighton today.

He got one for himself and a friend, too…but that's Ross's way. He's ever generous with my money. But he did it with good intentions, thinking he was being help- ful…considerate. He's watched me pining over a blonde for two weeks or more and daily becoming more frustrated and miserable. So he tried to ease my discomfort in the only way he knew how: by buying one for me. I didn't know about it. I hadn't arranged it and I wasn't laughing from pleasure. I was laughing because I couldn't credit that he'd actually brought that bawdy trio to my home. I was laughing because of the irony of wanting to speak to him about acting as my groomsman when I knew I was within an ace of hitting him. But mostly I was laughing in sheer disbelief that Ross imagined an expensive whore might be a substitute for even one tormenting thought of you. And I wasn't embracing her or any other damn thing. She had hold of me, but for no more than a few seconds. And she wasn't pretty… Well, she might have been, I suppose. I don't know. I hardly looked at her.' His eyes hungrily roamed Rebecca's perfect features. 'She certainly wasn't incredibly beautiful,' he said huskily. After a brief pause he demanded, 'Do you believe me?'

'I'm not sure,' Rebecca achingly whispered.

'Why aren't you sure?' he persisted, his tone hardening.

'Because I don't know you. I know so little about you…and you about me. All I'm certain of is that we have lived in different worlds. But I'm not so ignorant of polite society that I'm unaware how wealthy men behave.' She slowly slipped away from him and leaned back against the barn, her arms wrapping her shawl tightly about her chilled form.

'I know my uncle had other…relationships. I heard gos- sip about village children. I believe it was after my aunt had died. But I know it is not always just then…when men

live a bachelor existence. I understand that sometimes…men with power and status…can afford to also
have a wife and two or more households.' She paused,
sadly remembering him detailing his affluence and the
properties he owned throughout the country, when first
propositioning her. How many homes did he own? She
could not now remember the list.

She moistened her lips, feeling a racking pain clenching
her insides. She wanted to wail, to lash out at him for so
soon ripping away her golden happiness. Instead she quietly
stammered, 'I…I know it is deemed to be quite acceptable
by some to live that way. But it's not my way.'

She stole a quick glance at his expressionless profile. His
head was thrown back a little as he listened to her but she
wasn't fooled by his apparent calm. That dormant menace
she had already sensed beneath his urbane exterior was
strengthening. And it frightened her.

'I'm not very sophisticated, I know that,' she admitted
on a weak, shaky laugh, attempting to ease the unbearable
suspense between them. 'At times I have wished I were,
especially recently…' She trailed into silence and he turned
his head to look at her.

'Well, that's easily remedied, Rebecca, and right now,'
he softly promised. 'Young Lucy quite accurately predicted
my needs. Perhaps yours, too. Ten minutes in that barn
would help sophisticate you…and definitely make me feel
a damned sight better.'

Rebecca started quickly back towards the relative safety
of Ramsden Manor. She had hastened no more than three
paces when he dragged her in front of him. 'What are you
implying? That you now intend to reject my proposal because you believe I will be an inveterate adulterer?'

'I don't know you well enough. I need time to think…'

she quietly prevaricated, desperate to placate him so he
would allow her to get home to the Summer House.

He walked into her, forcing her backwards against the
barn wall. Her anxious eyes darted up to merge and plead
with his. But there was no reassurance or tenderness in his
hard, glittering eyes and thin compressed mouth.

'I would say that you've got no more to worry over now
than you had this afternoon. You believed in me then,
trusted in me, and I in you. I've told you exactly how that
farcical tableau you witnessed came about. I will not beg
forgiveness for misdemeanours I've not committed, Rebecca.' As her furtive evasion was thwarted by two fists
planted either side of her head, she sensed the rigid pulsing
of his touching body heating her.

'So, perhaps you need something genuine to fret over for
a day or two while I settle scores with my meddling
brother.'

His speciously controlled tone made her anticipate anger
and cruelty. Both her quaking hands shoved instantly
against the broad expanse of his chest, curling against the
reflexive leap of muscle beneath her palms. But when his
hand manoeuvred her face and his mouth touched hers, it
was with no more force than she recalled from earlier that
day.

She yielded immediately to the artful skill in his kiss,
but the knowledge that he had once again easily manipulated her made a humiliated sob jerk out of her and mingle
with his warm breath. Still her mouth clung to his, greedily
following every mercurial movement. Firm fingers
skimmed her silhouette, lingered tantalisingly at the sides
of her engorging breasts, thumbs catching almost uninten-
tionally against taut nipples.

The current of untasted sensation jolted her and even as
she arched towards those tormenting fingers, she grasped

them in hers and pulled them away. But she couldn't relinquish the kiss and as he took their clasped hands behind her to ease her closer she moved willingly between his spaced feet.

But when he eventually lifted his head there was no triumph or mockery and he breathed as hard and fast as she. He jerked her away from the barn and wordlessly started striding towards the house.

As they approached the carriage, stopped in the warm orange glow of light by the portico, Ross careered down the steps, glass in hand.

'I was just coming to find you,' he carefully enunciated, squinting at his grim-faced brother. 'You've been gone a while. I was worried.'

'Ah, Ross,' Luke greeted, far too cordially. 'Just the man I wanted to see. Come, tell Rebecca who those women are and how they come to be infesting my home,' he drily invited him.

Hazel eyes flicked from one to the other of them, detecting the proprietorial grip his brother had on the lovely young woman and the slick, swollen redness of her mouth. 'Oh, they're George's sisters,' he shrewdly explained, turning to George for confirmation, as that man joined him on the steps of Ramsden Manor. The conspirators faced each other to share a covert wink.

'George's sisters are harlots?' Rebecca couldn't help but acidly comment.

Ross glanced warily at Luke's forbidding countenance. 'So, you've heard that too. I'm sure it's just a rumour,' he dismissed, deadpan. He turned a clandestine grin on George who, in turn, glared, unsure whether to be outraged or entertained by this family slight. He reflected on his pair of vinegary spinster siblings, at home in Cornwall and was unable to prevent a lusty chortle erupting, before he hastily swigged his drink.

Ross swivelled back to his brother with a smug smile just as Luke's fist caught him on the chin and he collapsed like a rag doll.

George Dellon sobered immediately and stuck out both hands in front of him in a gesture of appeal. 'Sorry…sorry, Luke. We just thought it might help. Ross thought…'

Luke ignored him completely, his attention with his younger brother. 'Get those bawds out of my house right now. Get yourself out, too, and don't come back for at least two days. Stay away…I don't care where. Stay with George…stay with those damned sisters of his if you like. Just don't venture back here if you value your life…understand?'

Ross held on to his brandy balloon with one hand and his jaw with the other. His glass got the most attention as he examined the step to ascertain how much had been spilled. He nodded as he drained the glass.

'Can't you just abduct her?' he suggested with drunken forthrightness and then cowered back as Luke twisted menacingly back towards him.

'All right…just a thought,' he squeaked, but winked at George.

The perfume from the rose garden was enticing. As Lucy accompanied herself heavily on the piano but sang quite sweetly, Rebecca rose from the stool beside her with a sigh and quit the parlour. She walked out into the balmy air and threw her golden head back to survey the sky: cobalt blue and with just a hint of thin cotton cloud stretched high. It was mid-October now, yet the Indian summer continued.

The rose garden was situated at the back of the Summer

House and an open-windowed parlour benefitted from the sight and scent of it.

She collected the trug from Gregory's potting shed, and the sturdy knife he used in the garden. She selected two dark red blooms, not fully opened, and stripped away some of the superfluous greenery. Her fingertips slipped along the velvet petals of a pale pink bud and she cut that and another to match, inclining to breathe in their fragrance.

'Miss Nash?' Rebecca swirled about, pricking her finger on a thorn as she bumped into a rose bush. She hadn't even heard the horse and rider approach over Lucy's unharmonious trilling and plinking. She lifted a sap-stained hand to shield her eyes from the sun and squinted up at the man.

'I am Miss Nash. Can I help you?' she asked him pleasantly, as she sucked at her injured finger.

She had never seen him before. She guessed him to be a farmer or merchant of some description from his attire of sturdy, serviceable clothes. He was certainly no peasant. The horse he was riding looked a healthy thoroughbred. His pale blue eyes were regarding her with rather too fixed interest and Rebecca glanced about a little uncomfortably.

'I am looking for Simon Nash. Your brother?' the man questioned her as his eyes continued a raking assessment of Rebecca's slender figure.

His bold gaze was starting to unnerve her and she answered coolly, 'I'm afraid I can't help you. I have been desperate to find him myself for some years.'

The man laughed. 'My apologies for troubling you then, miss. I believed you must have been in touch with him since June when last I saw him. I thought he had possibly been lying low with a relative in some out-of-the-way spot. And this is out of the way...' he remarked as he gazed about him and then contemplatively at Rebecca.

The brooding look he turned on her this time passed

unnoticed as Rebecca breathed out, 'You've seen Simon as recently as that? In the summer of this year? Where? Please tell me, sir, I am quite desperate to find him.' When he made no attempt to respond to her entreaty, she urged, 'There are important family matters that need to be resolved.'

'Your brother and I had some business dealings, Miss Nash. The matter was never finalised,' he advised in a hardening tone, ignoring her request for information. 'Should he come by visiting, perhaps you would tell him I am urgently seeking him. He will know why and that it is better to settle with me sooner rather than later. Just tell him that's what Jake Blacker said.' He reined in his horse then as though about to turn its head and leave. Rebecca spontaneously stepped forward to arrest his departure.

'*You* are Jake Blacker?' she whispered, astonished. The infamy of the man had conjured up a coarse-mannered, evil-looking lout in her vivid imagination. Certainly not this clean-shaven individual with brown hair and the weakest blue eyes imaginable. He seemed quite inoffensive. Apart from that unsettling way he had of eyeing her.

'Indeed, I am,' he confirmed with a pleased smirk that his reputation had preceded him, even to a beautiful provincial miss living in this backwater. 'You've heard of me, Miss Nash?'

Rebecca moistened her parched lips, unsure how to reply. Admitting to knowledge of his criminal activities was hardly wise. Yet why else would she know him? His penetrating gaze shifted. She watched him frown towards the parlour window as Lucy struck up a new, discordant tune.

'I believe I recall Simon mentioning you once,' she blurted before those icy eyes could pin back on her. 'Would you tell me, sir, where last you saw my brother? Was it locally?'

'It was in Hastings, Miss Nash, where we dealt a little together. No doubt he has just omitted to conclude matters with me,' he informed her, but in a way that made Rebecca certain he believed no such thing. Her stomach plummetted and frosty fingers gripped her heart. It was true then, Simon *was* involved with these blackguards. And Jake Blacker was the worst of the bunch, if what she had heard was correct, however harmless he may look and sound. From his veiled threats, she could only conclude that Simon owed him money.

'Have you any idea where I might start searching for my brother?' Rebecca pleaded.

Jake Blacker regarded the lovely young woman gazing earnestly up at him with those astonishing sea-green eyes. He judged her the prettiest woman he had seen in many a long day. Certainly easier on the eye than his carrot-headed wife who was again beginning to thicken around the middle with her third child. He stroked his chin, scheming slyly that if he couldn't extract money from Simon Nash, he would now give him two choices: his life or his sister.

'Well, last I heard, miss, he was seen at the Bull and Mouth Tavern in Brighton,' he informed her clearly. 'When I looked for him there, I was told I'd missed him by mere minutes. I've heard it's a haunt of his in the evenings.'

'The Bull and Mouth Tavern,' Rebecca repeated in a low breath. 'Well, thank you, sir. And rest assured, if I do happen upon Simon, I shall relay your message.'

He dipped his head in acknowledgement and after another lengthy assessing stare, he turned his horse and trotted away towards Westbrook.

'Who was that?' Martha called inquisitively out of the open kitchen window.

Some innate caution made Rebecca casually dismiss the

visitor as, 'Oh, just someone looking for Simon. An old acquaintance, I believe.'

Martha withdrew her head, muttering inaudibly, but Rebecca knew the grumbled comments concerned Simon and Martha's disparaging opinion of him and his friends. The woman poked her iron-grey head back through the window and called, 'Jam tarts are done and so is the brew.'

She would have to go into Brighton and find this Bull and Mouth Inn, Rebecca mused as she bit into a raspberry jam tart and sipped at her tea. She desperately needed to find Simon. She wanted the money her father had bequeathed her before he handed it over to the likes of Jake Blacker…if he hadn't already done so. It was hers. It was her self-respect. It was her dowry. It was also her thinking time. Without it she might be prey to penury and unscrupulous people. And then she thought of Luke Trelawney.

She sipped at her tea again quickly. She had expected to see him by now. It was three days since she had searched for Lucy at the Manor. He had sent she and Lucy home in the carriage, with John driving them. A swift, hard kiss out of sight of Lucy, sulking in the carriage, and a cool parting statement that he would be in touch, was all the farewell she had received before he strode away and into the Manor. Why hadn't he been by? She had been so sure he wouldn't stay away more than a day.

No doubt he was also reconsidering the wisdom of his marriage proposal and was ready to withdraw it. The notion made an icy shiver race through her, even though she recognised the reason in it. He was wonderfully handsome; he was by his own admission extremely wealthy. So wealthy he could afford to disregard the entirety of his inheritance that brought with it a title. He was the sixth Baron Ramsden, a peer of the realm, and could pick a society debutante to marry if he wished. Perhaps he did now wish it, Rebecca reflected, chilled. Perhaps all she could now expect was a reinstatement of his original proposition.

Rebecca stared sightlessly into the steamy teacup. She was without money or status. But she had been gently reared; well-educated by Miss Arden, her governess until she was sixteen. Her grandmother, Grace, had been a Ramsden through marriage, but when Saul Ramsden died and Grace married Granville Nash, her grandfather had been the wealthiest businessman in the Brighton area.

She had heard tell that one of the reasons her father and Robin Ramsden had disliked each other so much was that the illustrious Ramsdens, who could trace their noble lineage back to 1630, had considerably less money at one time than the Nashes who had gained affluence and influence through common trade.

On his mother's remarriage to Granville Nash when he was eleven, her uncle Robin had chosen to stay with his paternal grandmother in straitened circumstances at the Manor, rather than move in with his stepfather and enjoy an easier life.

Her grandfather Granville had owned a terrace of houses in one of Brighton's most fashionable squares. He had bought them just as the Prince of Wales began transforming the farmhouse he had acquired into that most vaunted and elegant palace: Brighton Pavilion. As Brighton's reputation as a fashionable resort and gathering place grew, so did grandfather Granville's profit from renting out his Palladian terrace to the *haute ton* during the season.

Rebecca sighed a little wistfully. Although her father had inherited it all on Granville Nash's death, he had unfortunately not been blessed with that man's inherent business acumen. He was too gentle and trusting, her fiercely loyal mother had once told Rebecca, when they were packing up to leave the large house they could no longer afford to run.

How she wished now he had not been so trusting with her money, and left it to someone other than Simon to administer.

Her father had not owned a home of his own for several years before his death. But the leased property which was their last, on the outskirts of Westbrook, had been comfortable and spacious and was, on her father's insistence, one of the few which didn't belong to the Ramsden estate. She missed her parents dreadfully. Despite declining fortune, they had stayed a happy family.

Her father had provided Elizabeth with a very reasonable dowry on her marriage to James Bartholomew. Simon had inherited the bulk of the estate, and it simply wasn't fair that he had never released her money when he had received so much more. Had David been alive she would have had his love and protection, and no doubt her inheritance. She was certain Simon would never have attempted to gull her future husband.

Her fingers went to her locket and she unclasped it and laid it on the table in front of her. She ran a finger along its warm, silver surface. She had barely thought of David, she realised with a wrench. For the past five years she had recalled memories of him daily and yet... Now she dwelt on another man throughout each day, and long night. And he stirred in her something that dear David never had, something new that both disturbed and subdued her, something that had been with her from the moment he had taken her, dripping wet, from the pond.

She yearned desperately for him. She longed for the touch of his fingers on her face...in her hair. She craved the moist heat of his mouth on hers. She ached for that bitter-sweet knotting deep inside her at the sight of him or the sound of his voice...yet knew it was foolish, all of it. Everything she had said to him that night at the Manor was the truth. She didn't know enough about him...his life or background.

But she did know with utter certainty that the thought of enduring a faithless marriage was anathema. She would rather countenance a marriage of convenience to an elderly widower than discover that Luke Trelawney sought the company of other women while she was his wife. Sharing him would destroy her.

She needed to find Simon. Her five thousand pounds bought her thinking time. Time to perhaps discover if Luke Trelawney was the sincere gentleman she desperately wanted to believe him. Or whether he was an unprincipled rogue without an honourable intention in his handsome head, who might just carelessly crush her spirit before he returned to Cornwall.

Her time at the Summer House was coming to an end. She looked wistfully about the kitchen. She had had five good years but she knew with a quiet certainty there were to be no more.

'The Bull and Mouth'...the name ran through her mind. She hadn't been to Brighton since the summer. She rarely went because of her duty to her pupils. But she would go tomorrow afternoon and leave Lucy in Martha's care. Martha wouldn't mind: she was always trying to persuade her to get to town more. She would beg a lift with Kay and Adam Abbott. They made the trip to Brighton every Wednesday afternoon; Kay to visit her widowed mother while Adam attended to ecclesiastical duties. Kay had often previously tried to coax Rebecca to join her simply for the outing. And that's all Rebecca would explain it as, either to Kay or Martha, just an outing. For she knew they were sure to fret over the wisdom of it all...just as she was bound to herself.

Chapter Eight

Miles wasn't sure what worried him the most: the agony or the ecstacy. Choleric temper was certainly more common, he realised. That fit of euphoria three days ago had been unique and barely lasted the evening out. The following morning had seen a black mood once again settled over the man and therefore the household.

Miles had heard worrying tales of such behaviour: people with brain afflictions laughing and happy one minute and ranting in evil humour the next. He would have to take stock…keep a careful watch. He had no experience of the Cornish, but what he'd heard was not to the good. Even as he thought it he lifted his head a little and peered sideways into the enormous gilt-scrolled mirror at his master's handsome reflection.

Luke Trelawney stood just behind him adjusting his neckcloth with a steady, dark hand. As he noticed Miles squinting furtively at him in the glass, he gave the man a ghost of a smile.

Miles hastily blinked rheumy eyes and busied himself laying calf leather gloves on the hall table he stood by. He couldn't fool him with a smile. Oh, no. Not even that half a one he was fond of employing to dupe folk as to his humour. He knew the sixth Baron was in no better a mood this Wednesday evening than he had been this morning or yesterday morning or the one before that.

He scuffled away from the tall, dark figure that dwarfed him and ambled towards the kitchens, passing the snoozing figure of Ross, slumped in a hall chair.

Miles threw him a glance as he creaked on. It must be spreading. Even jolly young Mr Trelawney seemed affected now. He had been morose for three days or more and constantly lounging about the place. Very unlike him. Perhaps it was a family affliction. He had heard of that, too. Whole families addled in the wits.

Talking to oneself was a sign, so he recalled. And without a doubt he had heard Lord Ramsden cursing beneath his breath with no soul about. Sometimes several times a day. Laughing manically, that was another. Well, he didn't laugh much but he'd seen him grin off away at something on the ceiling and gaze through the window towards the woods, always the same spot too, as though someone stood there. Sometimes happy, sometimes as though he'd go out and rip every one of those trees up with his bare hands. Teeth grinding...pulling out hair...well, that didn't signify, Miles had to allow, as he shuffled on. He'd never seen two men with such perfect teeth and luxuriant manes. He gave a sour scowl as his tongue probed his lonely gums and an instinctive hand went to smooth down his own sparse, grey locks.

Absent-mindedness was a sign. They were still here. Perhaps they had forgotten to go home to Cornwall. So long as they didn't forget to pay the myriad merchants' bills that arrived daily, Miles was content keep his own counsel...and watch...and wait.

Luke critically surveyed his cravat in the mirror. He glanced past the perfect silver-grey folds at his neck and at

Ross, crumpled in the chair, allowing a small, hard smile. It was time to forgive him a little. Ross had been as well behaved as a five-year-old earning a treat for the past few days. He'd been wearing a pathetic, martyred look, reading books studiously in the library or wandering about as if lost. He'd hardly ventured from the house, which was a pity in a way, because whilst here he tended to get under everyone's feet.

Luke turned from the mirror, picked up his gloves and mildly called, 'Ross?' The lack of response made him whistle through his teeth at his brother. Ross shot up in the chair and rubbed his eyes.

'Come on. I'll take you into town for a drink and a game of cards before Miles sends for the physician. He's beginning to look at both of us as though we're mad.'

'What do you think of it now?' Kay asked wrinkling her pert nose.

Rebecca frowned consideringly, head tilted to one side. 'More ostentatious than when last I saw it,' she finally judged as she critically regarded the newest additions to the architecture at Brighton Pavilion. 'I dread to think what it has cost.'

Kay linked her arm through Rebecca's and they walked on. 'Will you come with me today to see my mama? She would adore seeing you.'

'I can't, Kay,' Rebecca hastily demurred. 'But thank you for the invitation and please convey my kind regards to your mother.'

'So how are you intending to spend your afternoon in Brighton? Shopping? Sea bathing?' Kay teased her.

'No. Actually, when last I saw Elizabeth in London, several weeks ago now, she bade me look up an old friend of hers who lives here,' Rebecca told her quite truthfully. It

was precisely what Elizabeth had asked her to do. Katherine Bates lived in Baker Street and Rebecca had, indeed,
promised to visit at some time. It wouldn't be today but
neither Elizabeth nor Kay need know that.

'We shall meet you in Ship Street then at seven of the
clock,' Kay said with a smile as she unlinked arms with
Rebecca to enter the quiet square where her mother lived.
'Adam will be finished with his meeting with the Bishop
then and we can be back in Graveley by eight.'

This was the part that Rebecca didn't relish. She had no
idea how long she would need to loiter at the Bull and
Mouth. She had decided to remain in the vicinity for some
while and watch for Simon. There was no point in just
leaving a message with the landlord. She was well aware
that if Simon did receive it, he would probably summarily
dismiss any request to contact her, knowing exactly why
she wanted him. She needed to confront him face to face.

'Actually, Kay, I'm not too sure when I shall be leaving.
If I manage to get away by seven I shall be only too pleased
to ride home with you and Adam. But please don't wait
for me. If I'm not there at the appointed hour, then leave
without me. I shall hire a conveyance of some sort to get
me home.'

She held up a silencing hand as Kay looked horrified at
the very idea. 'No, please. I get out so very little that I want
to make the most of my day.' She gave Kay a hasty peck
on the cheek. 'Please give my regards to your dear mama
and spend a pleasant afternoon.'

She drew her warm cloak about her as a gusting sea
breeze assaulted them. While Kay wrapped herself into her
own coat, Rebecca briefly waved, then walked briskly
away.

Rebecca knew she looked quite attractive today. She had
worn her best clothes, as she always did when taking a trip

to town, and although five years old, they were little worn and still quite chic. But she wished people wouldn't stare quite so much. Her beryl-blue velvet cloak nearly matched her eyes and the hood had loosened wisps of honey hair to fall in silky-soft ringlets that framed her face. It wasn't just the dandies eyeing her either. Several fashionably dressed women turned as she passed to give a hard-eyed scrutiny to her lone progress through the narrow streets.

She hastened on, hoping she was now on the right track for the Bull and Mouth Inn. She had twice asked the way: from a lamp lighter just beginning his rounds whom she barely understood and from a woman with a cart load of hot pies. The savoury aroma of mutton and onions had made her stomach grumble but she had kept her money safe, knowing that hiring a carriage home later would take all of her coins.

It had all taken much more time than she had anticipated and the breeze off the ocean was stiffening and the light was fading. She couldn't guess the time as cloud was prematurely shortening the day. She walked slowly the length of Brewer Street and hesitated on the cobbles by the wharf. With one hand firm on her velvet hood she threw back her head and looked at the sign: a garish smiling mouth was topped by a painted black bull and it oscillated whiningly in the wind. As she tarried there two gentlemen turned the corner. They ogled her boldly as they approached. Feeling her face heating at their scrutiny, Rebecca purposely peered over the harbour wall, apparently fascinated by the small craft bobbing on the oily swell.

The men disappeared inside the tavern. Once the promenade was again relatively quiet, Rebecca twisted about, wondering what was best to do. Believing she would be able to loiter unobserved and seek Simon had been hopelessly misguided. Obviously the worst possible interpretation would be put on her dawdling presence outside a men's gathering place.

She kept her head down and her hood forward as she discreetly but carefully surveyed another couple of gentlemen who made their jovial way into the inn. They gave her very little of their attention and she relaxed. Feeling reassured, she firmly decided she would have to venture inside. She had some extra money with her, in case the landlord hinted payment might jog his memory about this one particular customer. She would seek him out directly and ask him if he knew of Simon. She might find the landlord helpful and obliging, she encouraged herself.

Thus heartened, she drew her blue velvet cloak about her, settled the hood and walked confidently into the Bull and Mouth tavern.

The interior was danker and darker than she had imagined. It was noisy too and filled with narrow corridors; she stood now at a turnoff, wondering which way to venture.

She backed carefully away from an open doorway, having gleaned from a speedy peek that the room was filled with cigar smoke and gentlemen throwing dice or playing cards, and straight on to a foot.

'Oi, watch out,' a female voice declared none too amiably.

'I'm so sorry,' Rebecca murmured, staring down at the obese woman's slippered feet. She looked up into a red-veined, bulbous face topped by greying brown hair which was in turn crowned by a lacy mob cap.

The woman raised heavy blackened brows at her and pinched a rouged mouth together in her heavy jowls. 'Oh, yes... And what are you about, then?' Queenie Spencer demanded of the beautiful young woman hesitating nervously in front of her.

'I'm looking for the landlord,' Rebecca informed politely. 'I need to speak to him urgently.

'Oh, do you?' Queenie mocked her. 'And why is that, pray? Come along, you can tell me, girl. I'm his wife.'

'Well, perhaps you could help me, then,' Rebecca quietly ventured, hating to feel so intimidated by this florid-faced, rotund woman with reeking breath.

Rebecca moistened her parched lips, flattening herself against the powdery dank wall as two women clad in little more than gauze petticoats pressed past them in the corridor. They assessed her from velvet hood to daintily shod feet with open curiosity and Rebecca dropped her eyes away at once from their painted faces.

'I am looking for my brother. I have been advised to look for him here,' Rebecca said in little more than a whisper. Panic was beginning to curdle her stomach, and she realized with belated wisdom that it might after all have been safer to remain outside this establishment to search for Simon.

Queenie Spencer examined the beautiful young woman in front of her with commercial expertise. She raised a plump hand then and summarily flicked Rebecca's velvet hood back from her face. Tendrils of honey hair trailed her alabaster forehead and neck as the turquoise cowl draped her shoulders.

'Looking for a brother, eh? Well, we get 'em all in here, my dearie. Fathers looking for daughters, sons looking for mothers, brothers looking for sisters. We don't mind. You're looking for a brother, we'll find him for you, sure enough.' She stared transfixed at the classical beauty she knew she would only come in contact with once or twice in her working lifetime. 'How many brothers is it you want me to find you, my lovie?' she enquired hoarsely as she calculated the clientele likely tonight. 'Struth, but she could provide this one with enough custom to keep her on her back for the next fortnight.

'His name is Simon Nash,' Rebecca hastily informed the landlady, her tongue quickly slipping about her mouth to try to ease the croak in her voice. 'Do you know him? If not I'll apologise now for taking your time and be gone,' she courteously rattled off, gliding subtly along the distempered wall towards the exit.

Sensing her agitation and imminent flight, Queenie grabbed hard at Rebecca's slender arm. Soothing fat fingers rubbed back and forth against the soft blue velvet. 'There, there, my duckie,' she cooed. 'You come along with me to the snug. It's nice and quiet in there and we'll talk about this a bit more. You'll be so worried about your brother, then, I reckon...' Queenie solicitiously purred.

'Yes, yes, I am. I need to find him urgently,' Rebecca agreed, relaxing a little as the woman led her into a small, empty room.

'Well, sit ye down,' Queenie offered, still unable to drag her greedy eyes away from the vision of loveliness that tentatively perched on a crude wooden taproom chair. Her furtive gaze darted over Rebecca's body, trying to ascertain what was beneath the enveloping velvet cloak. If body and face matched...

'So, you've been told you might find him here...' Queenie said with a sugary, uneven smile, as her cunning brain started to work. If she was an apprentice bawd seeking work, she was a little too old to be getting started and a little too refined. Still, what a looker, and no mistake. She could still end up as top dog in this establishment within a very short time. Gentlemen looked for freshness and variety in a place like this and Queenie had just struck gold...no exaggeration, she reckoned, gloating over that thick hair spilling ringlets about the shoulders of the blue velvet.

Her mercenary musing was abruptly curtailed as a bloated man of middle years, with a greasy apron knotted about his distended girth, crashed into the room.

'What are you about, woman?' he growled at Queenie. 'I've a bar full of gents, a gaming room with nary a girl in sight and nor are you....'

He gawked at Rebecca. 'What's this? What's this?' he interrogated, glowering suspiciously at her. The only ladies of quality who ventured beyond his doors were those preaching charity or godliness and he could do without either.

Queenie licked her thick, rouged lips. 'This young lady's here a-looking for a brother. I thought as we would be sure to help her find the young gent she's after. Don't you think?'

Bertram Spencer looked at his wife for a long moment and then consideringly at the beautiful young woman, perched on the edge of the hard wooden chair. An inkling of something important stirred in his busy brain. 'Who is she looking for, did you say? What is his name…this brother?'

'Simon Nash, sir,' Rebecca supplied quickly, wondering desperately how she could extricate herself from this awful place and silently flailing herself for ever being idiotic enough to venture within it.

Bertram approached his wife surprisingly quickly, considering his swollen size, and whispered hoarsely in her ear. Rebecca watched the woman's pink tongue twice poke out and wet her lips.

Queenie pulled irritably away from her sibilantly hissing husband and scuffled towards Rebecca on her slippered feet. 'Well, seems you're going to be a lucky young lady. My good husband here has some idea of your young man you're a-seeking and thinks he can fetch him direct like.'

She coughed raucously. 'You'll be wanting to speak in private with him o'course and need a quiet room. I've just the place.'

'Simon's here?' Rebecca breathed, a smile of gratitude and relief softening the strain in her face.

'Er...not quite...but he will be soon,' Queenie assured her, nodding her head and wobbling several jowls. 'Bertram will fetch him. You come with me and we'll find you that nice quiet room.' She grabbed at Rebecca's arms and yanked her off the chair and towards the door.

She propelled her towards some narrow, steep stairs at the end of the corridor and began urging her up them. Rebecca attempted to swing about but the woman's bulk was mere inches behind her and her husband directly behind that.

'Come along now,' Queenie jovially encouraged. 'Let's get you off these stairs and safe out of trouble,' and Rebecca felt a none-too-friendly shove in the small of her back.

On reaching the landing, she immediately twisted around, desperately uneasy. But the Spencers were both still there, narrowed eyes in fleshy faces eyeing her with mercenary purpose.

Queenie scraped the key in a lock nearby and pushed open the door to a low-beamed room. With Bertram close behind her and Queenie at her side, pudgy fingers digging into her arm, she had no choice but to enter. Rebecca took in the daunting aspect in one horrified glance: the large bed, the lack of any other furnishing. She swung instantly about.

'There has been some mistake. I must leave this place right now,' she announced with an authority she was far from feeling.

'No mistake, dearie,' Queenie denied her, smiling smugly, as Bertram withdrew his gross bulk from the room.

'My husband is just off to find your young man for you. Then you can have…a nice long chat with him. For as long as you like,' she slyly chuckled.

Stabbing pinpricks of fear began frosting Rebecca's face and body. Her cynicism and suspicion had been honed lately and both were relentlessly cutting her to the quick.

'Let me pass,' she demanded of Queenie in a strident, wavering tone. But the woman simply roared with amusement and leaned her quivering weight back against the wooden door.

'There's five hundred and I'll raise five hundred,' Luke said impassively as he dropped the notes from dark fingers and they joined the untidy pile nestling in the middle of the table. This hand of brag was drawing onlookers and several inquisitive men gathered about the perimeter of the large circular table where he sat.

Sepia-coloured eyes raised to lock on to the golden gaze of his brother sitting opposite. Ross blew softly through his grimacing mouth, shook his head and folded his hand of cards. Several other men did the same, one or two throwing them forcefully and resentfully on to the baize.

Luke allowed a small smile to curl his mouth. He had nothing. His fingers tapped idly against the cards face down on the table. He couldn't remember ever drawing a hand quite as useless as this one, yet he'd just staked a substantial sum on it, bluffed, and could well take the pot. His eyes met those of the only opponent left and held them steadily. The man was young, perhaps twenty-one, and green. Luke could tell he was getting in up to his ears for a good reason. He most definitely held the winning hand but had empty pockets.

He watched him slip a nervous tongue about his lips and

glance around, obviously flustered by the attention the high stakes were attracting.

'Will you take my marker?' he asked Luke with a gruff hint of plea.

'Certainly.' Luke coolly qualified his generosity. 'For payment tomorrow noon.'

The man slid jittery fingers beneath his neckcloth and swivelled his head.

It was as Luke glanced away, bored by the delay, that the silver-blonde curls caught his restless gaze. They seemed familiar and redrew his attention. He frowned reflectively at Molly Parker and then, as his memory finally served him, he scowled.

Even irritated attention was welcome, Molly deemed, and she dimpled at him and weaved through the men thronging around the table now, making proprietorially for his chair. She had recognised him as soon as he had ducked through the low door of the Bull and Mouth with his cheeky younger brother. She had been about to accost them straight away, but Ross had noticed her and manically shooed her away behind his back. Well, the handsome devil had noticed her himself this time and she was going to make sure that she stayed noticed.

Tentative fingertips rested daintily, questioningly, on the black superfine cloth of his shoulders. When he didn't immediately throw her off, she became bolder. Her hands slid further around his neck and the sheer pink gauze of her gown grazed his cheek as she settled her hips close to his face.

Her musky scent was in his nostrils, her lust for him mingled with that expensive French perfume that reminded him of Cornwall and Wenna. He felt the tightening in his groin and knew it wouldn't wait too much longer. He'd come here tonight to play cards but had accepted subconsciously that three weeks' celibacy was all his starved, tormented body could stand. He hadn't been without a woman this long since…he couldn't remember when.

He wasn't married, he wasn't even officially engaged. It didn't make him unfaithful or any other damn thing. It just made him human. He needed the release every man did. He was also in need of some flattering female attention. He had grown used to admiring glances and willing bodies and unequivocal encouragement. He needed reassurance that he wasn't Attila the Hun but just the same attractive, successful philanderer he had always been.

He felt a soft finger slide possessively along the lean, abrasive side of his jaw and flicked his head impatiently away from it. He had a game of cards to finish first if the youth opposite ever decided what he was going to do about financing this last hand. His eyes slid past the young man with bored indolence. He frowned, grimaced, then swore aloud with such violence that every man seated around the table stared curiously at him, and Molly and her fondling fingers abruptly sprang away.

Ross anxiously studied his brother's face. Noting the direction of Luke's black-eyed stare, Ross swivelled his head. There was nothing…nothing apart from drifting smoke and an empty doorway.

Luke's fingers tightened on the cards he held and he glowered, rigid-faced, down at them.

This was lunacy…sheer idiocy. If Miles was beginning to suppose him addled in the wits he was well on the way to joining him in that worrying assumption. He was most definitely losing his mind. He couldn't sleep, he couldn't eat, he couldn't venture out for the evening to play a game of cards…he certainly couldn't contemplate taking a woman to bed, without Rebecca ethereally materialising in his mind. God, but she'd looked real.

He grunted a low laugh to himself, unaware of Ross's anxious narrowed gaze on him. She'd looked like a blue-clad angel. Why he'd imagined her dressed like that, he couldn't conceive. He'd never seen her wear that colour. The most extraordinary thing was that the gross pair who ran this establishment had been escorting her, walking into his delusion too. He shoved himself back in the chair, transforming Molly's wary return into hasty retreat.

Luke stared sightlessly and thin-lipped at the vacant doorway. Then Bertram Spencer nudged his bulk through it. Luke frowned. He was dressed as he'd just imagined him. But then he probably always dressed like that, he reasoned to himself. He watched the fat innkeeper sidle up close to one of the spectators at his table and mutter in his ear.

Luke watched the man's ice-blue eyes reduce to little more than slits and a smile of sheer satisfaction curl his mouth as he nodded slowly. The man turned away immediately, walking fast to the door with Bertram Spencer hard on his heels.

Luke's mouth thrust out in consideration as, just before they exited the room, money changed hands. The younger man turned right towards the stairs and Bertram Spencer hurried in the opposite direction, stuffing notes into his cavernous apron pocket.

Something heavy and stone-cold settled in Luke. It hadn't been a vision. It had definitely been someone. A regular, jaded customer, eager to be ahead of the pack, would be instantly drawn by a fresh new recruit. And would pay up handsomely for the exquisite harlot he'd just glimpsed.

How many women had hair that particular shade of honey? Had that cool beauty…pale skin…and were exactly that height? He felt a tic start its intermittent pulsing by his mouth and his back teeth ground together as the chill in him spread. The cards in his hands dropped from nerveless fingers to the baize. Just as the young man finished writing out his marker, Luke said hoarsely, 'Fold.' He pushed his chair back abruptly, sending a cautiously confident Molly crashing backwards again into the welcoming arms of an elderly gentleman behind her.

He was being ridiculous. It sang through his head as he passed where Ross sat. She was at home…at the Summer House. Probably retired for the evening already.

'Where are you going?' Ross hissed at him.

'Find a girl,' Luke told him huskily without losing pace.

Ross laughed then with sheer relief and several other men joined him. 'About time, too…' Ross muttered beneath his breath, relaxing into the sure knowledge that he was about to get his old, familiar Luke back very soon.

Good-natured bantering amongst the men followed his departure. That was some high instepper, the consensus of opinion went, who could lay a thousand pounds down on nothing at all, then walk off to find a girl without bothering to bluff the hand out.

Ross turned his laughing face from the man sitting next to him and caught sight of Molly. Christ, she looked as though she was about to cry. He got up and walked around the table to her. He hadn't had a blonde himself in a while.

'Mr Blacker!' Rebecca cried in a voice mingling astonishment and relief. 'Do you know if Simon is here this evening?' she asked quickly as the brown-haired man walked steadily into the room. At one time the thought and sight of this man would have filled her with revulsion. Now he seemed ridiculously welcome compared to the odious Spencers.

He gave Queenie an expressive look and jerked his head indicatively at the door.

'Well, I'll leave you to your gent then, dearie,' the obese woman smirked as she squashed backwards out of the room.

Jake Blacker proceeded into the room, his pale eyes never leaving Rebecca's face. Rebecca stepped forward to meet him and then hesitated, something in his silent attitude unnerving her.

'Have you seen Simon here tonight?' she repeated urgently. 'I'm sure the landlord and his wife hadn't the vaguest notion who I meant when I mentioned my brother.' She smiled at him appealingly, hoping for reciprocal friendliness.

'But I know who you mean, don't I,' he smoothly insinuated as he continued with his steady advance. 'Show me a little…gratitude on account, Miss Nash, and I'm sure I might find that brother of yours for you.' His tongue flicked to wet his lips. God, but she was beautiful. Dressed now in finery instead of those modest clothes he'd seen her in last, she was every man's fantasy: an angel in a whorehouse. His fingers itched at his sides. He longed to divest her of the garments he so admired. The blue velvet was handsome and set off her pale beauty and incredible eyes, but heaven only knew he'd love to see her out of it.

Rebecca swallowed quickly and then stood her ground. She had been imprisoned by Queenie Spencer in this spartan bedchamber for no more than ten uneasy minutes, yet it had dragged like sixty. She was, now, heartily sick of feeling frightened and intimidated.

'Where is my brother?' she demanded icily. 'Is he here at this establishment or not? If not, I shall…'

Further words were cut off as Jake Blacker unceremoniously grabbed at her arm and hauled her close to him.

The thick, frantic fingers of one hand were at her cloak, shoving it from her shoulders, while he thrust his other hand impatiently beneath it and grabbed at a breast. She simultaneously slapped at him, trying to evade him, but a spiteful hand sank into her hair and yanked her head around to his. A hard wet mouth pounced on hers, making Rebecca gasp in outrage and fight him in earnest.

'I think this must be where I say…unhand my betrothed, or suffer the consequences…' said a deadly quiet voice from the doorway.

Chapter Nine

'What the hell do you think you're about?' Jake Blacker growled furiously. He still had vicious hold of Rebecca and she was wrenched violently about with him. 'Get out of here and wait your turn. I suppose that grasping lard barrel of a landlord sent you up…'

'Luke…' Rebecca breathed in wonder and relief, fighting desperately to free herself to fly to him. Jake Blacker stared at her then more purposefully at Luke, standing with his back to the closed door, his eyes fiery coals in his tense, whitening face.

As though just recalling how this intruder had termed Rebecca, Blacker grunted a contemptuous laugh. 'What did you say just then? Betrothed…?' he sneered.

'I said…let her go…now,' Luke silkily advised in a lethally controlled voice, while pacing so lightly into the room, it was as though his feet skimmed the floor.

Jake Blacker easily recognised the danger signals. He faced him fully, abruptly releasing Rebecca. The instinct to protect himself was far sharper than his lust. He backed away, circling, assessing the small room's vantage points in flicking glances interspersed with challenging stares at the tall, athletic figure stalking him.

'Luke…' Rebecca murmured again as she rubbed at her bruised arm and rushed to him.

She wound her arms about him and held on tight, trying to still the shake in her body with his solid, familiar strength. But there was no expected comfort, no soothing words and he jerked her away and towards the wall without once looking at her.

Jake Blacker wet his lips. Everyone around these parts knew him and nobody dared cross him. Which meant that this man was a stranger and didn't know the rules. By the time he did, Jake worriedly reckoned it might be too late. He preferred teamwork…the unquestioning backing of the thugs who ran contraband for him. On his own in a fair fight, and weaponless, he wasn't nearly so cocksure. Especially not with a man like this.

The fellow wasn't that much taller or broader than himself, Blacker arrogantly decided, mentally enhancing his height and shoulders by inches, but his confidence and leashed rage were perilous. He'd been watching him downstairs playing cards and thought him a cool, callous customer and definitely well-heeled. Blacker found his mercenary mind veering off at a tangent, as he remembered that game of brag. He surmised whether this man had in his pocket the stack of bank notes he'd covetously watched mounting on the baize.

As Luke came within arm's length of him, Jake hastily evaded him. Fight or flight. He lived by that code and tonight the latter beckoned. He spread his hands in a brash, conciliatory gesture while sliding Rebecca a disparaging glance.

'If you're that desperate…you have her first. I can wait. There are plenty more downstairs.'

Luke continued his advance. His fists were balled so tightly his fingers were in spasm, yet through the red mist of his pain and fury he recognised the sense in letting him go. He wanted him out of the way so he could deal with Rebecca. And deal with her he would. He halted and one arm indicated the door, wordlessly inviting him to use it.

Jake Blacker sidled, back to the wall, towards it. He had been bested and this maddening outcome, together with the fact that he had vainly been parted from his money by Bertram Spencer, needled him mercilessly. Someone had to pay for this humiliation. It looked as though it would be the fat innkeeper.

'You're not from around here, are you, friend? If you were, you'd know not to cross me. Perhaps you'd care to tell me who you are so I can look you up at some time,' he blustered.

'Luke Trelawney, from Cornwall,' Luke introduced himself immediately and quietly. 'Find me there any time,' he added, as his narrowed, black gaze followed every movement of the man shifting towards the door.

'Luke Trelawney…?' Jake Blacker burst into genuine laughter. So the fellow did know who he was, and his profession, and was trying to be mocking and clever. *'Luke Trelawney?'* Blacker jeered again, as his ice-blue eyes derisively swept the elegantly dressed man in front of him from handsome ebony head to expensive, black-shod feet. He dressed and sounded like a member of the aristocracy. But at least he had a sense of humour. 'Well, if you're Luke Trelawney from Cornwall, I'm the Prince of Wales…from Brighton Pavilion.'

'I'd get back there, then,' Luke advised him with treacherous quiet. 'I believe you've guests waiting.'

'And you'd know, of course,' sniggered Blacker.

'I should do. I was one of the invited guests.'

'Luke…' Rebecca called his name again on a trembling

sigh. She felt icy cold and was desperate to be home and away from this foul place and this vile man.

Jake Blacker glanced uneasily at Rebecca. No, it couldn't be true…but it was the third time she'd used that name. But it was a common enough name. 'Who is he? Do you know of him?' he imperiously demanded.

'Luke Trelawney,' she managed to force out through frozen lips, as she numbly wondered why the name should make a criminal like Jake Blacker blanch and stare and then speed up towards the door. Why did it matter to him so much who he was?

'I'll settle with you another time,' Jake Blacker muttered but with little conviction in the guttural warning. He jerked the door open and immediately crashed it shut behind him.

'Luke…' Rebecca pleaded again as she wrapped her arms tightly about herself. She felt so cold and so tired. She just wanted to go home and sleep and sleep.

'Rebecca…' Luke parodied in a voice mingling steel and sarcasm. He walked to the door and locked it, removing the key which he dropped into his pocket. He slowly turned to face her and leaned back against the door, much in the same way he had done on first entering the room.

Rebecca took a tentative step towards him and then hesitated. She so much wanted him to hold and comfort her. But the wrath in his face was no longer hidden beneath that expressionless mask he employed, it was intentionally in evidence. She stepped back immediately against the wall, her cold palms hugging the damp distemper.

'Perhaps you'd care to tell me what you're doing in a gambling whorehouse?' he remarked in a voice so mild and pleasant it terrified her. But menace was nothing new to her tonight and she sensed a devilish anger of her own starting to burn. The memory of semi-naked women in the hallway downstairs was stoking it furiously.

'And perhaps you'd care to tell me what *you* are doing here?' she insolently returned in a tremulous voice.

'Gambling,' came his curt, chill response. 'And you…?' he silkily inquired.

Rebecca moistened her parched lips. She had felt so utterly relieved to see him. So immensely glad and fortunate and now… She walked wearily to the bed and collected her blue velvet cloak from where Jake Blacker had thrown it. 'I want to go home,' she defeatedly declared. She approached the door, halting just out of his reach and looked up into his handsome face. Rage was etched into each feature. Every harsh, lean plane was darkly, satanically set and so tense that a muscle pulled constantly at one side of his mouth.

'Are you going to imprison me, too?' Rebecca asked on a fatigued, shaky laugh. 'That will be the third time this evening I've been held in this accursed room.' His hand went to his pocket. He withdrew the door key and held it out to her, but didn't budge an inch. Rebecca looked longingly at it but didn't move closer to take it.

'Move!' she demanded, trying to ignore the traitorous blockage forming in her throat and the stinging heat at the back of her eyes. He thought the worst of her for being here and she couldn't blame him. She recalled the lascivious, disrespectful stares of the men she had seen outside this sordid establishment. They had believed the same of her.

However she explained it, it would appear ridiculous. She could barely credit that she'd taken such an appalling stupid risk herself. She had never so acutely or humiliatingly suffered for her naïvety. Jake Blacker had tricked her…baited her with the promise of Simon and she had suspected nothing, even knowing the man for a villain. She had simply gone like a lamb to the slaughter.

Luke pushed away from the door and walked towards her. Rebecca immediately side-stepped to pass him, but he followed her circumvention, forcing her back into the room with him, although he never once touched her. She felt the edge of the bed against her legs and as he kept coming and there was nowhere else to go, she abruptly sat down. Belatedly realising the folly in that move, she immediately attempted to spring up again but he was leaning over her, an arm braced either side of her on the bed, forcing her to angle backwards away from him.

'Tell me what you are doing here, Rebecca,' he requested in that deceptively mild voice.

To avoid him, she turned her head, presenting him with a view of artlessly draped golden coils of hair. She was determined to ignore him and his questions, and yet even as she garnered that courage, she complied unsteadily. 'I came here to find Simon. That evil man told me to look here for him.'

'Your brother Simon?' he asked quietly. Rebecca simply nodded without turning her head.

'When did he tell you to look here for him? When have you seen him before?' he rapidly interrogated her.

'He came to the Summer House yesterday. He was searching for Simon and asked if I knew his whereabouts. I told him that I also needed to find my brother and he appeared to want to help me. I foolishly believed him sincere when he stressed this place was a regular haunt of Simon's.'

'And why is he looking for this elusive brother of yours, Rebecca?'

'I believe Simon must owe him money. I think my brother has become involved with a fearsome band of criminals. I…I think he has joined a smuggling ring. That man, Jake Blacker, is their leader, so I've heard.'

She looked at Luke then as she recounted the full horror of her tale, and Simon's likely involvement, sure he would be disgusted by it.

She watched an odd smile alter the hard, thin line of his sculpted mouth and he repeated softly, 'Smugglers?'

'Yes,' she murmured, scanning his face, wondering why he found that amusing.

'So you needed to find your brother so urgently that you risked entering a place such as this?'

'Yes,' Rebecca told him in little more than a whisper.

'Why?' Luke asked in a voice almost as quiet as hers.

Rebecca glanced down at her shaking hands and gripped them together to still them. 'He has my inheritance. He has had it for five years. Had he not stolen it, I would never have been forced on my uncle's charity or been forced...' She broke off hastily, aware she had been about to mention his role in prompting her to desperately seek financial security. 'It is *my* money. My father left me five thousand pounds. It was to be my dowry when I married David.'

'You are not marrying David,' was the steely calm response to this information. 'And you have no need of a dowry.'

Rebecca turned her head then, sparkling aquamarine eyes clashing with chips of black onyx. 'No, I have no need of a dowry, for I have no intention of marrying. But I need the money my father left for my protection. It is mine and I intend having it to secure my future.'

'You have no intention of marrying?' he smoothly echoed her words as his eyes steadily held hers. 'Is this my answer? You've considered my proposal for a day or two and rejected me?'

'It's been more than a day or two,' Rebecca couldn't help but fling at him, recalling his prolonged absence. She now understood why she had seen nothing of him. No doubt he had spent a great deal of his time carousing in places such as this. She had been correct in her assumption of his morals and of the debauched scene she had witnessed at Ramsden Manor. In all probability it was a regular occurrence and had been since first he took up residence.

'Have you missed me, Rebecca? Been counting the days?' he taunted her with soft satisfaction and she immediately swung her flushing face away again, drifting honey curls catching his cheek.

'Not at all. I was merely hoping you would come by so that I could advise you of my decision and finally settle matters between us. I thought it best not to come to the Manor seeking you, lest I intrude on one of your…at-homes,' she taunted him with a honeyed-voice and bitter-sweet smile.

He caught at her face then and firm fingers kept her looking at him as he said, 'It still rankles, does it? Even though I told you there was nothing to it. Nothing at all for you to worry about.'

She shook her head free of his clasp, breathing hard, her turquoise eyes glittering shards of ice. 'I do not worry…I never think of it,' she lied. 'I care not what debauchery you seek. Just leave me alone. I'm going home now.' She half-rose from the bed but he was immovable. In her desperation to be free of him she slapped hard at his face while attempting to duck beneath one of his braced arms.

He pulled back a little, allowing her to stand before catching at her shoulders and partially lifting her backwards on to the bed so she was now sprawled across it rather than perched on the edge. Then he followed her down.

Her fists beat at his shoulders and were swinging for his face again when he restrained them, forcing them back either side of her head.

'This isn't the way to endear a new protector, Rebecca,'

he softly mocked. 'Gently at first. I'll let you know soon enough when I want things rougher.'

She closed her eyes and moistened her lips, her wrists straining against the weight of his pinioning hands. 'I hate you. Why can't you just leave me be?' she choked on a stifled sob.

'Because I can't. And whether you come to Cornwall with the benefit of a wedding ring or not matters little to me. But come with me you will.'

Rebecca flung her head around and glared up at him. She twisted her head this way and that, trying to clear the trailing silky tendrils of hair tickling her face. 'I'm going nowhere with you. I wouldn't even go willingly to the end of this street with such as you.'

'Perhaps you're right,' he agreed, feigning thoughtfulness, as he easily curbed her attempts to throw him off. 'It's a long way to take you only to discover you're a disappointment and need to be returned. It's as well to find out now if you're likely to show talent and be useful,' he said, mock solemn. 'It would save us both inconvenience and you an amount of unnecessary travel.'

He moved one of his hands, still clasped to her wrist, towards her face and carefully removed the irritating strands of hair, the backs of his dark fingers deliberately, caressingly, trailing the creamy satin of her cheeks and jaw.

Rebecca swallowed the ache in her throat. This was too much! Why was everything of late always a disaster? Why couldn't she have found Simon simply? Or simply not found him? Why couldn't the landlord have been a sincere or helpful fellow? Or, if neither, merely thrown her straight back out on to the streets? Why was she always prey to devious rogues and scoundrels who meant her harm? Why had David died? she cried silently to herself. He had cared for her; loved her in a gentle, respectful way. He had never forced her on to a bed and pinned her there while he taunted her with hateful words and tormenting touches.

She sensed rather than saw his mouth nearing hers and jerked her head away, forcing her cheek into the yielding softness of the mattress, her breathing fast and erratic. If he kissed her she was lost, she knew that, and that self-awareness squeezed the first tear between her lashes.

'Let me kiss you, Rebecca,' he softly requested as his mouth tenderly teased her face and rested close to hers. He slowly tantalised the sensitive corner of her firmly pressed lips. 'Please,' he coaxed hoarsely.

'No,' the word burst, strangling, from her throat, as she vainly renewed her efforts to rise from the bed.

'Why not? I've kissed you before.'

Rebecca choked a despairing laugh. That's why, she wanted to scream at him. That's the whole point. Instead she said unsteadily, 'You don't really want to kiss me. It's not what you intend at all. You just told me that.'

She sensed him smile, heard it in his voice as he murmured against her skin, 'I'll stop whenever you say, I promise.'

'No,' Rebecca quickly denied him, panic harshening her voice. He knew very well, as did she, that within minutes she would be rendered mindless and her mortification would scale new heights.

In response, his parted lips trailed her throat, warm and fluid, yet never resting to actually kiss. Rebecca sensed the treacherous coiling in the pit of her stomach as the lean, abrasive side of his jaw slid against the smooth silk of hers and her eyelids drooped and her breathing became shallow. The warmth of his breath stirred the hair close to her ear as he slid his open mouth across a sensitive lobe and she shuddered and reflexively turned into him. His face buried into her neck, fanning moist heat against the vulnerable crease between neck and shoulder and she sighed, closing her eyes and unclamping her mouth.

Luke drew back a little to look at her, while the gnawing ache in his loins and the incredible tenderness and protection she evoked in him did battle. He rested his face into her spread, honey hair. Even in this stinking hole she held the fragrance of fresh air and lavender, and he wryly realised that she truly had nothing to fear from him. He wanted her with a desperation that surpassed anything he'd ever experienced in his adult life, yet the thought of taking her virginity here, on some whorehouse bed, made him feel nauseated.

He'd only frightened her in retaliation, because she had terrified him so much. At one time, and not so long ago, danger and thrill had been a daily part of life and he'd adapted to it, eventually relished it to such a degree he recalled those days with nostalgia. But the thought of her certain fate tonight, had he not seen her, left a residue of fear that even now soured his stomach and caused his heartbeat to erratically strengthen. And he might not have seen her. He could have chosen to sit at the opposite side of that card table.

She might have passed the doorway earlier or later when he wasn't there. He might even now have been oblivious to her presence, while he eased himself with that blonde whore in a room nearby. He probably would have laughed, as would others, on hearing a scream coming from a chamber, imagining it to be fun and frolicking within. His head bowed close to hers and his hands tightened jerkily on her wrists at the sheer torture of it. Rebecca gasped with the painful pressure and he soothed her with careful fingers, nuzzling with apologetic tenderness against her cheek.

'You may kiss me if you don't move your hands,' she whispered in defeat, unable to deny the yearning longer.

'What?' he demanded, a smile in his disbelief.

'Don't move your hands…you mustn't move your hands,' she stressed as she twisted towards him. Their faces were inches apart on the bed as she murmured, 'Please don't move your hands. Promise me you won't.'

Firm, dark fingers slid from her wrists and entwined with her pale, trembling ones, as he said huskily, 'I swear,' just before his mouth touched hers.

Rebecca closed her eyes and tilted her head as he moved her on to her back and braced himself over her. She clamped her small, slender fingers purposefully around the considerable length of his as he carried their joined hands to bury in the silken softness of her hair.

He kissed her with slow, wooing sweetness and a hot urgent passion which made his fingers crush shakingly about hers, as he fought to limit his need. Clasped fists disentangled from luxuriant golden hair to mutually caress her body while skilful skimming knuckles deftly, covertly raised and disarranged her skirts.

Rebecca felt her own teasing fingers and her response to them and in feverish awareness pushed their coupled palms away across the covers. He controlled the sweep, taking them back up to her head, his thumbs free to soothe her face as the magical kiss protracted.

It was so slow and so deep their faces barely moved, fused together while his tongue made leisurely, probing strokes into her warm satin mouth, exploring and exciting. He could feel her small, intuitive movements jerking her hips up to meet his and discreetly shifted position. Reflexively her legs spread a little and a silken calf slid naturally over the black-suited, brawny length of one of his. Tiny panting sounds began breaking far in her throat, yet still she wouldn't relinquish his gripped fingers.

The erotic assault was calculated, unremitting, until she

was squirming against him, her tongue tentatively unfurling to seek and copy his. He manoeuvred her subtly; dexterously rearranging hampering skirts so a solid, trousered knee could wedge unimpeded between hers. It slid unhurriedly up, opening her thighs.

He abruptly lifted her, while rearing back to kneel on the bed and settled her relentlessly hard against him, so she widely straddled the iron-muscled rigidity of his thigh.

He had anticipated her immediate alarm at this sudden change in position. As she frantically twisted her mouth and hands against his to escape, he seduced her expertly, inexorably, until she quietened and accepted it. As she relaxed back into him she moulded herself breast to groin against him, with an innate rotation of hips. He encouraged her to do it again with insistent, guiding hands, meeting her movement with increased pressure of his thigh while eroticising the kiss.

Their mouths clung now barely apart and his tongue probed with deliberate, measured thrusts between her hot swollen, lips. She ground against him faster and then, fearful of the wild, enslaving sensations controlling her, fought again to tear her mouth and her body from his. But he was inflexible, pinning her against him with one clamped hand against her buttocks and the other behind her head maintaining hard sensual contact.

After a heart-thundering moment, Rebecca surrendered with a sobbing sigh, grinding her hips harder and faster against the reciprocating rock of his body.

Luke sensed her tense and then arch and deliberately jammed against her, heightening abrasive friction until she convulsed and shuddered. As her back bowed further and she moaned into his mouth, he finally released her lips, and relaxed. Her head lolled instantly back exposing the rose-flushed ivory of her throat. His face followed, dropping forward, his steamy mouth resting against the column of satin skin as she shook and gasped and her fingernails dug savagely into his hands.

Boneless languor bathed Rebecca and Luke lowered her gently back down to the bed. But as he tried to immediately remove himself, her arms and legs tightened about him and she whimpered. He did too. He wasn't sure whether to laugh or cry. He rested his face against hers while desperately trying to avoid contact with any other part of her. He felt sure he might explode at any moment and the excruciating torment was too much. He gradually disengaged himself from her clinging grip and touched his mouth to hers before he pulled away and stood up.

He walked to the window and looked out, then leaned his feverish forehead against the cold glass. He walked to the door and stared at the wooden panels, then rested his head and fists against that too.

He turned back to the bed and gazed at her. She lay quiet and sated, her golden head fallen to one side, with locks of hair coating her flushed face. In his demented desperation he wondered whether he had time to quickly find one of the tavern whores and relieve himself before reason reclaimed her drugged mind and body.

He watched her stir and turn on to her side, before resettling deeply into sensual torpor.

So this was love, he realised with an ironic little smile; this mix of tenderness and torture, elation and misery. There was a lot to be said for never having left Cornwall. God only knew why he had. He could have dealt with the whole Ramsden business from there if he had put a mind to it. But he hadn't; some irrevocable duty had brought him to Sussex and now he knew why. Destiny…fate, he'd never yet believed in them.

He walked back to the bed and squatted down on his

heels close to her. A fond finger came out to touch her cheek and rouse her.

Rebecca smiled against the finger that lovingly outlined her lips but she didn't open her eyes. 'I like it when you kiss me,' she murmured artlessly.

'I know you do,' he said gently. 'You'll like it even more next time. When you let go of my hands.'

Drowsy, large-pupilled turquoise eyes looked wonderingly at him, then she smiled. The dark finger by her mouth stroked along the bruised scarlet of her lips and she playfully caught it, bit down on it and then soothed it with her tongue.

Luke closed his eyes and choked a pained laugh at the innocent teasing and the images it evoked. Christ, it wasn't fair. Where was that hard-bitten, selfish bastard when he needed him?

He slid his hands under her and tipped her forward into his arms and stood up, holding her turned into him like a child. She immediately coiled her arms about his neck and nestled against him.

'We'll be married on Sunday,' he told her in a tone that was neither request nor dogmatic, as he stooped to collect her velvet cloak from the bed on his way to the door.

He placed her with her back to the door, facing him, blatant self-mockery and raw tenderness mingling on his darkly handsome features. Large, lean fingers settled the blue velvet carefully about her, drawing the hood up over her head and tucking in the strands of hair around her sensually flushed face. She looked up at him with wide aquamarine eyes and his steady, amused gaze never left her trusting face as he withdrew the key from his pocket and unlocked the door. He finally moved away, pulling her with him so the door could open.

'Let's get you home,' he said with a caress of a smile.

He scanned the empty corridor, grabbed at her hand, and then started along it.

He descended the stairs, keeping Rebecca shielded behind him, hoping to God that the silver-haired harlot didn't materialise out of the smoky atmosphere. The noise of gaming and revelry was becoming deafening: a raucous female chuckle was heard followed by uproarious male laughter and some lascivious banter.

'Found your brother then, my dearie,' came a lewdly insinuating voice from behind.

Rebecca made to swirl about, recognising it instantly to be Queenie Spencer, but Luke held her facing the exit as he turned to the woman.

Queenie goggled at him, wondering where the hell he had materialised from. 'Struth, but he was a big, handsome brute. Wealthy too, she reckoned, as her materialistic eye roved his impeccably styled black clothes. No doubt one of the Quality.

She wetted fleshy lips and smirked at him. 'Everything to your satisfaction then, your lordship?' she suggested with ferocious cunning and a meaningful nod at Rebecca's hooded profile.

Luke despised the woman openly with black diamond eyes and a curl to his mouth while he considered. He could ignore her, leave, and risk her causing an uproar and attracting the attention of every whore and patron within the place, or pay her. Not that the money bothered him in the slightest, it was the implication for Rebecca.

As another chorus of lusty laughing erupted, he wondered where Ross had got to, whether he had already left. As though in response to his silent call, his brother clattered down the stairs at that precise moment, a brandy bottle grasped in one hand and the silver-blonde in the other. Both spied him at the same time. Ross jovially called out his name, greeting him with a waving bottle and Molly narrowed spiteful eyes at Rebecca.

Rebecca heard Luke's name too. Sure she recognised Ross's voice, she made to turn and investigate. Luke slapped a fistful of notes into Queenie Spencer's humid palm, disgustedly shaking off the pudgy fingers that reflexively closed over his. He tightened his restrictive grip about Rebecca's shoulders and speedily ushered her outside.

With athletic ease, Luke swung into the saddle behind Rebecca and turned the black stallion's head towards the coast road. Rebecca settled back against him, instantly sliding her arms beneath his jacket seeking warmth and comfort. He drew her hood further forward on her golden hair as the wind whipped brine off the sea at their faces, then urged the restless animal into a trot.

Rebecca rested peacefully against him, closing her eyes as the evening's events ran through her mind in slow motion. Some made her shudder in recalled horror, others that she lingered over provoked trembling of a different sort, causing her body to heat. But there were niggling oddities that puzzled her.

'Were you really invited to Brighton Pavilion tonight?'

'Uh-huh,' he grunted on a smile. 'Are you impressed?' he asked softly against her velvet hood.

Rebecca considered for a moment. 'I suppose I should be. But I'm not sure. I know very little about the Prince Regent and his court.'

'Well, I know a little more,' he commented drily. 'That's why I decided to have a game of cards with Ross instead.'

'Am I supposed to believe you simply preferred the Bull and Mouth tavern and…*gambling*, to Brighton Pavilion and exalted company tonight?' Rebecca probed with more than a tinge of sour disbelief in her voice.

'I'm a country boy at heart, Rebecca. I'm happiest with simple pleasures. I've no need of such people.' He gave the top of her head a slow, indulgent smile. 'Besides, once we're married I won't be looking to go out and…gamble in the evenings. I shall be a model husband. And such society invitations will lessen. It's Lord Ramsden's eligible bachelor status which makes him sought after by scheming hostesses.' He added, mildly cynical, 'Not to mention the hundred or so thousand a year.'

Rebecca twisted to look at him. 'Am I a simple pleasure, then?' she asked, feeling illogically insulted, and apparently unmoved by his fortune.

'More hard than simple, I'd say, Rebecca,' he ironically remarked as glittering black eyes roved her beautifully solemn upturned face. But he managed a wry smile.

Rebecca returned him a contented one and again nestled back, reflecting once more on the thrilling evening's events.

'Jake Blacker seemed to know you,' Rebecca mentioned against the warmth of his chest, as her fingers began a tip-toeing, cautious exploration over hard ridges of muscle on his linen-covered torso. She hadn't been so casually close to him before and the desire to touch him, while he was otherwise occupied, was undeniable. His silence made her pull back a little and once more look up into his shadowy face.

She saw the flash of white in the dusk as he smiled. 'Lots of people know me, Rebecca.'

'But he seemed…disturbed by your name,' she persisted. 'Why?' She sensed him shrug and his hand slipped beneath her velvet cloak and a firm thumb caressed her midriff. She tried a different approach. 'Do you know him?'

'I've never seen him before,' he answered truthfully.

Rebecca relaxed back against him and as their fingers

touched beneath her shielding cloak and spontaneously laced, she quivered with recalled ecstacy.

'Jake Blacker has a fearsome reputation,' she told him in a voice muffled by his coat. 'He is a foul blackguard…a smuggler who runs the risk of hanging if caught. I hope Simon is not very involved with him. For all such criminals run that risk,' she whispered brokenly. 'And I suppose it is only fair they should pay for their crimes. Don't you think?'

'Absolutely,' he said but in an odd tone of voice that made her think he might be laughing. She immediately drew back to investigate. But he turned his head away, shielding his expression. His eyes were narrowed and intent when he looked back at her and then he bent his head to warm her wind-chilled lips with his.

'I'll find Simon for you. Don't worry,' he said soothingly against her mouth before he purposefully spurred the black stallion into a gallop so that any further questions were impossible.

Chapter Ten

Molly Parker slid a covert glance at Luke from the corner of one blue eye, trying to decide whether she could stomach yet another rebuff. Devil take him to hell! Why give him an opportunity to insult her for the third time?

But that bored, perfect profile turned to the leaded window of the taproom loosened her fine resolution, and tightened her fists around the mug of porter in front of her on the rough-hewn bar top. She glowered disgustedly at the bitter brown beer, wishing it a stiff French brandy instead of this cheap slop Bertram rationed his girls.

Why did this stranger, infuriatingly, have to be the most imposing, handsome man she could ever remember patronising the Bull and Mouth? She had worked in the place for nearly a year now and had entertained clients as diverse as an escaped French prisoner of war, fresh out of the sea in a last bid for freedom; to an octogenarian duke fresh out of his sick bed in a last bid for life.

This one was ridiculously wealthy too. Her heart thudded miserably as she remembered her last humiliation, when he had dismissed her and the pot of money laying in the centre of the card table, and walked away from both.

The French prisoner of war had been penniless...and

sopping wet, having swum a good deal of the ocean between the rotting hulk of the penal ship where he had been
incarcerated, off the Kent coast, and the pebbly shore of
Brighton. But Bertram Spencer had welcomed him quite
cordially, while bundling him upstairs into Molly's care.
'Général de Montfort' had been whispered about. So had
promise of generous payment when he was reunited with
his compatriots and country. Exhaustion and hunger had
taken their toll on the wretch, providing Molly with one of
her slackest evenings. A welcome night's rest always
sweetened her attitude.

She had worked at this den of iniquity long enough to
know when to play blind, deaf, and dumb. Thus she never
saw kegs and chests come ashore and cram the Spencers'
cellar. She never heard any hissing debate in the dead of
night as to payments due and owed, and she never uttered
a word about any of these oddities. Her reminiscence in-
evitably skewed to the decrepit yet lusty old duke. She
shuddered, recalling his fetid breath and decaying loose-
skinned body…and his energy… That foul memory did it
for her. She slid off her bar stool and was adjusting her
low-cut satin bodice and her coiffure when the taproom
door opened.

Her teeth ground in frustration. Another blond stealing
his attention! She watched Luke Trelawney's mouth curl
sardonically. But he raised a languid hand and curtly beckoned, encouraging the newcomer to join him.

Simon Nash walked forward hesitantly, a searching
glance about the low-beamed room settling briefly, interestedly, upon Molly as she fumbled behind her for her stool
and reseated herself.

Her professional interest quickened. Gawd! Another welcome, attractive man new to this dive. She gratefully acknowledged his attention with flirtatiously lowered eye-

lashes and dimpling pink cheeks. She swivelled on her stool to face the bar and took a satisfied swig from her porter before recalling, with distaste, what she drank.

'You got my message,' Luke stated evenly but the contempt he felt for the man was obvious in his cursory gesture at the chair opposite him.

Simon quickly seated himself, fidgeting with straightening the sleeves of his navy woollen jacket. He placed his hat on the table then removed it and arranged it carefully on the floor by his chair. Unsteady, work-roughened fingers raked a thick lock of sun-gilded hair back from his sea-beaten forehead. Anything to occupy himself and dodge those stone-cold eyes he knew judged and condemned him.

He gulped a steadying breath, blinked wide navy eyes, and summoned youthful brashness to his aid. 'I thought perhaps you got my message,' he boldly challenged the imposing man who was casually leaning into the carver chair, his powerful physique making its solid frame seem as insubstantial as matchwood.

Luke allowed a genuine smile to momentarily soften his mouth. So the lad was badly rattled and without the skill to adequately disguise it. But what championed his cause most, Luke wryly realised, was not his gaucheness, but his flaxen hair and blue eyes and an undeniable likeness to his beautiful older sister.

'*Your* message?' Luke queried, prepared to humour him for a while yet. 'You've been keen to seek me out?'

'Er…yes. I told Blacker I should like to meet with you,' Simon gruffly informed him. 'Blacker has told me that you and Rebecca are…er…very well acquainted. I knew it was my duty to introduce myself to you…in the circumstances.'

'Did you, now,' Luke remarked softly and smoothly, quelling an urge to reject sentimental indulgence in favour of gripping his prospective brother-in-law by the throat and demanding to know where he had hidden during more worrying circumstances affecting his sister. He steadily reined in his temper. 'Which circumstances?' he coolly invited through closing teeth.

'Those that made you leave messages at every local tavern that you wished to speak urgently with me,' Simon impulsively retorted, sensing he had a weak advantage but unsure why.

A humourless, thin smile cautioned Simon to quieten. He did so, swallowing further words with a visible jerking of his Adam's apple.

This was not going at all the way he had hoped. He had been cornered eventually by Blacker at Horsham and received, not the beating he had expected for his unpaid debts, but the first piece of good news in an age. A cut lip had been inflicted, almost as an afterthought, by Blacker before they parted quite amicably.

Simon was astute enough to realise the motive behind this leniency. Blacker's devious mind had already deduced what profit lay in a wealthy man becoming involved with the Nashes. And Simon couldn't deny he owed him a substantial amount. He couldn't deny either that he had been a naïve, gullible fool to ever have become hopelessly embroiled with scoundrels way out of his league. But that was another matter.

For the moment what monopolised his thoughts was that his reserved, homebody sister had ensnared a man such as this. If what he had heard whispered was true, Luke Trelawney was rich as Croesus, one of the landed gentry to boot, but most importantly…as dangerous as sin. Nobody, to Simon's knowledge, frightened Jake Blacker. Yet that felon had sweated merely rasping the name of the suavely dressed gentleman lounging opposite him.

Rebecca was extremely beautiful, no denying it, but

completely out of social circulation and apparently keen to stay that way. She was also without the artifice debutantes and demi-reps alike employed in hooking a sophisticated man of the world. Or so he had thought.

And he doubted men came more worldly-wise or sophisticated than this impressive aristocrat. Blacker had grudgingly admitted he was a fine figure of a fellow, when Simon had pressed him for a description so he would recognise him. It had been nowhere near as generous as it could have been. Part of him wanted to laugh aloud with glee and relief. But he didn't dare.

He was desperate to know more about Luke: exactly how deep his interest was in Rebecca. Not that he was about to fight for her virtue. She was almost twenty-six now and way past her marriageable prime. If this urbane man's interest was less than honourable, Simon was realist enough to know it was only to be expected and still to be gratefully encouraged.

But he was happily prepared to be optimistic. 'Blacker tells me you introduced yourself as Rebecca's fiancé. He also tells me that the name of Trelawney and…' he lowered his voice to a conspiratorial hiss '…free trading…have long been linked. In fact, he seemed keen to tell me more, but unfortunately we were unexpectedly interrupted that night…' He flushed and fidgeted, running a finger between his collar and his sticky neck.

'By the Revenue men?' Luke remarked, all feigned sympathy, before complaining with the same spurious commiseration, 'They've no sense of timing.'

Oblivious to Luke's sarcasm, Simon glanced swiftly about. 'Is it true?'

'Rebecca and I are to be married. Your sister will be leaving Sussex and removing with me to Cornwall,' Luke tonelessly supplied.

Simon gulped at this information, his mind in a delightful spin. 'And the other…is that true?' he demanded, unsure whether he wanted to hear it confirmed or denied.

'Why so concerned?' Luke quizzed sardonically. 'Are you going play the outraged protector? Raise fraternal anxieties as to my morals…my suitability as a husband for Rebecca?' he taunted and had the satisfaction of seeing the immediate guilty flush crawling the younger man's cheeks.

'I thought not,' he stated smoothly. 'Now I think it's my turn. Perhaps you'd like to furnish me with a few answers. Where is Rebecca's inheritance? Why haven't you done all in your miserable power to provide for her since your parents' death? Why haven't you risked your inconsequential life protecting her from harm and men…perhaps such as me…during the past five years? And, finally, perhaps you'd like to give me one good reason why I shouldn't teach you a painful lesson in family duty.'

Simon scraped back his chair, about to impulsively jump to his feet and flee, but Luke had unwound from his in a lithe second. He inclined menacingly towards Simon across the rickety taproom table. 'Sit still…there's a good lad. We're still barely introduced. We've a long way to go yet,' he mocked with a lop-sided smile and eyes as cold and hard as gravel.

'I think we've enough now,' Rebecca remarked as she lifted the basket, weighing the fruit with her hand. 'Martha is going to be pleased with you, Lucy; no doubt a blackberry pie will be coming your way at supper time and jam later in the week.'

In pleased response, Lucy's hand dived back into the basket, stole one of the largest, ripest berries and carried it immediately to her mouth.

Rebecca followed her away from the hedgerow, seeking

the rough track that meandered away from the woods towards the Summer House. They strolled in amicable silence, both absorbed with their own thoughts, and a quiet appreciation of the rustling, russett-leaved countryside.

Rebecca knew now was as good a time as was likely to present itself, to broach the subject of Lucy's imminent return to the village of Crosby and her family. 'I have some news for you, Lucy,' she introduced the subject lightly.

Lucy swished to face her and walked backwards with a smile. She tilted her head to one side so brunette curls trailed over one shoulder.

'Well, let me see,' the girl teased. 'Does it concern a local nobleman? Perhaps a very handsome certain gentleman?'

'In a way…' Rebecca admitted with a small laugh. There was certainly little that escaped this young lady's notice. She sobered; Lucy's premature return home at Christmas might not be at all welcome. Lucy could rarely be drawn into chatting about her family. Her stepfather she would barely acknowledge. Yet at Christmas Lucy must leave, for she and Luke were to be married.

The thought of her secret fiancé—for she had made Luke pledge not to announce their betrothal until Lucy had been told—made her stomach knot in that familiar, bone-melting way. He had been quite serious about marrying her on the Sunday following her disastrous rendezvous with Jake Blacker and the vile Spencers at that horrible tavern in Brighton.

But there was no possible way Rebecca could abandon her pupils so selfishly. The parents of the day pupils were entitled to some notice of the school's closure and more specific arrangements were necessary for Lucy. It had taken all her powers of persuasion to make him see that she had certain responsibilities to take care of prior to becoming a married woman.

Dwelling on the method of her persuasion made her heartbeat so erratic it was a bittersweet ache.

Noting the sturdy wooden stile to one side of them, the last on their trek home, Rebecca diverted to it. She sat down, leaving some space for Lucy to join her, and placed her basket on the springy turf by her side. 'I believe you've already guessed that Lord Ramsden has asked me to marry him, Lucy.'

'Indeed, no,' Lucy cheekily denied in a tone that made her tutor blush. 'That's not at all what I suspected.'

Rebecca sensed her colour heightening and steeled herself to regain her composure. That this fifteen-year-old girl was more experienced and worldly than she was was undeniable and regrettable. But Rebecca quietly acknowledged now that she had gained more sophistication in the last month than in the last five years. And she was thankful for it.

She had too long cocooned herself in memories of happy times with her dear parents and David. Now it was time to emerge from that nostalgic haven as a woman. Relinquishing all that was safe and familiar, and trusting Luke wholly with her body and soul, after so short an acquaintance was daunting, she had to admit. But she loved him. And she clung to the belief that he loved her and would soon tell her so.

So Lucy would no longer shock or worry her with crude innuendo. 'We are to be married, Lucy. We have settled upon Christmas as the date. Mr Trelawney wanted us to wed sooner, but…'

'I'm sure he did…' came Lucy's amused muttering.

'But I have decided,' Rebecca continued calmly, giving no hint that she had heard the sly aside, 'that we shall marry at Christmas. That way it gives your stepfather time to make alternative arrangements for your future. He might wish to place you at another small academy or appoint a governess for you at home.'

'You're sending me home?' Lucy choked, white-faced. 'You're sending me home…to him?' she repeated quietly now, with resigned bitterness in her tone and her pinched, chalky complexion.

Rebecca searched her face, confused. She had just been thinking how mature the girl was…how perceptive in all adult matters, yet something as simple as her tutor's marriage putting an end to her time at the Summer House seemed never to have entered her head. But the saucy miss had never believed her to be preparing for marriage. Becoming mistress to the lord of Ramsden Manor, while he remained in Brighton, need not have disturbed Lucy one iota.

'Naturally, I shall have to return you to your family, Lucy,' Rebecca gently confirmed. 'Mr Trelawney is determined to return to Cornwall and his estates there and I shall, of course, go with him.'

'I could come,' Lucy immediately seized upon the possibility. 'I could go with you. You will need a maid if you are to be a fine lady. I could be your maid. I know what to do. I had a maid of my own when my dear papa was alive. Not one shared between Mary, Mama and me because that bastard is so mean to us all.'

'*Lucy!*' Rebecca cautioned in a tight voice. 'Please do not speak in such a way. You do yourself no favours by using such language. Or me,' she ruefully admitted. 'What will your mother and stepfather think you have achieved here if you return home so coarse and ill-mannered?'

'He is a vile, lecherous bastard,' Lucy exploded, her face crimsoning now with rage. 'And I've told him so. Why do you think he hits me? Because I hate him creeping to my room at night when Mama is indisposed or huge with child? Because I hate his filthy hands on me?' A piercing laugh jerked out of her. 'No. That I can stand. Sometimes I even encourage it. Do you know why? Because then he leaves Mary be. No. It's my unruly tongue that earns me this!' She punched a screwed-up fist so swiftly and so savagely against her own face that she made herself flinch.

Rebecca instinctively reached out to enclose and comfort her in her distress while chilling, numbing shock drenched her. And shame, for Lucy had confirmed what she had partly suspected yet never had the courage to consciously confront. At that moment she detested Rupert Mayhew with a violence that shocked her.

Lucy roughly pushed Rebecca off. She gained her feet in an angry leap and was backing away from her tutor in a second. 'You marry your lover,' she hissed. 'And as soon as you like, for it makes no ·difference to me. I'm never going back there. Never.' She twisted angrily away and, gathering up her lemon muslin skirts, began running along the track in the direction of the Summer House.

'Is Lucy back?' Rebecca gasped at Martha before she was fully inside the kitchen door.

'Why, yes,' Martha told her, a worried crinkling about her eyes as she digested Rebecca's breathless agitation. 'Came in like a whirlwind she did, and stamped straight up them stairs to her room.'

Rebecca closed aquamarine eyes and sighed heavily, with relief at finding the girl home, and worry at the task that still lay in front of her: for there seemed no alternative to returning Lucy home.

Rebecca automatically tipped the basket of fruit into a colander and slowly poured a jug of cleansing water over the berries. She let plump fruit slide idly, soothingly, between her slender fingers.

Was it such an outrageous idea? Why could Lucy not accompany them to Cornwall? She could finish her year's tuition. Her piano playing might improve with perseverance. Would odious Rupert Mayhew care whether his stepdaughter gained her refinement fifteen miles away along the coast road or a hundred or so miles away in another county? He had made no effort to visit or enquire after Lucy's progress.

Implying that Lucy's prospects of finding an eligible husband might increase in Cornwall would be no small consideration to a man such as Mayhew, Rebecca decided, biting her lip and allowing herself a small smile as she recognised her first descent into sophistry. Perhaps she should parade Luke or Ross before him as examples of Cornish manhood, for she was well aware that no ambitious parent would object to such handsome, wealthy gentlemen. She enthusiastically warmed to the idea. Luke and Ross would be ideal allies in this. Both charming; and of good family she was sure, although she had to admit she had so far learned very little about the Trelawneys.

Luke had told her about his brother Tristan, at home in Cornwall, running the estates until his return. She knew he had a sister, Katherine, in her late teens. His mother was alive but, sadly, his father dead. These few tidbits of family information had been gleaned over the past few days, when he visited. But they never seemed to have a great deal of time to talk. The reason for that brought a simultaneous smile and sigh. And she knew she couldn't wholly blame Luke for their lack of conversation. It was a frightening new power she wielded over this strong, passionate man but its effect was addictive.

Rupert Mayhew, she briskly decided, dragging her feverish thoughts back to duty and Lucy's predicament, would probably welcome the idea. She was absolutely certain that he would not mind his stepdaughter's removal to Cornwall in the least.

But Luke was sure to, she realised with a wry grimace at that ridiculously overlooked consideration. She had an unshakable pessimism that her future husband might raise very great objections indeed.

'No!' Luke stated with an absolute finality that lost something when coupled with the tender look in his brown eyes.

'Come here,' he sighed out with mild authority, as Rebecca's chin came up in defiance. Long, lean fingers beckoned, as did his wryly charming smile. But Rebecca fought the temptation to go to him and jammed herself back against the sink. She was determined to make him hear her out.

'You've not listened to me properly,' she calmly began, still ignoring his outstretched, tanned hand. 'When I said I wanted to continue schooling Lucy after Christmas I didn't mean to imply that we had to postpone our marriage. Or that I would refuse to come with you to Cornwall and stay here in Brighton. That wasn't what I meant at all.'

'Oh, good,' Luke drily remarked, mock-relieved. 'Because there was never the slightest chance of any of that. I'm still not sure that waiting until Christmas is necessary. We should have been married yesterday as I planned. Travelling west now, while the weather is still fine, is far preferable…'

'Your motive has nothing to do with travelling in fine weather, and you know it,' Rebecca interjected, then she flushed. Dilating black pupils and heat stoking at the back of his eyes mesmerised her, for she knew too well what that intense look heralded.

'Indeed, it hasn't…much,' he admitted. 'But, nevertheless, it is a genuine consideration.' He strolled towards her and, taking one of her hands, led her through the kitchen and into her small parlour.

Luke gently pushed her down into the comfortable old fireside chair and then hunkered down beside her. 'Now…' he muttered on a drawn-out breath, as sepia-coloured eyes astutely watched her solemn profile, 'what's brought all of this about? Yesterday everything was settled between us: you would write to Mayhew and arrange for Lucy's return home…'

A dark finger trailed gently along an ivory cheekbone, urging her to face him. When she did not but continued to stare into the leaping flames in the hearth, he tilted her chin towards him.

'What is it, Rebecca?' he asked, concern hoarsening his voice as the tormenting possibility she would try to withdraw from their betrothal bedevilled him. He'd come to see her at the Summer House this evening, as he did every evening, with the excellent news that he had at last located Simon and found him well; yet now he felt the time was not right to impart any of it.

'Why won't you let me deal with Mayhew?' he probed gently. 'I can tell, from the way you've spoken of him in the past, that you've no liking for him. It's high time I introduced myself to my neighbours. And I suppose he could be classed as one. I'll ride over tomorrow and explain the situation to him.'

'No,' Rebecca cried, a cloud of silky-gold hair rippling about her shoulders as she twisted to face him. 'No, don't do that,' she wheedled with a disarming, wavering smile.

Immediate suspicion narrowed his eyes at her vehemence

but she wasn't ready for explanations yet. The whole situation whirled chaotically in her head—whether to scour her mind for more plausible reasons why Lucy should accompany them to Cornwall than those already voiced; whether to simply tell Luke of Lucy's awful accusations; whether to vent her own suspicions as to the vile nature of the girl's stepfather.

What would Luke do? Feel similar outrage and want to help Lucy? Or take the view that the matter was none of his or his future wife's concern? Turquoise eyes soberly searched his hard, handsome face. He was a man, after all…one of strong passion as she knew.

Soft colour flowed into her face at those delicious yet fearsome memories; her wonderous yet incomplete knowledge of his sensuality. For there was more to love-making than she had tasted so far. The magical closeness of kissing and cuddling enchanted her, yet she knew this left him sometimes unbearably tense and frustrated, and prone to a disturbing self-mockery.

His slow smile made it obvious he'd a hint of the reason for her protracted silence and rosy complexion. 'What are you thinking?' he demanded, brilliant eyes half-concealed by long, lush lashes as they targeted her lips.

'I'm thinking I should like to know more about you and your family. About your background…' she told him speedily. 'And that it's very warm by the fire,' she lied, shielding her glowing cheeks with a cool hand. 'But I'm mostly thinking that we never talk enough…'

A low oath made her pause. He twisted about and was, within a second, sitting on the floor by her chair. One knee was raised and he idly rested a hand upon it, opening his broad palm to the warmth to be had from the ruddy embers.

'Talk to me now then, Rebecca. Tell me what's worrying you.' Brooding dark eyes abruptly relinquished the smouldering coals and burned into her exquisitely demure face. 'You have to trust me…and you won't, will you?' His mouth slanted while he waited for her reply, his eyes hungry for every nuance of telltale emotion.

'I barely know you, Luke.' As she saw his head jerk back in frustration, she quickly added, 'But…but I'm glad we're to be married.' She sighed, knowing those few feeble words in no way conveyed the depth of emotion this man aroused in her: the conflict of logic and love; the need for independence and support.

She put out a conciliatory hand to touch his sleeve. He seemed unaware of her gesture, so her slender fingers moved to tentatively stroke the abrasive side of his jaw, copying the caress she had received from him minutes before. She felt the flexing of lean muscle beneath her timid fingers as his teeth closed and he half-smiled into the fire.

'Well, don't do that, Rebecca. I thought you wanted conversation instead this evening.' Her fingers made to spring away but he caught them and held them firmly within his.

'So…what shall I tell you?' he quietly began, almost as though he spoke to himself. Her slender, pale fingers resting within his dark, broad palm, received loving attention as he divulged, 'I'm thirty-two years old and have spent the majority of those years in Cornwall. The countryside there is dangerous and rugged…but beautiful. The people…very similar. I've never felt the need to move anywhere more fashionable. Bath draws me but rarely now. I liked it better before it gained such popularity with the *haute ton*, but I still have a fondness for it because of happy memories.

'At one time, Tristan, Ross and I were sharing lodgings together as students. Tristan and I at college and Ross at Grammar School. We had some fine times,' he recalled with a smile that turned to such an infectious laugh it made Rebecca join him.

'It was probably simply nostalgia for those days which prompted me to buy a mansion there, for I rarely use it. I'm nearly always at Melrose. But I shan't pretend I've lived a quiet, uneventful existence on a remote countryside farm. I'm not going to insult your intelligence by claiming to have lived a blameless life; yet neither have I done anything deliberately evil to feel ashamed of. My adult years have been spent in the way of a fairly typical Cornish bachelor.

'As to my family, as you know, my father died some eleven years ago and left me Melrose, still unfinished after thirty years. Not that he didn't have the money to finish the building…he and my mother were always squabbling over how to do so.' He glanced at Rebecca and smiled. 'It was the breath of life to them to argue about paint colours or window symmetry or the style and pitch of the roof to the east wing addition.'

'Did I tell you how the estate came to be so named? It was taken from my mother's maiden name—Demelza Penrose. When she was seventeen and they began courting, they came upon a tumbledown house while out walking. He promised her that one day he would buy the whole of that dilapidated estate that spanned two miles along the Cornish coast and that they would marry and live there. For they both fell in love with it straight away. They could see the potential in its setting and acreage that other, more experienced landowners, could not.'

'A year later when she married into the Trelawney clan, they moved into that ramshackle cottage and lived in what was little better than a hovel. Yet they classed it as a wedding gift, each to the other. My father worked on it tirelessly, enlarging and improving it. And when his three sons were able and old enough, we helped him. Hence Ross's enthusiasm for carpentry,' he informed her with a smile. 'He really is rather good, actually.'

'What a lovely, romantic story. Your father must have thought the world of her,' Rebecca wistfully sighed.

'Indeed,' Luke confirmed with a faraway gaze. 'And she of him. His stipulation that the house should be willed to the eldest male son gave me more anxiety than she. But he had prepared well: she has an elegant dower house on the estate which was built with her blessing. It was a long-standing family tradition for he came from a landed family, but being the youngest son, he inherited very little.

'At the time of his death it was approaching being the finest house and grounds in the county. It now is. And it has been enlarged again and finished. My mother assures me that what I have done, with her guidance and advice, would have found favour with him. She tells me she loves its graceful elegance.

'She is now in her fifty-first year and still very beautiful. She was barely nineteen when I was born and still enjoys very rude health. She and my sister Katherine walk the clifftops close to Melrose most days. Even the rain rarely keeps them inside. The winds tend to since a couple of sheep were lost over the edge. Katherine is made in her image…just as beautiful and quite a problem with her eager gentleman callers. I hope Tristan is rationing her favours fairly while I'm away.

'What I told you a month ago about my ability to provide for you is completely true. My father left the majority of his estate and stockholding to me. I've considerably increased his bequest. My shipping interests have been especially profitable…' Noticing Rebecca's slight withdrawal and her increased colour as he obliquely referred to propositioning her as his mistress, he frowned. 'I never apologised for that, did I?' he rebuked himself.

'It doesn't matter…' Rebecca began in a thready voice.

'It does and I do regret it. I'm sorry. I badly misread the situation between you and your uncle. It was idiocy to jump to such a ridiculous conclusion about you. But then perhaps I should add,' he mentioned drily, 'if I have a failing, it's that I'm an incorrigible cynic. Apart from that, I'm not such a bad fellow. Sociable, generous…' He paused thoughtfully. 'But now I shall have to be less accommodating and find them all alternative housing. I've no intention of sharing you. It's high time I had some privacy. Don't worry. They'll all love you,' he reassured her with a tender smile.

'Will you?' was sighed unbidden and immediately regretted from Rebecca.

Chapter Eleven

'I'll send Gregory over to the Manor,' Martha asserted. 'He can bring her back with a flea in her ear. That miss is the most wilful, selfish minx…'

'Hush, Martha,' Rebecca began, but Martha was not to be quietened.

'It's time there was some plain speaking about that…that young woman,' Martha spat. 'She's run off again, that's what she's done and she knew you was going with his lordship to town. My guess is that she's done it on purpose. And it's about time that you had a day away, too. And off she goes bold as brass. Straight to that young carpenter, I'll lay a pound to a penny—'

'Enough, Martha,' Rebecca cut determinedly into her disjointed tirade, a hand held up, begging silence. But Martha's chins wobbled indignantly, readying for another attack.

'I believe you're right,' Rebecca placated her. 'She probably has gone looking for John. She was very upset yesterday and, I have to admit, I was expecting her to hide straight away… Oh, heavens, what is the time?' She sped through to the parlour and looked up at the ancient wooden wall clock. It was practically one o'clock in the afternoon and Luke was expected at any minute.

Martha stomped through into the parlour after her. The kitchen door opened and Gregory shuffled in, feathery carrot tops quivering in his fists.

'Boots off!' Martha ordered with a grim cursory glower over her shoulder. Gregory was then ignored. 'Don't you go making his lordship start searching for her as soon as he gets here,' she warned Rebecca. 'You two need some time to yourselves. I reckon as he might have some pertickler reason for wanting to take you to Brighton and you might never know of it if'n you send him off on a fool's errand. We got Gregory for that,' she emphasised with a nod, shelving her crossed arms on her bosom.

There was intentional intrigue in Martha's tone. 'Such as?' Rebecca probed with a smile.

Martha tapped the side of her nose, wagged her head, and bustled back to the kitchen and her husband. The cosy kitchen, and its warm aroma of spiced buns, drew Rebecca too, but her mind was again with Lucy. Martha was probably right. It was likely that Lucy had done this today, of all days, out of spite, to ruin Rebecca's first proper outing with Luke.

Rebecca was to shut school early today and they were to lunch and shop in town, he had stated yesterday before departing. Rebecca had walked the lanes of Graveley with her young pupils, just before midday, delivering messages about her new circumstances and her school's closure.

She had taken a few precious minutes chatting to Kay Abbott over the parsonage gate, finally confiding her exciting news to her friend, and had received joyful congratulations. On her return from that pleasant interlude, Lucy was nowhere to be found and Rebecca had been gone barely an hour. She saw no harm in doing as Martha suggested and allowing Gregory to take the trap over to fetch her. It was a bright yet autumn-fresh day. A brisk walk across the meadow to the Manor might have tired Lucy and dispersed some of her mischief. Rebecca had the greatest sympathy for the girl's predicament and hadn't given up hope yet of persuading Luke to help her in some way.

She had been prepared to persevere with the subject last night before he left, but... A small, wistful smile slanted her full mouth, for the very last words she had spoken to him remained unanswered.

Why hadn't he answered her? Why had he said nothing when she had so needed his reassurance? Why had he looked at her in that smouldering, intense way that made her feel she was the centre of his universe and yet not confirmed what she longed to hear? Just one small word would have enchanted her. Had he simply said 'yes' she would have been in heaven. In desperate confusion at his silence, she had been about to compound her mistake: pretend it a joke, even apologise, for she knew that after such a short acquaintance as theirs, to speak of love too soon could be foolish and humiliating.

And so it had proved. But no further words were necessary...or possible. He had, within a moment, kissed her deeply, skilfully into silence. He had manipulated her body and mind in the way he knew best. And when the hour was late and he gazed down into her rosy, swollen-lipped face and told her of today's arrangements for their outing to Brighton, she surfaced just enough from her sybaritic languour to sigh and smile agreement.

'Look at you,' Martha clucked at Rebecca, spoiling her reverie. Spinning her about, she neatly rearranged the silken hair into a twisted golden coil that neatly trailed the blue velvet cloak she wore. Martha stood back and assessed her young mistress with a critical eye, nodding her satisfaction.

'Handsomest couple in the whole of Sussex,' she muttered to herself, before turning to Gregory and giving strict instructions regarding Lucy: the speed of the fetching and the strength of the lecture on the way home.

'I'm not sure that this is really proper,' Rebecca advised her fiancé with a mischievously demure raising of her delicate dusky eyebrows.

Luke leaned towards her in the carriage rocking its way carefully down the slope to the town of Brighton. Sartorially splendid black-coated forearms rested on equally elegant knees.

'I can't imagine you ever doing anything that wasn't proper, Rebecca,' he gently mocked her as his eyes caressed the beautiful sight of her. With golden hair, creamy skin and turquoise eyes matching that soft velvet she wore, she looked radiant. The difficulty was keeping to his seat opposite her rather than joining her and taking up where they had left off last night.

Rebecca smiled through the window, well aware of his fixed attention and relaxing into a warm contentment because of it. 'I may be of somewhat advanced years, my lord, but I am still a spinster and we are not even officially betrothed. I really ought to have a chaperon when abroad with you,' she teased, knowing he hated it when she addressed him so formally.

'I believe you're probably more in need of one, Rebecca, when we're within doors…' He smiled at her immediate blush before remarking in an odd, sardonic voice, 'Besides, you will have one, when we reach Brighton, and the most appropriate one there is for an unmarried, orphaned woman.'

Rebecca gazed enquiringly at him. When he said nothing, but merely leaned back against the comfortable, cushioned interior of his travelling coach, surveying her through sleepy eyes, she shifted forward on her seat towards him. Turquoise eyes searched the hard, angular planes of his handsome face but he gave nothing away. The wonderful possibility entered her head and her soft lips parted to voice it, but she dismissed it. It couldn't be…not so soon…but he had promised he would…

She sighed out uncertainly, 'You've found Simon.' When he said nothing, but his sooty lashes momentarily touched his cheeks and his mouth thrust in something akin to agreement mingled with ironic regret, she flung herself across the carriage. Silken, lavender-scented hair clouded his face, velvety arms twined about his neck and soft lips found a hard, dark cheek.

'I knew there had to be some advantage in unearthing him,' he muttered hoarsely as muscular arms immediately entrapped her against him.

The sudden violent rocking of the carriage made two pairs of eyes widen, then roll. The groom and driver grinned knowingly at each other; the driver's tongue poked into his cheek and his thick, straggly eyebrows disappeared beneath a similar fringe. He started to tunelessly hum, then shrilly whistle, anticipating his diplomatic duty to drown out any embarrassing noises that might, any moment, issue forth from within.

'Simon!' Rebecca exclaimed as soon as she was within the doorway and spied his bowed sun-streaked blond head. Simon sprang up from the chair by the roaring fire, immediately stepping a pace towards her. But the mix of anger and relief sharpening his sister's voice made him hesitate. Neither moved or seemed capable of breathing for a moment; they gazed at each other as though frozen in a tableau. Simon's blue eyes shifted to the man standing a little behind Rebecca, his chiselled features set in an impenetrable look.

'Simon!' Rebecca breathed again as her eyes closed and she allowed the wonder of his presence to douse her fury a little. Within a second she had propelled herself the length of the room towards him and enveloped him in a hug. 'It's so good to see you…so good,' she murmured into his rough woollen shoulder, a betraying shake in her voice and dew glistening on her lashes.

'It's good to see you, Rebecca,' Simon gruffly responded. As he sensed the watery sting in his nose and his arms shaking about her, he realised just how sincerely he meant it. Overwhelming shame swamped him so abruptly that he dipped his head to rest atop hers, attempting to conceal glossy navy eyes from the tall, silent man, so closely watching their reunion.

'I'll see if lunch is ready. I'll be but a moment,' Luke said quietly from the doorway before quitting the room.

Rebecca gazed out of the window upon the busy Brighton street scene. This hotel was situated in the most exclusive area of the town and their beautifully furnished private room on the first floor had an excellent view of the fabric warehouses, beyond which could be glimpsed a sparkling grey ribbon of sea. Her attention was momentarily arrested by two young ladies alighting on to the cobbles from a smart phaeton. They giggled together and waved to the dandy driving their transport before hastening into an emporium displaying exotic silks, satins and laces.

'Why didn't you write then, if you didn't want to visit?' Rebecca demanded of her brother, as she swung back towards him, watching him now, as he gazed morosely into the fire. 'Can't you imagine how worried I've been? Not knowing what dangerous scrapes you might have been in?

Don't you realise what terrible rumours there have been about treacherous villains in the area?'

In response, Simon sighed and threaded ten nervous fingers through his thick blond hair. He seemed about to reply but the door opened at that precise moment. He fell back in his chair, thankful for the distraction.

Luke approached them and sat in the gilt-framed wine brocade chair by the window. Firm, tanned fingers, briefly, imperceptibly, sought Rebecca's in a touch that was both reassuring and affectionate.

The hotel manager then glided in, silently traversing the luxurious carpet. There followed a stream of phlegmatic servants dressed in darkest black and crispest white. The long mahogany table set against a creamy watered-silk wall had its sleek surface decked with a delectable array of cold meats, fish dishes, pastries, pickles and salads within what seemed to Rebecca little more than a minute. The staff filed out in the same mute orderly way, the manager the last to go, after he had set out wine and crystal glasses to his absolute satisfaction. He bowed low into the room before pulling the door closed behind him, without having uttered a word.

Sure she had not seen so much food on one table since her sister Elizabeth's wedding breakfast, Rebecca was drawn slowly to it to investigate.

'Are more people to arrive and lunch with us?' she enquired quite seriously of Luke as her eyes roamed the sumptuous spread. It had arrived and been deposited so quickly, yet was beautifully prepared and arranged on the highly glossed table, with fine silverware fanned for use and lace-edged linen intricately folded by snowy porcelain plates. A magnificent swan, carved from glistening ice, shimmered centrally, and was encircled by slivers of smoked salmon, trout and other seafood delicacies. A warm finger stretched out to touch the glossy sculpture, and Rebecca gasped as it immediately slid down the bird's gracefully arched neck.

Luke watched her indulgently, before admitting, 'I hope you are both hungry, for there is just us to do justice to it.'

Simon couldn't remember when last he had feasted so well. On arrival at this place his stomach had been gurgling from neglect. The last proper meal he'd eaten had been that other bought for him by this man at the Bull and Mouth two days ago, while they discussed financial matters. His blue eyes lifted from his plate to watch the extraordinarily attractive couple seated close by him as they chatted and laughed intimately while eating. They had both done their utmost to include him in their conversation. Simon smiled to himself; but one couldn't help but feel intrusive: their eyes rarely left one another. It was a real love match, he suddenly realised, quite surprised, for he knew very few of those between couples, engaged or already wed. A delicious morsel of sweet pastry found its leisurely way to his mouth; he chewed and considered.

This relaxed, cosy atmosphere couldn't last. The matter of the missing five thousand pounds was sure to soon raise its ugly head. When it did, he hoped he would perform well and sound convincing. If not…he gave no further thought to the consequences of upsetting such a powerful, enigmatic man.

Perhaps he should be the one to introduce the topic; that way he might be able to control the way the discussion went and still be able to relax and enjoy to the full this pleasant afternoon with Rebecca. His crystal goblet of ruby wine once more touched his lips and a warm glow of alcohol hit his stomach and fired his courage.

'I know I have been despicable, witholding your inheritance, Rebecca,' he catapulted into their brief lapse in conversation, wincing as two pairs of eyes immediately fixed on him.

'Yes, you have, Simon,' Rebecca quietly confirmed, glad that her brother had had the decency to mention her inheritance and that she hadn't been the one forced to broach the subject. 'Have you any of my money left?' she directly asked him, pushing her plate away from her a little, her tasty lunch forgotten.

Simon's eyes shifted momentarily to Luke before seeking his plate. 'Very little, I'm afraid,' he carefully answered. 'But I'm confident I've just enough of it left to invest and recoup all that money of yours that I've lost,' he quickly added.

Rebecca continued, frowning at him, 'Surely not another harebrained scheme to get rich quick, Simon,' she chided. 'For the moment, I'll settle for what is to hand. It's better than nothing at all. If you intend to get proper employment, perhaps back with Gillows, then you can repay me in the future. For I should have all of what Papa left me. It was my due and my dowry,' she stressed with a minimal sideways glance at Luke's unreadable face.

'Yes, I know,' Simon agreed, unperturbed. 'But I've no wish to pay you back in instalments. I should like things sooner set to rights between us. I've behaved unforgivably and want to make amends as quickly as I can.' Another discreet sliding look took in Luke's bland expression: his lowered eyes examining the silverware with which his long, dark fingers casually toyed.

'What money of yours I had left, I have invested,' Simon said, relieved it was only half a lie. He dwelt on the banker's draft that had yesterday found its way into his account, astounding the bank manager. But the money certainly had been invested for Rebecca.

'Simon, no!' Rebecca rebuked in disbelief. 'Don't you

dare… You've not squandered even that residue on some hopeless venture?'

'I'm assured it's a certain winner,' he stressed quickly and truthfully. 'A reputable company was looking for a few select backers to import spices and fruit and the return, I'm told, is guaranteed and phenomenal. I'm very fortunate to get this chance. There's also a possibility…if I satisfy certain requirements…that they might employ me.'

'It's illegal importing, isn't it?' Rebecca accused him in a tight voice. 'You're again involved with criminals…smugglers, aren't you?'

'No…I swear, I'm not,' Simon emphasised, then hesitated and qualified the assurance. 'To the best of my knowledge, the company is reputable and the proprietor an honest businessman,' he avowed, avoiding looking Luke's way at all. He thus missed long dark lashes screening sepia-coloured eyes and the very ironic smile twisting a narrow mouth.

'Please believe me, Rebecca. I swear to you that I regret what I have done over the past five years. When the money came to me from Papa's will it seemed like a godsend. I believed I would be able to escape that interminably boring job he had arranged for me at Gillows and make a career at sea, as I had always wanted. He should never have forced me into that apprenticeship. He knew I hated being imprisoned indoors… I was slowly suffocating.'

'He did what he thought best, Simon,' Rebecca righteously defended her father. 'He wanted to secure your future with a worthy profession. He did it for you.'

'He did it for him,' Simon snapped. 'Because he was always so financially useless he wanted me schooled to take over the accounts, to try to recoup some of the losses he had made since Grandfather Nash died. *He* would have taken me to sea. Grandfather always promised me my own ship, but Father lost them all…every one.'

He repeated with quiet wistfulness, 'So, when my bequest came, I thought I would at last get my way; purchase a small vessel… But Father misjudged my potential,' he mocked himself with a bitter laugh. 'Commercially, I am just as useless as he was. I not only lost all my inheritance but all yours, too. Almost all of yours, too,' he hastily corrected himself. 'It made me panic and listen to unsound advice. One night in Hastings when I was losing at cards to Blacker, he hinted he knew how I could make a tidy sum for very little outlay. You can guess the rest. He fleeced me of any profit by telling me that my booty had been lost at sea in bad weather or seized by the Revenue men. Strangely, his never was,' he admitted with a self-deprecatory grimace. 'I guessed his plan, but how could I go to the magistrates with such a tale? Blacker knew that, of course. He pretended sympathy; lent me money at an extortionate rate. You can imagine just how deeply embroiled I was. I have been running the length of the south coast…back and forth…trying to keep one step ahead of him and those batmen he employs.'

Rebecca went to her brother. She leaned over his shoulders, enclosing him in a comforting, forgiving embrace, her lips brushing the top of his head.

'Well, what's done is done and no use crying over spilled milk,' she unconsciously quoted one of Martha's favourite sayings. 'If Luke thinks this business proposition quite proper, I will not object to you using my money.' She smiled over the top of Simon's head at her fiancé. 'Do you know of this company, Luke? Tell Luke who they are, Simon. He may know of their reputation and be able to advise you as to their past successes or failures.'

'I know of them. They are very successful,' Luke economically supplied, giving Simon no chance to speak. 'I would have no objection to my money being invested in this venture,' he reassured, with a warm smile for her; it cooled to sardonic humour as it included her brother. 'Now…' he said, with abrupt finality, as he approached Rebecca and proprietorially drew her arm through his, 'if you have eaten enough, it's time we did some shopping. It's past three o'clock already,' he mentioned with a cursory glance at his gold pocket watch.

'Are you to come shopping with us?' Luke addressed Simon with an odd inflection to his voice which made the younger man hastily shake his head.

'No…no, I believe I might stay here and do further justice to some of this delicious food,' Simon excused himself.

Rebecca gazed at the burgundy-shot silk draped in intricate folds across the counter. Her fingertips slid across the fabric reverently, back and forth, loving the luxurious feel of it. She glanced up enquiringly at Luke.

'I like you in blue,' he said softly, intimately. 'But I dare say any shade would suit you.'

The hovering draper must have heard his quiet compliment for he hoisted on to the counter bolt after bolt of blue materials, from winter-weight midnight velvet to cobwebby cornflower muslin. With a flourish he swirled a little off each roll to display its quality and hue.

As the counter became crowded with jostling ladies, all apparently keen to see the sumptuous display of fabrics, Rebecca pressed possessively closer to Luke. Many of these over-perfumed, under-dressed women, she realised, with a new stomach-churning pang she recognised as jealousy, only really intended gaining the attention of the tall handsome man by her side. She began to feel hot, bothered and indignant at their blatant, inviting stares and sly proximity.

A tall brunette's hard dark eyes slid from avariciously stealing across Luke's powerful physique to challenge and poison Rebecca.

'Perhaps a quieter shop might suit. It's like a common meeting-place in here,' Rebecca pointedly said, with a freezing look at the provocative, impenitent woman.

'Well, what are you buying? Everything?' a familiar voice called across the throng.

As a groaning oath escaped Luke, Rebecca spun round with a ready smile, welcoming Ross through the hostile females. He approached with a rather plain young woman dangling on his arm.

'Nothing personal, Ross, but we were just leaving,' Luke good-naturedly rebuffed his younger brother.

Ross quickly introduced them to Miss Arabella Stone, who smiled coyly and retained a limpet-like grip on his arm. 'We'll walk outside with you,' Ross immediately decided, seizing the opportunity for other company. The diffident young lady with him had been summarily foisted on him by her scheming mother earlier that afternoon. He had been looking to return her for the past hour or more, but the elusive woman was nowhere to be found.

Strolling towards the sea-front in amicable silence, Rebecca suddenly half-turned and waved to a woman in a pretty pink bonnet on the opposite side of the street. She was promenading with an elderly lady and they both raised gloved hands and beamed and hesitated. Luke tightened his hand over Rebecca's, resting in the crook of his arm, rightly anticipating she might want to rush off to greet them more lengthily.

'I'm keeping you to myself today,' he wryly excused his possessiveness. 'Who was that?' he mildly enquired

Rebecca looked up at him. 'Kay Abbott, the vicar's wife,

with her mother. You have met Kay. She was at the Summer House on the day you...' She trailed into silence, unable to say, *Came to proposition me*, and unable to think of any other purpose to his visit.

'Ah yes, I remember now,' Luke said with a smile at the sea to the side of him. An affectionate thumb brushed satiny skin on the hand resting through his arm. 'Nice woman,' he economically summed Kay up.

'She is my best friend. Is that all you have to say?' Rebecca teased in a horrified voice. 'I told Kay today about our betrothal and that I would soon be leaving Brighton. I shall miss her so when I leave here,' she sighed wistfully.

Large fingers comfortingly enclosed smaller ones. 'She can visit us. You needn't lose touch.'

Rebecca laced her fingers into his, fascinated by the mingling of light and dark, large and small. 'Lunch was wonderful. It must have cost a fortune. But there was far too much. You should have invited Ross to dine with us,' she brightly suggested, quite disturbed by the waste of such splendid fare.

'I want today for us, Rebecca. I just manage to free us from your brother and we get saddled with mine. I want some privacy so I can talk to you.' As though an idea had just occurred to him he said, 'Actually, tempting Ross with a free lunch and as much as he can drink might just distract him enough...' He slowed his pace and made to turn but Rebecca pulled him on.

'You can't do that,' she hissed, horrified. 'You can't send him back now. He'll know it's simply to be rid of him.'

'Good...' Luke mildly began but the rest of his conversation was cut short.

'Let's go down to the shore,' Ross called from behind, having speeded up to join them with Miss Arabella Stone still an unwanted appendage.

Diverting to the beach, Ross suddenly unthreaded Arabella's arm from his and placed her close to Rebecca. 'I'm sure you two ladies must have things to discuss: fashions and bonnets and such,' he suggested in desperation. 'Luke and I need some bracing ocean air.' He unceremoniously dragged Luke ahead with him towards a wide wooden groyne that ran down to the sea. Luke grimaced his exasperation and apology at Rebecca before the two men picked their way past small battered boats, nets and pots and walked towards the smooth silvery water.

Arabella wrinkled her pert, freckled nose. 'Awful smell,' she said as a briny whiff of tar and seaweed stirred their hair. 'That's Lord Ramsden, isn't it?' Arabella queried immediately when Luke and Ross were out of earshot. Her grey eyes narrowed on the men some way ahead of them now.

'Yes,' Rebecca said, uncertain what else to add, yet sensing Arabella's steady, piercing gaze on her. There was probing interest in her eyes and voice and Rebecca knew that she was being proved correct in fearing fashionable young ladies of good families would target Luke. Just as those shameless women had so recently tried to do in the fabric emporium!

'Mama says he's terribly rich and such a good catch. And he and his brother are so handsome. But nobody seems to know much else about them.'

Rebecca choked a melancholy laugh and murmured, 'Exactly.' She stared ahead as Luke and Ross leaped from the wooden groyne on to the shingle and strolled to the sea. She studied her fiancé: his tall athletic figure and long dark hair whipping about his beautiful face. He suddenly threw back his head and laughed at something Ross said before he looked back to where Rebecca and Arabella stood on the promenade. Even at that distance Rebecca could sense his eyes exclusively on her, and when his hand raised and he beckoned, she instinctively obeyed and walked forward.

'You're not going on to the beach, are you?' Arabella gasped disbelievingly.

'Yes…come on,' Rebecca encouraged the younger woman. 'We can stay on this wooden jetty. Your gown won't get dirty,' she reassured Arabella.

'Mama will kill me if she discovers I have behaved in such a hoydenish manner. This dress…' she swirled the lilac skirt of her walking dress out from her legs '…cost a fortune.' She grinned. 'But never mind. I believe she is still with Mrs Pettifer taking refreshment at Dilly's Tearoom. She will never know. I haven't seen her in an age. They gossip for ever when they get together,' she confided as she followed Rebecca along the wide wooden slats, taking great care to avoid touching the fishing nets.

Luke started to stroll to meet them. Realising he was about to lose his companion and again be encumbered with Miss Stone, Ross intercepted him and started skylarking. He shoved Luke close to the water's edge, into the frothy tide. He then backed off, whistling, and casually skimming flat pebbles across the glinting waves. Luke walked out of the surf, shaking brine from his calf leather shoes, but laughing. He swiped out at Ross, then abruptly grabbed him, throwing him further into the sea, so foam sprayed up his brother's immaculately clad legs.

'Oh, my goodness,' Arabella breathed, horrified, before she giggled. 'I hope Mama does not see this…or ever hear of it. Such outrageous behaviour would have her fainting dead away.' She turned excited grey eyes on Rebecca as though they were conspiring in a marvellous plot.

Rebecca couldn't believe it either…but she watched fascinated as two expensively dressed handsome men frolicked quite unselfconsciously, and uncaring of being observed or ostracised. As Ross lunged at Luke and Luke dodged, evading him, Rebecca glimpsed two young boys playing naturally on a Cornish beach. She relaxed into the wonderful moment, mesmerised by their antics and the quiet realisation she had never loved Luke more.

'Arabella!' The screech came from behind them and Arabella's shining eyes and dimpled cheeks were replaced by a disappointed grimace. She lifted a hand to greet her mother even before she turned and spied the woman.

Ross walked back nonchalantly towards them and vaulted on to the wooden walkway. He politely offered Arabella his arm and began sedately escorting her back to her mother, a picture of masculine sophistication despite his damp trousers.

Rebecca gave Luke a worried smile as he approached. 'I hope Ross is not in trouble.'

'Ross is always in trouble,' he said, breathing hard from exertion. His dark skin was tinged a healthy pink, his black hair streaking his face in thick, glossy strands. He loosened his perfectly folded cravat and said, 'I could do with a swim.'

'You're surely not going to...' Rebecca pleaded and threatened.

He laughed. 'No. We could take a boat out fishing. The sea's calm.'

'That's a joke,' she whispered.

'No,' he answered her with a smile. 'Have you ever been sea fishing?'

She shook her head. 'I wouldn't dare. I can't swim. Simon loves fishing. He loves eveything about the sea...'

Rebecca searched her mind, desperate to think of something to say to distract him from any other bizarre ideas. But his rugged yet awesomely attractive appearance dominated her mind and she could think of no conversation at all. She could only look at him. For there was something undeniably appealing in the contrast of expensive finery and careless dishevelment; and the way he was so at ease with both.

'You look like a gypsy ruffian who has done well for himself,' she softly said. She had intended keeping it as a cherished secret description but it somehow escaped.

He looked up at her from the pebbly beach. 'Do I, now?' he challenged, dark eyes gleaming and the start of a smile pulling one corner of his mouth.

'Indeed,' she chided. 'And not at all a suitable fiancé, I'm afraid. I might have to rethink....' Her words were cut off as he vaulted back on to the wooden jetty and swung her up into his arms in one swift fluid movement.

He walked down the landing stage towards the sea. 'Would you like to learn to swim, Rebecca?' he asked with deliberate insinuation.

'Put me down...someone will see,' she half-laughed and squealed, outraged, as her fists beat against his arms. 'Please put me down,' she wheedled, her mouth close to his face. 'Mrs Stone will faint dead away; poor Arabella told me such a scandalous sight would give her an attack.'

'Arabella and her mother have gone,' Luke said, with a cursory glance over his shoulder to the promenade, 'and there's no one else about apart from Ross. He won't care if I throw you in.'

Rebecca tensed uncertainly in his arms. 'Luke? You won't...you wouldn't dare...would you?'

Sensing her genuine fright, he tipped her comfortingly into him and murmured against her face, 'Returning home dry must be worth at least a kiss.'

She struggled in his arms. Realising she was instinctively nestling further into him, she abruptly gave up. 'I don't find this at all amusing. Put me down,' she ordered primly but with a betraying smile in her voice. Her mouth was temptingly close to an earlobe and in mischief and frustration she nipped at it with her small teeth. Remorseful in case it hurt, a lingering flick of her tongue soothed his warm, salty skin.

He immediately removed his arm from beneath her legs but still held her close so that she slid slowly down his long, hard body. 'That was a very nice alternative to a kiss, Rebecca,' he softly praised and tutored her. A long dark finger emphasised his pleasure by stroking her warming face and an intimate smile increased her colour and her confusion.

'I thought I was saddled with her for the rest of the day,' Ross exclaimed as he reached them. He exhaled a deep, satisfied sigh at having at last jettisoned Miss Stone. 'Where her mother's been hiding herself all afternoon, I've no idea.'

The problems of searching for someone determined to remain concealed jogged his memory of something important. 'Oh, I nearly forgot. I meant to look out for you earlier today. I have some news.

'Before I left the Manor this afternoon, Miles bade me give you a message that John was nowhere to be found. John…the young carpenter,' he explained when Luke looked mystified. 'Oh, and he thinks that young Miss Mayhew from the school may be with him. Apparently Gregory Turner and Miles searched for some while; all the outbuildings have been investigated. They couldn't find hide nor hair of either of them. Do you think they might have eloped?' he suggested quite cheerfully.

Chapter Twelve

'I thought I told you never to come here,' grated an icy irate voice.

Jake Blacker twisted about and a snake-quick flick of his tongue wet his dry lips. 'You don't think I would have come unless the circumstances were exceptional, do you?' he flung back.

A thunderous look received this impertinence, making Blacker wince and avoid those feral eyes that raked him from head to toe. 'If you need to contact me, you use the crypt as postbox, as always,' snarled the small, squat man, glaring up from his inferior height into Blacker's face.

Blacker bit down on his lip and his temper. 'No one saw me; I've tethered my horse out of sight. Besides, I've a notion that the authorities are wise to the churchyard's use: any proper investigation will reveal it.'

Mayhew allowed a ghost of a smile as he dismissed Blacker's fears. 'Those dragoons will soon tire of staking out a desolate graveyard in favour of a jug in the snug of the Red Lion. But forgive me if I don't offer you a seat or a drink,' he sneered. 'I'm sure the only reason prompting you to risk my good reputation…and therefore your life…'

he smoothly interjected '…is desperation to pay me what is long overdue.'

His sarcasm and contempt weakened Blacker's nerve. 'I cannot extract one penny from that wastrel who owes me so much,' he whined. 'Paying you my share of that last consignment of brandy is presently impossible. Chipping in on the gold shipment bound for Calais this week is quite beyond my means.'

'Indeed? Is that so?' Mayhew spuriously commiserated as he stalked closer. 'Who is this man you cannot seem to deal with? Shall I have to do it for you? Do you want that favour added to what you owe me?'

Blacker gave a bitter, jeering laugh. 'It might not be quite so easy as you, or even I thought. This youth suddenly has a very dangerous champion.'

Mayhew swung back towards him, intrigued. 'A knight in shining armour?' he mocked. 'You are a dolt, Blacker. Where is this unassailable reputation you boast of? Where are these thugs you brag do your every bidding? The Falconers gang in Kent, where I lately was, have batmen who are mine for the asking. Give me this young puppy's name and I will settle it. But you will pay. Indeed, you will pay.'

'Simon Nash,' Blacker immediately supplied.

'Nash…Nash?' Mayhew rolled the name off his tongue, scouring his mind for the reason it sounded familiar.

'And the man who gives his protection to that family is…Luke Trelawney,' Blacker added, maliciously satisfied by Mayhew's stunned expression.

Then Mayhew's ugly features faced the ceiling and he howled, 'Luke Trelawney? Of course,' he scoffed. 'Why didn't I think of that? Luke Trelawney has come from Cornwall to champion some ne'er-do-well milksop.'

'This ne'er-do-well milksop has an extremely beautiful sister,' Blacker hissed. 'She is one of the most beautiful women I have ever seen. And now Trelawney's seen her. They are betrothed.'

'Not Rebecca Nash, surely?' Mayhew dismissed, reflecting on that beautiful face and body, yet prim and proper attitude. But for his blasted wife's ailing health following her confinement, and a month of pressing business matters that had taken him from Bournemouth to Kent, he would have visited the delectable Miss Nash at the Summer House school. After all, he had the pretext of checking on the unlikely progress of that hoyden of a stepdaughter.

'The same,' Blacker righteously confirmed.

'Trelawney is involved with that virtuous schoolmarm?' Mayhew stated, amazed. 'Trelawney?' he repeated with an incredulous snort, ruminating on the last voluptuous beauty he had seen draped about the man in Penzance. The memory of that full-bodied, dark-haired wench made him sweat. 'You're mistaken. It must be an imposter. He rarely leaves Cornwall; or ventures further east than Bath.'

'It's Trelawney and his brother Ross. They're at Ramsden Manor. Luke Trelawney inherited the Ramsden estate, by some quirk of lineage.'

Mayhew stood stock still. It could not be true! Yet while he had been away he had heard noised abroad that Robin Ramsden had his estate entailed on some distant relative from the west country. He had not been bothered enough to probe further. Knowing Robin for a philanderer, he had not been surprised at gossip of his sordid death, or that the new owner of the estate would, at first, choose to keep to himself until rumours quietened.

Trelawney! How he hated the name and the man. Luke Trelawney had forced him from successful free-trading in Devon and Somerset, to seek new pastures and coastlines. Four years ago, having fled Somerset and the Revenue virtually penniless, he had covered his tracks sufficiently to make a new identity and life. And he had been lucky and done remarkably well for himself in duping a wealthy widow into believing him a personable, trustworthy fellow. Now she knew differently, it hardly mattered. They were married and he had gained this beautiful house and substantial funds in the bank. She and her two brats were a minor hitch.

He was sure Trelawney knew nothing of his whereabouts, his new name or his business with these local smugglers. It was ironic. It was fate. Fate had decreed his revenge could now be taken on the unsuspecting enemy. And perhaps very sweetly, he grinned to himself, as Rebecca Nash dominated his mind.

'Trelawney is now Lord Ramsden and is betrothed to Rebecca Nash?' he asked, almost lyrically.

Jake Blacker nodded curtly. 'And Simon Nash is now quite brazen about what he owes me. I've not had the opportunity to warn the pipsqueak of all I know of his prospective brother-in-law. He continually avoids me.'

'Well, we shall have to do something about that,' Mayhew purred. He hated Luke Trelawney with a vengeance. For it was only luck and cunning that had put him in this genteel house rather than in gaol...or on a gibbet. He resented Trelawney's wealth, his good looks and his sexual conquests. He always had the most attractive women fawning over him.

Whether Trelawney intended Rebecca Nash to be his wife or mistress, her chastity was sure to be of vital importance. His thin smile turned to a lusty laugh.

'I do believe that the virtuous governess and I are overdue for a talk. My stepdaughter's progress is suddenly of immense concern to me. There is a way you can repay me, Blacker, and perhaps keep your purse in your pocket. Assist me in a little...conversation with Miss Nash tonight at

Devil's Cove. I warrant Trelawney might pay hand-somely…even beg…to get that blonde angel back intact.'

It was impossible! How could he have found out so soon?

Rebecca stared, flabbergasted, at the stooped, elderly man propping ancient joints against the kitchen doorframe at the Summer House.

'And master says as ter be as quick as yer can fer it's terrible important that he speaks to yer,' Bert Morris impassively advised through the clay pipe clenched between stained teeth.

Re-reading the note in her hand, Rebecca tried to extract some inkling of the writer's mood and purpose. The only detectable tenor was the urgency apparent in the phrasing of two brief lines of scrawled script which summoned her immediately to Crosby.

Bert Morris stuffed horny hands into fraying pockets and stood morosely, waiting. When Rebecca simply continued staring at him in astonishment and consternation, he gave a backward nod of his bedraggled head. 'Sent the coach and pair fer yer,' he said proudly, drawing Rebecca's attention to the smart carriage, so different from the last creaky contraption they had shared.

Could Rupert Mayhew have so soon found out that his stepdaughter was missing? Rebecca had known herself for barely five hours, and it was only the last two of those which had given her real cause for concern.

After Ross's staggering news in Brighton about the absent couple, they had all returned immediately to the Ramsden estate so that Luke and Ross could join the search for them. Although unbearably restless, Rebecca had obeyed Luke's ruling that she stay at home and wait for news, recognising the sense in it: for there was little she could do as dusk approached. She had never forgotten coming so terrifyingly close to the smugglers trekking through the woods some weeks ago.

How on earth could the news have travelled fourteen miles to the girl's stepfather so speedily? She just could not imagine. Or could she…? Of course! Rebecca gave a little blow of annoyance at her stupid lack of comprehension. Lucy might not have run away at all, but rather taken it upon herself to return home at once. Perhaps she had, after all, become resigned to her fate and decided to hasten to it rather than fearfully anticipate it. Rebecca could understand that; she was wont to rush to meet the inevitable herself. Her memory skittered over the day she had walked the meadow to the Manor in trepidation of confronting Luke with his proposition, yet unable not to.

Oh, Heavens! Rebecca threw back her head in despair at another excruciating possibility. Had John gone with her to Crosby? Perhaps to speak to her stepfather of his intentions? Rebecca dare not even imagine how the young carpenter would be received by the vile man who had harboured such lofty ambitions for his stepdaughter some six weeks previously.

'Is Miss Lucy back with her parents?' Rebecca immediately interrogated the dour-faced man before her, yet dreading his answer.

'Dun't know,' the man laconically advised with a chomp on his pipe that sent foul smoke wafting Rebecca's way. 'Been in stables most of day. Jest been arst ta come and git yer. Best be gittin back, too. Light be going pretty quick. Best ta travel wi' some light,' he announced before taking the pipe from his mouth, inspecting it, then knocking smouldering ash on to the ground.

'Who is it?' Martha demanded over Rebecca's shoulder. 'Not them peddlers back again, I hope. I told them…'

'It's Bert Morris, Martha,' Rebecca quickly told her. 'He's come from Lucy's stepfather.'

Martha instinctively covered her mouth with a hand, unconsciously betraying her horror at this awful turn of events.

'I shall have to go and speak with Mr Mayhew,' Rebecca defeatedly sighed. Despite her antipathy for the man it was her duty to go and face the music. If Lucy and John had been too indiscreet…or intimate…or both…and Rupert Mayhew had discovered it, God help them all!

'I will probably not be more than a few hours. I'm sure Mr Mayhew will provide me with transport home later this evening,' she quaveringly reassured the woman, noting Martha's unusual pallor. Privately, she had little confidence in what she uttered. Mr Mayhew, she was certain, would oblige her with nothing other than blistering accusations, if her alarming suspicions proved correct.

'Luke will be back soon, I'm sure.' Another unlikely prospect, she dejectedly realised, for he had been sent on a fool's errand, after all. The last place he would think to search for Lucy and John would be her parents' home.

As the coach swayed to an uneven tilted halt fifty yards into the densely wooded track that wound to the main coast road, Rebecca didn't bother investigating the shadowy dusk, so lost was she in her own hectic thoughts. When the coach door jerked abruptly open, and Jake Blacker leapt in, slammed the door, and rapped for the driver to resume the journey, Rebecca barely had sense enough to breathe, let alone act.

'Mr Blacker!' she finally burst out in a mingling of fright and outrage.

'Indeed it is, Miss Nash,' he jeeringly greeted her before

proceeding to settle himself comfortably into the cracked leather squabs.

'Well, don't just sit there like that!' Rebecca exploded after two stunned minutes, on realising he apparently meant her no bodily harm, but intended to snooze. 'What on earth do you think you're about?' she demanded as he did no more than stir enough to flex his legs. Perhaps the odious man simply thought he could hitch a ride to Brighton or one of the surrounding villages.

Unable to stifle a hysterical laugh from jerking out of her at the farce of it, Rebecca closed her tired eyes and a shaking hand pressed to her mouth.

This should have been one of the happiest days of her life. Her first outing with Luke had started so promisingly. The long-awaited meeting with Simon had brought wonderful release; their lunch had been exquisite; and loving and trusting Luke had become more natural with every contented moment. She had felt so joyful on the beach...so carefree. But that happiness had been cruelly curtailed. This marvellous day was changing into blackest nightmare.

She breathed slowly and deeply, composing herself. Fear and fury were the enemies of common sense, she knew. Sparking aquamarine eyes fixed on Jake Blacker with a resolution that made him curl a lip in a travesty of a smile.

'I am on my way to see a Mr Mayhew in the village of Crosby,' she detailed icily. 'And I would be grateful if you would remove yourself from this carriage and find your own transport.'

'Why should I? This is my transport, too.' Slitted eyes slithered over her body as he mocked her. 'By lucky chance, Mr Mayhew also has business this evening with me. It was at his suggestion that we now travel together,' he quite truthfully informed her, his tone tinged with sly amusement.

This news was so startling and enfeebling that for a long moment Rebecca merely gaped at him. Then the chill started to creep and crawl over her skin. She wound her black-fringed shawl more tightly about her, feeling frozen to the marrow, yet knowing that very little of the cold was attributable to the ill-fitting coach windows. She wished now she had taken the time to fetch her heavy cloak before leaving, for she sorely needed its soft comforting warmth.

Something was not right. Something was not right at all. Despite her coldness, her golden hair clung to her neck in damp tendrils and beads of moisture stuck wispy curls to her forehead. Warm perspiration trickled down her back despite the shivering of her body and her icy hands. She tried to force her numb brain to logically sort and process information but it constantly rebounded from this monumental task to simply focus on escape.

Turquoise eyes spontaneously flicked to the coach door before she shot a glance back at Blacker and noted his grin. He was well aware of her thoughts of bolting and seemed entertained by them. 'I've seen a man nigh on cut in half by coach wheels when he tried that,' he recounted with morbid relish. He rapped imperiously on the coachwork and roughly commanded Bert Morris, 'Get going, man…faster.' But his glacier-blue eyes never left Rebecca as he silently challenged her to defy him.

'They won't do you no harm.' The young man emphasised his reassurance by nodding his large moon face at Rebecca. He lurched away from the boulder he leaned on, the flare in his hand throwing disjointed wobbling shadows on to the rocky wall.

Rebecca shrank back into a sitting position on smooth stone as his gigantic frame lumbered closer to her. One shapeless mass of a hand was gripping the flaming torch and the other huge paw, she breathlessly noted, was clenched by his side. Her heartbeat seemed to fail completely as he crouched down close by her. 'Here…throw these at 'em. They'll leave you be,' he knowledgeably said, but with a blank expression. He raised his fist then abruptly spreadeagled fat fingers. Pebbles scattered around Rebecca's skirts and she jerked her trembling legs closer to her body, simultaneously wrapping her shawl and skirt yet tighter.

The dank odour of the cave made her stomach churn, but it was the squealing, inquisitive vermin that occasionally emerged, streaking from behind boulders lining the rocky prison, that really nauseated her. She did as the giant said and unsteady fingers launched pebbles into corners shrouded in blackness. The scurrying and squeaking increased and a flash of long whiskers, teeth and string-like tail helped her aim increase and improve. When finished with her missiles, her arms hugged quickly about her shins and her forehead sank forward to rest on her knees. Despair and fury made tears tingle hotly at the back of her eyes but she was determined not to break down.

She had been delivered to this isolated beach spot by Blacker what now seemed like several hours ago, though Rebecca realised that it could have been less than one. A permeating salty stench mingling with boat oil, seaweed and rotting fish clung to her nostrils, so that every breath heightened the dreadful sickness swamping her.

She had no chance of escape: not only had she this monstrous simpleton to get past, but the evil-looking ruffians standing guard outside this coastal dungeon and along the clifftop. The prospect of risking an encounter with any of those leering thugs made her throat clench and her heart achingly pulsate.

When Blacker had forced her roughly down the shifting

shingle path to this desolate place, she recalled passing some four or five shadowy figures. From their sibilant hissing with Blacker, she gleaned that each one of them wanted the task of guarding her. But that popular job had been entrusted to 'Clarkie', as this mountainous half-wit was called, until Blacker returned. She also overheard the dire consequences threatened by Jake Blacker should any man lay a finger on her person. Her teeth ground together as she prayed that every one of them would heed his warning. The idea that she would gladly set eyes upon Jake Blacker again was totally illogical yet, compared to those batmen outside, he seemed ridiculously welcome.

From where her head rested upon her clasped hands, she glanced assessingly up through her lashes at Clarkie. Although he was oafish he seemed relatively inoffensive, even showing her some kindness: once Blacker had left she had easily persuaded him to unbind her hands. But Rebecca was sure he would do all in his immense power to prevent her escaping.

'Is Mr Blacker coming back soon?' she asked Clarkie with an amity she was far from feeling. She was desperate to draw some information from him as to why she was being held prisoner. A hysterical bubble of laughter choked in her throat. Rupert Mayhew might be upset at his daughter's behaviour, and hold Rebecca responsible for it, but this was taking retribution to ridiculous extremes.

Rebecca's forced smile faded: Clarkie was avoiding looking her way at all. Grasping at what reason her exhausted mind retained, she realised that her abduction and imprisonment might have little, perhaps nothing, to do with Lucy. His daughter *was* an uncontrollable hoyden and Rebecca had failed to improve her, but Rupert Mayhew would need to be insane to risk punishing Rebecca so harshly. But Mayhew was involved, for she had caught his name mentioned in gruff asides, several times, by the men outside. And Jake Blacker had spoken of him in the coach.

Blacker would divulge nothing, and the longer she pleaded with him to tell her the purpose of it all and her fate, the more evil pleasure he seemed to gain from keeping her in ignorance. The only connection she could make out was Simon. Simon knew Blacker and owed him money. But why Rupert Mayhew, an apparently respectable businessman, was embroiled in it all, was beyond her fright-limited powers of deduction. And why holding her would aid them was even more of a mystery—they must know she had no money.

An exasperated sigh warmed her clasped, cold fingers and Rebecca determinedly tried to catch her guard's eye. 'Do you know if Jake Blacker is returning soon?' Rebecca repeated, mounting frustration sharpening her voice.

'Ain't to say nothing,' Clarkie dolefully said, wagging his head.

'Is there a blanket about this draughty hole somewhere?' Rebecca demanded through chattering teeth. She was freezing and her shawl did little to ward off the November sea breeze. Merely the whoosh of tide rushing in over shingle induced uncontrollable shivering in her.

Clarkie shambled towards her, awkwardly removing his tar-and-sweat-stained jacket. He clumsily draped the enormous tattered woolen garment about her quivering shoulders. The reek from it made Rebecca's stomach heave but she gave him a grateful smile. 'What's in those barrels?' she asked, desperate to get him talking on any subject: it might perhaps lead to another.

'French brandy,' he briefly informed her but with a shy, rather sweet smile.

The thought of a warming drink consumed Rebecca's mind and would not be shaken off. She had drunk brandy once or twice on special occasions with her papa, and a drop when she had been ill once with a severe chill. She reminisced on the fiery warmth and sense of relaxed well-being it had instilled. Rising from her cramped position on the smooth bed of rock, she gingerly flexed stiff limbs before approaching the barrels ranged against the cave wall and tapping the one closest. It thudded dully. 'Have you a cup? I should like some,' she said with the most charming smile she could muster.

'Can't drink that,' Clarkie warned harshly. 'It'll kill you. Kill you down dead,' he stressed agitatedly. 'It be made specially too strong to drink so's we get more in each of them barrels. We got to mix it up with water afore we sell it. Men been found dead as can be on the beach from opening up them barrels and drinking it,' he gruffly explained.

Rebecca trudged away, but couldn't face huddling down again on the stone-cold seat. 'Why am I here?' she pleaded. He avoided her eyes and stared out into blackness in the direction of the moon-silvered sea.

'Nobody tells Clarkie nothing. Clarkie's dunderhead.'

'You shouldn't believe what others say about you, Clarkie,' Rebecca said gently, with a butterfly touch for a beefy hand. 'You have fine qualities. You are a better man than those ruffians outside and Jake Blacker. All wish me harm. Yet you have been kind to me. You have kept me warm with your coat, you warned me not to drink that deadly alcohol and you untied my sore wrists.'

'Exactly why he is a dunderhead, Miss Nash,' a deceitfully smooth voice stated from the shadowy cavern entrance. 'And why he will later pay for his disobedience…as will you for leading him to it.'

Rebecca's heart leapt, lodging in her throat, as she twisted immediately about and squinted into blackness. Rupert Mayhew stepped into the flare of yellow light, only his face illuminated near Clarkie's gross middle, making him seem disembodied and miniature.

'But enough of this unpleasantness,' he chided himself, bestowing a reptilian smile on Rebecca. 'How very nice it is to meet with you again, my dear. I had hoped to renew our acquaintance sooner, and under more agreeable circumstances, but 'twas not to be.' He gazed smilingly around the cave interior as though it held some happy memories for him. 'I hear from my acquaintance Blacker that you have a rather foolish brother. I also hear that you have acquired an extremely dangerous lover. Quite unexpected…nay, astonishing…Miss Nash, I must say. You must tell me all about it while we await his arrival at my house.'

'This is quite outrageous, Mr Mayhew,' Rebecca bit out through her chattering teeth, the bizarre reference to Luke passing unnoticed in her wrath. Far from feeling terrorized by this repugnant little man, as she had anticipated she would, she was incensed. For two pins she would have flown across the dark void that separated them and slapped that smirk from his ugly face. Her small fingers curled so tightly that savage fingernails scored her palms. But she steeled herself against such folly: she was going to need every ounce of composure and logic.

'I imagine that your stepdaughter, Lucy, must have told you by now,' she enigmatically mentioned with admirable self-assurance.

'Told me? Told me what?' he demanded, uncertain whether to dismiss it or show curiosity. 'Why would my stepdaughter tell me anything? And how? I've not seen her. I've received no letters…'

Rebecca swiftly masked her expression of heartfelt relief. So Lucy was safe…at least from him…and he knew nothing of her elopement, if indeed that was what she and John had attempted. She threw her captor a disdainful look.

'Why, told you that you are the most repulsive man I have ever had the misfortune to meet, Mr Mayhew,' she clearly announced. So much for logic and composure, she regretfully acknowledged, as Mayhew's stunted body recommenced stalking very purposefully her way, fists curling at its sides. As he drew level with Clarkie, the giant began clumsily gesturing and grunting for clemency on Rebecca's behalf. Mayhew contemptuously shoved double-handed at the barrel-like figure.

'Don't you dare touch her,' threatened a hoarse, familiar voice.

'Simon?' Rebecca croaked. Her throat was so parchment dry with fear she could barely articulate her mingled query and relief. She dodged Mayhew and fled to the cavern entrance where her brother was detained, with his arms pinioned behind him by Jake Blacker.

'Ran the pipsqueak to ground at last,' Blacker sneered as he cuffed the side of Simon's head. Blacker's pale eyes shifted to Rebecca, lingering on her dishevelled yet still beautifully appealing person. 'Well, here's one of the Nash family I've a softer spot for. Or should I perhaps say a harder one...?' He roared at his own lewd banter, restraining Simon as he fought to physically remonstrate with him.

'You keep your lecherous hands to yourself,' Mayhew hissed menacingly. 'And make sure that those pillaging louts outside do likewise. Do you think that Trelawney will pay for spoiled goods?'

Simon managed to extricate an arm from his captor's painful grip and grabbed Rebecca close, desperate to comfort her.

'I'm sorry,' he whispered into her soft hair. 'I'm so sorry.'

Rebecca gazed anxiously up into his strained shadowy face. Her shaking white finger soothed a graze close to his ear, from Blacker's knuckles.

'What is this all about? Is it the money you owe Blacker? Why is Mayhew involved?' she whispered urgently.

Simon shook his head, signalling ignorance and defeat. 'I've never seen that ugly dwarf before. And I never believed Blacker would stoop to this…imprisoning you to force my hand.' His voice cracked and he bit at his lip to steady it. Rebecca felt prickles frosting her as she realised just how close to disaster they must be: Simon was very near to breaking down.

'What a touching little scene,' Mayhew mocked. 'Well, make the most of it, for it will surely be your last unless I have what money is due me.'

'Due to you?' both Simon and Rebecca uttered, astonished.

'Naturally,' he scoffed. 'Obviously whatever money you owe Blacker the dolt has already pledged. Partly on this consignment of brandy we see all around us, but more importantly on one of gold soon due to cross the channel to Napoleon to pay his mercenaries. Because of Blacker's outstanding debts I am now becoming embarrassed for funds myself. And needs must when the devil drives,' he grated.

'You will never get away with this,' Rebecca vibrantly challenged him. 'Abduction and imprisonment are serious offences, Mr Mayhew. You will be arrested and tried…imprisoned.'

Mayhew howled, head back, in genuine, raucous laughter. 'Indeed, I shall, if caught,' he agreed, wiping a mirthful tear away with a stubby finger. 'Well, it is to be expected, I am afraid, my dear Miss Nash. There has been a noose with my name on it for some twenty years or more. Abduction and imprisonment? Small fry compared to smuggling and murder…oh, and treason. For the crown takes a rather dim view of my providing our old foe Napoleon with the wherewithal to pay his rag-tag troops; or returning to him prisoners of war so they may rejoin the fray. Buonaparte paid up rather well for a Général de Montfort. But it is all purely business, of course. I have no political allegiances, and no love for the *monsieurs*. The *mesdemoiselles*, of course, well, that is a different story,' he lasciviously chuckled. 'The French mademoiselle…yes… Which brings me in mind of another matter.' He addressed Blacker. 'Where is my nemesis? Has Trelawney had my message?'

'I left it with a doddering old cove named Miles at Ramsden Manor. Neither Trelawney nor his brother were at home. A young couple had gone missing from the estate and they were searching the locality for them.'

Mayhew swore beneath his breath and Rebecca held hers, the mention of Lucy and Luke vying for priority in her whirling, incoherent thoughts.

'Well, let's hope for the sake of *these* young people that he arrives at my house at the appointed hour and is amenable to my plans.'

'Why do they mention Luke so often? It is almost as though he is implicated other than by his relationship with me,' Rebecca whispered to Simon before noting her brother's odd expression.

'Blacker told me once that the Trelawneys and smuggling had long been linked,' Simon reluctantly sighed out. 'I believe these two miscreants have known of him far longer than you or I.'

Rebecca felt as though she had received a physical blow. She clung to Simon while struggling for breath. It couldn't be true. Luke involved with smuggling? Luke a criminal? Never! But her frantic mind raced back over the past weeks and pounced on the evening she had sought Simon at the Bull and Mouth tavern in Brighton. Blacker had recognised the name of Trelawney, if not the man, and Luke's reputation had greatly worried him. And then, on their ride home, when she had quizzed him about it all, he had seemed oddly amused and had evaded answering her. Pieces of a puzzle which had niggled at the back of her mind seemed to suddenly converge and, harrowingly, fit. There were the tubmen she had seen trekking through Graveley woods. In the direction of Westbrook! Surely not to the Manor? No, it must be coincidence. They were in the area because of Blacker being once more local. But there *was* something menacing about Luke…a ruthlessness he screened with urbane manners. She couldn't deny that, for she had glimpsed it; had sensed it as long ago as when he had first propositioned her.

'Ah, I see Miss Nash looks concerned that I know her lover's history. And I'll wager better than she does herself,' Mayhew perceptively guessed, gratified by this new discovery and how he might use it to wreak further damage on the man he feared and hated. Making this lovely woman despise his old enemy might be the sweetest revenge of all.

'Why, let me enlighten you a little, Miss Nash. Luke Trelawney and I are old acquaintances. Very old. I knew of his father, Jago Trelawney, of course, before I knew him. In fact, I like to take credit for hastening that man's death. For he wouldn't see sense,' he impassively recounted. 'Then, when his son Luke took over the family business, we never saw eye to eye. There was enough sea and trade for both of us to make a good living. But he wanted more…too much…' His yellow eyes gleamed demonically and Rebecca realised that the man was insane. 'He did his level best to ruin me. And nearly succeeded,' he softly admitted, nodding, with a faraway look in his feral eyes. 'But

I have come back to haunt him for I'll warrant that after the skirmish at Lizard Point, he honestly believed me dead. And it certainly suited me to disappear from Devon…and the Revenue.' He gave Rebecca a twisted smile. 'He is a perilous man, my dear, not at all a seemly husband for such a sweet innocent as you. One of his Cornish trollops would prove a far better consort. That lush brunette he keeps in Penzance especially, for I swear the lovely Wenna considers them already wed…in all but name. No doubt she will be keen to make your acquaintance and seek you out if you remove there. She has a fiery temper, as I recall.'

'I will listen to no more of this,' Rebecca choked breathlessly across his speech, her body stone-cold yet her heart afire with a dreadful, caustic fear. 'You are an evil man. You are lying to poison my mind against my fiancé and ruin our lives. By your own admission you hate him. I will listen to no more of your malice.'

'I swear on the life of my sweet baby son that all I have just told you is the truth. If I have ever loved at all, I love him,' Mayhew said, in a voice made husky with sincerity.

'Pay him no heed,' Simon gruffly ordered Rebecca, frightened by the intensity with which she was now quivering in his arms and the glossy wideness of her eyes. 'He is a madman too full of bitter grudges to know night from day, let alone truth from falsehood.'

A careless shrug and expletive met Simon's insult. Then without another word, Rupert Mayhew curtly indicated by flapping his hands that they should all move outside. He shoved at Clarkie, wordlessly gesturing he should go in front and light the way back to the clifftop.

Luke had been more tolerant and philosophical than he would have believed himself capable: certainly more than the terrified pair had expected. He might even have been a

little amused, had it not been for the fact that his day with
Rebecca had been so rudely shortened. And he had so much
planned for today…so much to finally tell her on what he
had chosen as his perfect day.

The young runaways had been apprehended at the King's
Head at Guildford, as Ross had guessed, on their way north
to marry at Gretna Green.

On arrival back at the Manor, famished and thirsty after
setting such a cracking pace home, they had all rested in
the hallway. As Miles greeted them and limped over, Luke
gave the butler an immediate order for refreshments and
Miles immediately gave him…the greatest shock of his life.

Luke stared at the note. He raised sightless eyes to the
sheepish young couple huddled close together on hall
chairs. Black eyes dropped to the paper again, stark white
against his unsteady dark fingers. His grip tightened, making the paper quiver and the black script dance out of focus.
He felt blood leeching from his face and that well-
remembered raw fear torturing him, as it had once before
at the Bull and Mouth tavern.

A mere scribbled note, yet, insignificant as it seemed, the
seconds taken reading it were the most harrowing moments
in his life. Even the time his mother had run to the shore
to find him and tell him his father was critically injured
had never wounded him with such aching force. And now
the source of that day's pain had unbelievably…
impossibly…brought him this, too. The raging mix of despair, fury, guilt and dread burned indelibly into his soul
and he knew the taste and feel of it would remain with him
until he died.

He sprang out of his velvet-seated chair and paced aimlessly to the stairs, half-aware of Ross's anxious hazel eyes
on him and the young couple warily tracking his every
move.

Ross walked over and prised the folded paper from his rigid fingers, digesting the few lines within a second. He gazed at the side of his brother's face, noting his back teeth grinding, misaligning his jaw, and the tic by his rigid, compressed mouth.

Luke swung back to regard Lucy, strode to her chair and hunkered down by her in one swift fluid movement. The frightened young woman tried to pull back close to John for protection. Luke firmly took her chin in gentle fingers. 'Now think hard, Lucy,' he stressed hoarsely. 'What I am going to ask is very, *very* important and I'm hoping you can help me. If you have an inkling of anything at all that may help you must tell me, even if you feel it is of little significance or that you are betraying members of your family. You *must* tell me…I *must* know it.' He paused before asking huskily, 'If your stepfather wanted to hide something away from home…something very valuable to him, where would he put it?'

Chapter Thirteen

An odd stillness, interspersed only by the sucking and rushing of sea on stones, at first made no impression. Rebecca felt so exhausted and so emotionally drained that sinking on to the shingle to weep and sleep beckoned.

Nearing the clifftop, Blacker suddenly grunted in exasperation and shouted to Mayhew.

'What now?' Mayhew gutturally hissed and then froze as moonbeams picked out a flash of gleaming steel in his comrade's hand.

'Where are the others? Where are my men?' Blacker demanded and warned in one breath, shifting his knife from hand to hand.

'Fool, I told you they were not to be trusted. Where are they? Throwing dice, I'll wager. Or playing cards. You leave them for a moment and they skive off to their own devices.' His muted tirade was interrupted by Blacker cupping his mouth with his hands and emitting a low, melancholy hooting. The plaintive sound induced a violent shivering in Rebecca and she nestled into her brother.

Blacker prodded urgently at Simon and Rebecca, wildly gesturing at them to scramble the last few paces to the craggy clifftop, before again issuing that eerie call. The silence thereafter seemed impenetrable as they all listened and waited: even the ocean music seemed to have diminished.

'I don't think they'll hear you in the Red Lion,' mentioned a sardonic voice that made Rebecca's heart leap and pump frantically.

'Well, this one might, but I doubt he'll be a lot of use,' Ross added to Luke's comment as he strolled out of a thicket, shoving a stocky, balding ruffian in front of him, a blade at his throat. The fist gripping the knife raised suddenly and the heel of it came down savagely on the back of the man's head, knocking him out cold.

Luke's black-clothed figure detached itself from the rock he was resting back against, and he walked into the pool of yellow light thrown by Clarkie's flare. 'Come here, Rebecca,' he ordered softly, his dark eyes engulfing, seducing her across the flickering patches of dark and light. But the fleeting chance of escape was lost as love and suspicion warred within her, making her hesitate and cling to Simon.

'I think not, Trelawney,' Mayhew grunted, striding to Rebecca's side. One cruel, stubby hand wound into her long, silken hair and yanked it back, exposing her creamy throat to the night air and the gleaming blade in his fist. 'She's wary of the smuggling fraternity, my old friend. Something in your history, perhaps, that frightens her?' he scoffed, while the silky steel caressed tormentingly up and down her moon-pearled skin.

'Shouldn't you be dead, Merrill?' Luke rasped bitterly, his black eyes fixed unwaveringly on Rebecca.

'Tut…tut. You shall confuse everyone, Trelawney. My name is now Mayhew…Rupert Mayhew. Ronald Merrill is certainly dead and buried…or drowned, should I say? At Lizard Point…remember that night?' he taunted him. 'And I hear that yours is now Lord Ramsden of Westbrook. Who

would have thought such nobility of a man so closely
linked with free-trading? But then you always were unpredictable,' he allowed, grudging admiration quietening his
voice. 'Tell me, how did you find out about Devil's Cove?'
he interrogated, with a backward nod of his head indicating
the tide-lashed rocks below.

'Your stepdaughter told me, Merrill. She told me lots of
things. Things that make me ever more determined to see
you hang from a gibbett and die very slowly.'

'Not a sensible comment, Trelawney,' Merrill snapped
as the knife tracing Rebecca's throat stilled and the flat of
it pressed down making her jerk and gasp. 'I knew that
little bitch was spying on me. And I never could teach the
slut to guard her tongue.'

'And you'll get no more chances,' Luke vehemently told
him.

'I've no need of any,' Mayhew sneered. 'After tonight,
I shall be long gone from the area. That drab I married has
no money left and the house is mortgaged to the hilt. Why
stay? I believe I would have been gone a year sooner but
for the promise of a son, and the ambition Lucy might
whore her way into some rich roué's affections. She
showed some potential…' he said with chilling gravity.
'But we need never again meet. I will leave you in peace
if you accord me the same favour. Tangling with you was
never wise,' he reluctantly admitted with a grimace. 'The
continent beckons, I think. All I require from you is money
to send me on my way, then you get your bed warmed by
this blonde lovely.' He grunted a sly laugh. 'I suppose you
didn't bring your buxom Cornish doxy with you to Sussex,
Trelawney? Pity,' he answered himself after a long second
of singing silence in which turquoise and black eyes fused.
'For I'll wager that dark-haired beauty knew a trick or two

to keep a man happy. Forgoing the cash and swapping Miss Purity here for that wench might even have appealed…'

'Where are my men? Have you killed them?' Blacker suddenly cut across Mayhew's lecherous musings.

'Dead drunk only, I imagine,' Ross interjected quietly. 'By the time they've run through the money I gave them, though, they possibly might have poisoned themselves. Such loyalty you two inspire,' he sarcastically sneered. 'I wonder why that is?' He stirred the body of the unconcious man at his feet with a disdainful boot. 'One only prepared to stay here on duty.'

Mayhew glared his contempt at Blacker at this news, mouthing an obscenity. But he politely said to Luke, 'So glad to hear you're being generous with your money. One thousand of your pounds will buy you back sweet Miss Nash. Oh, she is untouched.' He slid his free hand tormentingly, insolently inside Clarkie's jacket that Rebecca still wore, pulling it wide to expose his intention as he roughly clutched at a softly rounded breast, making her shudder and try to break free. 'Almost untouched…for the present…'

'Merrill…' Luke harshly warned him, fear and rage in his voice as he stepped two paces closer.

'But I have a crew who have seen nothing of a woman for a month or more,' Mayhew racked him further, as the silver steel recommenced its lethal fondling along Rebecca's neck. 'I'm sure this little angel would make a very welcome addition on their next channel crossing. See how she quakes at the thought?' he taunted Luke. 'No doubt afeared she'll never find her sea legs. Not to worry, my dear, you'll never need them, you'll be spending the voyage flat on your back.'

'Let her go now, right this minute, and you can have more money than even you can run through in a lifetime, and that racing sloop you coveted,' Luke desperately offered and then realised his mistake. In his panic to get Rebecca safely free of the blade, he was firing the man's insatiable greed and malevolence. He could sense Ross breathing fast and shallow by his side, impatiently waiting for the signal to go. But they were too far away from the weapon at Rebecca's throat. He didn't dare risk it until they were closer and he was sure Simon perceived what he had to do.

'Well, well, who would have thought it?' Mayhew derided softly. 'That I would eventually hold within my grasp Luke Trelawney's downfall. You'd pay me anything...give me anything, wouldn't you?' His spiteful fingers again grabbed intimately inside Clarkie's coat making Rebecca jerk then freeze in his arms with her eyes tight shut against the nausea rolling in her stomach. 'Well, I'll take your money, Trelawney, and your sloop and you can beg me on your knees to stop pleasuring her...see how she likes it?'

The patch of light haloing Luke wobbled and Mayhew ground out at Clarkie, 'Hold the flare still, you damned fool.' But Clarkie lowered the torch and speared it into the sandy ground.

'What are you about?' Mayhew hissed anxiously at the simpleton, as Clarkie lumbered closer with swaying head, scrunched-up face and a weird moaning wringing from his throat. 'Get the horse and cart now, you dullard, or you'll get it,' Mayhew screamed at him, gesturing wildly at the old farm vehicle tethered nearby. But his threats and rage did nothing to halt the giant's inexorable progress towards him.

Clarkie's hand closed over the blade at Rebecca's throat and an animal growl of physical pain and rage erupted. He shoved the dimunitive man back from Rebecca with such force that Mayhew actually ran backwards several yards before he sat down heavily in the darkness.

The abrupt removal of Mayhew's support had Rebecca sinking quite gracefully to the ground. Simon was on his knees beside her before he was roughly pulled away and Luke lifted her in his arms. Across her swimming head she heard Luke's guttural threats and commands to Simon, before he kissed her hard and swift, removing what little breath she had left. His dark hands were at her face, in her hair, reassuring, trembling touches for them both and then he tipped her into Simon's waiting embrace and was gone.

Running with her in his arms, Simon swiftly deposited her in the waiting cart. He jumped up to the driver's seat, croaked urgent encouragement at the old cart horse, and they began rattling away along the coast road. As Rebecca pulled herself to a sitting position on the splintery boards, she realised that they were escaping pandemonium. Blacker and Ross were locked in combat, each gripping blades and looking for deadly openings to use them, and Mayhew was now on his feet and running towards the battling men.

Rebecca watched in horror and fascination as Luke raced towards his brother. She gasped aloud as the smuggler Ross had previously knocked out scrambled up from the gritty ground. He lunged at Luke and they scrapped for little more than a few seconds before the batman once again hit gravel and Luke was sprinting to Ross's aid. Ross swiped his dagger in a vicious arc in front of him, making his two assailants back off a few paces.

He lobbed a weapon over Blacker's head and moonlight glanced off the lengthy blade as Luke's hand arrested it mid-flight. The expression on Ross's face fascinated her. He was smiling…no, laughing…as though he were thoroughly enjoying himself. He gestured a warning to Luke of more opposition, and Rebecca twisted about too, as the cart rumbled further away from danger. A rabble of about four men was running up the hill having exited a dimly lit building. As they got closer, Rebecca recognised them. They were Blacker's men and, no doubt, now fired with Dutch courage purchased at the Red Lion tavern.

Simon yelped and whipped the old cart horse into some speed and rounded the wooded bend in the track. Under the canopy of trees both moonlight and the affray were lost from sight. After about a minute of frantic driving, Simon pulled up sharp and clambered quickly into the back with Rebecca. He took her ashen, chilled face between his palms, feeling the chattering of her teeth through her cheeks and the incessant quivering of her whole body.

'I have to go back and help them, Rebecca. I know Luke bade me deliver you to the Manor and I know he'll probably want to kill me as much as those ruffians for not obeying him. But I have to go back. They are badly outnumbered, even if the giant rallies enough to aid them; his hand was nigh on cut in half.'

Rebecca merely nodded her acceptance and understanding, incapable of speech.

'If you keep heading along this road, and as fast as this old nag will go, you will eventually come to Brighton. After that you know the way. You can drive that old trap of yours as good as I can. This will give you no problem.' He embraced her hard against him, and then he had vaulted over the cart edge and was sprinting back towards Devil's Cove.

Rebecca clambered on to the seat and groped about for the reins with clammy hands. She wanted to stay; to go back to the two men she loved. But she knew she was close to hysteria or fainting. She would be a perilous hindrance, not any help. The old cart horse swayed its head about and looked at her and for some reason, in filtering moonlight, she recognised the animal and remembered its name. It was old Bessy, the mare who had delivered her and Lucy to the Summer House what seemed now aeons ago.

'Come along, Bessy old girl,' Rebecca quaveringly encouraged. 'I'm sure you know this road, even if I don't. I'm trusting you.'

The old mare whinnied softly and the merest flick of the reins had her breaking into a reasonably steady trot.

The last dying embers collapsed into the grate, sparking a dull orangey glow from flaking coals. Rebecca rested her head back into the fireside chair in her parlour and again allowed exhaustion to overtake her. But the old wooden clock behind her on the wall chimed two o'clock, defeating her and making weary eyelids flutter up.

She had been back at the Summer House for two hours; arriving at midnight, she had found Martha and Gregory still waiting for her, frantic with worry. She had felt incapable of furnishing lengthy explanations: she was still too close to hysteria herself to cope with it in others. But with the promise that all would be explained in the morning and assurances that she was absolutely fine, they had eventually left her to desperately needed solitude and rest.

She had decided not to go to the Manor despite having heard Luke's explicit instructions to Simon that that was where she was to be taken. As the chill night air cleared her shock a little, she had realised that the Turners, already worried, would wait up to see her safely home. With immediate peril at bay, the quiet solitude of the journey freed her mind. All Rupert Mayhew's malicious talk of Luke's Cornish past monopolised her thoughts…and so she went to her own home.

She now felt so emotionally drained that the thought of Luke and her brother and perhaps Ross lying injured or dead at that isolated coastal spot evoked no more than a whimper and a tightening in her already sandpapered throat. She had wept all the tears she possessed, she was sure, and after two hours of utter desolation only an aching emptiness remained.

But even that raw listlessness would not prevent her again torturing herself with what Mayhew had revealed of Luke's life in Cornwall. All had been divulged in spite and anger, but there was truth in it. In a strange way, as Mayhew had spouted his venom and Luke had denied nothing, Rebecca realised she never expected him to, for part of her already knew. And it was not the thought of her fiancé being a criminal that seared into her soul, but the thought of him being with another woman…kissing and touching someone else in the way he did her. Smiling and joking with her in that intimate way she believed was uniquely theirs. And to her shame, she realised she hated and envied that beautiful, faceless mistress with a passion that ground her teeth and made her shudder, weeping, in her chair. And she hated him, too, for bringing her so low.

Her thoughts returned to yesterday evening when she had obliquely asked him if he would love her. He had said nothing and now she knew why. There was a woman he already loved and, by Mayhew's reckoning, she classed him as her property. They were practically wed…in all but name, Mayhew had said.

She had been a naïve fool trusting in him, believing in his implausible explanations. Everything had pointed to him being a dangerous philanderer…and a liar, too. Besides the scandalous incident with the bawds at Ramsden Manor, he had been at the Spencers' tavern where harlots strolled about in their petticoats and where rooms were provided for men to pay to do business with them. Because she so wanted to believe him a fine gentleman, she had accepted he gambled rather than whored. She had been a total ingenue and there was no excuse for such self-delusion in a spinster of nearly twenty-six.

He had been ruthlessly tricking her. She was sure now that he never truly intended them to be man and wife and his suggestion that they marry in Brighton had merely been a sham. He probably knew very well she would object to such a rushed affair, but might be seduced into travelling to Cornwall as a besotted fiancée. The tears started again as she bleakly wondered just how many *chères amies* he intended collecting. They flowed freely as she realised, despite it all, she still loved him and so wanted him to come safely back to her.

What little warmth was to be had from the parlour fire finally expired and the chill surrounding her feet seeped upwards. She wearily stood and made her way to the kitchen, taking comfort from the residual warmth in the cooking stove before she climbed the stairs to her bedroom.

The familiar redolence of dried lavender calmed her and she instinctively breathed deeply of its soothing fragrance. Removing her shawl and her shoes, she kneeled on her thick mattress, her arms self-comforting, as she simply pitched forward into the luxury of its yielding comfort. She gathered the soft, plump quilt about herself and rolled into it, holding it high and tight about her, and within a few minutes was deep in dreamless sleep.

Long dusky eyelashes swept against her warm feathery nest then weightily drooped closed. They brushed abruptly up again. It had been a sound…and there it was again. Rebecca shoved back on her elbows and strained to listen. A faint, recognisable click made her heart leap up and hammer into her throat. It was her parlour door closing, in the same quiet, careful way she shut it herself, when not wanting to disturb Lucy at night.

She scrambled from the bed, perching on the very edge of it, still woozy and befuddled from deep sleep. A trembling hand cleared tumbling golden hair from her face while the other tried to straighten her crumpled clothes. Her frantic mind attempted to weigh up possibilities. It might be Simon or Luke…or Mayhew or Blacker. Despite the viciousness in the way the Trelawneys fought, there were overwhelming odds against they and her brother being victorious at Devil's Cove. That horrifying fact made her spring from the bed and seek the wall close to the door. She hugged its cold hardness and listened again: soft footfalls in the kitchen below her bedroom were quite audible, despite the distorting, pulsing blood in her ears.

If Luke and Simon were injured…or dead…then Blacker or Mayhew would come for her and God only knew what awaited her at their hands. Her terrified mind tormented itself with Mayhew's threats to put her aboard one of his smuggling boats, yet it was the thought of Luke or Simon or even Ross laying dead that made her stuff a fist into her mouth to stifle a sob. She silently sped to the window. Scudding clouds had freed the moon and its silver glow illuminated the smooth marble top of her washstand…and her small scissors. She tiptoed back to the door and stood quaking just behind it, the cold metal gripped in one of her hands.

Her bedroom door slowly, silently swung inwards towards her and a flickering candle glow danced high upon the ceiling. A wavering male figure was traced gigantically on her wall. He had halted just out of sight behind the door, as though he too were waiting, taunting her with his presence. It was the sort of fiendish cat-and-mouse game Mayhew would revel in, she was sure. Unable to bear the suspense longer, Rebecca emerged with a sobbing cry, and lashed out wildly with her weapon, just as the man turned to go.

There was a thud and a curse as the intruder dropped the candle, plunging the room into moon-dappled darkness and then her hands were imprisoned and she was roughly pulled against a broad, black-clad torso. The familiar lemon-fresh scent and powerful feel of him was so marvellous that Rebecca's small hands fought to freedom just to clutch voraciously at him in undeniable love and stupendous relief.

An innate sensuality in the way she clung and wound herself about him forced a groaning, throaty laugh from Luke. 'I believe you missed me, Rebecca,' he murmured. One of his dark hands threaded into her hair, guiding her shadowy face towards his. And then he was urgently, deeply kissing her, as his unsteady fingers circled her neck and smoothed up and down, seeking damage.

'Are you hurt?' he broke the kiss to gasp against her mouth. 'Did they hurt you at all?' She shook her head against his face, her open mouth sweeping with unintentional allure close to his. Thumbs at her jaw tilted her face back to his and he groaned thankfulness and relief into her mouth before the kiss rekindled.

Despite the wonder of his presence and his gently erotic kiss, the spectre of Simon's fate and Ross's, and every other suspicion and fear cramming her mind tonight, began to roil and surface again. The temptation to shove them down, submerge them beneath this anodyne bliss that enveloped and subdued her whenever Luke touched her, was so enticing. But Simon's fate was paramount. And so was her pride.

Her clinging mouth and body tore from his with such abrupt force that she fell back a few paces into the room and sat upon her bed. 'Where is Simon? And your brother?

What happened to those felons...Mayhew and Blacker? And what about Clarkie? Poor brave Clarkie.' She barely paused before exclaiming, 'Lucy!' She had completely forgotten about her pupil's plight in all of this. It was difficult to reconcile that so many disasters had occurred within the space of not yet one day. 'Where is Lucy? Is she safe?' she tremulously demanded.

'Hush...' Luke soothed her, immediately reaching to gather her close again. Rebecca swiftly stood up, evading him, wrapping her arms tight about herself, instilling warmth and courage. She would never again be a mindless fool she fervently vowed, avoiding eye contact with the man who could bring her to it, oh, so easily. But she needed to know the outcome of this terrible night and to extract that information in a calm, sensible way.

Luke's dark eyes narrowed on her, his intelligent gaze steady and assessing. 'Lucy is very safe and in Judith's care at the Manor,' he quietly informed her. 'She and John were en route for Scotland, hoping to wed. They hadn't travelled very far when we caught up with them.' His eyes shifted to the crumpled quilt as he said huskily, 'I thought I'd chosen the wrong room. I didn't expect you to be behind the door, armed and dangerous.' His eyes caressed her dishevelled appearance. 'I'm sorry if I disturbed you. I tried to be as quiet as I could, I guessed you might be asleep. As for your brother, he went to the Manor...as you were expected to,' he grimly reminded her. 'As to how he is...he looks a bit of a mess...'

'Is he badly hurt?' Rebecca whispered, trepidation widening her eyes to glossy stars.

'Split lip...black eye. Oh, that was me, when I discovered you weren't at the Manor where I had specifically ordered him to safely deliver you...on pain of death. So, all things considered, he got off very lightly. Apart from that, he and Ross suffered a few scratches. I think Simon might need the physician to stitch a wound in his arm but it can wait till daylight. They both seem in excellent spirits…mine, actually,' he sardonically reflected. 'The first place they headed when we got back to the Manor was the liquor store. They're no doubt still outdoing each other with tales of their past heroics…fuelled by my brandy decanter… Come here,' he tacked on the end, extending long fingers towards her.

'And you?' Rebecca quickly sidetracked. 'Are you hurt?'

'A few minor scrapes…oh, and a pair of scissors stabbed in my arm…apart from that I'm fine.'

'Oh, I'm sorry,' Rebecca breathed and rushed forward a few paces as though to investigate what damage she had wreaked. She pulled up sharp. If she was to maintain her self-possession, keeping her distance was vital.

'Don't stop,' he softly prompted. 'You were doing just fine. Come here.'

Rebecca turned and walked away, her heart thumping as she put the bed between them. Her fingers ran along the smooth marble top of the washstand. 'And Mayhew and Blacker?' she asked in a gulp. 'What of them?'

'Mayhew's dead and Blacker wounded and delivered to the local magistrate with two of his batmen who didn't make good their escape. The magistrate wasn't too happy about being woken in the early hours. The Revenue will also have some questions for them, I've no doubt.'

'For you, too, *I*'ve no doubt,' Rebecca bitterly observed and then immediately regretted the unguarded comment. She was determined to retain her caution and composure.

The ensuing, pulsating silence between them seemed interminable. 'Well, come here,' Luke eventually said wryly. 'I can't tell you if you stay over there. Let me hold you and I'll explain. I wish now I had told you sooner. I didn't want you to hear fragments of it that way. I know I've been a bit reticent about a lot of things: the danger in my past, our family's link to smuggling…and the Ramsdens. I've been foolishly waiting for the perfect moment. I thought I had it this afternoon. Everything was going so well. I can't remember a day I've enjoyed more…'

'A *night*, perhaps…?' Rebecca scathingly snapped.

'Come here and I'll explain that too,' he gently said, but on a grunt of rueful laughter.

'You have explained before,' Rebecca spat at him, infuriated by his mild amusement and unruffled manner when she was so desolate. She gathered her golden hair away from her face in icy, nervous hands, twisting it neatly over her shoulder. 'You explained about other things that troubled me and so very persuasively that I actually questioned what I had seen with my own eyes and began to believe ludicrous stories. What was I to you?' burst furiously, unstoppably, from her. 'Some cargo to carry off home? Some quaint rustic novelty for you to toy with until you grew bored? What would have become of me, I wonder, when that day came, and I was far from home and friends who truly cared for me? Ross told me you were very generous to your discarded mistresses. He told me you would happily return me to Sussex…secure my future and reputation…I think that was how he put it.'

'Ross knows nothing of my affairs.'

Rebecca choked an hysterical laugh. 'What does that mean? Was I to be sent back, then without your financial help? Is that how you conduct your *miserly affairs*?'

Luke threw his head back, frowning regret at his thoughtless phrasing at the silver-flecked ceiling. 'Rebecca, my patience with this is near ending. Mayhew…Merrill, as I knew him, is a criminal of the worst sort…thief, rapist, murderer, traitor, inveterate liar. The list is endless and I've no intention of expounding it all now.' With a muttered curse and a few strides he was round the bed and reaching for her.

Rebecca jerked away, crashing into the washstand, slapping out furiously at his outstretched hands. 'Don't you dare touch me. Don't…you…dare,' she choked, silent tears slowly dropping from her eyes. 'I believed you…I trusted you…but no more.' She feebly tried to disguise her distress and regain her composure with conversation. 'You didn't say how Clarkie is,' she pushed out through the tears blocking her throat. 'Will his hand heal?'

The silence between them seemed interminable. Just as Rebecca gave up hope of a reply, he told her quietly, 'Clarkie is dead. He was a very courageous man…he deliberately gave his life ensuring that Mayhew lost his. I envy him, too. Mayhew was mine. I wanted to kill him and was about to. For some reason he wouldn't let me. He ran at Mayhew and his weight took them both over the cliff. Without him close to you tonight…' He sighed deeply into silence and bowed and shook his head.

'You're overwrought, Rebecca,' he said soothingly. 'And understandably so. We'll talk about all of this in the morning. We both need to sleep before we say any more.'

'And don't you dare patronise me either,' she raged at him. 'I might have been a childish idiot thus far, but not any more. I have nothing to discuss with you in the morning, Mr Trelawney. Or at any other time. If you would just tell Simon I should like to see him directly he rises, I would be grateful. If you would now quit my bedroom and my house, I would be more grateful still.'

Moonbeams filtered across his perfect features, highlighting his expression. There was a chilling hardness intermingled with the humour about his eyes and mouth. 'You don't want to see me any more, Rebecca?' he softly enquired. 'Are you sure?'

'More positive than I have ever been about anything,' she tremulously asserted.

'Well, I think you're probably right,' he dulcetly concurred. 'I told you once before that I will not apologise or beg forgiveness without just cause. You refuse to have faith in me; without trust and loyalty, there can be no marriage. Whatever I say…whatever I tell you about my past life, my behaviour here, there, wherever…it all meets with your suspicion. You want to believe the worst in me, don't you? Why is that? Is it safer that way?' he perceptively suggested. 'Are you frightened of what we're getting closer to? I want a wife…children. What do you want from me, Rebecca, apart from the Summer House and a goodnight kiss? I trust you. I believe everything you tell me. Yet you'd rather listen to that malicious pervert Mayhew than me.'

He paused for a long moment before saying, 'Which prompts me to ask why you felt you couldn't tell me about him abusing Lucy. You knew, didn't you? It's why you wanted her to accompany us to Cornwall. Why was it she could confide in me yet you couldn't?'

'Why would you care?' Rebecca threw recklessly up into his dark face. 'You're a lecher, too, aren't you?'

He smiled slowly and she knew she had backed herself both physically and verbally into a corner.

'If that's what you insist I am, Rebecca. Anything to please you.'

Rebecca sensed ice stinging her face and body. She had lost all advantage, all control, and was way out of her depth and floundering. She hadn't anticipated this. She had expected he might be forced on the defensive, not that this showdown might require her apologies.

Rebecca glanced fearfully up at him. She hadn't seen him move yet he seemed closer, mere inches away now and towering over her. The moon escaped the cloud once more, brightening the room. She threw her silver-gilt head back and met his eyes squarely, implying a courage she was far from feeling.

'You're no better than those villains at Devil's Cove, are you? And masquerading here as a gentleman has all been too much for you, hasn't it? I can understand now why you never intended staying. Maintaining the sham must have been so arduous…quite beyond you,' she uttered scathingly, starting to slide away from him. As a dark hand propped idly against the marble top of the washstand, she shifted in the opposite direction. As his other casually leaned for support too, trapping her between rigid muscular arms, she became quite still.

'I take it with that little character assessment you're terminating our betrothal,' he drily observed.

Rebecca managed a brief nod of her head, not deigning to bestow on him speech.

'Well, I'd rather we didn't finish on bad terms,' he said.

'There is no other way for us, I fear,' she breathlessly rejected his conciliation.

'Surely a kiss then before parting, Rebecca?' he lazily suggested, not bothering to hide his amusement or confidence.

The knowledge that he was still laughing at her and she was still utterly despondent made her swing a hand up at his face with all the bitter pain of humiliation and betrayal and loss. The blow knocked his head sideways but, that apart, his stance remained unflinching. He turned back slowly to look at her, then straightened, and his hands removed from the marble top to cool her flushed face. His thumbs brushed her pearl-satin skin as dark eyes travelled her features and settled on her mouth. Her lids lowered as his face neared hers with tormenting leisure. He kissed her with thorough expertise, imprisoning her between the washstand at her back and his strong immovable body.

For one whole minute she fought him, standing frigidly, until the heat moistening her mouth and her loins spread and betrayed her, tenderly filling her breasts and liquifying her limbs. She sobbed in anguished surrender to it, rested into him and allowed him to swing her up in his arms. His mouth was still fused to hers in a kiss of calculated seduction as he carried her to the bed, lowered her gently and followed her down.

By the time their slick mouths slowly unsealed, Rebecca's breathing was shallow and erratic. Luke raised himself on his elbows to look at her and she followed him up, as though magnetised, eyes closed and slender throat arching temptingly towards him. His hands supported her head, long fingers digging deep into the silky mass of hair as he gently, abruptly made her look at him.

'Do you realise how terrified I was today, Rebecca, when I found out Mayhew had you?' he demanded hoarsely. 'I have lived most of my adult life in danger but, today, when Miles gave me that scrap of paper and I thought I might have lost you...' His husky voice cracked and Rebecca gazed up wide-eyed at his first loss of control. He sat up properly, pulling her with him so she half-straddled his lap and their faces were inches apart.

'Don't do this to me, Rebecca. I told you yesterday that I've lived the life of a typical Cornish bachelor...I'm neither saint nor sinner. Just a man. And if I've been drawn into smuggling because of my heritage, you shall have to blame those damnable Ramsdens you revere. For they started it all.'

The shock and disbelief in Rebecca's face made him give

her a lop-sided smile. 'It's true,' he said with mild emphasis. He settled her more comfortably against him, his chin resting atop her golden head as he recounted the story.

'When my great-grandmother Charlotte Ramsden eloped to Cornwall with my great-grandfather Jago Trelawney her family were outraged. They believed it was he who had seduced her. But he was simply a respectable, but devilishly handsome—oh, it runs in the family—' he interrupted himself to tease her 'young man in Brighton visiting a relative. But Charlotte saw him in town and the rest, as they say, is history.

'Family folklore has it that, in fact, it was she who seduced him and when he left for Cornwall, she followed him home. But he loved her and they were happy despite being quite poor and living frugally. Coming from a well-to-do family, Charlotte was used to pretty things. So she bought some French lace from an itinerant smuggler…then French perfume and brandy. She had a good business brain and realised that if her fisherman husband crossed the channel for her, luxuries would be cheaper still and she could have more of them. He did anything to please her…another family tradition, perhaps,' he reflected with dry self-mockery.

'Anyway, that was the founding of one of Cornwall's greatest smuggling dynasties. One hundred years later my father was the finish of it. The free-trading Trelawneys died with him.

'He and Merrill were bitter adversaries, although in the same trade. My father smuggled and made a fortune from it but there were things he would never do: take payment from the homeless *émigrés* escaping the French revolution who pleaded for passage to England, or betray his country in any way. Merrill had no such qualms. He would do anything for money and only for money and, if payment was not forthcoming, he would kill without compunction.

'A French aristocrat and his family fleeing persecution were unlucky enough to be brought over by Merrill. They had nothing apart from the clothes they stood in. When he realised that they couldn't pay him, he killed the count and raped his wife and daughter. My father happened to be on the same stretch of beach that night, unloading. So was I.

'I was eighteen then and in the family business although, even at that time, I preferred our Bristol shipping office. There was always a legitimate side to Trelawney shipping, more as a screen than an enterprise, but only I saw its potential. Tristan and Ross…especially Ross,' he grunted on a rueful laugh, 'always preferred the excitement of night runs and skirmishes with the Revenue. Well, to be honest, they were quite exhilirating times and useful, for we all learned to fight young and well.'

He sobered and sighed. 'My father and I came upon the distraught French women and the count's body just as Merrill was setting off again. A vicious fight broke out between the Merrill camp and the Trelawneys. My father sustained a serious back injury inflicted by Merrill's dagger, for the cowardly bastard had knifed him from behind. But he seemed to recover.

'While he was out of action, recuperating, I had started to put more emphasis on legitimate transactions and expanded our fleet at Bristol. He began to see that there was colossal profit to be made. But that same injury killed him three years later. Almost to the day.

'Finding Merrill and killing him was always a priority. I thought I had done so four years ago, at Lizard Point in Cornwall when the Trelawneys and the Revenue ran his motley crew to ground. I have some fast cutters I allow the Revenue to use against the smugglers. I have been getting personally involved in a lot of skirmishing…more than I need to. But old habits die hard, I suppose, and then there's Ross to keep entertained and on the straight and narrow. Sometimes I worry that a smuggling life might seduce him back. He continually craves for adventure. Perhaps it's in his blood.'

Rebecca felt his warm breath on her neck a moment before the moist heat of his lips touched behind a sensitive ear, making her lids droop and her head sway.

'I'm not going to pretend that I'm morally outraged by the principle of free-trading; but for the most part it is operated by vicious thugs, and commercially I lose. Legitimate trade always suffers when smuggling is rife. It is impossible to compete with contraband prices and I was always determined to be a wealthy shipping magnate…and I am.'

He raised a caressing hand from her hip to touch her golden hair. Taking a thick, silky strand, he smoothed it between his long fingers and thumb before they threaded up close to her scalp, turning her to face him. His hard narrow mouth rested close to hers as he softly enquired, 'Do you believe me, Rebecca, or still suspect me a villain?'

Interminable silence throbbed between them. Tell me about your mistresses too, she wanted to scream at him. Tell me you don't love this dark-haired woman who believes you wed. She merely murmured, 'I'm not sure.'

'Well, I'm sure you know what an incorrigible reprobate would do with you next.'

Rebecca swallowed and moistened her lips, unwittingly drawing glittering eyes to her glistening mouth.

'So who am I, Rebecca? Your fiancé or a marauding Cornish smuggler?' was breathed warmly, softly against her chilled face.

'You're the man I was betrothed to,' she finally said.

Chapter Fourteen

'Good to see you again, Simon,' Mr Johnson greeted the blond man before turning his attention to Rebecca. He cordially extended a large hand and solicitiously found her a chair.

Simon watched the gallantry with a jaundiced eye. Not so long ago he had been plain 'Mr Nash', and not nearly so welcome as he appeared to be now his account was bursting with almost six thousand pounds.

'Miss Nash, you are aware that your brother is today to transfer your inheritance into your own account and henceforth you may use those funds as you choose?' the bank manager asked.

Rebecca smiled vaguely. 'Yes, I am aware of that,' she confirmed. She simply wanted these niceties over and to be back out into the refreshing seaside air, for her interminable headache seemed worse today. Worse than it had for the past week. It had come upon her when she had cried herself to sleep the night Luke had slammed out of her life for ever. She hadn't had a day free of it since. She pushed those hurtful, humiliating memories aside and concentrated on Mr Johnson's droning advice.

'…at compound rates of seven per centum,' his voice

penetrated her mind. She smiled and nodded, adopting an expression of what she hoped passed for intelligent interest befitting a spinster of twenty-six as he advised on stocks, bonds and other investments. For she was, indeed, now twenty-six, she sadly realised. Three days ago, she was miserably sure, was the date she became a confirmed old maid.

'But I'm sure your brother will advise you on such matters…' Mr Johnson's nasal speech cut into her melancholy.

Rebecca noticed with a small, wry smile that Simon had the grace to blush at the unhappy inference that he be her trusty financial adviser.

Mr Johnson pushed papers across his desk towards her. 'Just sign these please, my dear, so all the formalities are taken care of.' As Rebecca finished with the documents, he convivially remarked, 'A young lady of such independent means will doubtless want her own property. Perhaps even two. For renting one in the season could bring you a nice income. And you must make your money work for you, you know. I have heard your grandfather made excellent profits as a landlord. I could put you in touch with a property agent I know…'

'Thank you but, at present, I am not ready for such commitments. I need some time to think…'

'Of course…' He gave an apologetic smile. 'No doubt you'll want to wait and see who your new landlord is. He may be kind enough to sell you the Summer House, for I know from what your brother has told me, you have a particular fondness for that little building.'

'True, but as the ownership of Ramsden Manor is still so uncertain, Rebecca will not want to wait for ever,' Simon interceded, quite swayed towards the bank manager's idea that Rebecca should find a new home and a business venture to boot.

'Oh, the matter of the Ramsden estate is finalised. I hear

from my acquaintance, Willoughby, that the matter is now settled. But I know no more.'

'The Trelawneys are soon moving out?' Rebecca demanded in one shaky breath.

'Packing up to go even as we speak, so I have heard. Now, if I can be of any help to you, Miss Nash, with investments or advice, please do not hesitate to come and see me.' The encouragement was sincere: female clients were a rarity. One of such stunning good looks was definitely a sight for sore eyes in his dusty office. She had quite brightened his day; a pity he seemed to have dampened hers. The pretty lass had been in better spirits on first meeting twenty minutes ago.

'Well, that's now done and out of the way.' Simon sighed his satisfaction as they gained the cobbled street and the warmth of a pale November sun. 'Let's go to Dilly's teashop for a brew and a bite to eat before I take you home. Oh, I have some news for you,' he mentioned in passing, as he took Rebecca's arm and they strolled on.

Rebecca lifted her cup absently to her mouth, then replaced it untasted. 'Did you know that Luke and Ross were readying to leave for Cornwall?'

'No,' Simon admitted. 'They've said nothing to me. But then I've not seen a lot of Luke recently, and Ross and I…well…' he grimaced uneasily.

'You mean when you two get together you're both usually too in your cups to discuss anything sensible,' Rebecca mildly censured him.

'He is grand company…' Simon excused his excesses with a boyish smile.

'What news have you for me?' Rebecca asked, before sipping her tea and gazing through the teashop window.

She watched an urchin flower seller accosting strollers and children playing hopscotch in patches of autumn sun.

Three months ago this would have been one of the happiest, most fulfilling days of her life. After five anxiety-ridden years, struggling to earn enough to live, her future was finally secure. She had enough money of her own to live free from worry for the rest of her days. She could even afford small luxuries, yet she felt empty and depressed.

'I shall be leaving the area soon, Rebecca.' Simon cautiously broke the news of his departure. 'I have employment,' he proudly finished. 'Luke has offered me a position at his Bristol shipping office. If all goes well, I might get aboard a vessel.'

Rebecca stared at him, stunned by the fact that he was going away again and who was responsible for her loss. 'Luke has given you work? Why?'

'He said he might some while ago and he has proved true to his word.'

'I thought you were promised a chance of employment with the investment company you used....' Rebecca's words tailed off. When would she grow up? When would she stop being such a credulous idiot? Her fingers tightened about her cup as her brain sifted information and found answers. She watched the hopscotch games as she said bitterly, 'It was his company you invested with. Was it his money, too? Was nothing left of my inheritance?'

'No,' Simon quietly admitted. 'I didn't have a penny, so he loaned me two thousand pounds and I made a ridiculous profit on it. I've paid him back,' he quickly affirmed. 'Every penny I borrowed has been returned. His only stipulation...command...was that your money was to be repaid, and that I should let you think that the scheme was my idea.'

'I see…' Rebecca breathed, knowing she didn't really see at all why Luke would go to such lengths to help her or why, having done so, he would try to hide such generosity.

Probably her independent means ensured she would never be a financial burden once she was discarded. She closed her eyes and ground her teeth. It was probably nothing of the sort. He was kind and generous and the honest gentleman she had always wanted to believe him. All that he had recounted about his fight against smuggling on the last fateful night she had seen him had been confirmed to her the very next day…and by her own brother. Luke had been right. Luke was always right, she wistfully acknowledged. Had she done as he said and slept before making accusations, by the following day she would have had the validation she required.

For Luke, Ross and Simon had been summoned back by the magistrate to give evidence and information of the circumstances of the affray at Devil's Cove. The Revenue men were there too, Simon had told her. He had also told her in what high esteem Luke Trelawney was held by those men and how grateful they were for his loan of vessels to aid in ridding the south coast of treacherous free-traders.

She was so ready to believe him mean-spirited because accepting she had lost him through pride and jealousy was anathema. She shook trailing curls of honey hair back from her face and gazed through the window at the laughing children, desperately rallying and summoning back those very failings. He was still a philanderer. He had no excuses that night for the women he kept. No denial or sweet words of explanation there.

'You won't tell him we've spoken of this, will you, Rebecca?' Simon broke into her self-torment. 'He was adamant you shouldn't know of his part in reinstating your inheritance. If he found out I had betrayed his trust...I don't want to jeopardise my opportunity with Trelawney Shipping. I'll never get another as good...'

'I shan't say anything, Simon,' Rebecca cut in. 'In all probability I shall never again see Luke; even a chance meeting is unlikely if they are soon to return to Cornwall.' The truth in this statement made her voice brittle and a sheen enhance the brilliance of her aqua-coloured eyes.

'It's just a tiff,' Simon dismissed lightly, quite genuinely bewildered by his sister's distress. 'Ross knows nothing of any rift between you and Luke or that your betrothal is over.'

'I would rather you didn't discuss this with anyone, Simon,' Rebecca emphasised in a hiss, white with shock. 'It was never an official betrothal. If Luke has said nothing, probably he too feels it concerns no one else.' Or probably it bothers him little, she sadly thought.

She was aware of Simon's dark blue eyes scanning her face. Lowering his voice, he said, 'It wasn't anything to do with what that fiend Mayhew told you...about...'

Simon halted and cleared his throat. Discussing another man's mistresses with a female relative was almost as embarrassing and unheard of as discussing one's own. But he was her brother: she had no mother to advise her and he guessed that their self-centred older sister Elizabeth had never bothered to put her straight on such matters. A surge of affection softened him. He did owe her so very much. He wanted to see her happy and settled. A subtle tack was required.

'You know very little of what goes on in the world, Rebecca,' he began gently. 'You have shut yourself away for too long in Graveley...with just the Turners and the vicar and his wife as adult company. Because you have no experience of…umm…society and…er, men and the way they go on…'

Rebecca raised limpid turquoise eyes to her brother's kindly blue gaze. 'If you are trying to say that Luke has mistresses and I shouldn't let that bother me for it's commonly accepted behaviour…' Her voice faded away.

Simon blushed to the roots of his blond hair but he managed to stutter, 'I'm sure he loves you, Rebecca, no matter what he does…or who else he… Dammit, Rebecca,' he groaned, 'you're not supposed to even acknowledge such…things, even if you do hear about them.'

A pained laugh escaped Rebecca. 'I have a splitting headache, Simon,' she cut into his confusion with the quite truthful complaint. 'Would you take me home?'

'I've packed up the rest of Lucy's things,' Martha told Rebecca as she walked in through the kitchen door, removed her bonnet and discarded it on a kitchen chair. 'Gregory can take the trunk over in the morning, if you like.'

Rebecca gave the woman a grateful smile and thought of Lucy, back at home now with her mother. Simon had returned Lucy home the day after the fracas at Devil's Cove, and she knew by the time they arrived late that afternoon, the woman would already have had a visit from the authorities regarding her dead husband and his nefarious activities. Rebecca could only guess how poor Mrs Mayhew must be feeling. She only hoped that the removal of that odious man from her life was accepted with the same quiet contentment that Lucy had received the news of her stepfather's death. Rebecca had an instinct that Rupert Mayhew would have treated all the women in his life in the same appalling manner.

'Has your headache cleared?' Martha interrupted Rebecca's thoughts.

'A bit better, thank you, Martha,' Rebecca lied. If she told the truth, Martha would fuss the evening through, trying to ply her with potions, instead of returning to her cottage with Gregory.

'I heard today from Mr Johnson at the bank that the Trelawneys are packing up to leave. Do you know if that's true, Martha? Have you heard?'

Martha removed her apron and carefully folded it. 'I believe it is, Miss Becky.' She raised her grey eyes to study Rebecca's tense features. 'If he won't come to you, you should go and see him,' she prompted. 'Perhaps it can't be put right…but you won't want him going away thinking bad of you, now will you?' She sighed and shook her greying head. 'Supper's in the oven,' she added, then hesitated at the kitchen door as though about to say more, but with a sad grimace was gone.

Rebecca swallowed, then swallowed again, trying to clear the blockage forming in her throat. She would not cry. She would not cry again, she threatened herself and abruptly stood up. She walked through into her parlour and then aimlessly back to the kitchen. It was so quiet and lonely now Lucy had gone. Simon now used the Summer House as lodgings, but she rarely saw him. He only used her home to sleep and eat, she wryly realised. She sat at the table and looked about her kitchen, pondering on what Mr Johnson had said about the possibility of buying the Summer House from the new landlord. Or purchasing a larger property in town, perhaps to rent. A shaky hand went to her face. She couldn't concentrate on anything.

With a cloth protecting her hands, she withdrew the earthenware dish from the oven and looked at the tempting chicken and vegetable hotpot. She put it on to the draining board to cool for she knew she would never eat it. Her stomach rolled, but with nausea, not hunger. She automatically covered the meal with the cloth in case Simon wanted it when he arrived home.

Her eyes shut tight against the abrupt sting of tears. Her golden head sank forward and with every ounce of her being she willed Luke to come to her. Even the haunting mortification of their parting could not diminish her desperate need to see him.

Her body flamed at the memory of their final hour together when he had tantalised her inch by squirming inch with sweet seduction and ruthless passion into such fevered surrender that she had actually pleaded for release, not once but twice before he finished with her. For she had tasted the ecstasy of fulfilment on a tavern bed; and he had promised her, when his hands were at liberty, it would be rapturous. But it was such bitter pleasure. Those long, hard fingers had merely been instruments of torture, as had his cruel mouth. He had not once kissed her. Even when she desperately sought to intercept his mouth with her own before it could recommence plundering her body, he would not allow it. Leisurely, punishing torment would ensue until she clung and writhed and raised herself against him.

That was when he would deliberately break contact with her raw, aroused body and stroke her face or her hair until some of her aching need died and her shame and pride renewed and she would fight to spring from the bed. And he would start again.

As dawnlight flushed the sky and he straddled her once more she had finally found the will to lash out but not to stop the tears. His pitiless mouth teasingly lowered, just touching hers when she no longer cared. Firm fingers slid against her wet face forcing her to look at him as he tauntingly enquired, 'Is that enough to remember your Cornish smuggler by?' before he left her with the sound of the door crashing closed, echoing in her ears.

Rebecca gazed through the kitchen window at the fading light. If she was going she ought to go now to return before dusk. And she knew she would go. Just as two months ago she had had to go and apologise for her immaturity, so she had to go now, before he went away, and do so again. For she was still lacking in worldliness, as Simon had so rightly judged earlier today.

Martha was right, too. She couldn't bear the thought of him returning to Cornwall and thinking ill of her. Her insults that night made her head bow now with shame. He was also due her thanks. For without him she would be still penniless and perhaps even dead or worse by Mayhew's hand. She owed him so much, and so wanted to see him, just once more; her pride was a small price to pay.

The grass felt damp against her legs as she hoisted her silver-grey skirts and nimbly climbed the last stile. The countryside was so different to the last time she had walked this meadow, with thundering heart, to speak to him. Then the weather had still been warm and sultry, the grass still short and dry from a long hot summer. But it was mild weather for this time of year, she impressed upon herself, her thoughts cleaving to any topic rather than the coming encounter.

She shook her skirts to straighten them as she gained the parkland that abutted the driveway to the Manor and began calmly walking across it. In the distance she glimpsed John, recognising him by his fair head. The sight of that young man made her wonder whether he and Lucy would again see each other now she was back home. John was leading that coal-black stallion Luke rode. So Luke was at home. Her pace didn't falter. Her eyes closed and she threw back her head a little, instilling courage. Her hands impulsively tidied stray locks of honey hair and she smoothed her skirts. She approached the corner of the mellow brick house and rounded the corner to the great door. And froze.

It couldn't be happening to her. Not again. The scene that greeted her removed her heartbeat and her courage. But it was too late to quietly withdraw, she realised, panic-stricken, for he had raised his head away from the woman he embraced, and seen her.

Their eyes locked across the brunette's glossy head. His expression terrified her. He looked pleased...almost triumphant. He put the woman away from him and walked towards her.

'I'm sorry,' Rebecca murmured, admirably controlling her voice and her spontaneous need to flee. 'I...I didn't mean to intrude. I have simply come to bid you farewell. Goodbye,' she managed before twisting swiftly away and heading back towards her meadow.

A dark hand on her arm halted her and turned her about. The overwhelming urge to lash out at him was just curbed. Aware of the young woman curiously watching them, she simply jerked her arm free of his grasp.

It was impossible not to stare. She was very pretty, Rebecca realised. Very pretty and very young, nothing like she would have imagined from Mayhew's lewd description. This woman—girl, for she looked still to be in her teens— had a fresh beauty, not the voluptuous appeal that had tormented her. Somehow that made it all so much worse. And Luke did love her. She had witnessed not a quick affectionate hug for a friend but a close leisurely embrace for someone cherished.

'I'm glad you've come over, Rebecca,' Luke soothed her, taking her arm to draw her forward. 'I'd like you to meet my sister.'

Wide, disbelieving turquoise eyes immediately sought his face, making his mouth twist in bitterness. Rebecca glanced back at the pretty girl, remembering the last time she had been at Ramsden Manor and strange young women were explained away as someone's 'sisters'.

As though recalling the same incident, a grunt of hard laughter choked in his throat and he stared off into the distance. 'Shall I find my mother to confirm her identity?' he sardonically suggested and so quietly that only Rebecca heard.

'Katherine,' he called, beckoning to the young woman. She approached straight away with a friendly smile.

'Katherine, this is Rebecca Nash, a very dear friend.' Initially Rebecca's eyes searched his for sarcasm at this introduction. Then, as though the French translation occurred to them both at the same time, Rebecca blushed and looked at the gravel drive and he pivoted on his heel with a savage curse. 'Where are the others?' he bit out to his sister with steely control. 'I should like to introduce them all to Rebecca.'

Katherine was distracted from answering.

'My lord,' Miles huffed out, as he hobbled down the stone steps. 'Mr Willoughby wants to speak with you… Hello, Miss Rebecca,' he broke off to greet Rebecca immediately he laid eyes on her. 'I haven't seen you for a while. Why haven't you been by to see us? Judith was only saying the other day, Where's that Miss Becky been? My lord, he says it's urgent you inspect these documents,' Miles's meandering discourse turned on his master.

'Tell him to wait,' Luke enunciated carefully through closed teeth.

Undeterred by his master's odd moods, which he was now quite coming to terms with—for over the past week Miles had experienced everything from blackest rage to saddest despair—he ignored this mild testiness and continued about his business. 'And young Mr Trelawney says he wants to speak to you about which mount is best for Miss Katherine. The grey mare or the…'

A low string of oaths trailed in Luke's wake as he stalked off a few paces, hands thrust deep in his pockets, as though to steady his temper.

Miles was unperturbed and smilingly took Rebecca's hand, patting it affectionately in pleasure at seeing her after all these weeks.

Luke watched them for a moment before approaching again. 'Come inside the house. I'll apologise now for it's like a lunatic asylum in there,' he said tightly. 'But Katherine will keep you company until I have dealt with Willoughby. Please,' he urged softly as she hung back. 'I'm very glad you've come to talk to me.'

'Rebecca and I will be fine, Luke,' his sister said with a smile. 'I shall find Mama…oh, and Sara and Jago.'

The names washed meaninglessly over Rebecca as Katherine linked arms with her as though she had known her for years and lead her to the steps of the Manor. But Rebecca's eyes were fixed on Luke's tall athletic figure as he took the front steps two at a time, his tense speed denoting great exasperation.

Entering the familiar cool hallway was like walking into mild chaos and explained Luke's odd apology for the state of his house. There were packing cases lining the walls and large documents strewn around on hall tables. There were several men of business perusing the paperwork.

As she took two paces into the house a young boy of about five careered into her. Rebecca automatically steadied the child on his feet.

He grinned mischievously at her as Katherine swung him up into her arms and planted a kiss on his forehead.

He struggled to be put down again and she complied, ruffling his jet-black hair.

'That's young Jago, named after his grandfather and his great-great grandfather,' Katherine helpfully supplied as the young boy dashed down the stone steps. 'He's my nephew, Tristan's son. Tristan couldn't come. He's looking after Melrose. But his wife, Sara, is here. There she is,' Katherine said, indicating a petite brunette who was ascending the stairs, carrying an armful of colourful gowns. 'She came along with us to keep Jago happy. He does so love his two uncles. I'll introduce you to Sara later. I wonder where Mama is…' She gazed searchingly around the strewn hallway. 'She's probably gone to lie down in a darkened room,' Katherine giggled, surveying the disorder. 'I think it's all been too much.' She turned amused, hazel eyes on Rebecca and at that moment her likeness to Ross was quite undeniable.

'As you might have guessed, Luke wasn't expecting us. Do you know, in all the time he has been in Sussex he has sent us only two proper letters,' she complained. 'The rest were all business missives for Tristan about the mines and shipping and boring suchlike. No gossip. But we knew there must be something vital keeping him away from Melrose. He likes to think he's indispensable. So we decided to come and investigate, and make it a surprise. And here we all are on the very day he is packing up to move out. I don't think he's very pleased about the timing of our surprise.' Katherine grimaced.

'I'm sure you all meant well.' Rebecca managed to edge a few words into the chatty monologue, before her eyes once more anxiously sought Luke's face. Katherine was right: he didn't look pleased at all, she realised, biting her lip. He probably wasn't very pleased about the timing of her surprise either. She must have considerably worsened his temper by turning up unexpectedly at such an inopportune moment. He obviously had important business matters as well as his family to deal with.

Because he was such a gentleman he had tried to make her feel welcome; but it must be inconvenient and embarrassing for him to have her around right now. No wonder he looked so irritated.

It was impossible to detach her hungry eyes from his lean profile. The angular planes of his jaw looked sooty and she realised he was unshaven. He looked a little haggard too, probably lacking in sleep, she guessed. She discreetly watched him listening, head bowed, to a middle-aged fair-haired man who was indicating something on a large, unwieldy document, while trying to position the flapping chart against the wall for support. Luke shifted position at that precise moment and looked up straight at her.

The noise and bustle in the hallway seemed to recede and Rebecca was aware of nothing for a long moment but the intense dark eyes trained on her with such relentless force that she felt her knees weaken.

'You have lovely hair...and eyes.' The compliment finally penetrated through her trance and Rebecca tore her eyes away.

'Thank you,' she said graciously to Katherine, frantically wondering how she could extricate herself and slip away. She was sure it was what Luke really wanted, despite his well-mannered insistence she stay.

'Ross said you were very beautiful,' Katherine added, making Rebecca wonder why Ross would have bothered mentioning her at all.

'Oh, look, here's Ross now,' Katherine said, spying her brother exiting the library into the crowded hall with a glass in one hand and a large piece of cake in the other.

Catching sight of Rebecca, Ross immediately walked

over. 'Hello, Rebecca; nice to see you,' he said with a genuine warmth. He looked about for Luke then back at her and seemed about to say something, but decided against it.

'You didn't say Simon was still here,' Katherine chided Ross.

Rebecca had already noticed her brother and was staring, amazed, as he too emerged from the library with a slice of cake in his hand. 'This is Ross's friend, Simon,' Katherine said in a low, excited breath. 'I met him earlier today. Isn't he so handsome?' she quietly squealed.

'Note the family likeness,' Ross drily hinted with a private grin at Rebecca. When his sister looked mystified, he relented. 'Simon is Rebecca's brother.'

Katherine looked from one to the other of them. At Rebecca's wry confirmation, Katherine blushed, mortified, and actually punched Ross slyly on the arm. 'Why didn't you say?' she hissed, with her head down, before another crafty thump made him spill his drink and a quarrel start.

'You young people…you do love a rumpus,' Judith scolded, unsuccessfully suppressing a smile. 'Hello, Miss Becky…now why haven't you been by before to see us?' She proffered the tray she held laden with slices of madeira cake, treacle biscuits and glasses of pale wine.

'I planned to,' Rebecca told her quite loudly over the warring siblings, shaking her head to decline anything from the tray. 'There have been so many unexpected turns of event…'

'It's all been so exciting, hasn't it?' Judith said with shining eyes. 'What with smugglers…and fighting…and the Revenue. And I'm so pleased that young Simon's back from his travels. It's so nice to have a houseful like this.' She chuckled. 'Just like the old days. We used to have some wonderful times years ago. I've catered for hundreds in my time,' she impressed upon Rebecca, before turning to offer her refreshments elsewhere. Her foot kicked against a wooden toy boat discarded on the marble tiles and it skidded noisily away. She gave a little screech as her tray tilted.

A firm hand drew Rebecca backwards, out of the chaos just as she heard Katherine demand, 'What smugglers? Ross, you haven't... If Mama finds out you've been involved...'

The last Rebecca saw as Luke wordlessly lead her away was Simon steadying Judith's tray while helping himself to a glass of wine. As they passed the men of business, Luke bid them terse farewells. But his pace didn't slacken until he reached his study door.

'I'm sorry,' he quietly said. 'The whole place is bedlam.' He leaned against the door, head tilted back, and sighed as he turned the key in the lock behind him.

Rebecca's eyes immediately latched on to the movement.

'To keep them out, Rebecca, not you within,' he drily reassured her before he pushed away from the door.

'Sit down, Rebecca,' he quietly, politely invited her. As he seated himself behind his desk, she took the wing-chair she had used the last time she sat before him in trepidation. He looked at her and started to speak but a child's cry cut across the words. It escalated to a scream, then changed to laughter.

Luke swiped a hand about his shadowy, angular chin, stifling a muttered imprecation and Rebecca knew he was about to apologise again for his family.

A rush of tenderness swamped her. She had never seen him so vulnerable...so tense. It made her want to rush around the desk and hold him, comfort him. She felt warm blood suffuse her face at the very idea. His reaction to such a show of affection might wound her battered pride yet further. He had made it quite clear that their relationship was over when he had taunted her with having something to remember him by. Memories of what he had done to her before his callous abandonment shattered her fragile self-possession completely. Another rush of blood stung her face and she could bear no more.

'I'm sorry, I've arrived at a bad time,' she tremulously said, hastily standing up. He stood too, as though to prevent her leaving.

'*They*'ve come at a bad time, Rebecca. Not you. I was hoping you would come over once you found out I was moving out.' He allowed self-mockery to twist his mouth. 'For if you hadn't…I would have given in later today and come to you, and I didn't want that.'

His words and wry expression confused her. But she was aware he wouldn't yet let her leave. She searched for conversation to mask her wavering courage and her desolation. For he really *was* leaving. The evidence was scattered about his hallway and now he had confirmed it to her. 'I like Katherine very much…Ross, too. You're very lucky to have your family about you. Sometimes I long for those days when Simon, Elizabeth and I were all at home together as a family, arguing and fighting,' she wistfully told him.

'Arguing and fighting, Rebecca? You?' he softly mocked.

Rebecca blushed but defended her tomboy days. 'Of course. Elizabeth and I would run Mama ragged with our constant bickering. She was always saying she would box our ears if we didn't stop. I hit Elizabeth once with my hairbrush when she stole my favourite doll. I suppose I was about twelve then,' she said, a reflective little smile curving her soft mouth. 'Mama was furious…she thought I'd knocked one of her teeth out.'

Aware of his amused interest and unnervingly steady attention, she fell awkwardly silent. He seemed in no hurry to say anything, so to lighten the expectant tension, she continued, 'And Simon and I were always squabbling over who won games. One day, when he accused me of cheating, I punched him and threw the chessboard at him.' This time she had nothing further to add to break the quiet. She stood before him, unsure why on earth she had just confided those private, precious memories.

'Did he hit you back?' Luke eventually asked, not quite so amused.

A sweet, nostalgic smile met his anxiety. 'No. Simon used to indulge me; and I did cheat sometimes,' she softly admitted. 'But he nearly always let me win…even when I didn't deserve to.'

'Strange…you have the same effect on me, Rebecca…' he slowly, sardonically, said.

Rebecca raised searching eyes to his. There was no sign of vulnerability now.

Chapter Fifteen

'What have you come to say to me, Rebecca?' Luke asked with such quiet determination that even an excited shriek from his nephew echoing around the hallway didn't elicit any change in his expression.

Clammy hands gripped together behind her back. She had come to take her leave and she would. She had come to apologise and thank him too, and she would do so, she exhorted herself.

'Shall we sit down again?' he suggested with a wry smile.

Rebecca gratefully sank into the chair, relieving legs that felt too weak to support her. 'Simon and I were in town…at the bank. I learned that you are moving out and came to say goodbye,' she said quickly. 'I didn't want you to leave and…'

'And…?' he tonelessly prompted.

'And think I was ill mannered enough not to…to… I—I didn't want us to part on bad terms,' she stammered.

'I thought there was no other way for us, Rebecca? Wasn't that what you told me?' he remorselessly reminded her.

Remembering the words she had tossed at him in her

bedroom a week ago made her colour rise and her eyelids lower. She banished the mortifying memories and hastened on. 'I also…I owe you an apology. I said some unforgivable things. I insulted you, and I am very sorry. I was wrong to suspect you…accuse you of consorting with smugglers or with…people who are none of my concern.'

'Which people?' he relentlessly probed.

She tossed her golden head back then and glared at him. She would not mention his mistresses. She would not give him the satisfaction of glimpsing her distress or jealousy. But she hadn't yet finished. She still owed him thanks and she would complete what she had come to do. 'I also wish to thank you for the return of my inheritance.' She froze. She had completely forgotten that Simon had charged her never to speak of it, that it might affect his future employment with Luke's shipping company.

Wide turquoise eyes darted anxiously to his face. 'I guessed you had helped Simon return my money…that he invested in your company,' she breathlessly added. 'And I am extremely grateful.'

'When did you guess? Before or after he told you?'

Rebecca winced at the heavy irony, then again at his next curt words.

'I don't want your gratitude, Rebecca…or your indebtedness…or your sense of duty.'

His eyes roved her beautiful wan face. It was time to give in. He'd gained nothing by staying away: the strain of it was nearly killing him. Now she was before him in all her delicate golden glory he wasn't sure how he had managed it. This absurd situation was as much his fault as hers. His pride, her jealousy…her distrust, her immaturity…well, almost as much his fault, he wryly thought.

But then it was her artless innocence that had endeared him in the first place. He should have told her that he loved her weeks ago. Had he spoken sooner, he was certain their estrangement would never have come about. For it was all she had ever desired. Just the words—not possessions, material tokens of his honourable intentions. He'd waited, wanting perfection for her and ended up giving her nothing. And damn Merrill to eternal hellfire, for his malicious, lecherous tongue.

She now wouldn't rest easy until it was all brought into the open. Yet there had been no reason for her to know. The irony of it: none of those women had been of any real consequence, yet the fact that she knew they existed, and her knowledge was incomplete, was devastating her.

'Which people?' he gently demanded.

Rebecca ignored his persistent question. 'Simon didn't tell me, I swear. I…I'm glad he is to work for you in Bristol,' she added for good measure.

'If I don't employ Simon, it's likely he'll end up in gaol,' he casually imparted to her.

'What do you mean?' Rebecca gasped, her complexion chalky.

'Blacker let the Revenue know your brother was an associate of his and had been runnning contraband. The only way to appease them was to imply Simon had been spying on free-trading along the south coast at my behest. Were I to withdraw that…?' The subtle message drifted between them.

'Which people, Rebecca?' he very deliberately repeated, leaning across the desk towards her, hands lightly clasped in front of him. His warm gaze on her chilled face was obdurate and determined to exact an answer.

She moistened parched lips. 'Your mistresses,' spilled out, but so weakly she prayed he wouldn't expect her to repeat the hateful words.

'My mistresses? Women I consorted with before I even knew you? Why would they concern you?'

His enquiry was so mildly curious, she felt foolish. 'They don't,' she choked, rising immediately. She was reaching for the handle when she remembered the door was locked. And the key was removed. 'I want to be home before dusk…'

'Come, tell me why they trouble you,' he insisted. 'Should I worry that you were once engaged to a man you loved? It is in the past.'

'David is dead,' Rebecca whispered. 'He is gone from me forever. I will never see him again.'

'And neither will I see again any of the women I kept in Cornwall…except by unlucky chance. Do you believe me?'

'No,' she flung back at once, twisting about. 'Mayhew swore your current mistress considers you already married to her…in all but name.'

'Perhaps she did stupidly believe that,' Luke allowed quietly. 'But she wisely never said as much to me. I choose who is to become my wife and it would never have been a courtesan for whom I felt a passing fondness. I've never before met anyone I've wanted to marry. I've never asked anyone…even in jest. I've never before loved anyone. I've more cause for jealousy, Rebecca. I know you cared deeply for David and that's not easy to bear.' After a brief pause he asked huskily, 'Do you believe me?'

'Yes.' The word was immediate and whispered. Turquoise eyes limpidly attached to a steady dark gaze. She allowed herself the luxury of staring. Even when she saw him acknowledge her avid attention by relaxing back into his chair with a private smile, she still couldn't look away.

If only…ran wistfully through her head. Her inexperience had made her imagination run riot. Emotions she had never previously tasted had overwhelmed her: jealousy, passion; she knew nothing of them and could control neither. He could control both. She knew now what caused that self-mocking look that accompanied his goodnight kisses and gentle caresses. She knew why he shook and gripped the chair they sat in or the wall they rested against when she clung, reluctant ever to let him go.

He looked like that now, his jaw tense, his mouth twisted and his eyes sleepy: more so than ever. And he had deliberately shown her how easily he could change the tenor of his lovemaking and her pleasure; that her fulfilment was his to withhold as well as bestow. He was honest; he had never lied to her.

Yet she had lied to him on several occasions; had done so minutes before when asked why his mistresses bothered her. He wouldn't lie to her now if she asked. But she didn't want to know…she didn't… 'Since in Brighton, have you…?' she burst out.

'No one,' he said, without allowing her to finish or his expression to alter.

The next thought stopped her heart beating and she panicked and chased it out. But when it sneaked back she allowed it to rest, for living without him in Brighton, torturing herself daily with what she had needlessly thrown away, would be impossible.

It had been good enough for Charlotte Ramsden to selflessly follow the man she loved and Rebecca knew she could find the humility to do likewise. Jago Trelawney had married Charlotte, it was true. Her own chance of such happiness was now destroyed and there was no one but herself to blame. She had childishly terminated their betrothal and he had wisely pointed out the sense in it.

But while she breathed she wanted to be by him wherever he was, wherever that took her and in any way he would have her. She was sure he still wanted her. She recognised desire in those jet-fringed velvet eyes that ceaselessly caressed her.

'When you go home to Cornwall, may I come with you?' The shy plea hung, pulsating, in the quiet room. Just two months ago she had come here, stood by this door and despised him for propositioning her. Now she was back, voicing the exact proposal she had deemed an insult. She was begging him not to abandon her. 'I will be no trouble to you, I swear. I am a woman of independent means.' Her fragile pride made her stumble over her coaxing, 'If I…if we…don't suit, I will have money enough to travel to Brighton or Bristol where Simon is or—'

'You're not going to Cornwall,' he cut into her persuasion in a harsh, strangled voice. He wasn't sure whether to laugh or wail at the farce of it. But he felt racked, not only by what he'd brought her to, but his physical state. Unremitting sexual frustration coupled with the recent savage fighting and the heady exhaustion from lack of sleep had taken their toll on his mind and body. Lack of sleep, laughably, because he lay restless the night through in a waking dream of Rebecca…and what she was now sweetly willing to put at his disposal.

In her quiet, graceful way she was offering herself to him because she loved him. He knew that now for certain. Just as he knew that she was close to tears at what she thought was his rejection. But her dignity wouldn't allow her to weep or plead or attempt seduction. Wenna would have tried all three. He wondered how his brief note had been received. No doubt the banker's draft and deeds to the house in Penzance had sweetened her temper. He watched Rebecca reach for the door again, forgetting in her distress that he still had the key. She would simply try to remove herself; failing that, talk about trivialities until she could escape. And she did.

She had to get away now. She had to get away from this house, from the people chatting in the hallway, without breaking down. She was desperate for home and solitude. She retreated into conversation. 'So the matter of the Ramsden Estate is now settled,' she blurted out brightly. 'Who is to live here?'

'Newlyweds.'

'Are they from Sussex…local people?' she said distractedly, trying the doorhandle again just in case by some miracle it came open in her hand.

'She is…very local and he is new to the area.'

The information washed over her. She didn't really care who had this house, all she cared at present was how to speedily remove herself from it. She stared at the mahogany panels, feeling the hot burn of tears at the back of her eyes. 'May I have the key now?' she said in a rush. The sound of his footsteps behind made her move politely aside so he could reach the lock.

'Don't you want to know any more about these people?' he asked softly.

A swift hand slipped inconspicuously across her damp face. 'Not really. I shall move away to town so it will not affect me who lives here.'

'Well, I'll tell you about them anyway,' he said in such a deep, honeyed voice more betraying tears sprang to her eyes.

'The man's a bit of an arrogant fool,' he quietly began. 'He's not even told his beloved fiancée just how much she means to him. That the prospect of a future without her would make his life meaningless. Or that he's willing to live anywhere with her. In a hovel or a palace…anywhere so long as they are together. He's been waiting for the perfect moment to tell her all this and, of course, there never is one. He never believed he would remain long here in Sussex. While still arrogant, he thought he could take this beautiful, enchanting woman away from everything that was dear to her, treat her as though she was a precious trophy. But in his defence,' he added hoarsely, 'he always loved her…from the very first moment he saw her dripping wet in a woodland pond.'

Rebecca half-turned towards him, pain and uncertainty shadowing her delicate alabaster features. She suspected him of cruelly joking, he realised.

'Do you know what made him decide to settle here, Rebecca? Apart from the need to please his adored fiancée? It was the Summer House. That small unobtrusive building. He couldn't take it with him and couldn't leave it behind. And where else would his children play?'

She faced him fully then, wide wet turquoise eyes flying to his face.

He raised a slow, dark finger and the back of it wiped the tears from her cheeks with feather lightness. 'And he wants the manor restored…made splendid again, a fitting wedding gift for her…for them both. A gift each to the other to live in till the end of their days. Then for their children and their children's children. Renovation is about to start, so they'll have to live elsewhere for a short while. Perhaps the Summer House. What do you think she'll say, Rebecca, when this arrogant fool finally tells her all this? Will she forgive him? Still want him?'

'I think she'll say she loves him so much she would have followed him home…humbled herself just to be near him,' Rebecca solemnly murmured, her eyes fused to his.

The dark hand caressing her cheek sank, spear-fingered, into her silken honey hair and he cradled her against his shoulder. 'God, I love you. I love you so much it's like insanity,' he choked. 'I'm sorry. I should have told you sooner. I wanted everything to be perfect. It was idiocy, just pride. I wanted to give you something valuable too.'

He drew her backwards with him to the desk and sat right back in his chair, settling her on the seat in front of him, so that his muscular thighs enclosed her slender, soft ones. He slid open a drawer and withdrew two small elegant boxes and a folded paper.

'Open them,' he said hoarsely.

Unsteady white fingers raised the first lid. An exquisite ring nestled against snowy velvet: an aquamarine gem surrounded by diamonds sparked rainbow lights at her. She had never seen a jewel so awesomely lovely and she told him so. She raised the lid of the other box: a plain gold band gleamed softly.

His fingers unfolded the paper. 'A marriage licence. I've had it for weeks. I wanted to give you your betrothal ring on our day out in Brighton. I thought, as soon as we got rid of Simon and found a quiet spot. Then Ross and his young lady arrived. I was so desperate to get you alone and tell you I loved you, and talk to you about things, I probably would have hired a fishing boat and taken you to sea just for privacy and peace and quiet.' He dropped his head forward so their glossy black and honey-gold hair mingled. 'I can't wait any longer for you, Rebecca. I swear I can't.'

She swivelled against his body to look at him, aware, as he winced, of his tension and the heat radiating from him. 'I don't want to wait either. I didn't want to last time…' She flushed, and her dusky lashes screened her eyes. 'You could have stayed. I wanted you to stay,' she whispered.

'I know…and God knows, I nearly did,' he huskily told her, kissing her forehead. 'Seducing you was always easy. I could have done that two months ago. Sexually, you were made for me. You respond and fit against me as though it's the most natural place in the world for you to be.' He soothed her heating face with cool fingers. 'Don't be shy,' he said softly. 'It's right it should be that way. But I want all of you, every part. I want your heart and soul. You believed you hated me that night. You might have truly hated me if I'd stayed. For I wasn't thinking straight. I was still insane…jittery from fear of losing you and from fighting. Mostly, I was furious because you wouldn't trust me. I wanted to punish you. As ever, I ended up punishing me more,' he wryly admitted. 'I had sense enough not to want your first time to be that way.'

Long, strong arms wound her back hard against his rigid, throbbing body. She relaxed against his shoulder, her eyes closing while she dwelled on that leisurely teasing punishment. But it made her fidget and her breathing shallow.

'Which time will be that way?' she artlessly demanded.

Immediate laughter burst from him, shaking her in his arms. He kissed her neck through lavender-scented hair. 'See what I mean? You were made for me,' he growled. 'When I left you that night,' he reflected aloud, 'I rode off in a daze, unaware of where I was headed, and found myself by that woodland pool. In my lunacy, it seemed somehow fitting. It started here, I thought, so it might as well end here too. I just walked into it, at dawnlight, to cool off.' He nuzzled her neck as he continued, 'More absurd still, when I got back here and walked in dripping, Miles gave me a towel and a newspaper and didn't say a word. I'm sure he thinks I'm an escaped bedlamite.'

'Miles is a very good man. All the staff here are fine people.'

'And they love you too, Rebecca. You have that effect on people. Ross adores you. Clarkie loved you,' he said distantly. 'How long were you with him? An hour? Two? Yet he gave his life for you on that short acquaintance. I shall have to ensure that his family are cared for. I just wish he had lived so I could have properly shown him my eternal gratitude.'

They sat in blissful silence for a moment, Rebecca wrapped back against his torso with her arms covering his.

'What of Melrose?' she tentatively posed. 'What of your businesses in Cornwall? Are you truly intending to stay here permanently?'

'Yes. Tristan can take control of the mines. He has done so while I have been away and deserves as much. The shipping is my concern and operates from Bristol. I can get there as well from here as from Cornwall, when I need to. As to Melrose, it was never really mine. It belonged to my parents and I always felt that. It is a beautiful estate and we shall visit. I shall show it all to you. The cliffs, the coves, the beaches...the smuggling haunts of my youth...all of it.

'But I am a Ramsden as well as a Trelawney, and I've never felt that more than I do now. I never needed to come here and oversee the sale of this estate. But come I did. It was my destiny. Time for one of the Cornish Ramsdens to come home. Time for the Ramsden line to have new life breathed into it...babies, nurseries...a fresh dynasty...my dynasty. I'm sure the first Jago Trelawney and Charlotte Ramsden would have approved. Aren't you?'

She nodded slowly, her face softly grazed by his unshaven jaw. 'Today when in town I reflected on my destiny. This morning I was resigned to remaining an old maid, for I was sure you no longer wanted to marry me. I am twenty-six now,' she hesitantly, regretfully told him.

He turned her face to his, suppressing humour as he read genuine concern. 'Twenty-six? It's high time you were married Rebecca,' he solemnly warned. 'Where is it exactly that your best friend lives? Close by?'

'Kay Abbott?' Rebecca queried, surprised. 'In Graveley at the vicarage. A few minute's walk from the Summer House. Why?'

'Is her husband—Adam, isn't it?—is he at home, do you think?'

'I imagine so. Yes, I saw him heading home on horseback earlier.'

'Good,' Luke said and abruptly stood up, lifting her with him.

An inkling of his intention penetrated her blissful languour. 'Surely, arrangements have to be made? He may be busy or unwilling…' she breathed.

'Is his church roof leaking?'

'Why, yes…' She broke off, noting his humour at her gravity.

'I'm sure he won't be too busy to accept the gratuitous loan of my builders to work on his church.'

'Well, what of your family? Your mother? I've not yet met your mother,' she anxiously reminded him, looking at the door.

'This is about *us*, Rebecca, not them. I've no real desire for pomp. Just for you. I want you…right now. If they become involved…' he tailed off. 'We can celebrate properly later in the week. Give them a reception. Can't we?'

She nodded, her eyes sparkling twin jewels that rivalled her glittering betrothal ring. Luke removed the aquamarine from its velvet nest and slipped it on to her slender finger. The other box was snapped closed and with the licence put into his pocket.

Rebecca looked down at her silver-grey skirts, creased from sitting so close to him and an anxious hand went to the trailing tendrils of honey hair about her face and neck. 'I look a mess,' she wailed.

'You look beautiful. You always look beautiful.'

She smiled up at his extraordinarily handsome face, the blue-black stubble shading his lean, angular jaw, making his appearance more piratical than usual. 'So do you,' she shyly whispered.

'Why, thank you, Rebecca,' he said with gracious sincerity, dipping to kiss her, as though no woman had ever before complimented him on his outstanding good looks.

He took her hand and lead her to the door and opened it with the key.

'Are you ready, Lady Ramsden?' he asked her softly with a wicked smile.

'Yes, Mr Trelawney,' she breathed.

'Say nothing,' he charged her with gentle warning, as they walked the corridor side by side. 'I'm just hoping Mother is still reclining with her smelling salts above stairs. Dammit! I've not shaved,' he muttered, wiping a testing hand across his face.

He held her elbow lightly as they traversed the hallway. The scene looked the same, Rebecca realised. Her life was perfection yet nothing in the littered hallway had changed. Ross and Katherine were still bickering. Simon was sipping from a glass of wine, one elbow propped idly against the wall as he indulgently watched them. Young Jago was crouched on the marble-flagged floor, skidding his boat against its smooth surface. Miles and Judith were bending over packing cases and discussing their contents as they moved items from one box to the other.

They walked quietly on and as Rebecca glanced again at Ross she saw he was watching them. Watching them intently. And then a slow smile just tipped his mouth and, unobtrusively, he moved his crystal goblet, toasting her, before he returned to his conversation with his sister.

They lightly descended the stone steps of the Manor and it wasn't until they reached the parkland that Luke's hand moved from her elbow to her waist and he pulled her close. Rebecca's arms immediately enclosed him in a loving hug, stretching to clasp together around his broad torso. He lifted her hard against him, kissing her and then in sheer joy spun them both about so her hair streamed out like a shining golden banner behind her and then they were walking on, in the direction of the Summer House.

*   *   *   *   *

Modern Romance™
...seduction and
passion guaranteed

Tender Romance™
...love affairs that
last a lifetime

Sensual Romance™
...sassy, sexy and
seductive

Blaze™
...sultry days and
steamy nights

Medical Romance™
...medical drama on
the pulse

Historical Romance™
...rich, vivid and
passionate

30 new titles every month.

*With all kinds of Romance for
every kind of mood...*

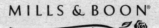

MILLS & BOON®